Dear Reader,

So, things got pretty dark there for a while. And while I loved my time in the Ottoman Empire and Frankenstein Manor, I was ready for a little more wonder in my life. I hope you feel the same way, because it is my genuine pleasure to welcome you to Camelot. But not the Camelot you know . . .

I've always been fascinated by the Arthurian legends, but I find the same problem there that I have with most classic tales: a stunning lack of compelling female characters. We have brave, noble Arthur. Honorable Lancelot. Conniving Mordred. Baffling and powerful Merlin. But I wanted a Guinevere who was more than the fickle, feckless love interest. A Guinevere with agency and longing, adventures and fierce friends. A Guinevere who perhaps *isn't* Guinevere, but a mystery to everyone—including herself.

You know what they say: when you want something done right, write it yourself. I needed an escape, so I ran away to a wondrous and treacherous and deeply romantic Camelot. Losing myself in this story was one of the most delicious writing experiences of my life. I hope reading it gives you the same magical escape.

With love,

Kiersten White

RANDOM HOUSE
CHILDREN'S BOOKS
A DIVISION OF PENGUIN RANDOM HOUSE LLC

TITLE:	The Guinevere Deception
AUTHOR:	Kiersten White
IMPRINT:	Delacorte Press
PUBLICATION DATE:	November 5, 2019
ISBN:	978-0-525-58167-3
TENTATIVE PRICE:	$18.99 U.S./$24.99 CAN.
GLB ISBN:	978-0-525-58168-0
GLB TENTATIVE PRICE:	$21.99 U.S./$28.99 CAN.
EBOOK ISBN:	978-0-525-58169-7
AUDIO ISBN (download):	978-0-593-10481-1
PAGES:	352
TRIM SIZE:	6" x 9"
AGES:	12 and up

ALSO BY KIERSTEN WHITE

THE GUINEVERE
DECEPTION

KIERSTEN WHITE

DELACORTE PRESS

Text copyright © 2019 by Kiersten Brazier
Jacket art copyright © 2019 by artist

GetUnderlined.com

Educators and librarians, for a variety of teaching tools, visit us at RHTeachersLibrarians.com

Library of Congress Cataloging-in-Publication Data
Names: White, Kiersten, author.
Title: The Guinevere deception / Kiersten White.
Description: New York : Delacorte Press, [2019] | Summary: Sent by a banished Merlin to protect King
Arthur, a sixteen-year-old impersonating the deceased Guinevere struggles to fit in at Camelot where
the magic she practices is banished.
Identifiers: LCCN 2018041028 (print) | LCCN 2018047967 (ebook) | ISBN 978-0-525-58169-7
(ebook) | ISBN 978-0-525-58167-3 (hc : alk. paper) | ISBN 978-0-525-58168-0 (glb : alk. paper)
Subjects: | CYAC: Characters in literature—Fiction. | Guenevere, Queen (Legendary character)—
Fiction. | Magic—Fiction. | Impersonation—Fiction. | Arthur, King—Fiction. | Knights and
knighthood—Fiction. | Camelot (Legendary place)—Fiction. | Fantasy.
Classification: LCC PZ7.W583764 (ebook) | LCC PZ7.W583764 Gui 2019 (print) | DDC [Fic]—dc23

The text of this book is set in 11-point Fairfield LT.
Interior design by Ken Crossland

Printed in the United States of America
10 9 8 7 6 5 4 3 2 1
First Edition

To Steph and Jarrod, for opening

their home as a magical portal,

and to Mister Tumnus,

for tolerating me there

CHAPTER ONE

There was nothing in the world as magical and terrifying as a girl on the cusp of womanhood.

This particular girl had never before felt the power she held by existing in a space of men, but today, surrounded by them, it radiated from her. *I am untouchable.* They revolved around her as though she were the Earth, and they the adoring but distant sun and moon and stars. It was a type of magic in and of itself.

A veil obscured and dimmed the world around her. She sat back-achingly straight in her saddle. She did not wriggle her toes in the boots they were so unaccustomed to. She pretended she was a painting.

"I cannot believe the convent had no nuns willing to travel with you," Brangien complained, brushing at the fine layer of dust that baptized their journey. Then, as though unaware she had spoken aloud, she bowed her head. "But of course I am very pleased and honored to be here."

The smile offered in response to Brangien's apology went un-acknowledged. "Of course," the girl said, but the words were not quite right. She could do better. She had to. "I do not love travel, either, and I appreciate the kindness you have shown by being my companion on this long journey. It would be lonely without you." They were surrounded by people, but to them, the blue-and-scarlet-wrapped girl was goods to be guarded and safely delivered to the new owner. She hoped desperately that Brangien, eighteen years to her own sixteen, would become a friend.

She would need one. She had never had one.

But it would also complicate things. She had so many precious hidden things. Having another woman with her at all times was both unfamiliar and dangerous. Brangien's eyes were black like her hair and hinted at cleverness. Hopefully those eyes would see only what was offered them. Brangien caught her staring and offered a tentative smile.

Focused on her companion, the girl did not notice the change outright. A subtle shift, a lessening of tension, her first breath fully drawn in two weeks. She tipped her head back and closed her eyes, grateful for the leafy green reprieve from the sun. A forest. If she were not barred on all sides by men and horses, she would hug the trees. Run her fingers along their veins to learn each tree's story.

"Tighten the circle!" Sir Bors commanded. Under the heavy arch of branches, his shout was hushed. He was a man unaccustomed to being muted. Even his mustache bristled at the offense. He moved his reins into his teeth to grip them and drew his sword with his good arm.

The girl snapped out of her daydream to see that the horses had caught the fear of the men. They shifted and stamped, eyes rolling to search as their riders did. A gust of wind lifted her veil. She met the gaze of one of the men—Mordred, three years older than she, and soon to be her nephew. His subtle mouth had twisted up at one corner as though he was amused. Had he caught her reverie before she realized she should not be pleased by the forest?

"What is it?" she asked, turning quickly away from Mordred, who was paying far too much attention. *Be a painting.*

Brangien shivered and shrank into her cloak. "The trees."

They crowded in on either side of the road, twisting trunks and grasping roots. Their branches laced overhead to form a tunnel. The girl did not understand the threat. No crack of a twig, no rustling. Nothing disturbed the beauty of the forest. Except her and the men around her. "What about the trees?" she asked.

Mordred answered. His face was serious, but there was a song-like quality to his voice. Playful and low. "They were not here on our journey to retrieve you."

Sword still drawn, Sir Bors clicked his tongue and his horse moved forward again. The men clustered around her and Brangien. The peace and relief the girl felt at being among trees again disappeared, soured by their fear. These men claimed every space they went into.

"What does he mean, the trees were not here?" she whispered to Brangien.

Brangien had been mouthing something. She leaned over to adjust the girl's veil and answered in a whisper as well, as though afraid the trees were listening. "Four days ago, when we passed through this area—there was no forest. All this land had been cleared. It was farms."

"Perhaps we took a different route without realizing it?"

Brangien shook her head, her face a blur of dark eyebrows and red lips. "There was a jumble of boulders an hour back. Like a giant had been playing a child's game and left his toys behind. I remember it very clearly. This is the same road." A leaf drifted down from the trees, landing as lightly as a prayer on Brangien's shoulder. Brangien squeaked with fear.

It was a simple matter to reach out and pluck the leaf from Brangien's shoulder. The girl wanted to lift it to her face, to study the story in its lines. But, touching it, she instantly sensed that it had teeth. She dropped it to the forest floor. She even checked her fingers for blood, but of course there was none.

Brangien shuddered. "There is a village not far. We can hide there."

"Hide?" They were a day from their destination. She wanted this to be over with. Everything to be done and settled. The idea of huddling with these men in a village while they waited to—what, fight a forest?—made her want to tear off her shoes, her veil, to beg the trees for safe passage. But the trees would not understand.

They were on opposite sides now, after all.

I am sorry, she thought, knowing the trees could not hear her. Wishing she could explain.

Brangien cried out again, putting her hands over her mouth in horror. The men around them stopped abruptly. They were still surrounded by green, everything filtered and unclear through the veil. Shapes loomed out of the forest, enormous boulders covered in moss and trailing vines.

Modesty be damned. She tore off her veil. The world came into startling, perfect focus.

The shapes were not boulders. They were homes. Cottages much like ones they had passed before, made of lime-washed cobs and beams with thatched roofs sloping down to the ground. But where smoke should have been drifting up from the roofs, there were flowers. In place of doors, trailing curtains of vines. It was a village reclaimed by nature. If she had to guess, she would say it had been abandoned generations ago.

"There was a child," Brangien whispered through her fingers. "He sold me bread weighted with stones. I was so cross with him."

"Where are the people?" Sir Bors asked.

"We must not linger here." Mordred veered his horse toward hers. "Surround the princess! Quickly!"

As she was carried by the momentum of her guards, she saw one last vine-covered boulder, or perhaps a tree stump. Just the right size and shape for a little boy, offering bad bread.

They did not stop until dusk claimed the world far more gently than the forest had claimed the unfortunate village. The men regarded the fields around them with suspicion, as though trees would spring forth, impaling them.

Perhaps they would.

Even she was unnerved. She had never before viewed the green and secret things of the world with fear. It was a good lesson, but she wished that the village had not paid the price for her education.

They could not go much farther in the dark without risking injury to the horses. Their first night together, they had stayed in an inn. Brangien had slept beside her in the finest bed the inn had to offer. Brangien snored lightly, a friendly, companionable sound. Unable to sleep, the girl had longed to pad down the stairs, to find the horses in the stables, to sleep outside.

Tonight she would get her wish. The men divided the watch. Brangien fussed setting up bedrolls, complaining about the lack of proper sleeping arrangements.

"I do not mind." The girl once again offered Brangien a smile that went unclaimed in the darkness.

"I do," Brangien muttered. Perhaps she thought the veil obscured hearing as well as vision.

Even with the fire crackling in defiance of night, of cold, of beasts and creeping things, the stars were waiting. Men had not yet figured out how to beat those back. The girl traced her favorite constellations: The Drowned Woman. The Swift River. The Pebbled Shore. If any stars winked a warning, she did not see it through the sparks the fire sent heavenward.

They pushed the horses harder the next day. She discovered she was less afraid of the forest behind them than of the city awaiting them.

What peace she could find was in the sway and bump of the horse beneath her. Horses were deeply soothing to touch. Calm and purposeful. She stroked her mare's mane absentmindedly. Her own long black hair had been plaited that morning by Brangien, woven through with threads of gold. "So many knots!" Brangien had said. But she had not seen their purpose. Had not suspected. Had she?

There were too many unforeseen complications already. How could the girl have known this young woman would explore her hair so carefully? And Mordred, always watching. He was beautiful, smooth-faced, with mossy-green eyes. She was reminded of the elegance of the snake gliding through the grass. But when she caught him staring, his smile had more of the wolf than of the snake.

The other knights, at least, cared nothing about her except out of duty. Sir Bors pushed them ever faster. They passed tiny villages where the homes huddled together like the men had in the forest, protecting each other's backs and staring outward at the land around them, fearful and defiant. She wanted to dismount, to meet the people, to understand why they lived out here, determined to tame the wild and exposing themselves to threats innumerable. But all she saw were hazy forms and green and gold hints of the world around her. The veil was a more intimate version of her guards, sealing her away.

She stopped disliking Sir Bors's pace and wished they would go even faster. She would be happy to have this journey behind her, to see what threats lay ahead so she could plan for them.

Then they came to the river.

She could make up her mind about nothing out here, it seemed. She was glad for her veil now. It hid the winking treachery of the water from her, and hid her panic from those around her. "Is there no way around?" She tried to make her voice both light and imperious. It did not succeed. She sounded exactly how she felt: terrified.

"The ferryman will see us safely across." Sir Bors delivered it as a fact. She longed to cling to his certainty, but his confidence flowed swiftly past her and out of her reach.

"I would be happy to ride longer if it meant we could avoid the crossing," she said.

"My lady, you tremble." Mordred had somehow slid next to her again. "Do you not trust us?"

"I do not like water," she whispered. Her throat closed around how inadequately that phrase captured the soul-deep terror she felt. A memory—heavy black water over her head, around her, pressing in everywhere, filling her—surfaced, and she pushed it away with all her strength, pulling her mind from it as fast as she would her hand from a burning brand.

"Then I am afraid you will not find your new home to your liking."

"What do you mean?"

Mordred sounded apologetic, but she could not see his features well enough to know whether his face matched his tone. "No one has told you?"

"Told me what?"

"I would hate to ruin the surprise." His tone was a lie, then. He hated her. She felt it. And she did not know what she had done already in their two days together to earn his ire.

The rush of the river drove every other consideration away, its only competition the beating of her heart and her panicked breaths, trapped by her veil in a humid cloud of panic. Sir Bors helped her dismount and she stood next to Brangien, who was lost in a world of her own, distracted and distant.

"My lady?" Sir Bors said.

She realized it was not the first time he had addressed her. "Yes?"

"The ferry is ready."

She tried to step toward it. She could not make her body move. The terror was so intense, so overwhelming, she could not even lean in that direction.

Brangien, finally realizing something was wrong, moved in front of her. She leaned close, her features sharpening beyond the veil. "You are frightened," she said, surprised. Then her voice softened, and for the first time she sounded like she was talking to a person instead of a title. "I can hold your hand, if you would like. I can swim, too. Do not tell anyone. But I promise I will see you safely to the other side." Brangien's hand found hers, squeezing tightly.

She took it gratefully, clung to it as though she were already drowning and this hand was all that stood between her and oblivion.

And she had not yet taken even a step toward the river! This would all fail before she reached the king, because she could not get over this absurd fear. She hated herself, and she hated every choice that had brought her here.

"Come along." Sir Bors's words were clipped with impatience. "We are expected before nightfall. We must keep moving."

Brangien tugged gently. One step, then another, then another.

The raft beneath her feet dipped and swayed. She turned to run back to the bank, but the men were there. They moved forward, a sea of broad chests and unyielding leather and metal. She stumbled, clinging to Brangien.

A sob escaped her. She was too afraid to be ashamed.

Brangien, the only solid thing in a world of turmoil and movement, held her. If she fell in, she knew—she *knew*—she would be unmade. The water would claim her. She would cease to exist. Sealed in her fear, the passage could have lasted minutes or hours. It was infinite.

"Help me," Brangien said. "I cannot move, she clings so. I think she is insensible."

"It is not right for us to touch her," Sir Bors grumbled.

"God above," Mordred said, "I will do it. If he wants to kill me for touching his bride, he is welcome to, so long as I get to sleep in my own bed one last time." Arms lifted her, reaching beneath her knees and cradling her like a child. She buried her face in his chest, breathing in the scents of leather and cloth. Never had she been more grateful for something solid. For something real.

"My lady." Mordred's voice was as soft as his hair, which her fingers were tangled in like claws. "I deliver you safely to dry land. So brave in the forest—what is a stream to you?"

He set her down, hands lingering at her waist. She stumbled. Now that the threat was past, shame claimed her. How could she be strong, how could she complete her mission, if she could not so much as cross a river?

An apology bloomed on her lips. She plucked it and discarded it. *Be what they expect.*

She straightened carefully. Regally. "I do not like water." She

delivered it as a fact, not an apology. Then she accepted Brangien's
hand and remounted her horse. "Shall we move along?"

On her way to the convent she had seen castles of wood that grew
from the ground like a perversion of a forest. Even one castle of
stone. It was a squat, cross-looking building.

Nothing had prepared her for Camelot.

The land was tamed for miles around it. Fields divided the wild
into orderly, neat rows, promising harvests and prosperity. In spite of
the presence of more villages and small towns, they had seen no one.
This did not inspire the same fear and wariness as the forest. Instead,
the men around her grew both more relaxed and more agitated—but
with excitement. And then she saw why. She removed her veil. They
had arrived.

Camelot was a mountain. An actual mountain. A river had carved
it free from the land. Over too many years for her mind to hold, the
water had split itself, pushed past on either side, and worn away the
land until only the center remained. It still cascaded violently on
either side. Beneath Camelot, a great lake lurked, cold and unknowable, fed by the twin rivers and giving birth to a single great river on
its far end.

On the mountain, surrounded on all sides by water, a fortress
had been carved not by nature but by generations of hands. The gray
rock had been chipped away to create fanciful shapes. Twists and
knots, demon faces with windows for eyes, stairs curving along the
outer edge with nothing but empty space on one side and castle on
the other.

The city of Camelot clung to the steep slope beneath the castle.

Most of the houses had been carved from the same rock, but some wooden structures intermingled with them. Streets wound through the buildings, veins and arteries all leading to and from the castle, the heart of Camelot. The roofs were not all of thatch, but mostly of slate, a dark blue mixed with thatch, so that the castle looked as though it were nestled into a patchwork quilt of stone and thatch and wood.

She had not thought men were capable of creating a city so magnificent.

"It is something, is it not?" Envy laced Mordred's voice. He was jealous of his own city. Perhaps viewing it through her eyes, he saw it anew. It was a thing to be coveted, certainly.

They rode closer. She focused only on the castle. Tried to ignore the ever-present roaring of the rivers and waterfalls. Tried to ignore the fact that she would have to cross a lake to get to her new home.

Failed.

On the banks of the lake, a festival awaited them. Tents had been erected, flags snapping and whipping in the wind. Music played, and the scent of roasting meat tugged them forward. The men straightened in their saddles. She did the same.

They stopped on the outer edge of the festival grounds. Hundreds of people were there, waiting, all eyes on her. She was grateful she had replaced the veil that hid her from them, and that hid them from her. She had never seen so many people in her entire life. If she had thought the convent crowded and the company of knights overwhelming, that was a trickling stream compared to the roar of this ocean.

A hush fell over the crowd, which rippled like a field of wheat. Someone moved directly through the crowd, and the people parted, closing in again behind him. The murmur that accompanied his procession was one of reverence. Of love. She sensed they had come there to be near him more than they had come to see her.

He strode to her horse and stopped. If the crowd was hushed, her body and mind were anything but.

Sir Bors cleared his throat, his booming voice perfectly at home in this environment. "Your Grace, King Arthur of Camelot, I present to you Princess Guinevere of Cameliard, daughter of King Leodegrance."

King Arthur bowed, then extended his hand. It engulfed hers. It was a strong hand, firm, steady. Calloused, and with a sense of purpose that pulsed warmly to her through him. She began to dismount, but with the rivers and the lake and the travel, she was still shaky. He bypassed that effort, lifting her free of the horse, spinning her once, and then setting her on the ground with a courtly bow. The crowd roared with approval, drowning out the rivers.

He took off her veil. King Arthur was revealed like the sun breaking free of the clouds. Like Camelot, he looked as though he had been carved straight from nature by a loving and patient hand. Broad shoulders over a trim waist. Taller than any man she had ever met. His face, still youthful at eighteen, was firm and steadfast. His brown eyes were intelligent, but lines around them told stories of time spent outside, smiling. His lips were full and soft, his jaw strong. His hair was cut startlingly short, clipped almost to the skin. All the knights she had met kept theirs long. He wore a simple silver crown as easily as a farmer wore a hat. She could not imagine him without it.

He studied her as well. She wondered what he saw. What they all saw when they looked at her long hair, so dark it shone almost blue in the sun. Her swift and expressive eyebrows. Her freckled nose. The freckles told the truth of her life before now. One of sun and freedom and joy. No convent could have nurtured those freckles.

He took her hand and pressed it to his warm cheek; then he lifted it and returned his attention to the crowd.

"Your future queen, Guinevere!"

The crowd roared, shouting the name Guinevere. Over and over.

If only it were actually her name.

Finger on leaf. Leaf to forest floor to root. Root to root to root, interlocking webs crawling through the dirt. Root to soil to water.

Water seeping and creeping through the soft black loam. Rushing over stone. Falling and breaking and rejoining, flowing, flowing.

Water to water to water to root to tree to sap.

Sap to dirt that held the absence of a body.

Arthur's queen does not taste the way a queen should taste. What does she taste like? The true queen, the dark queen, the generous and cruel and wild queen, wonders. She has no answer. But she has eyes. So very many eyes. They will see the truth.

CHAPTER TWO

There were so many people.

Too many people.

Arthur led her through the crowd. Hands reached out to touch her. She tried not to shudder, tried to keep herself pleasant and regal. There were jugglers, minstrels. Children running madly through the crowd. Those she found fascinating. She had never seen a child before.

Tables had been set up and they overflowed with food. There was no money being exchanged. Free food probably accounted for much of the attendance. They passed a miniature wooden stage. Two crudely carved imitations of humans bowed dramatically at her, and she paused. For one confusing moment she thought they were moving of their own free will, but then she saw the arms and hands behind a curtain, controlling them. No magic.

"Oh, this." Arthur smiled with weary tolerance. It was obvious he wished to move on, but she was intrigued.

"We now present," one of the puppets cried out in a squeaky, exaggerated voice, "the story of our great King Arthur!"

Children pressed in, eager to watch. The two puppets disappeared, and in their place were puppets of a battered knight, a child, and a baby. "I am Sir Ector!" the battered knight said, weaving drunkenly around the small stage.

"I am Sir Kay!" the child said.

Sir Ector bopped Sir Kay on the head. The children watching roared with laughter. "You are not Sir Anything yet, rat!" Their fight continued until they noticed the baby. A booming voice from offstage declared, "This is Arthur. He is yours now. Take care of him."

Sir Ector and little Kay looked at each other, then looked at the baby, then looked at each other, then looked at the baby, continuing the repetition for far too long. The children giggled, shouting, "Take the baby! Take the baby!"

Finally, the puppets complied. They wandered offstage.

Interesting that there had been no puppet for Merlin, only a disembodied voice. And it had not happened exactly like that. There had been violence, pursuit, simmering threat. There had been those who wanted to kill the baby simply for existing. And Arthur's mother was left out entirely. Though Igraine's sad fate was hardly fodder for a children's play.

Various stages of puppets progressed through Arthur's childhood as a servant to Sir Ector and Sir Kay. Then they came to a tournament in Camelot where Sir Kay's sword broke. Desperate to replace it, Arthur pulled Excalibur out of the enchanted stone that held it fast against all other attempts to retrieve it. The stone that would only release the sword to the true future king.

The audience gasped and clapped when the tiny puppet held up the knife-sized sword. Then they laughed as he tripped and the sword skidded away. Sir Kay and Sir Ector chastised Arthur for a dizzyingly silly few minutes.

In reality, the three had fled. Uther Pendragon, the king, wanted no heir. No usurper. Sir Ector had thrown Excalibur into a lake to get rid of the evidence of Arthur's right to rule. The inky depths claimed it. Until . . .

The backdrop of the puppet play was replaced with a blue cloth. The Arthur puppet was larger now. A hand—a real hand—shot up out of the blue cloth, holding the miniature sword.

This version acknowledged the magical elements—the story could not be told without them—but made them so minor they were afterthoughts. The Lady of the Lake was merely a prop to get the sword back to Arthur. Not one of the few magical beings who had sided with him against the Dark Queen was present. But Camelot had abandoned magic; perhaps even its stories were pushing it away, as well.

A huge puppet with a black, spiky crown roared onto the stage. The kids screamed, jeered, and shouted curses at Uther Pendragon.

"Come." Arthur took her elbow. His eyes were still kind, but there was something hard there. "There will be gifts."

She wanted to see the rest of the play, see how Arthur's citizens decided to interpret and spread his story. See if Merlin ever came back into it, if they acknowledged his part in the next scenes after ignoring his role in the first ones. And she was very curious as to how puppets would re-create the Forest of Blood and the battle with the Dark Queen. Not to mention the banishment of Merlin.

But she could not very well demand to be left with the children. She followed Arthur.

The lakeshore was lined with boats. Flat ferries, narrow vessels made of hollowed-out logs, rowboats that looked as steady and dependable as a leaf caught in a maelstrom.

"Are you nervous?" Arthur asked. For the last two hours, he had celebrated among his people while she sat with Brangien at her side, bowing her head and smiling as people laid gifts on a table. Food, mostly, though some lengths of cloth and cleverly twisted pieces of metal. She had touched each item. None bit her. None sang to her. They were all safe.

Now it was evening and the festival was being dismantled. The boats awaited. Camelot awaited. No king would be married on the shore of a lake.

"Our Lady Guinevere does not care for water." Mordred's voice winked brightly as the daylight faded. Somehow he always ended up at her side.

"Is that true?" Arthur asked.

She nodded, wishing she could lie and pretend to be strong. What would he think of her?

Arthur turned to their company. Though Mordred was closest, all Arthur's knights were gathered around them. She had already lost track of which ones had accompanied her here and which ones she had only just met. So many faces! The forest had seemed lonely, but now she longed for the simplicity of her life there.

Arthur's voice was as warm as his smile. "My bride and I will take another boat. We wish to arrive first so we can watch the procession."

"But my king, is it proper?" Sir Bors frowned dubiously, his mustache drooping. "To be alone with her before you are wed? Women's passionate natures cannot be trusted."

Annoyed, she forgot to be a painting. "I shall protect his honor with my life," she answered drily. There was a brief silence, and then the men broke out into raucous laughter at the idea of this slip of a girl protecting their king. If only they knew. Sir Bors, however, did not seem amused.

Mordred clapped him on the back. "Fear not, valiant Sir Bors. I will attend them."

"Thank you, nephew," Arthur said. It was odd, hearing Arthur call Mordred—who was a year older than the king—*nephew*. Arthur's family tree was gnarled and diseased, filled with twists and betrayals and pain. How it had produced him, she did not know.

Well. She knew some of it. She wished she knew less.

Arthur had his horse brought. He lifted her onto it, and then mounted behind her. She did not know how to respond to this startling intimacy; she was buzzing with awareness that every eye was on them. So she sat as primly as she could while Arthur waved and then spurred his horse forward.

He leaned his head close to her ear. "There is another way. It is known only to Mordred and me. I share it with you as a wedding gift, since I forgot to get you anything else."

"Saving me from a boat is the kindest gift imaginable." She tried to dampen how attuned she was to the feel of him behind her—his broad chest, the rise and fall of his breaths. She had had more direct physical contact with other people in the last two days than in all the years of her life combined. Brangien. Mordred. Now Arthur. Would she get used to it? She would have to.

They rode along the lakeshore. Mordred's horse was pure white, almost glowing in the darkness beside them. The rush and roar of the nearest waterfall became deafening. She felt it through her body. Even knowing she did not have to go through the water did little to alleviate her panic at the nearness of it all.

Arthur dismounted and lifted her down as easily as if she were a child. He seemed so comfortable in her company. There was none of the proper distance his men had maintained. She had been instructed not to so much as touch a man's hand—though she had broken that spectacularly on the way here. But Arthur did everything without pause. No lingering, like Mordred had done as he released her after their river crossing. Arthur wanted her off the horse, so he lifted her off the horse. It was as simple as that.

He took her hand and guided her through the dark. His steps were assured, his path known, though invisible to her. Her racing heart would not let her forget how close the lake was, how ravenous the waterfall right beside them. A fine coat of mist settled on her and she shuddered, holding his hand too tightly, pulling as much of her sense of *Arthur* into herself as she could. If her fear was like the water—pounding, rushing, coating everything—Arthur's strength was like the rocks. Steady and immovable. No wonder he was the foundation on which a kingdom was built.

"Here," he said, releasing her hand. With the loss of his touch, she felt diminished. He struck flint and a torch burned into life. Mordred drew a curtain of vines aside to reveal a cave. The smile Arthur shot back at her was pure boyish delight, betraying his youth in a way his bearing and manners had not. "It was how I first entered Camelot. Merlin showed it to me."

She felt a pang at Merlin's name. It should be him here. He was so much better suited to this. Smarter. Stronger. But he was not exactly marriageable material for a young king.

"Uncle king, may I remind you not to speak the banished demon spawn's name."

Arthur sighed. "Thank you, Mordred. Yes."

She hoped she had not reacted to Merlin's name in any way that Mordred might have noticed. She could betray no connection to the wizard.

"Your soon-to-be queen knows, does she not?" Mordred asked. "Things might be different in the south."

"Ah, yes." Arthur cleared his throat. "We have banished all magic from Camelot."

"Why?" Guinevere asked. Merlin had never been clear. He had referred to his banishment with a derisive but resigned puff of air from between his lips, and then talked to her at length about a type of frog that could change from male to female if a situation required it for survival.

Mordred answered. "We worked and fought to push the Dark Queen and her fairy forces back. But leaving any magic here was like sowing tares among the wheat. The tendrils grow and choke out what we are trying to do. And so it was decided that there would be no magic allowed inside Camelot. Which meant our resident wizard was no longer welcome, and cannot be referred to with anything other than the sternest dismissal." Mordred turned so he was walking backward, facing them. "And any who are found to be practicing magic are banished from the kingdom. Or worse." Mordred lingered as lightly as a spider's touch on that last sentiment, then moved quickly on. "My uncle king rules with justice and order. He is bringing the kingdom forward from the chaos of its birth to the peace of its future."

Arthur's smile was tight. "Yes. Thank you, Mordred. There is no magic within our borders. It is an absolute rule."

She shivered as the cave tunnel sealed them off from the night. The rock was black, slick with moisture. Arthur did not stumble or slip, but he walked more slowly than she suspected he could. She appreciated it. Mordred's words lingered like the chill around them. Banishment. *Or worse.*

"I have never had a queen before. What shall I call you?" Arthur's voice was soft, so the echoes surrounded only them, not reaching Mordred where he walked ahead. The way was narrow and close, forcing them into single file.

"Guinevere suits me very well, thank you."

"Only Guinevere? Nothing else? I know the power of names."

His words hit her with two meanings. Names that were titles gave power among men. True names gave power among the things that came before men. She focused on the torch to make her voice cheery, like it. "Guinevere, when spoken by you, has power enough."

She would hold her true name to herself as a talisman. A secret. In the horrible inn, claustrophobic and desperate, she had whispered it to herself in the middle of the night. It did not feel real. She wondered if, with no one else to say it back to her, it would cease to exist. *Guinevere,* she whispered. The cave swallowed it whole, carrying it away toward Camelot.

Guinevere. Guinevere. Dead and buried. What had she been like? Who was she?

Me, she thought. *Guinevere.* She imagined stepping into the name as she had stepped into the clothing. Putting it on sound by sound, piece by piece. Draping it over herself, and then cinching it up tight so it would not slip away. It was a complicated name. So many pieces. She would have to be very complicated to fit it.

"Guinevere" followed Arthur through the cave.

They emerged into a cramped storage room filled with barrels. Arthur helped Mordred shift a large one to get them through. Mordred levered it back in place while Arthur produced a key and unlocked the door. When they had all stepped through, he locked the door behind them.

They were outside, on one of the walkways that twisted around the exterior of the castle. Guinevere stared up at the castle, dark and soaring above her. She put her hand to the stone, but it was old. So old it had forgotten what it was before it was a castle. Mordred put his hand next to hers. His fingers were long and finely shaped. They looked as soft as a new leaf. But perhaps a leaf with teeth, like the one in the forest.

"We did not build Camelot," he said. "Neither did Arthur's father, Uther Pendragon. He did what men always do. He wanted it, and so he claimed it. And then we took it from him."

She did not know if he sounded proud or sad, and the night around them offered no clues.

"Look!" Arthur drew her attention away from the past that had been bloodied and defeated on the edge of his father's sword.

She turned outward and the rest of the night was revealed. The city of Camelot knelt before them, and past the buildings and homes and walls, the lake carried sparks of fire. Hundreds of boats were crossing the lake with illuminated lamps. The lamps reflected with rippling beauty off the black water. It was like the night sky, burning with stars.

She could almost love this place, even with the lake.

"They are bringing light to Camelot in honor of their new queen."

Guinevere watched. Her smile was like a reflection, too. Not quite real. They offered her hope and beauty in return for a deception.

She was draped in red and blue. A belt of silver hung low across her hips. Her hair was heavy with jewels. It was the last time she would ever wear jewels there, as married women never did. It was also the *first* time she had worn them, but no one knew that. A fur collar adorned her cape, the ghost of the animal tickling her. If she touched it, what story would it tell?

She did not touch it.

They knelt in front of an altar. A priest recited words in Latin. The words meant nothing to Guinevere; they were as meaningless as the vows she spoke. But Guinevere, dead Guinevere, was a Christian princess, and so Guinevere, false Guinevere, had to be the same.

When they were finished, Arthur led Guinevere to a balcony overlooking the city. The lights had moved to the streets now. People thronged, crowding to get close to the castle. Guinevere smiled, even though they could not see it from that distance. Why did she constantly offer smiles when none were demanded? She raised her hand and waved.

A cheer erupted. Arthur—a hero from Merlin's stories three hours ago, her husband now—nudged her in the side. "Watch." He gestured to a man standing nearby, who called out an order. There was a rushing noise, and then the people cheered with such delight and ferocity that Guinevere saw how weak their cheer for her had been in comparison. They scrambled, laughing, lifting each other up to long, winding troughs set over the streets.

"What is it?" she asked.

"Water, usually. We divert it from the river so it flows down through the city and people can siphon it from the aqueducts. But tonight we blocked the water and my men up there are pouring barrel after barrel of wine to toast our wedding."

Guinevere covered an inelegant snort of laughter. "I shall be a very popular queen indeed. Until they awake in the morning in agony."

"Pain is often the price of pleasure. There is a feast awaiting us, with all my best men, where you can experience both as you meet their wives."

Guinevere wished very much for her own aqueduct of wine then. This would be the great test of her hasty instruction, her clumsy costuming in another girl's life. And if she did not pass, everything would be for naught.

While everyone was watching the wine spectacle, she pulled a few strands of her own hair, tying them in intricate knots. Each twist and turn and loop secured the magic to the hair. To her. Sealing it in. It was a small, finite magic. The only safe kind for now. She reached up as though adjusting Arthur's crown and wrapped the knotted hairs there. He smiled at her, surprised by her apparently spontaneous gesture. Satisfied, she took Arthur's offered elbow and walked with him into the castle.

Knot magic was fragile and temporary. Merlin did not use it. But Merlin did not need to. He walked through time, trailing the unknowable future, cloaked in magic. He could ask the sun to change color or command the trees to join him for breakfast and she would not be surprised if they obeyed.

Guinevere—the true Guinevere—was not a wizard. Guinevere was a princess who had been raised in a kingdom far enough away that no one here had ever seen her. She had spent the last three years in a convent preparing herself for marriage. And then she died, leaving a space in her wake. Merlin saw the space, and he claimed it.

He also saw to it that no one knew or remembered the Guinevere-who-was. He erased her from the convent's memories. That was not a finite or controlled magic. It was a wild and dark and dangerous magic. It was a violent magic, undoing the record of a life and giving it to someone else.

The new Guinevere wanted, desperately, to whisper her own name to herself, but she could not risk its being heard. *Guinevere,* she whispered. Instead imagining the name as her dress and cloak, she imagined it as armor. But when she and Arthur walked into the feast, she forgot her fear.

This, finally, was something Guinevere could enjoy. She had lived on so little in the woods. She and Merlin ate whatever nature decided to give them. Sometimes it was berries and nuts. Sometimes a falcon would drop a fish on their doorstep. Once, a falcon dropped the fish on her head. Perhaps she should not have teased him. Falcons were such terribly prideful birds. But occasionally nature decided they would like nothing more than a meal of grubs. The grubs would bubble up from the ground outside the shack. Merlin never minded. She went hungry those days.

At King Arthur's table, there were neither grubs nor petulant falcons. There was food the likes of which she had never seen, and she wanted to try it all.

She had to be careful and measured. The real Guinevere would have been accustomed to such fare at her father's castle before she was sent to the convent. But eating also meant not speaking, which was good. The ladies at this end of the table—wives of the knights, mostly, with a few ladies-in-waiting and some visitors—were content to chatter and gossip around their new queen. They were politely distant as they tried to get a feel for what she would be to them.

What she would be to them did not matter. What she was, was famished. The first course was all meat. Ground venison in wine sauce. Succulent cuts of fowl. All things she and Merlin had never eaten. She tasted everything. She was careful not to touch the food with her hands. Probably the animals would not speak to her, but she did not want to risk it.

There was a pie filled with something she could not place. "Eels," Brangien whispered at her side. "You may not have had them as far south as you were. We raise them in the marshlands. Whole acres of eels. Living, they seem like nightmares. But baked into pies, quite nice." She took a bite.

Guinevere did, as well. The meat was chewy, the pie having soaked up the oil. It was an unusual taste. She preferred the other dishes. A piece slid off her knife and she snatched at it to catch it before it fell onto her dress.

Darkness. Water. Sliding and slipping and curling around a thou-

sand siblings, a thousand mates, hungry, snapping, so cold, and the water, always the water—

She dropped it as though burned. She did not want to touch eel ever again.

Once those dishes were cleared, the second course was delivered. This, Guinevere was more familiar with. Fruits and jellies and nuts, displayed artfully. She eagerly reached forward and took several pieces, then froze. No one else had taken any. They were all just . . . looking.

"The second course," Brangien whispered, "is generally more to appeal to the eye than to the tongue. Though if you are not going to eat all those cherries, please slip one onto my plate."

Guinevere was startled by this new, brash Brangien. Then she saw how far into her very deep cup of wine Brangien was, and it made more sense. Guinevere put two cherries onto Brangien's plate. A minstrel played while his companion sang, the songs competing with the general chatter and happy noise of the room. Guinevere felt invisible. It was not unwelcome.

The courses continued. Guinevere was more careful to take her cues from the women around her. The table was divided between men and women. Arthur, surrounded by his men, was across from her. They laughed raucously, trading stories and commenting on the quality of the meat. She found herself wishing he would look at her. Even with Brangien next to her, by the sixth course she was beginning to feel truly alone. She was marooned in a sea of falsehood, and among celebrating strangers, she felt it most keenly. She meant nothing to any of these women. She only meant something to Arthur. But he meant something to everyone in Camelot. She had so little claim on him.

But someone *was* looking at her. Mordred raised his cup in a toast, eyes glittering in the candlelight. She did not answer his toast.

"Do not meddle with that one," Brangien whispered, nibbling on the roasted nuts Guinevere had passed along. "He is poison. Sir Tristan says Arthur should banish him, but Arthur is too kind."

"Sir Tristan?"

Brangien subtly pointed out a man sitting several people down from Arthur. He had black hair cut close to his head like Arthur's, though his was coiled in tight curls. His skin was deep brown, his face handsome in a way Guinevere could not help but appreciate.

"Sir Tristan brought me here and got me a position in the castle." Brangien smiled, but it was a smile burdened by a deep sadness Guinevere was not privy to. Why would Sir Tristan have a young woman as a maid in the first place? They could not be family. They looked nothing alike. "Like most of Arthur's knights, he is not from Camelot. Arthur took him in when he was banished. Took us both in."

"Why was he banished?" Guinevere asked it casually, but she needed information about everyone close to Arthur.

"Isolde." Brangien said the word as reverently as a prayer. This time she did not even pretend to smile. "She was my lady. She was betrothed to Sir Tristan's uncle. An old lecher." Brangien's hand tightened around her knife.

"Sir Tristan loved her?"

There were tears pooling in Brangien's eyes.

"Are you well?" Guinevere reached out a hand, but Brangien brushed at her eyes and then smiled brightly.

"The dim light in here. It makes my eyes weak. You must try the roasted fruit." She scooped damsons onto Guinevere's plate, too many for one person to eat. "Sir Tristan is a good man. You will like him. Sir Bors means well, but he is prideful and quick to anger. His arm was withered by his father."

"How did his *father* do that?" She could not see much of Bors's arm. It was not unusual for men to be injured in battle or even to lose a limb. But Bors's hand was twisted and gray, more like bark than skin where it stuck out from his sleeves.

"Sorcerer." Brangien popped a damson into her mouth. "Not a kind man. His father, I mean. Sir Bors is not kind, either, but he would never harm an innocent. And he fought back the forest with the ferocity of a man with four arms. He was one of the first to call for Merlin's banishment." Brangien dropped the information as easily as roasted meat fell from the bones in front of them. Guinevere tried not to react.

"Did you know him? Merlin?"

"He was gone before I arrived. There was a purge of anyone who practiced the old ways."

Guinevere wanted more details, but Brangien moved on in hushed tones about Sir Percival's sister, who had never married and who depended on her brother for everything, much to the chagrin of her sister-in-law. Since Guinevere knew nothing about either of them, the stories had no impact and her attention wandered to the more important bits.

Mordred, always watching, distrusted among the other knights. Tristan, banished and in love with his uncle's young wife. Bors, loud and brash, with his arm withered by magic. She would have to be most careful around him. Several other knights whose names she struggled to remember. The ladies whose names she actually remembered: Percival's wife, Blanchefleur, and his sister Dindrane, the two of whom seemed to be in an aggressive game to get the best cuts of meat before the other. Most of Arthur's knights were young. Sir Tristan, Sir Gawain, Sir Mordred, all unmarried. But the wives who were present were all older than her by at least a decade. So much experience. Despair overwhelmed her; she had taken on too much. The bottom of her cup greeted her. She wanted to whisper her name into it, to carry herself safely pooled in a cup.

She realized several moments too late that everyone else was standing. She stood, too, to find Arthur beaming at the room. "Never has a king been so blessed with friends as I have. You are more than my friends. You are my family. We are Camelot, and on this night, I am filled with hope for the future."

"And hope of a good night with a fresh lass!"

Guinevere's face burned. The knight who had spoken—Sir Percival?—was red-faced, too, but flushed with wine, not embarrassment. The men laughed. The women primly ignored the comment. Except his sister Dindrane, who glared at Guinevere with undisguised malice.

Brangien leaned near. "I will be close tonight," she whispered.

Arthur came around the table and held out his hand. Guinevere put hers in it. Cheers and whistles followed them out of the dining hall all the way to Arthur's bedchamber. He closed the doors behind them, sealing them in. A bed waited, its four posters draped with muted cloth. The room glowed dimly in the candlelight, everything soft and dark with anticipation.

She had known being queen was necessary. That only by being Arthur's wife could she have the freedom to be close enough to do what needed to be done. But . . . she was his wife now.

She had not thought this through.

"So, my queen," he said, turning to her. "Who are you really?"

CHAPTER THREE

Arthur gestured toward the sitting area of his wide, stone-walled room.

Guinevere was grateful to move in a direction away from the bed. "You should not have asked what to call me when we were in the cave. What if Mordred had heard?"

Arthur leaned back, stretching. "Many men have special names for their wives. What if I called you your real name as a sort of endearment?"

For a moment, the idea of hearing her name in Arthur's mouth was more tempting than any delicacy at the feast. Maybe then she would feel at home here. But no. If she was to be Guinevere, she would be Guinevere all the time. "You may call me 'My Queen.' Or 'Loveliest of Women.' Or 'Ruby of Unimaginable Value.'"

Arthur laughed. "Very well, my sun and moon. Tell me, how is your father? I miss him."

Guinevere squirmed, uncomfortable with thinking of Merlin as her father, just as she was uncomfortable in the chair. Fatherhood fit Merlin even more poorly than her body fit this seat designed for a much taller person. "How is he ever? Half the conversations I have with him leave me more confused than I was to begin with. But I am fairly certain he sends you his best wishes."

"He sent me his best student and his only possession, which is better than wishes."

She felt a blush, and prayed the dim candlelight would hide it. "I hope I am enough."

"Banishing him was idiocy. I cannot believe I had to do it. I trust that he knows what is best, but pretending to hate him, allowing my people to hate him is . . . wrong." He shifted in the chair, burdened by the invisible weight of the deception. Merlin had said Arthur was the most honest of men. The most true. Even though she had met him mere hours ago, she could *feel* that. It was as though she had known him before. Like if she reached deep enough, she would have memories of him.

But that was Merlin's doing. His words were so laced with magic that even his tales created pictures. She knew Arthur because Merlin knew him. She trusted him because Merlin trusted him.

A threat is coming, he had said. *We need more time. I need to give you more. But it is nearly here, and I dare not delay. You must go to Arthur.*

But why me? she had asked. *Your power is so much greater than mine. What if I cannot protect him?*

You are afraid of the wrong thing, he had said. And then he had looked at her, the way he did when he was searching for something in her eyes. He never found it. He twitched into a smile, and then wandered away. *I will find some horses. There is a convent waiting for you.*

Guinevere sent silent anger and curses toward Merlin. That was all the preparation he had given her. Something was coming, it was nearly here, and she had to protect Arthur. Alone.

"We should talk about my role here," she said. "I am sorry you had to marry me." It was the only way for her to stay close to him, and to have access to the castle. To the people around him. To every threat that his knights could not dream of, that swords could not save him from.

Arthur was trying to carve a nation of ideals from the wild and hungry land, and the land was not giving up without a fight. Only someone who knew the subtle paths and seeping reach of magic could ever hope to protect him against it. She had seen his knights in the magical forest. Their terror gave her some hope. She was no Merlin and never would be, but she knew more than these men. She would see things they never could. Merlin had not told her what the threat was, but she would know.

"Do not apologize." Arthur took her hands in his. She dampened her sense of him; it felt intrusive right now. She could control it, a little, if she concentrated and it did not catch her by surprise. "It is a great sacrifice you have made for me. And I needed to marry soon anyway. Percival has been arranging for me to unexpectedly run into his sister."

"She is ten years your senior!" Guinevere coughed to cover up the force of her exclamation. "And lovely."

Arthur grinned. "She is a jewel among women. But a lesser jewel. Perhaps more of a shiny stone. Certainly not a ruby."

Now she was sure he saw her blush, because he looked away and spoke quickly. "Then there are the Picts to the north, who would have me wed one of theirs and use it as an excuse to expand south-ward into our lands. Better to have military treaties than marital trea-ties where the Picts are concerned. Besides, marriage to a distant king's daughter renews my southerly bonds of friendship without any of my borders fearing I am trying to expand. It is ideal."

"But I am not a distant king's daughter." She was surprised by the subtle longing in her voice. If she were really Guinevere, how much simpler her life would be. How different this night would be. Though she suspected she would have been just as terrified had the marriage bed awaited, rather than a discussion on how to keep Arthur safe from fey assassins and magical attacks. Perhaps those aspects of being a queen had been covered in the convent. If so, the real Guinevere had taken them to the grave. And Merlin certainly had not given her an education in romance. She was sixteen, and this was the first time a boy had held her hands. Rather than being thrilled by it, she was fighting magic to avoid invading his mind.

"You are Merlin's daughter. And that makes you far more valuable than any princess."

"I hope I am a better protector than he is a father."

She meant it in jest, but Arthur's face darkened. He nodded. "We all of us must be better than our fathers. At least Merlin leaves you nothing to atone for. Only to live up to."

It was a relief to see how much Arthur missed Merlin. It confirmed Merlin's stories of him, how much they trusted each other.

She tried to understand why Camelot would demand Merlin's banishment. It was true that he was closer to the wild magic of the forest than to the orderly rule of Arthur. Merlin was not quite human, not quite other. He was inscrutable and confusing and often somehow absent even when he was right next to her. But he was also the reason Camelot existed. The reason Arthur was alive. If Camelot could reject that, what would they do if they found out she was no princess, but rather a simple forest witch?

Arthur was king because of magic—a magical sword, delivered by the Lady of the Lake. A life protected by a wizard. But his role as king was to push back magic in order for mankind to thrive.

Until magic was truly gone, it could threaten him. She would be the shield against any magic seeking to destroy what Arthur was doing here. As ill-prepared as she felt, she would not fail him. She would live up to Merlin's legacy. "I am honored to serve you, my king."

"And together, we serve Camelot." He smiled wearily, leaning back and rubbing his face. "I am glad I do not have to get married every day. It is exhausting."

Guinevere, too, was more tired than she could remember being. She felt as though she had lived a lifetime in the last few days. And, in truth, she had. An entire new life as she became Guinevere.

There was one thing left to discuss, though. She did not want to, but she needed to know the boundaries of their agreement. The things the real Guinevere would have known.

"What do . . ." She hesitated, then changed tactics. "What do the people expect of your wife?"

Arthur, honest Arthur, sweet Arthur, did not understand her meaning. "I have never had a queen before. I think you should be at my side for formal events. When greeting other rulers. Perhaps even for hunting, if you wish."

"I will need privacy to do my work."

He frowned, scratching the back of his neck. It was obvious he had not considered this yet. No wonder Merlin had sent her. Even with her there to protect him through magic, Arthur hardly thought about it. "Hunting parties could be a good way to get you out of the confines of the city without arousing suspicion. I will see to it that you have everything you need, and privacy to do your work without being noticed. We can figure out reasons why you need to be out and about instead of always in the castle. I—" He paused, then smiled. "I want you to be happy here."

"I am here to work. To serve you, as Merlin did."

Arthur nodded, something shifting in his warm, open face. "But you can still be happy. It is important to me."

Guinevere did her best to suppress her own brilliant smile. "Very

well. I will add happiness to my list of duties, alongside protecting
the king from magical threat." She stood. Arthur stood. They both
stood there, unmoving. The bed awaited. Their marriage was legal
only upon consummation. "But it is not legal anyway, since I am
not actually Guinevere," she blurted out, continuing her unspoken
thought.

Arthur raised an eyebrow, puzzled. Then, at last, he understood
what she was unwilling to say. He blushed in a confusingly gratifying
manner. "You are here as Merlin's daughter, and I ask nothing more
of you. Neither do I expect anything more."

Her relief was . . . complicated. "But eventually they will want heirs."

Arthur's gaze seemed to turn inward, a shadow of old pain crossing his face. Perhaps he thought of his mother. "We will worry about
that when it comes. Besides, I am fully confident that you will root
out every magical threat to my life within a fortnight."

She was grateful she could tell he was joking. She did not expect it
to be so quick or so easy. The urgency of Merlin's demand, the lengths
he went to in order to establish her here as Guinevere—it all made
her certain that the coming threat was not to be underestimated.

But she was also grateful that Arthur expected her to be a wife in
name only. He was a stranger to her, still, no matter how familiar he
seemed and how instantly she trusted him. She would die for him.

The thought startled her. It felt like it was coming from far away,
like an echo. She accepted it as it presented itself, though. She
would die for Arthur. But that did not mean she wanted to share his
bed on the first day they met. Though here, without the trappings of
kinghood, he was just as handsome and far more *real* in a way that
made her feel light and unsteady inside.

She had met more men in the last few days than in all the other
days of her life combined. It would take some time to decide how
she felt about them in general, and him in particular. Though he was

by far the best of them. She suspected she could meet every man on the entire vast island and still find Arthur the best.

He pulled aside a tapestry of a woodland hunting scene. Like everything in his bedroom, it was faded with age. There were no luxuries here. Everything was serviceable or old.

Behind the tapestry, a heavy door was revealed. "It connects my rooms to your rooms. We will visit each other enough, so there will be no cause for suspicion." He grinned. "Perhaps I can learn how to plait your hair, and you can teach me some magic."

She laughed, finally at ease. "Plaiting hair *is* magic. That is why men cannot do it. It is women's magic alone. Which reminds me!" He would not sleep in his crown, after all. She needed to do more than the knots she had left there. She went to the nearest window, the thick, uneven glass cool to the touch. She breathed on it, then traced her knotting patterns onto it. When her breath fog faded, so, too, did her tracings. But they were still there. It was weak magic, like the hair knots, but it left a bit of her here. It would keep minor things out, and she would feel the break if any knot was undone.

She did the same on all the windows. With each bit of breath magic, she felt more winded, as though she had been running. It would fade with time. The door was not right for breath, so she spat on it. Arthur laughed at that. She shushed him, but she was secretly pleased. Though Arthur smiled easily, it still seemed a very fine thing, making him laugh.

At the bed—which she could view without fear knowing it expected nothing of her—she pulled threads free from the worn coverlet and twisted them into the correct knots. More permanent, but less personal. The sacrifice was not in her body, but in the risk that the magic would come unbound without her knowing. But it was enough for now.

"Did Merlin teach you this?" Arthur asked, curious.

"No, he—yes." Guinevere paused, trying to remember. Merlin would never stoop to knot magic, even to demonstrate it. It was far too human. Frail and temporary. She tried to conjure a memory of Merlin explaining it to her, teaching her. It would have been at their sturdy table. Or in the forest? She remembered her neat bedroll, the cottage she kept tidy. The trees and the sun and the birds. Staring at her own hands in wonder. Night and day, sleeping and waking, hunger and food and everything swirling and obscured as though she were searching through fog . . .

Merlin, frowning, pushing his fingers against her forehead. "This should be enough," he had said. *"Do not look for more."*

She rubbed at the spot on her forehead. He had pushed the knowledge into her brain. Willed it to be there, rather than teaching her himself. He could be *very* lazy. "Yes, he taught me, in his own way." She finished the knot.

Satisfied, she turned and almost ran into Arthur. He had come up behind her to watch her work.

"Sorry!" Her hands were on his chest. She pulled them back quickly. "I am sorry. I should go. I am tired."

He walked her to the tapestry, pulling it aside again and holding it for her. "Thank you. I am glad you are here, Guinevere."

"Me, too," she whispered, surprised to find how much she meant it. And surprised by how much she wished she had told him her name after all.

As the door closed behind her, leaving her holding a candle in the dark passageway, she closed her eyes and leaned close to the flickering light. She whispered her name directly into the flame.

And then she blew it out.

The spider dies on the windowsill.

The centipede withers, legs twitching in agony, at the space between door and stone floor.

A dozen other things that creep and crawl and skitter try and fail to visit Arthur that night. None intends harm, so the magical bonds are not broken and no one is alerted to the dark queen's attempt. But those same magical bonds mean that the queen cannot see.

Not seeing, however, is just as telling as seeing.

The usurper king has a new wizard. Merlin is gone, but still has his claws in the kingdom. She calls back her legions that have not yet perished. There will be other times to see. Other ways to spy. She has hands and eyes in Camelot yet. Let the king and this wizard sleep.

She is the earth, the rocks, the forest. She is patient.

She plucks the life from a hundred spiders in a twitch of anger.

Perhaps not too patient.

CHAPTER FOUR

The problem with being a lady was that a lady had a lady's maid, and a lady's maid never left.

Brangien had been sleeping on a cot in the corner when Guinevere crept from the passageway into her own bedroom. If Brangien was startled to wake up in the morning and find Guinevere, she did not show it. She bustled about, drawing curtains and tidying. There were windows along only one side of the room. The back wall was against the secret passage, which itself was against the rock of the mountain. The way the castle clung to the cliff was unnerving to Guinevere. There was so little between her and falling. And the lake lurked, waiting beneath to swallow her whole.

No wonder Merlin had never described Camelot to her. He had filled her instead with stories of Arthur. His goodness, his bravery, his goals. If she had been aware of the particular geography of the place, she might not have agreed to come.

Come to think of it, she had never explicitly agreed to come, because he had not asked. He had told her the threat was imminent and whisked her to the convent. That was his way, though. For all she knew, ten years in the future he would sit down and explain the whole thing to her, including what the threat was, how she was to fight it, and why it had to be she, and she alone.

After she had already done it.

She tried to have compassion for him. It was like he lived every moment of his life all at once, his mind slipping through time. Which meant that he knew things were coming before they happened, but it also meant that he had a hard time landing on what needed to be said or done at any given time.

And it made her own life very frustrating. Nothing to be done for it, though, but to get to work.

She stood and stretched. The bed, at least, was comfortable. It seemed new compared to Arthur's. The coverlets were dyed deepest blue. The ropes across the bed frame tight enough that they did not so much as creak when she moved. And the mattress was softer than yellow-green tufts of new spring grass. The bed at the convent had been a straw mattress, itchy and lumpy. And her bed at home had been . . . She could only picture it, not remember sleeping in it. It felt like a lifetime ago. She had only the memory of dreams, which was fitting for a home shared with a wizard.

Cloth draped over the four posters of the bed could be drawn closed like curtains at a window, sealing her in to sleep. She had not done that the night before. She did not like the idea of being confined in her dreams.

In addition to the bed, there were several chests in the room, sent ahead by the convent. They were the real Guinevere's. She wondered what was inside them. It felt wrong to open them, but she had already claimed Guinevere's name. How much guiltier would claiming belongings make her?

She tore her eyes away from the chests, which had begun to feel like caskets. There was a table with a single chair, and Brangien's neat cot in the corner. A door led out to the hallway, and another door to a side chamber.

Two tapestries brightened the wall without windows; one of them hid the secret door. The tapestries were both old, like the one in Arthur's room. The pastoral scenes could have been hanging in any great man's home.

"Why does he have no tapestries of his life?" Guinevere asked as Brangien bustled around.

"Beg pardon, my queen?"

"Arthur. The king. All the tapestries I have seen are meaningless. Does he have none of the miracle of the sword? Of his victory over Uther Pendragon? The defeat of the fairy queen and the forest of blood?"

Brangien paused where she was laying out fresh underclothes. "I had not thought of it before. But he has never commissioned them. And there are no tapestries of Uther Pendragon, either. I think he had them destroyed."

"Is he— Am I supposed to eat breakfast with him?" Guinevere did not know the rules yet. Could she go over to his room to bid him good morning? Should she?

"I believe there is a trial this morning. A woman caught practicing magic." Brangien said it as perfunctorily as her movements making Guinevere's bed were. It was a routine matter. Guinevere forced a neutral *hmm* in response.

After Brangien was satisfied with the items she had chosen, she bowed and left. Guinevere hurried to the windows, repeating for herself the same work that she had done last night for Arthur. She would need to redo it all at least once every three nights. And there were bigger, stronger magics to work. But those would take time as well as supplies.

She had just finished tracing the knots on the window when the sitting room door opened. She hoped it looked like she was trying to see the view through the thick glass.

Brangien bowed neatly. "Everything is ready, my lady."

Ravenous, Guinevere followed, eager for breakfast. Instead, she was greeted by a tub of steaming water in the center of her sitting room.

"No!" she exclaimed.

"My lady? Did I do something wrong?" Brangien was standing next to the tub. A table held various tinctures and soaps, a soft length of cloth, a scrubbing brush. Brangien's sleeves had been tied back, her pale arms exposed.

"What is this for?" Guinevere looked everywhere but at the bath. She had seen something reflected on the water. Something not in this room. She did not want to know what it was. Water was the best tool for seeing, better than any of her paltry tricks. Water touched everything, flowing from one life to the next. With enough patience and time, water could lead a skilled magician to any answer.

But it could also lead them astray. Water shaped to whatever container held it. Not all containers were benign. The Lady of the Lake had long ago claimed water magic as her own, and it all flowed back to her in time. The Lady of the Lake had been Merlin's ally against the Dark Queen, but she was ancient and unknowable, and Guinevere could not risk invoking any of her power within Camelot. Better to be small. Contained. Knotted.

She could justify it all she wanted to, but magic aside, the bath was *water*. Guinevere would not climb into it.

"I think the temperature is pleasant, but if it is not to your liking, I can change it. Shall I help you undress?"

"No!"

Brangien flinched, wounded at the vehemence of Guinevere's response. Her face turned scarlet and she stared at the floor.

"It is perfectly customary, my lady. I have bathed many women before you. And you need not put your face under if it frightens you."

"It is not that." Guinevere scrambled, grasping for a reason why this ordinary task for a lady's maid would not—could not—ever happen. "At the convent they taught me that my body is only for my husband. Even I am not to look at myself while naked." It sounded reasonable for a society that forbade her from showing her wrists. "I could not bear if anyone else saw me. You are a fine lady's maid—the best I could hope for. But I must bathe myself."

Brangien frowned, but at least she no longer looked wounded. "I have only recently become Christian. I have not heard this."

"I think it is particular to the convent where I was instructed on how to be a wife. There are so many more ways for a queen to sin." She tried not to grimace at all the falsehoods coming out of her mouth. Certainly in her three days at the convent, she had learned a great deal about sin and guilt, which seemed a powerful type of magic in its own right. A magic of controlling and shaping others. The nuns wielded it deftly, experts in their craft. They were also kind and loving and generous. Guinevere would not have minded more time among them, trying to understand this new religion that was pushing back the old in much the same way men were pushing back the forests.

Arthur had embraced Christianity, too. She would have to learn it. If only Merlin were here to place it all inside her head like he had the knot magic.

"So," Guinevere said, "I would like to bathe myself. When I am finished, I will call you and you can dress me—and care for my hair? You are much better with it than I am!"

This seemed to placate Brangien, or at least make her less afraid for her position. She nodded. "I will retrieve your undergarments. If you need any help getting into them, please call for me." She hurried to the bedroom, then brought the linen undergarments in and set them gently on the table beside the other supplies.

Guinevere smiled until Brangien left again. Then she dropped the smile with a shudder as she dropped her nightclothes. She did not look at the bath. She could feel the water there, steaming, promising magic she did not ask for and would not explore.

She stepped out of the ring of her nightclothes. Her feet were bare against the stone floor and she curled her toes, missing the soft give of soil. Luckily, Brangien had left a candle on the table. Guinevere breathed it into life. It was a dangerous trick, but the wick contained the fire before it could escape.

Fire magic was Merlin's specialty. Not hers. She needed the limits of knot magic, the security of the loops and ties. But she had to get clean, and she could not bring herself to sit in water.

She put her finger to the flame, whispering. It jumped from wick to flesh, stinging just shy of burning. She spun in a circle. The flame followed the path of the circle to form a shimmering ring, encompassing her. It took all her concentration to hold it, to forbid it from the chaos that was its nature. Unlike water, fire had no master. No lady or queen who could rule it.

It rushed over her hot and hungry and dry, devouring anything unclean. When she could no longer stand it, she pushed away the air so the fire had nothing to feed on. It reluctantly faded and died.

It left her skin itching and her whole body tired. But she was clean and the water left undisturbed. As difficult as it was, fire magic was relatively safe. It devoured whatever it touched, leaving no evidence of itself or its user. And when it was extinguished, it was gone. It could not carry news of her magic to anyone who knew where to look.

The first time she had tried a cleansing, Merlin had to extinguish her. She had been seconds away from being devoured. She frowned, as stung by the memory as by the fire itself. Merlin had found it *hilarious*. She wished he could see how well she had handled it now. But at least he had given her the tools she needed to avoid water. It was uncharacteristically thoughtful of him.

She pulled on her underclothes and surveyed the room. The table of bath supplies was undisturbed. Chagrined, she broke off a piece of the petal-pressed soap and tossed it into the water behind her. She took the brush and backed closer to the bath, carefully dipping it in without looking at what she was doing. Then she hastily replaced it on the table. The other supplies she rearranged messily, assuming a princess would never worry about neatness with so many people to be neat on her behalf.

Her hair was dry, but hair was washed infrequently. She would figure out how to trick Brangien when the time came.

Now all she had to do was wait a reasonable bath period. She sat on the floor so the surface of the water was above her eye level and she could not see it and the lies it told. When the steam finally stopped drifting, she called for Brangien.

Brangien did not notice anything amiss about the unused bath. She undid Guinevere's hair, redoing the braids and carefully removing the jewels Guinevere had not remembered to take out the night before. Brangien placed them into a gilded box, which was then closed and locked.

"I have the key, unless my lady would like to hold it herself." There was a challenge in Brangien's voice, as though daring Guinevere not to trust her. The bath rejection had done damage. Guinevere needed to repair it. She could not have someone in such constant contact suspect or dislike her.

"I would lose it, I am certain! Thank you for taking care of it. What is expected of me today?" Guinevere asked.

Brangien shook her head, deftly twisting and braiding Guinevere's long, thick hair. "It is assumed the queen will be tired after her wedding night, so none of the other ladies will call on you."

Guinevere did not comment on the basis of that assumption. At least it gave her some peace. "And Arthur?"

"I expect he will be busy all day."

"Good!" Guinevere turned, smiling in unfeigned excitement. "Will you take me into the city? Show me Camelot as you live it?"

Brangien looked taken aback. "What do you mean?"

"This is my city now. I want to walk the streets with you. See how it works, how the people live. Please take me on an adventure?"

Brangien's face softened with friendliness. She finished pinning a twisted braid to frame Guinevere's face. "I forget sometimes what a wonder it is. When Sir Tristan and I arrived, it felt like the journey across the lake had transported me into a dreamland. It was the first time in months I could feel something like hope again." She leaned back, admiring her work before nodding to herself. "But do you think it is appropriate for us to explore today?"

"I have not been given any instructions on what I am to do. And if no one has told me no, they cannot be angry with us!"

Brangien laughed. "If we are leaving the castle, we will need different clothing than I picked."

Guinevere followed Brangien into the bedroom and waited patiently as Brangien cinched and tied her into her clothing. Today's dress was a cheerful yellow. The hood draped over her shoulders was deep blue. After checking to make certain that Guinevere's sleeves went all the way to her fingers, Brangien knelt and helped Guinevere get into her shoes.

"Would you like to wear a veil?" Brangien asked.

"Must I?"

"It is not unusual for ladies, but it is not so common that it will cause gossip if you do not."

"I would much rather they get used to my face than expect a veil."

Brangien nodded and stood. Her maid's clothes were nicer than any Guinevere had ever owned before now, but the cloth was not so finely woven, and she had no fur trimming her hood. The dyes were duller as well. Brangien's clothes said that she was important, but not royal.

There was an entire language to this city that Guinevere had to learn. She was grateful she had Brangien to navigate it for her, and even more grateful for Merlin's wisdom in choosing a princess from so far away for her to impersonate, so that any errors could be excused by her foreignness.

Brangien hurried her through the hallway. Guinevere suspected her maid was half-worried they would be caught and not permitted to leave. They both sighed with relief as they exited the castle through one of the side doors; then they turned to each other and laughed.

Guinevere followed Brangien down an unnervingly narrow flight of stairs that wound from the midsection of the castle all the way down to the city below. Having so many doors into the castle initially seemed like a safety flaw, but only one person at a time could navigate these stairs. And they were so twisty and treacherous, no one in armor and wielding a weapon could climb them with any haste.

The base of the castle featured the only door wide enough to accommodate more than one person. It was open, but guarded ten men deep. They passed alongside it. Guinevere half expected the men to call out to them to stop, but they paid the two women no mind.

Feeling freer than she had since she entered the convent, Guinevere linked her arm through Brangien's, and together they walked down the steep path into Arthur's city. The streets were not what she had expected. They were not cobbled or made of dirt, but were channels in the rock itself. The centers were flat, but the sides sloped gently upward. Almost like the aqueducts above their heads, but on a far larger scale.

They passed the homes closest to the castle, which were also the nicest. Brangien chattered happily about them. Sir Percival's, Sir Bors's, Sir Mordred's. Mordred's was by far the largest and finest of them.

"Where does Sir Tristan live?" Guinevere asked.

"Most of the knights who flocked to Arthur left behind everything they had to fight at his side. He claimed them as brothers and gave them rooms in the castle." She turned and pointed to the lowest level. "They all live there, in their own chambers. Arthur says they are the foundation of his strength."

"He values them very much."

"He does. And his love is reciprocated." She returned her attention to the city. "Doubtless you will be forced to sit through many meals at these manors. No reason to linger here. I want to show you *my* Camelot. Pull your hood a little closer. If no one recognizes you, we will move easier."

Brangien's happiness was contagious. Guinevere's own feet moved faster, nearly dancing down the path. "Do you spend a lot of time in the city?"

"I do! Or, I did. There was not much for me to do before the castle finally got her lady." Brangien turned to Guinevere. "But do not take that to mean I am not glad you are here! It is a relief to be useful again. It has been so long since I lost Isolde."

"You were Isolde's maid? I thought you were with Sir Tristan."

"I was hers first." She cut off the conversation with another determined smile. Brangien offered smiles in place of explanations. "The aqueducts are back to water today." She pointed upward. Guinevere followed the lines of them, twin tubes going alongside the road and then veering to either side down through the city.

"It is a clever system. I have never seen its like." Guinevere had never seen a city, period, but Brangien did not know that.

"We do not have wells. The rivers provide our water. It would be such a chore going down to the lake and then hiking to the heights of the city or the castle. There is a saying among servants when things go wrong. 'Could be buckets.' Their way of reminding each other to look on the bright side of things. At least they are not breaking their backs hauling endless buckets of water up these streets!"

Guinevere understood. She had to step carefully to avoid breaking into a run, pulled as they were by the slope of the streets. The homes and shops were all built at an angle. Most doors were on the lake side of the hill. She peered into an open one to see a tiny entry, the floor sloping sharply upward toward the castle. Shelves had been put there, a clever use of the space. The streets seemed unplanned, like tributaries branching out from the castle. Houses and buildings had been put in wherever they could be.

As she and Brangien got lower, the buildings grew closer together, jostling and nudging each other for space. Barrels of water were placed at regular intervals.

"What are the barrels for, if you have the aqueducts?"

"Fire," Brangien said. "There are bells on every street. If they ring, everyone runs out and commands their assigned barrels."

A fire would eat up this hill with terrifying speed. Many of the buildings were stone, but they were mingled with enough wooden structures that it would be devastating and deadly.

"Mind the little shit," Brangien said.

Guinevere looked at her, shocked. Brangien laughed, covering her mouth in embarrassment. "Oh, I am sorry, my lady. That is his title." She pointed to a scrappy boy pulling a cart straight up the hill. "He collects the night's chamber pot offerings and disposes of them out beyond the lake. In Uther's day, these streets ran with piss and offal. Actually, they called this Pissway. Arthur imposed fines for dumping into the streets. He uses the money to pay the little shits. Now the streets are clean, but the old names are harder to wash away. Some have started calling Pissway the Castle Way, which is nicer. And the merchants on Shitstreet have been campaigning vigorously for people to call it Market Street. But it is so much less satisfying to say."

Guinevere laughed. She could not help it. Perhaps a princess would not have found this funny, but she certainly did. She had never thought through the sheer logistics of this many people in a small space. Nor had she ever considered that a king would have to figure out how to deal with the chamber pots of a thousand citizens. In her head, it had been all swords and battles and glory and magic.

A city was its own kind of magic, though. Complicated and filled with ever-moving parts. Arthur was responsible for all of them. Guinevere was already overwhelmed with the city, and they had barely come across any people. It was wonderful and terrible and *new*.

Perhaps Merlin should have spent more time taking her into cities than giving her knot magic.

Brangien pointed out various shops. Most of the buildings had residences on the upper floors and a shop on the bottom. Smithies were all on the plain beyond the lake, along with slaughterhouses and anything else that either could not fit in the limited space of Camelot's slopes or was too offensively scented to intermingle with homes.

"Every third day, one of which is tomorrow," Brangien said, "we have a market beyond the lake. People come from all the hamlets and villages to trade and buy. Special markets happen every new moon.

That is when you can find more unusual things. Spices. Silk, sometimes! My father and uncle were silk traders. They walked across the world to get here, hiding their wares the whole way by taking turns in the cart pretending to have the plague." She looked both sad and fond. "My father bought a better life for himself. My family was well-to-do and respected thanks to him. That is how I got a position as Isolde's lady's maid." Forcibly breaking free from the past—though Guinevere wanted to hear more—Brangien continued. "Special markets also have horses and weapons and food and shoes and anything you can imagine. Traders come from all over. King Arthur's fees are fair, and everyone knows they will be safe in his borders. Last time, there was a juggler, and acrobats. I cannot wait to show you."

"It sounds wonderful." It sounded chaotic. And like the perfect place for a magical attack against Arthur. The more she walked through Camelot, the more she saw how inhospitable it would be to the Dark Queen's fairies and minions. All these people, this ancient, sleeping stone, the metal on doors and windows. What threat had Merlin seen coming? Why could he not have been more specific? The Dark Queen was dead and defeated, but her type of magic— wild and devouring—lived on. Guinevere had seen it herself on the way here.

"Is there anything you need today?" Brangien asked. "Most things we will have to get at the markets, but some of the shops might have a ready supply."

"No, thank you. I cannot think of anything I lack." Nothing that any of the shops would sell, anyhow. Though she would have to go through her box of jewels. Certain stones held magic in special ways. And no one would look askance at a king wearing jewels.

It would be her next task. For now, they were midway through the city. The shape of the slope evened out here before dropping again dramatically closer to the lake. It was the flattest ground they had been on. Guinevere heard shouting and whirled, alarmed.

"Oh!" Brangien said. "I can show you something truly exciting." Brangien turned down a side street and they came to a round building. It was the largest Guinevere had seen besides the castle.

"This is newer than the castle, but still old. Before Uther Pendragon. He built nothing." Brangien led her through a dark stone arch and into the brilliant sunlight.

It was not a building, exactly. There was no roof. The walls encompassed a flat, dirt-packed circle. Several levels of seats were built into the walls. Those seats were nearly all filled, and they held the source of the roaring shouts. Around the circle, various rings had been set up, marked by chalk in the dirt. Weapons lined the walls. And within the rings, men battled.

"Come on, there is a special box. I have never been able to sit in it before!" Brangien pulled her swiftly past the steps and benches. They climbed to the top of the wall, nodded at a guard there, and entered a wooden structure. It was built out so that when they reached the open front, they were suspended above the fighters. Between the cushion-covered benches and the roof above to provide shade, they were the most comfortable people in the arena.

Certainly more comfortable than the men beneath them. The warriors pounded and hacked at each other. Their thick leather armor, sewn with metal plates over the most vulnerable areas, absorbed the blows. But Guinevere screamed and covered her mouth as a man near them took a brutal hit.

"The swords are blunted," Brangien said, patting her hand. "There are still injuries—sometimes terrible—but no one has died."

"What are they doing it for?" There were more than a dozen men down there, performing war like a minstrel performed songs.

Guinevere's heart raced. It was terrible, and exciting, and she did not understand the purpose of it.

"Training, some of them. See, there are Sir Tristan and Sir Caradoc. Sir Bors is directing the fights." Brangien deftly identified each man, though to Guinevere they all looked the same: like helmeted, armored death.

"Is Mordred down there as well?"

"Oh, no. He never fights. He thinks much too highly of himself to train with his brother knights, even though King Arthur often joins them."

"And who is—"

Brangien gasped, clutching Guinevere's hand. "He is here!"

"Who?"

Brangien pointed to a new knight who had entered the ring. He was tall and broad-shouldered, and he wore a leather mask that obscured his entire face. His armor was unusual, too, a jumble of metals of different colors. The variety made it look less like armor he wore and more like it was a natural part of him.

"The patchwork knight! That is what they call him. No one knows who he is or where he is from! He comes sometimes, wins every fight, and then disappears. Oh, he is terribly popular. It cannot be long before he earns a tournament and becomes a true knight of the king."

"Would Arthur do that? Offer a position to a stranger?"

"That is how Sir Tristan got his knighthood! Through his valor in the ring."

"So anyone could perform well enough and then have a place at the king's side? A place in the castle?"

"Yes, but aspirants can only compete here once a week. And there are always so many of them. It is only a matter of time before the patchwork knight makes it through, though." Brangien's tone was distracted, her attention entirely on the ring as she leaned forward, breathless with anticipation.

Guinevere had a reason to pay attention now, too. Because there could be anyone—or anything—behind that mask. Using it as a way to get close to Arthur.

CHAPTER FIVE

Though a dozen other fights were happening at the same time, it was clear who the crowd was there to watch. Every move the patchwork knight made was met with cheers, shouted advice, even a few jeers from those loyal to the unfortunate opponent being mercilessly pounded. The fight lasted only a few minutes before the patchwork knight's would-be rival stumbled out of the ring, admitting defeat. The loser took off his leather armor and threw it.

His theatrics were lost on the crowd. They only had eyes for the patchwork knight. But rather than raise his arms or exult in his victory, he stood perfectly still, his sword tip resting on the ground, both hands wrapped around the hilt. He looked like a statue that would come to life only when challenged.

Another aspirant—Brangien clarified that was what they called those who tried their hand at besting the knights—entered the ring. The aspirants for the week's matches fought each other. Only the winner among those would be allowed to fight one of Arthur's knights.

"Most days there are so many aspirants that the knights never end up fighting one. The sun sets before they work through each other," Brangien explained as another aspirant strode confidently into the ring with the patchwork knight.

"There are that many trying to become King Arthur's knights?"

"Oh, yes. Those who do well enough can enter his service as a standing army. They are given lodging but still have to work for food and train on their own. Only a handful have made it to his actual circle of knights. And those who have were all trained in other courts. A man used to planting fields would have to work for years to best a lifelong knight. But Arthur's system gives them training and creates an army of men we can call on in times of peril."

It made sense. What did not make sense were the patchwork knight's skills. In the time it took Brangien to explain the system, he had already defeated the confident aspirant. This one had to be pulled insensible from the ring. And again the patchwork knight went back to perfect stillness. It was almost inhuman.

Guinevere leaned out over the balcony, squinting as though she could penetrate his mask that way.

"That is what is so unusual about the patchwork knight," Brangien said. She was embroidering a strip of cloth, scarlet thread pulled through in a pattern Guinevere could not see yet. Brangien barely looked at it, her deft fingers knowing their business. "He has obviously been trained. All the other trained knights who competed, like Sir Tristan, announced themselves. Their names, their titles, where they came from. The patchwork knight has never said so much as a word."

"Interesting."

"Be careful," a voice said behind Guinevere, startling her so she nearly fell forward. Slender fingers grasped her waist. She looked up into Mordred's face. He released her, stepping back to a respectful distance. "You should not lean too far out. You might fall. Perhaps the queen should not be so invested in the fights that she risks her own neck to see them better."

Mordred sat on Guinevere's right side. Brangien scowled on her left. "Most of the men," Brangien said, directing her voice to her embroidery, "do not sit in the box. They are too busy training."

Mordred laughed. "*Most* of the men have something to prove down there in the dust and the blood, playing at war with blunted blades."

"Do you watch the fights often?" Guinevere asked, trying to keep the conversation banal and civil.

"Only when there is someone worth watching." He stared directly at her. She narrowed her eyes, but before she could reprimand him, he nodded his head toward the patchwork knight. "I could not miss this."

The second aspirant was still on the ground. No. It was a new one. The patchwork knight had defeated his third opponent. His actions were like the other men's, but more forceful, more efficient. He moved faster, he struck harder, he anticipated every blow before it came. When he did get hit, he twisted away from the pain as easily as if the swords were reed switches.

Guinevere had never before seen fights. Even knowing the swords were blunted and the blows not fatal, she cringed and ached in sympathy at every one. And several times she almost found herself joining the elated shouts of the crowd when the patchwork knight defeated yet another aspirant.

After perhaps an hour, she allowed herself to glance to the side. Mordred was leaning forward, his eyebrows drawn low in concentration or concern. He, too, watched the patchwork knight. Not admiringly, or excitedly, like the crowd. But as though he was studying a foe. Or a threat.

"You seem quite intrigued by the patchwork knight." Guinevere sat up straight and delivered an artfully fake yawn to imply she was not just as invested in the knight. "If you do not fight, why the interest?"

Mordred leaned back. "Look at the way he moves. Every fight is the only fight for him. He does not want this. He *needs* it. Anyone that intensely focused on a goal, anyone with a purpose that single-minded, is dangerous." His words surprised her; it must have shown on her face. He smiled. "Not all of us protect my uncle king with fists and swords. And I am always watching."

She wanted to look away from the intensity and the intelligence she saw in his mossy-green eyes. This time she did not question his meaning. He was watching the patchwork knight, yes. But he was also watching her. And he wanted her to know.

A cold prickle of danger passed over her. She was here to protect Arthur, like Mordred was. But her methods of protecting the king had to remain secret at all costs. She turned deliberately back to the fights. "I am glad my king has you on his side, then."

"On his side and at his side, whenever he needs me, however he needs me. Did you ever hear the story of the Green Knight?"

"No," Guinevere answered.

"Well, you are not likely to because it features a knight who is not quite human, and definitely not Christian. And we do not tell these stories anymore. Do we, dear Brangien?"

"We do not tell that story because you tell it so often there is no need," Brangien grumbled, not looking up from her work.

Mordred laughed. "Tongue like her needle, just as clever and twice as sharp. But our queen has not heard it."

Brangien heaved a sigh and dropped her sewing. "Before the Dark Queen was defeated, Arthur and his earliest knights were questing, looking for supporters. Sir Mordred, Sir Percival, and Sir Bors came to a path through the forest—the only safe one—and found their

way blocked by a knight. Green armor, green skin, beard of leaves."
She waved a hand dismissively. "All green."

"You are terrible at telling stories." Mordred frowned, sounding
hurt.

"He would not let them pass unless they found a weapon that
could defeat him. Sir Percival tried a sword, but the blade got caught
in the thick wood of the knight's arm, and Sir Percival could not pull
it back. Sir Bors tried a mace and chain, but the dent in the Green
Knight's chest blossomed and re-formed."

"They were at a loss," Mordred cut in. "Their weapons had no
effect, and they could think of no way around a problem other than
hit it and hope it bled. Not everything can be solved with iron. So
while they were occupied trying and failing to hack the Green Knight
apart, I crept into the forest and—"

"A deer," Brangien interrupted. "He brought a deer back to eat it.
The Green Knight thought it was hilarious and let them pass."

"Brangien." Mordred put a hand to his chest as though wounded
himself. "You have the soul and imagination of a hammer. Stories are
not nails to be driven home. They are tapestries to be woven."

"Your stories are burdens to be endured. Now can we please
watch the match?" Brangien retrieved her sewing, belying her words
by focusing on that instead.

"What happened to the Green Knight?" Guinevere asked, intrigued. No one here spoke about the time before the Dark Queen
was defeated. It seemed a wondrous and strange landscape. One she
felt more akin to than the order and stone of Camelot.

"Excalibur happened. And that was a far more permanent end
than being nibbled on by a gentle doe." Mordred's tone was wry.
Whether he was mocking himself or Brangien's storytelling, Guinevere could not tell. He stood and bowed. "Allow me to find refreshment for you."

Brangien hissed softly after he walked off. She looked up, then smiled and tucked away her embroidery. "Oh, there! He has defeated another. That makes fifteen. I believe there are only thirty vying today. He may yet get to the knights, if you wish to stay that long."

"Is he likely to meet King Arthur tonight, then?"

"No. If he gets to the knights, it will be an official tournament. Each knight will choose his preferred form of combat, and meet him on the field. He does not have to defeat all of them to win his spot. But he does have to defeat at least three."

"And if he defeats all of them?"

"That has never happened. But if it did, then Arthur himself would challenge him in combat."

Guinevere felt ice in her stomach. "Here?"

"No. Past the lake, in the meadows."

The meadows. Where Arthur had pushed back the Forest of Blood and reclaimed the land. That dirt was soaked in the blood of magic. If the patchwork knight was a fairy creature, he would be more powerful there than in this ancient, dead city. And Arthur would be vulnerable, ensnared by his own rules. If Guinevere were planning to attack the king, that is where she would do it. Where the knights still felt comfortable and at ease, but the protection of their city was not around them.

Guinevere stood. "I am feeling faint. I would like to return to the castle."

Brangien scrambled to pack her things back into her satchel. On their way out they passed Mordred, who was carrying a goblet of wine and a plate of bread and cheese.

"Leaving so soon?" he called. Guinevere did not answer. She needed to speak to Arthur. And, more importantly, she needed to break free of her maid in order to follow the patchwork knight after he was done fighting for the day.

"The king is not in the castle." Brangien offered the explanation with
an apologetic tone. Guinevere had sent her to find Arthur as soon as
they returned to her rooms. "He is often gone. He travels his lands
constantly, checking in with the farmers, ensuring the roads are
clear. He is not one to sit idly on a throne."

"Where is he now?" Guinevere tried not to be hurt that he would
leave the day after their wedding. Obviously *she* knew it was not a
real marriage, but no one else did.

"The forest," Brangien said, her eyes lowered. "The one that took
the village. He left with men to burn it back."

"But it is not within the borders of Camelot."

"He does not turn away from a fight. Even when it is not his own
fight."

Guinevere admired that about him. He was king to his people,
yes, but he extended that responsibility and protection wherever he
could. Even when there was neither threat nor benefit to himself.
Arthur was . . . good. That was the burning warmth inside her when
she thought of him.

She was glad for it. But today it was inconvenient. She wanted to
warn him about the patchwork knight and her suspicions. Perhaps
the delay was better, though. She needed more information.

"Brangien, thank you for taking me out. It was wonderful. But I
am afraid I have overtaxed myself. My head aches, and I would like
to lie in the dark. Is there a meal I am supposed to attend tonight?"

"Of course you should rest. Feasts only happen once a month. A
few nights you may be expected to dine with the knights and their
wives, but no one has inquired about you for tonight. If anyone does,
I will tell them you are—" She paused, looking for the right word.

"Overwhelmed with love for my new king and country and insensible with joy." Guinevere smiled slyly, and Brangien laughed.

"Unconscious with joy, even."

"Perfect. Thank you."

Brangien drew the curtains and pulled down the covers. Then she helped Guinevere undress, unlacing her from her sleeves and outer gown. "I will be in the sitting room, sewing. I will not disturb you or enter unless you call for me. If you fall asleep for the night, rest well."

Feeling silly and deceitful, Guinevere climbed into bed. Brangien adjusted the blankets over her, and then slipped from the room.

Guinevere climbed out of bed.

She checked the first trunk. No woman of her status would be in the streets alone. Neither would a lady's maid of Brangien's caliber, but there was more room to improvise there. The queen needed a tincture, or requested a special spice for her food, or some such thing that would demand the urgency of a maid rushing into the city alone. Surely even the queen's maid could get away with being out after curfew if it was under a direct order from the queen.

Then again, Guinevere had no idea what—if any—authority the queen actually had in Camelot. It had never had a queen. She would have to ask Arthur about that, as well.

The first, second, and third trunks all held her things. She paused, her hand hovering over them. Not her things, not really. How quickly she forgot. The fourth, a small one in the corner, held Brangien's possessions. Her clothing was simpler. Guinevere could put it on alone.

Guilt twisted inside Guinevere as she pulled out a dress and a hooded cloak. Clothing was expensive and valuable. This was the bulk of Brangien's material wealth, and Guinevere was stealing it. But she would return it all unharmed.

Relatively unharmed. She pulled a seam from the cloak, knotting and tying the broken thread in a confusing mess. It would be impossible to untangle. And when she pulled the hood over her head, the knot magic would extend so that anyone glancing at her face would find themselves unable to untangle who, exactly, she was.

Guinevere pulled on the hood, then swayed. A little of herself went into every knot, every piece of magic she did. And she had done more in the last twenty-four hours than she used to do in a week. She really would have loved to crawl into bed and sleep away the evening. But much like faithful Brangien, she had work to do, and she would not neglect it.

She stepped into the hallway and walked with the hurried efficiency of a woman on a mission. She followed their path from this morning, navigating the stairs in the low afternoon light. Hopefully she would be back before nightfall.

There were more people out now, errands being run and business being finalized before they lost the sun. The masses in the streets, gossiping and calling to each other, buying and selling and haggling, meant she was just another person in the crowd. She loitered outside the arena. There had been some women in the seats, but only accompanied by husbands. She knew she would stand out if she were to go inside alone. The roars and cheering told her that the combat was still going strong.

Needing something to fill her time, and not wanting to miss the patchwork knight through an error of her own, she walked the circumference of the arena. Houses were built close to the walls, and she skirted puddles and crates. Arthur's little shits did their jobs well, though. It was remarkably clean.

On the far side of the arena was a small door, inconspicuous and nothing like the great gate that would open to spew spectator and combatant alike onto the main street of the city. She could be wrong—in which case all her efforts were wasted—but this seemed like a door for someone who wished to go unseen. Someone like the patchwork knight. She found a crate in the deep shadow of a leaning stone building and sat there.

She was very good at waiting. She had once spent an entire day lying perfectly still on the forest floor, unmoving, to lure a doe to her side. It had worked. She smiled, remembering the velvet nose as it nudged her face. Less pleasant was what she had needed the doe for.

She paused.

What *had* she needed the doe for?

The memory seemed to stop, cut off. As though she had turned a page and found the next one blank. She pushed at it, but nothing revealed itself. There was a dull ache behind her eyes. Maybe the confusion knot had done more than she had counted on.

The roaring from the arena reached fever pitch, and then quickly died. The sun had set. The day's fighting was through. She did not know the results, but she did not need those. She only needed the knight. The voices faded, drifting away. Everyone was returning home. And no one had come through this door. She had guessed wrong. Disappointed, she moved to stand and stretch her cramped muscles.

Furtive footsteps made her freeze and twitch back into the shadows. A woman wearing a shawl over her head hurried to the door. She stumbled, and the bundle she carried in her arm spilled free. Crying out softly in dismay, the woman knelt and gathered the things as swiftly as she could.

But Guinevere saw. Burlap-wrapped packets. Some fruit. And, inexplicably, several smooth stones.

The woman knotted the bundle together as tightly as she could. The door opened. With a quick bow of gratitude, the woman passed the bundle to the knight. He tucked it into a bag at his side and then walked past Guinevere without seeing her and swiftly turned down a narrow alley. The woman went back the way she had come.

Whom to follow?

The knight. Guinevere shadowed him as he snaked through the back alleys of the city she had not yet been introduced to. These did not smell as pleasant as the main areas. The homes were closer together. They were not necessarily older, but they were not as well maintained. The wooden structures seemed less stable, and jammed in wherever there was a hint of space.

The knight had not removed his helmet or his mask. He kept to the alleys between and behind houses. No doors opened into the spaces back here. The windows were shuttered. He and Guinevere might as well have been alone.

He paused next to a crumbling foundation. Then he reached up and removed his mask. She was too far away to see. She could not hurry forward without risking discovery. She looked to the side to see if there was a better vantage point, but when she glanced toward the knight again, he was gone.

Cursing herself, she sprinted to where he had vanished—and nearly tipped over a sheer edge of cliff that greeted her. It was the end of Camelot, the side shorn neatly to the black water a hundred feet beneath. She swayed, dizzy and sick, and caught a single glimpse of the patchwork knight, climbing straight down the side as though he were an insect.

The new queen cannot be seen.

It vexes the dark queen. Because the new queen should not matter—should be less than nothing—but the leaf said that the queen was not the queen, and that is intriguing. Her resources are better spent on Arthur, but so little is intriguing anymore. Even death has lost its sheen. So if the queen-not-queen is something new, she will discover what.

The queen's bedroom is protected the same as Arthur's, petty knots, base tricks. They insult her. They are not a magic of life, creation or unmaking. They are a human trick. A border. A barrier. Humans and their walls. She has humans to take care of those. They will do their work in time.

But she can feel another space. More windows. Her moth throws itself against them, beating its life against the glass. Inside, a heartbeat. Not the queen-not-queen's heart. Someone else's.

And that heart is racing. That heart is—

Magic. There is magic in that room.

The moth expires. The true queen, the dark queen, the queen of stone and soil and tree, is pleased. Camelot has gotten very complicated. Complicated is close to chaos.

And chaos is her realm.

CHAPTER SIX

That the castle was directly uphill seemed a cruel punishment for Guinevere's failure to catch the patchwork knight. She trudged up the streets. Candles illuminated shops being closed for the evening, families shuttering themselves against the night and the things that held sway in the dark dreamspaces it brought.

The curfew bells had not yet rung. When showing her around the city, Brangien had mentioned them. Anyone found in the streets after the bells was escorted to a holding cell for the rest of the night. It prevented mischief and crime, but it made Guinevere's life more difficult. And sad. Weaving a cloak of shadows was one piece of magic she relished. It did not bite or sting like the cleansing fire, or ask pieces of her like the knots. She had done it every night to escape the convent. When she slipped into shadows, flitting from pool of darkness to pool of darkness, each one claiming her as its own, she felt almost at home in her own skin. She loved the night. In the quiet stillness, she suspected, even a city could feel like a forest.

What had dead Guinevere loved? What would she think of this wondrous mountain city? What would she think of her handsome, valiant husband, who wandered his lands constantly to maintain peace and justice, building a kingdom where all were welcome, so long as they fought for Camelot?

Would dead Guinevere have loved the castle? Would she have missed her home? Would she have had a simpler relationship with Arthur? Perhaps one day they would have grown to love each other. Perhaps she would not have minded this endless, wretched hill.

Who had ever thought to build a city into a mountain? It was a terrible idea. No wonder Camelot was impossible to invade. An army would have to rest before they got halfway to their goal. And that was after crossing a lake with no cover or navigating one of the thundering waterfalls. No, Camelot could only fall from within. Which was how Arthur had taken it.

As though summoned by her thoughts, Arthur appeared from a side street. He swept onto the main thoroughfare, silver crown catching the light of his torch. At his side were several knights. They moved as one in his wake, a scent of smoke hanging from them like second cloaks. Arthur's own cloak fell back to reveal his hand resting on the pommel of his sword.

The sword.

Excalibur.

She had that same nebulous sense of recognition she had felt about Arthur. He looked over at her, his eyes passing her easily and disinterestedly as they scanned the buildings.

Then he paused mid-step, turning to look at her once more. His eyes met hers, and he raised one eyebrow in question. Shocked, she shook her head. She did not want the men with him seeing her. As though nothing had happened, he continued up the hill toward the castle.

But he had *seen* her. She reached up to the thread. Her knots still held. She could not explain how he had pierced the veil of her magic.

But after these long days of being someone else, the sheer relief of being seen by the one person who knew her lifted her spirits enough that she was able to finish the climb to the castle. The stairs winding up the side, however, were too much to ask. She entered through the main gate, the soldiers there not bothering to look under her hood. She would have to talk to Arthur about that. And figure out a way to secure every door in and out of the castle. She did not expect an attack there, but Merlin's infuriatingly vague instructions meant she could leave no opening unguarded. It would be tedious, wearying work. Far less exciting than chasing a mysterious knight through the city.

Though she also planned on doing that again.

Guinevere slipped back into her bedroom, relieved that the sitting room door was still closed. Brangien had not missed her. All her protection knots were in place as well, though she could feel that some of the tension coiled inside her was lessening. The knots would have to be redone tomorrow. How annoying that the physical relief of the knots coming undone meant they had to be remade.

She bit off the tangled thread from Brangien's hood, then carefully replaced the clothing she had taken. She pulled on a fur-lined robe. It was difficult not to touch the fur with her fingers. It was not that she did not want to feel what the animal had felt. Rather, the opposite. The brief spark of life and freedom made the walls unbearable. She would have to ask Arthur for some clothing without fur.

And then she realized—if she could not follow the patchwork knight, she could take something of his!

Merlin had not taught her touch magic. He did not seem to understand it—but in truth, she did not, either. It was unlike the knots, or the fire, or any of the other tricks in the handful she had at her disposal. For those, she had to concentrate. She had to perform them deliberately, and in certain ways.

The touch magic simply happened. Most often with people, though it was hard to interpret. A person was constantly changing, even their skin always shedding and renewing itself.

She did not like it. When it had been only her and Merlin, everything was familiar. It had been jarring in the convent, all the new sensations and feelings and people flooding her. Objects were less confusing. Like the fur, they usually held something of their origins. A sense of what they were, or what they could be. It was not always clear which she was feeling. However, if an object was important, it almost always whispered to her. And if she pushed, she could get more than a fleeting sensation. Though it felt intrusive and wrong to do so with people. She had tried it on one of the nuns and was met with a well of sadness and compassion so deep she could scarcely catch her breath.

She did not understand the borders or the purpose of the touch magic, and that made her nervous. She liked the security of the knots. Still, she might be able to arrange a way to touch something of the patchwork knight's. Most preferably his mask, which she sensed was more vital to the knight than his sword or his armor. Anything with a purpose to obscure could not help but reveal in equal measure.

And she would try to find the woman from the alley, as well. Something about the exchange she had seen nagged at her.

Arthur was back, though. Her eagerness to see him surprised her. It had been only a day since she met him, but he was the center of her life here already. She slipped past the tapestry and through the passageway to Arthur's room. She knocked lightly on the door, waiting in the frigid space between stone wall and mountain rock. The cold radiated with an intensity that felt personal. She put her hand against the mountain, but it was too old and too immovable to react to her. It feared only—

Water. It did not like water. She could feel it in the stone. It cared nothing for the men who crawled on it, nothing for the castle carved into its surface. But the water, the constant, relentless water, would someday unmake it. She felt how it had diverted the river, forced the water to split when it wanted to remain whole. How many more thousands of years the mountain would survive because of it. But not forever. It would be worn down and would disappear. The coldness mourned the future. Even mountains do not want to be unmade.

"I understand," she whispered, patting the stone.

The stone pulsed back with—sullen recognition? She yanked her hand away, surprised and unnerved. She was about to return to her rooms when the door opened.

"Come in." Arthur stepped aside and held the tapestry so she would not have to duck. "I was hoping you would visit. I am not sure what Brangien would think if I came into your rooms."

"Whatever she thinks, I doubt she would criticize you. She is very fond of you."

"She is a good girl. Sir Tristan thinks highly of her." He sat and she followed suit, trying not to show how amused she was at Arthur calling Brangien a girl. Brangien was the same age as he. But Arthur wore the weight of a nation on his shoulders. Perhaps he had earned the right to feel older than those around him.

"Are you well?" he asked, leaning closer.

She had not intended to bring it up, but her body had slumped into an arc of exhaustion, betraying her. "The next few days will be difficult. But once I have the foundations of the protections in place, maintaining them will require less of me."

"Please let me know if there is anything I can do."

She appreciated the offer, but if Arthur could do this for himself, she would not be here. Arthur had always needed magical protection. He ruled Camelot, but she had skills he never could have.

"I have a few thoughts," she said, reinvigorated by her confidence. She was no Merlin, but she had Merlin's trust. And Arthur's, too. "First, tell your guards at the gates that women can be threats as easily as men, and they should check everyone who comes in."

Arthur frowned as if it had never occurred to him. Even though he himself had fought a queen of tremendous power. He nodded. "I will instruct them. Though, will that not make your tasks harder?"

"All my efforts will be for naught if an assassin in women's clothes can walk right through the front gate."

He poured two glasses of watered wine and passed one to her. "I would like you to tell me if you are leaving the castle, though. What if something had happened to you? I would not know where to look."

Guinevere raised an eyebrow. "You forget your place, my king. You are not to worry about me, I am to worry about you."

"Ah." Arthur's brow darkened, and he took a sip from his glass. "What else?"

"What do you know of the patchwork knight?"

Arthur's whole demeanor shifted as he gestured with so much animation he nearly spilled his drink. "Did you see him fight? Oh, he is *magnificent*. I have longed to declare a tournament for him, but the problem with rule of law is that you have to abide by your own silly ideas. If I made an exception for him, the knights who earned their places would be resentful, and those who were not given the same accommodation would be angry. Every day I hope there will be fewer aspirants so we can finally set the tournament. I did not expect the opportunity to fight for me to be quite so popular."

"Arthur. You are the greatest king in generations. Of course men want to fight for you. For what you are building here."

He ducked his head, rubbing the back of his neck. "Well. There must be a reason you mentioned him specifically."

She did not want to dampen his enthusiasm, but it had to be addressed. "He might not be human."

"*What?*"

"The way he moved. His incredible stillness between fights. If he makes it through, the tournament ends with you on a field watered by fairy blood. If I were an assassin fueled by magic, I would come at you in just such a way."

Arthur seemed reluctant with his next words. She thought it was because he did not want to give up his dreams of a new treasured knight, until he finally spoke. "You are wrong."

"What?"

"You are wrong. He is not fairy or using magic."

"But I saw him fight! And I followed him after the fighting was done. A woman gave him an odd package, and then he went to the sheer cliff face on the southern side. He climbed straight down."

"Really? That is remarkable!" Arthur was again more delighted than concerned.

"I know no human who could do such a thing!"

"I have seen men display feats of strength that seemed magical. It is what I believe in most deeply. The ability of men to be greater than themselves. Everything here is aimed toward building on that."

"That is all well and good, but—" Guinevere stopped herself. She slowed down, smiling. "That *is* all well and good. The best. But you cannot say he is not a creature of magic unless you have met him. Have you?"

"I do not have to. I learned from Merlin as well, if you recall. He could not teach me magic—I have no skill for it—but he taught me about it. We spent so many hours together." Arthur smiled, then squinted. "Who took care of you when Merlin was with me? He spent months at a time instructing me during my childhood, and then he was at my side here for two straight years before being banished."

Guinevere reached for the memory. There were the birds, and the deer, the creeping sly foxes, the rabbits burrowing beneath the earth. And Merlin. But surely there had been someone else? She would have to use that wretched confusion knot more sparingly. She could feel the spaces of her mind, distant and unreachable through a fog. She shook her head. "Do not change the subject. How can you know the patchwork knight is human?"

"No aspirant is allowed to bring his own sword into the ring. Every sword provided is iron. Even the pommels are made of it. None of the fair folk could hold one."

"Oh." Guinevere leaned back in her seat, all her suspicions and her night's work wasted. Iron bit fairy flesh. Fairies could not stand to be near it, much less hold it and fight with it. "That was very clever of you."

He laughed. "Do not sound so surprised. I know how to use my brain in addition to my sword."

"Of course! Of course you do. I am upset with myself, not with you. What about the woman with the package?"

"Doubtless an admirer giving him a gift in hopes of winning his favor."

"Mmm." It made sense. If only she could have seen what was in the burlap packets. And why rocks? She could not shake the movement of the patchwork knight from her mind, either. It nagged at her. He might not be fairy, but he was different. Fundamentally. Maybe he was something new. Maybe the fair folk had discovered a way around their aversion to iron and the fear of biting death it brought.

She was not done suspecting the patchwork knight. But she would do it in private rather than challenge Arthur and make him think she doubted his intelligence again.

He nudged her knee with his. "You said you had a few thoughts to discuss. That was two. What else?"

She *had* said *a few thoughts*. But the last one she had not meant to include in the list. She wanted to know how he had recognized her. How he had found her face even when she was hiding it. It felt precious. A gift of grace in the midst of turmoil. And she did not want to spoil it by pulling it apart like one of her failed knots. She snatched at another issue to bring up.

"Oh, yes. I will need to visit every door in and out of the castle. You have given me the solution I lacked for how to secure them. I need threads of iron, melted and stretched so thin I can twist them." Those knots would not need replacing. They would ask more of her to put in place, but then she could forget about them. The cost would be paid up front.

"Of course. I will have them made as soon as possible. Do you require anything else?"

"A way to store supplies without arousing Brangien's suspicion."

"That is easily done. I will get a trunk for the secret passageway between our rooms."

She yawned, unable to hide it. Her eyelids were heavy. A touch as light as a moth's wings alighted on one of her coiled, aching muscles. No. Not a real muscle. Something else inside her. She sat up, alarmed. The knots were all intact. She would know if they had broken. Had she really felt something? Or was she so tired the barrier between sleeping and waking was crumbling?

"Is everything all right?" Arthur asked, responding to her expression. She felt through herself. The space on her scalp where it always felt like three hairs were being yanked out. The tickle of missing breath in her lungs. The dryness on her tongue. The sore ache that never quite faded. All the knots were still tied to her. If something had brushed against them, it had accomplished nothing.

"Yes. I think so." But she redid all the knots under his patient gaze. She would seal them with iron soon. Bidding Arthur goodnight, she stumbled, exhausted, back into her bedroom and gratefully crawled under the blankets.

She did not see the moth waiting, soft and patient, where it had been carried into her rooms on Brangien's stolen cloak.

The dark queen has seen this Guinevere, the queen-not-queen, already, carried to her on a hundred wine-tinged dreams. Arthur can seal his people away from her, but dreams and nightmares are still her realm, and she is free to come and go as she pleases.

The queen-not-queen is small, more like a sparrow than a falcon. Her hair is as black as tar and, depending on the dreamer, is worn in a plain braid or a tremendous crown of plaits.

In some of the dreams she is regal. In others, a mere girl. In a few, she is small and ugly, with sneering lips and vicious eyes. In most dreams, she barely exists, overshadowed by the usurper king, the boy with his sword, the figure even the dark queen cannot escape though she no longer sees with eyes herself.

But she does not care how those hundreds of borrowed eyes see the queen-not-queen, because none of their eyes matter. None of their eyes see truth. Even their dreams cannot pull apart what they see to understand what is.

That is why she finds the queen-not-queen's dreams. A moth dusting the girl's sleeping eyes, her lips, her ears.

She slips from the dust into the dream.

There is a steady plink-plink-plink *of water. The dark queen knows darkness, but in the black, the claustrophobic fear of the dreamer snags her, tries to overtake her. She is the darkness, though. She has nothing to fear there. She cannot be trapped.*

There is a girl. Naked. Pale and trembling, arms wrapped around her legs, face buried in her knees. She has made herself as small as she can, and still she is not small enough.

The dark queen pushes through the dream toward the girl. The dream pushes back. Eventually she is as close as she cares to be. What she had taken for pale skin is more complicated. There are knots everywhere, woven into the very veins, webbed over the skin like scars, binding and holding. Strands of blue-black hair flow down the girl's back, and the queen can almost see what the knots are doing there. Can almost tell what—

The girl looks up. Her eyes are bottomless. Empty. The dark queen recoils. The cave is not the trap. The girl is the trap. Because in those eyes, she sees—

"It will unmake us," the girl whispers. "And I will let it happen."

The moth dies.

The dark queen claws her way out of the darkness screaming after her, the darkness wanting to swallow what is left of her. She feels something she has not felt since the usurper king drew his cursed sword.

The dark queen is afraid.

What did Arthur bring into the castle?

CHAPTER SEVEN

"Market day!" Brangien chirped, throwing the bed curtains wide. Guinevere had not recalled drawing them. Perhaps they were the reason her dreams were all of darkness and being trapped. "The king requests your presence at his side."

As much as she was determined to spend every moment preparing and hunting for the impending threat, she had to admit a day at a market sounded *fun*. With people there for a reason other than her wedding, it would be less overwhelming than their time at the lakeshore. And she would have to get used to crowds. People were mysteries to her, which would not do for a queen.

She had gone so long without knowing them. It had only been Merlin before the convent. This reminded her of Arthur's question. Merlin had been with Arthur until a year ago. Guinevere had been with—

"My lady?"

"Yes?" Guinevere snapped to attention.

"I said, what colors would you like to wear today?"

Guinevere smiled. "Something joyful. Unless you think I should be somber?"

"The people love their king. They want to see him happy. Showing them a joyful queen at his side will endear you to them." Brangien hummed softly to herself. Her voice was clear and sweet and sad. Guinevere liked it immensely.

Brangien laced and tied Guinevere into a long flowing under-dress of green, then draped a delicate yellow robe over it. A silver belt cinched them together.

Frowning, Brangien held up several hoods. The hood would en-gulf Guinevere's head like a cave, with two long strips of cloth com-ing down nearly to the floor on either side in the front, keeping the hood anchored.

They all looked the same to Guinevere. Like ropes to bind her.

Brangien shook her head. "Not quite right. As a married woman, you can choose whether or not to cover your head. And there are no rules for your hair. The style is plaited, of course. Elaborate braids crowning your head are in fashion. But your hair is so striking. What if we braided it back from your face but then left it long and undone, trailing down your back like the waterfalls of Camelot?"

Guinevere did not like imagining her hair as waterfalls. But she trusted Brangien to present her well. "That sounds perfect."

Brangien got to work. By the time she was done, Guinevere's hair glistened and rippled. There was a burnished metal mirror in her room. It gave more of an impression of her looks than truth, but the impression was pleasant.

After a careful examination, Brangien nodded. "There is no rea-son to try and make you look like a stuffy old wife. You are young and lovely. Oh, Sir Percival's sister will simply loathe you." Brangien smiled wickedly. "She used to snatch me up every time she found me alone, treated me like I was a common servant. I do not seek pleasure in others' unhappiness, but I might accidentally find some today."

Guinevere laughed, taking Brangien's elbow. "I fully support that accident." Brangien was already been dressed, so they were ready to leave. It was odd, being the latter to wake up. In the forest, she had woken with the dawn. So many long conversations with Merlin. Lessons. Sweeping the cottage. Running from rain and sheltering in a cave.

She could not quite remember the details of the cave. Or she did not want to. It was as though the girl she had left in the forest had ceased to exist. Just like dead Guinevere. They had both of them been replaced. Perhaps the source of her memory gaps was that simple. She had to fill her mind with so many new things, the old got pushed out. And every magic had its cost. She knotted away tiny parts of herself constantly. What had Merlin pushed out when he pushed in the knowledge of knot magic?

Trying to shake off her troubled thoughts, Guinevere let Brangien escort her down several flights of stairs to the main hall of the castle. Because the castle was shallow and had been painstakingly carved from the mountain, it had been built upward instead of outward. Everything was stone. The steps, the walls. And most of it was seamless. It was not plastered together around openings. Instead, the openings were dug from the stone.

"Who made the castle?" Guinevere asked.

"I do not know, my lady."

"Does anyone know?"

Brangien shrugged in apology. "It is older than anyone here. Uther Pendragon discovered it. But I doubt even he knew who carved it free from the mountain."

They entered the great hall. Arthur was there already, standing in conversation with Sir Bors, Mordred, Sir Percival, and a few knights Guinevere did not yet know by name. A slight pang hit her: they spent more time with him than she ever would. She was his wife, after all.

She was not his wife.

How quickly she forgot! Playacting had muddled everything. There was a dangerous magic in pretending. Pretend long enough, and who could say what was real?

But when Arthur looked across the room and his entire being lit up with happiness at seeing her, she forgot again. She beamed at him as he rushed to her and gave her an exaggerated, silly bow. In the space of crossing the floor, he had transformed from conquering king commanding men twice his age to . . . Arthur.

"I thought we could visit the smithy tents today." He took her hand and put it on his arm. Brangien walked several steps behind them. The knights fell in as well, orbiting Arthur. If the way they had orbited her on their journey here had been dutiful, the way they orbited Arthur was determined. Purposeful. He was not a task to them. He was *everything*. "I wanted to have something made for you. You can give the instructions yourself." He winked at her. Not jewelry for his queen. Iron thread for his secret sorceress.

It suited her better. And it would help remind her that she was not a queen. She was a protector. Protectors, like the knights around Arthur, did not take days off to celebrate trips to the market.

Still, she smiled and waved prettily as they walked down the streets. She had just as much protecting but far more pretending to do than any knight.

Though some horses were stabled inside Camelot's city, they were very rarely ridden there. The streets were too steep. Brangien had explained the previous day that the horses kept here were ferried across the lake to be exercised. Most people in Camelot had no horses, or the horses they had were stabled on the plains beyond the lake.

Guinevere could see a great flat ferry ahead of them was already packed with horses. The horses were perfectly calm, used to their transportation. Guinevere was not calm at all. She had not considered how they would *get* to the market.

Her body froze. Arthur felt it. He held up a hand for his men to stop; then he leaned close, putting his mouth next to her ear.

"Trust that I will let no harm come to you."

She did. She truly did. But who was Arthur to water? Arthur was a king. The wielder of Excalibur. That mattered nothing to the lake. It was dark and deep, cold and eternal. Someday it might dry up, but the water would flow elsewhere. It could not be unmade.

And they were fragile, breakable, one choking breath away from death.

She stumbled numbly forward, Arthur leading her. When they got to the edge of Camelot, the lake gnawing at the shore, she could go no farther. Arthur scooped her up into his arms, laughing brightly to cover the necessity of his actions. He was cloaking it in jest.

"My queen is so light, I could swim her across the lake myself!"

His men laughed as well. A hand was on her back. Brangien. Guinevere buried her face in Arthur's chest. He talked and joked with his men as though carrying his queen onto a ferry was a perfectly normal action for a king to take. And because Arthur acted as though it were normal, it became normal.

Guinevere stayed curled against him; she was trembling, hiding herself from the water. She felt it in the sway of the raft, heard it in the hungry slapping of the water against the wood. Arthur directed the ferryman to cut to the side of the lake, shortening their journey and meeting up with the horses instead of steering directly to the market. "I would like to ride in," he explained.

He did not put her down until they were on dry land again. Brangien stepped in front of her, blocking everyone's view and pretending to fix one of Guinevere's braids. "Take your time," she whispered. "Wait until you can breathe again. Wait until you can smile." She held Guinevere's eyes. And soon, Guinivere could breathe. Soon, she could smile.

"Thank you," she whispered. Brangien squeezed her hand, then stayed with Guinevere while the horses were made ready. Brangien's touch felt like dusk or dawn—something was nearly in view, but Guinevere could not tell whether Brangien would be illuminated or hidden completely given enough time.

"I think," Guinevere said, making her voice as light and breezy as the summer day around them, "I have found my new preferred form of transportation. I will never walk again. Nor shall I ride horses. I want to be carried everywhere by a king."

The men laughed.

"The queen has expensive tastes," Mordred said. "Imagine how many kings we will have to find to take turns so my poor uncle king can rest on occasion."

"I am up to the challenge." Arthur picked Guinevere up by the waist and spun her around. She laughed at the surprise, aware of how they were being watched. If Arthur pretended to adore her enough to want to hold her all the way across the lake, she would make certain everyone knew the feeling was reciprocated.

He set her on a horse. She settled herself, but had a moment of disappointment when he mounted his own horse instead of riding behind her as he had on their wedding night.

Brangien directed her horse to Guinevere's side. Arthur was on her other. Around them, Arthur's most trusted knights escorted them along the wide, curving shore of the lake. Guinevere would have preferred more distance from the water, but she hoped that for the return trip Arthur could think of an excuse to break away and take the tunnel instead of another wretched ferry.

Her thoughts were overtaken by the market ahead of them. Already it was bigger than any village they had passed on their journey here. It was *acres*. Far more people were there than Camelot could ever hold.

"They come from all around for the markets," Arthur said. "On market mornings, I send men to the roads and make certain passage is safe. Everyone who wants to buy, sell, or trade is welcome."

"For a fee," Mordred added.

Arthur smiled. "For a fee. I have to pay the men who guard it, the ones who make the roads safe. But a safe market is a prosperous market."

"Are all markets like this?" Guinevere asked Brangien as Arthur and Mordred discussed something to do with a border.

"Have you never been to market before?"

Guinevere flinched. Her voice had been filled with wonder. She had spoken like a wild thing from the forest, not like a Guinevere. She covered with a lie that would give her excuses for future mistakes as well. "I was never allowed. My father did not think it appropriate. I rarely left our home at all, and then I was in the convent."

"Well, you have started with the best. There are no markets in the world like Camelot's market. Our king has seen to that. He speaks of the safe roads as though it is a simple task. I assure you it is not. He has fought these last three years to create this kind of far-reaching safety."

It was no hard thing to pretend to be delighted with and proud of Arthur. Who could not be proud of such a man? Of such a king? Her fears of losing herself in the pretense were unfounded. She was *allowed* to think the best of him.

They rode up to the edge of the market. Guinevere searched the borders, but saw nothing menacing. Brightly colored strips of cloth were raised on poles, like flags. Some had images painted on them, advertising where certain wares could be found. Music and laughter and the general chatter of people in a celebratory mood surrounded them.

Arthur helped her dismount. "Go and explore. I will meet you at noon to visit the smithies."

"But what about you?" She scanned the crowds nervously. "How can I protect you if we are not together?"

Again, he looked surprised. "Oh. Is there . . . a knot? Something to connect us? I must be with my men. And I am afraid your presence would be too remarkable."

Guinevere plucked out three of her hairs. Arthur leaned close as though whispering something to her while she knotted them around his wrist. His breath was warm and pleasant against her ear, the prickling sensation on her scalp connecting her to the hairs almost unnoticeable in comparison.

"Done," she said, though she had lingered a bit longer on the knots than necessary.

Arthur squeezed her arm, then turned back to his men. A few more, wearing the dust of many miles, had joined them. Their faces did not hold the happy ease of a market day. They held the weight and strain of news.

Guinevere wanted to hear what it was. But Arthur had said this was not a place for a queen. If any of it was a threat from magic, Arthur would tell her. If it was matters of men, Guinevere could not help. She had connected them for the time being. If something magical menaced Arthur today, she would feel it.

She had wanted to explore the market with him. Now it felt pointless. Her mood was dampened further when she and Brangien stepped into the tents . . . and Mordred was still beside them.

"Did you need something?" Guinevere asked.

"I have been tasked with accompanying you and making certain you have everything you need." He delivered the news as though they should both be pleased with this arrangement.

"Surely you have something you would rather be doing!"

Mordred's smile grew. "Not a thing."

Now she was truly vexed. Away from Arthur *and* under the ever-watchful gaze of Mordred. But it was hard to hold on to her frustration amidst the sights and smells and sounds of the market. She could not imagine what the big festivals must be like, if this was the smaller market. There were tents and wooden stalls. Shoes, clothing, cloth. Sewing supplies. Fur. How was there this much *stuff* in the whole world? And this many people to buy it!

"This is the textiles section," Brangien explained. "Point out anything you like. I can make you any style."

Brangien did always have a needle in her fingers. Guinevere liked everything, but she needed nothing. She preferred to study. There was so much more here than in any of the paintings she had looked at in the convent. This was real. This was life. And it was *vibrant*. With no focus directly on her, she was less overwhelmed than she had been at the marriage gathering. She let the chaos wash over her like the warm summer breeze.

Brangien steered her in another direction. "That way was the livestock section. We do not want to go there. We should head to the bakers. There are fines and lost stall space if they weight the bread with stones or sell bad flour, so everything is delicious."

"Oh, but I want to see the animals!" Guinevere hurried past the butchers and fishmongers. The fish wriggled in barrels of water. Women haggled, arguing and demanding better prices. There was an entire wooden tub writhing with eels. Guinevere looked hastily away, remembering how they had felt when she touched one from the pie.

The animal pens were wonderful, though. Brangien wrinkled her nose, holding a handkerchief there. Guinevere loved the smell, the intense and warm life of it all. Sheep and goats bleated, horses stamped their feet, pigs basked in the sun as their enormous bellies rose and fell with each breath. A young girl, shouting threats, chased a chicken. It ran straight for them; the girl chased it around Guinevere's skirts.

At last the girl caught it, then looked up in triumph. Her eyes went wide and her jaw dropped when she saw whose skirts she had been trampling around.

"That is a very fine chicken," Guinevere said. "Does it have a name?"

"My pa calls them all the same thing."

"And what is that?"

The girl's eyes grew even wider. "I cannot say in front of a lady." Then she whispered it, unable to stop herself. "He calls them Shit-for-Brains."

Brangien coughed. Mordred looked away. Guinevere laughed. "I think that is an excellent name for a chicken. Go and return Shit-for-Brains to where she belongs."

The girl grinned, gaps where her front teeth should have been. Then she ran away.

"Poor thing," Guinevere said. "So young to have already lost teeth."

Brangien frowned. "She is exactly the right age for that."

"She will go her whole life without teeth!" Was it that common among the poorer classes to have no teeth?

Mordred and Brangien shared a puzzled look. "They grow back," Brangien said. "You remember losing your baby teeth. The small ones fall out to make room for the big ones."

Guinevere remembered no such thing. The idea that children

were running around with two sets of teeth in their mouths—one lurking beneath the gums, waiting to burst free—was horrifying. She must have lost hers too young to remember. She was glad.

But Brangien and Mordred still watched her. She needed to redirect. She could not explain to them why she had so many gaps in her memories. She shied away from the thought that she could not even explain it to herself.

"Look! Horses." Guinevere hurried over to them, leaning against the wood planks that had been erected as a pen. "They are lovely."

She had never ridden a horse before leaving the convent. While the first days had been incredibly painful, she loved the great gentle beasts. A velvet nose appeared, nudging her hand to explore for treats. She rubbed its head, pleased to find that she got a sense of it. It was subtle. Nothing so dramatic and horrible as the eel.

The horse seemed to find her . . . familiar. There was the slightest hum of kinship. "Hello, friend," she whispered. The horse neighed in gentle reprimand, fixing one large brown eye on her as if expecting something.

Brangien held out an apple, but the horse paid it no mind. It stared at Guinevere for a few more seconds, then huffed and turned away.

"My queen likes animals," Mordred said. He was leaning against the fence turned outward, watching the crowds. Anyone noticing him would think he looked bored. But Guinevere saw the way his eyes never stopped moving, never stopped taking in information. He was *protecting* her. She did not need a guard. Her annoyance at the charade of queendom resurged. She was here as a protector, not someone needing protection.

"I like them very much," she snapped.

"Me, too." The horse had begun nudging Mordred's shoulder.

Mordred leaned his face in and whispered something. The horse nuzzled him, pushing gently so that Mordred would wrap his arms around the horse's neck. Mordred rubbed the horse's neck, then patted it and whispered something else.

Mordred straightened. "Shall we find something to eat? There is a spice merchant here who sells roasted nuts the likes of which you have never experienced."

"Very well." Guinevere let Mordred lead them back through the crowds. Brangien did not trust him, and Guinevere herself felt him a threat. But he had been genuinely loving with the horse, and the horse had seemed to trust him. Animals could sense things where people could not. Perhaps she had been wrong about Mordred. Arthur, too, trusted him. And she could not resent him for protecting his queen. Allowing herself to be guarded was a necessary part of her deception.

Mordred procured the nuts for them. The first one burst on Guinevere's tongue like sparks of flame. "Oh!" She put a hand to her mouth. She did not want to spit out the nut, but the sensation was so surprising.

Mordred laughed. "I should have warned you. It is not to everyone's taste."

"No, I—" Guinevere could not manage to get the words out. Her tongue was burning. Mordred handed her his own leather canteen, and she drank far faster than was feminine.

He reached into her packet of nuts and took several. She passed the entire thing to him. It was an acquired taste, apparently, and one she had no interest in acquiring.

After that, things were different. Easier. Mordred was very good at pretending to be at ease instead of guarding her, so she resolved to pretend, too. Mordred pointed out various merchants he knew. They all seemed to like him, or at least to like how free he was with his purse. Everyone around them haggled and bickered over prices, but Mordred always paid the first price they asked.

"You are being taken advantage of," Brangien complained as he handed her a length of pretty yellow cloth he had noticed her eyeing. Two women standing in the shadows of a stall were having a furtive conversation. One held something clutched in her hand. Guinevere narrowed her eyes, trying to see what it was.

It looked like . . . a rock. The woman who had taken it hurried away. Guinevere took a step to follow. There was something familiar about her.

Mordred shifted, blocking her view. By the time she glanced around him, the woman was lost to the crowed.

"*Am* I being taken advantage of?" Mordred asked. "If I can afford to pay it, and they can use the extra coin, why should I not agree to their prices?" He waved to a hat merchant, who returned the gesture with affection.

"Brangien," Guinevere asked, keeping her voice low, "is there something special about . . . rocks? Some value?"

"Rocks?" Brangien frowned. "What kind of rocks?"

"Just . . . rocks. Any reason to sell or trade them?"

"Cobblestones, perhaps. A farmer might trade them as wall material, I suppose. I cannot think of any other value."

"Mordred!" a voice shouted through the din. Mordred closed his eyes, his face twisting in disdain. Then his smile slipped back into place, but it was no longer a genuine smile. It was an eel, twisting and sliding and straining.

"Sir Ector. Sir Kay." Mordred bowed to two men. The first was older, in his forties. He was shaped like a gourd, with four twigs stuck in for arms and legs and a head balanced on top. He blew a gust of air through a tremendous mustache. Guinevere could smell the ale from this distance.

The second was a younger man, probably in his twenties. He had a long face and a long nose, thin lips, small and squinting eyes. He was a younger version of the first man. His belly had only just begun to expand and his arms and legs still seemed in proportion, but Guinevere could see his future. Father and son.

"So you must be our Art's new bride." Sir Ector looked her up and down as though she were in a stall and he were debating whether she was worth the price asked. "Small, you are. Nice hair. Nice teeth. From the south?"

Guinevere did not know how to respond. She nodded dumbly, not wanting to talk and show him more of her teeth lest he find something he did not approve of. The rocks worried at her, but she could not very well go chasing after a woman in the crowd. Besides, it could have been something else. An apple. A hard, gray apple. That seemed likely. What threat was a woman with a rock, though? Guinevere was here to protect Arthur from magic. Not from stones.

"Queen Guinevere," Mordred said, annoyance making his voice thin and tight. "May I present you to Sir Ector and Sir Kay, knights of Camelot."

"And father of the king!" Sir Ector said, puffing his chest out so it almost matched his belly.

She knew who they were, of course. Merlin had taken Arthur when he was a baby. And, when he realized he could not raise a king, he had given the young boy Arthur to a knight to be trained in the things he would need to know.

But . . . *this* knight? Merlin was a mystery, certainly, but nothing he had ever done had made less sense to her than the man he had delivered the future king to.

"Sorry we were not at the wedding," Sir Kay said, smiling. He was missing several teeth. She did not think they would grow back, but she refused to ask. "We were crusading. And the marriage was such a hasty affair! We got word too late."

"Crusading," Mordred repeated, his tone dry.

"Yes, crusading. We heard of a lord to the southeast, holding maidens captive. So we went to investigate."

"And?"

Sir Ector shrugged, his leather armor creaking. It was cracked and worn. Several stains looked less like blood and more like wine. "It turned out he has a lot of daughters. Many, many daughters. He tried to convince us to take a few with us. But who has time for women?"

"Who indeed," Brangien muttered.

"Do you live in Camelot?" Guinevere asked, knowing as queen she should be able to make conversation with Arthur's adoptive father and brother, but at a loss for topics.

"No, not for us." Sir Kay eyed a stand of ale appraisingly. "We are traveling knights. Always have been."

"Mercenaries," Mordred said.

"Mercenaries hire themselves to kings and tyrants. We provide our services to the lowly. To the needy."

Mordred leaned close so only Guinevere heard his words. "To those so desperate they cannot afford better."

"Come." Sir Ector clapped her on the shoulder. Though his arms were spindly, his hands were huge and the blow was unintentionally jarring. "Sit with us. I want to get to know Art's wife."

"I thought she would be taller." Sir Kay signaled to the ale merchant that they would be purchasing.

"Pretty enough, though, if you like them small."

Guinevere's face burned. Did everyone talk about her this way, but they were too polite to let her hear it? Brangien glared at the knights' backs. Mordred looked longingly toward the center of the market.

"We could lose them in the crowd," he whispered.

"They are my husband's family."

"*I* am your husband's family. *They* are an embarrassment."

Sir Ector waved for them to join him and Sir Kay. "I found us a tent! We can have a nice drink in the shade."

Guinevere really did want to continue exploring with Mordred and Brangien. But it would be rude. And while *she* was fine with being rude, the queen could not be. With an apologetic grimace for Mordred, she followed Sir Ector and Sir Kay into a cramped tent. The men sat on the floor, leaving the two chairs for her and Brangien. Brangien immediately pulled sewing out of her bag, cutting herself off from the conversation. Mordred lingered at the entrance to the tent.

"I will be right outside," he said, apparently deciding he preferred the glare of the sun to the company of Sir Ector and Sir Kay.

Guinevere did not find either of them appealing. But she was intrigued. What had Merlin seen that made him think Arthur would best be served by being raised by them? It took nearly thirty minutes for them to get drunk enough that their stories became interesting. Then Guinevere's patience was rewarded and she understood Merlin's decision.

"Back, what, ten years ago?" Sir Ector asked.

"Ten years." Sir Kay nodded, staring into his empty tankard.

"Uther Pendragon was still in charge. And I am not saying I am unhappy with Art being king. Makes a great king."

"A pretty good king," Sir Kay said with a shrug.

"But our lives were much easier under Uther Pendragon."

Guinevere frowned. "I thought he was a terrible, violent tyrant."

"Oh, he was! Absolutely. Meant there was a lot of work for knights-for-hire such as ourselves. When the king thinks nothing of using a sorcerer to help him, ah, *conquer* another man's wife—meanwhile having that man killed—well, you can imagine what was going on in the countryside."

"Not to mention the fairies," Sir Kay added.

Sir Ector blew a noisy, wet blast of air between his lips. "Fairies. Bah." He patted his sword affectionately.

Sir Kay raised his glass. "Poor Igraine, though. I hear she was beautiful."

"Had to have been, for Uther to go to all that trouble."

Brangien stabbed her needle into the cloth. Guinevere did not blame her for her silent rage at the way these men were speaking of Arthur's mother. Merlin had told her the story. Uther Pendragon, warlord king, had seen the Lady Igraine during a treaty negotiation. He had tried to get her to his bed, but she refused him. She loved her husband deeply. And Uther wanted that more than he wanted her. He wanted to feel what it was to be so loved by a woman. Uther lured Lady Igraine's husband into a battle, trapping him there. Using dark magic, he disguised himself as her husband and entered her chambers in the middle of the night, declaring the battle won. And then he took what she willingly gave to the husband she loved. But it meant nothing, changed nothing, because she did not love him. Who could?

He left her husband dead and Arthur in her womb.

Igraine had older children. Mordred's mother was among them. Morgan le Fay, Mordred's mother and Arthur's half sister, wanted vengeance. When Arthur was born, Lady Igraine died of a fever. Morgan le Fay planned to kill the child and deliver the body to Uther. That was when Merlin found him and whisked him away.

"Art was too young to fight back then, so we brought him along as our page. Oh, he cried when we found that slaughtered village, you remember?"

Sir Kay nodded, wiping his nose. "Cried all night. No use in crying. They were already dead. He was always soft."

"If you stopped to cry over everyone who died because of Uther Pendragon, you would have your own lake."

"Might be where Camelot's lake came from!" Sir Kay slapped his leg as though he had made a funny remark.

"Maybe the Lady of the Lake was dribbled out of his snotty nose!" Sir Ector laughed so hard he turned purple. Finally he caught his breath and took another drink. "Anyway. I was saying. We showed Art what the world was like. Village to village. Even fought a few fairy knights."

Brangien made a doubtful noise in the back of her throat.

"No one was more surprised than us when he pulled the sword from the stone," Sir Kay said. "You know about that, right? A great hulking stone with a sword in the middle used to be in the center of Camelot. Old as time. No one knew where or when it was from. But the sword never dimmed or rusted. And on the stone, it was written that only the true king could have the sword. Made old Uther Pendragon furious. He could budge neither the sword nor the stone that held it. No one could. The great mystery of Camelot. And to think! All that time we had the true king with us. Polishing our boots and feeding our horses and cooking our meals!" Sir Kay grinned proudly. "Not many can say they used to whip the king for burning their breakfast. Do you remember that time—"

Guinevere let their storytelling meander. They were lost in their own reminiscing, each filling in details about a time they had been hired by a village to kill a dragon and had tricked the villagers into thinking it was done.

As she heard about what they had seen and done in the years

under Uther Pendragon, Merlin's choice to leave Arthur with them re-formed itself with crystal clarity in her mind. If Arthur had been raised in seclusion in the forest, under the tutelage of a kind wizard, how would he have known the work there was to be done?

He had seen the suffering under his father. He had seen what a tyrant inflicted on the land. He had seen how little use men like Sir Ector and Sir Kay were. And rather than letting that break him, rather than letting the tragedy and violence of his very existence turn him bitter and angry, he had decided to do something about it.

He had decided to become the king his land needed.

Merlin never walked a straight path. His choices often seemed to be absurd or wrong. But he saw through time, pierced it with the arrow of his magic, and always hit his target at the other end. It was reassuring. He might not have armed her with as much knowledge as she needed regarding the coming threat, but if he had sent her here, this was where she should be. Time would prove it.

"Thank you, good sirs." Guinevere stood, cutting them off mid-story about lighting pigs on fire to scare a charging band of thieves. "This has been most informative."

They hurried to stand. She inclined her head to them and they bowed. Brangien lifted her eyes in relief, packing up her sewing. Guinevere stepped into the now-blinding light of day, followed by their voices.

"Breasts are rather small," Sir Ector said.

"Pretty enough face, though. He can always find big breasts elsewhere."

She repented of any kind thoughts she had had toward them. Merlin might have made the right decision, but that did not mean she had to like them. Ever.

CHAPTER EIGHT

"I feel like livestock," Guinevere hissed to Brangien as the tent flap closed behind her, sealing away Sir Ector and Sir Kay.

"At least they are all talk and no hands." Brangien glared at the tent. "With the exceptions of Sir Tristan and King Arthur, I could do without men entirely."

"You wound me, fair maid." Mordred stood from where he was leaning against a stall. He held out two perfect plums.

Brangien snatched her plum and aggressively bit a chunk out of it, turning her back on Mordred. Guinevere held hers, rubbing her fingers against the smooth skin. It had no stories to tell. She had had enough stories for the day, though.

Mordred pointed their way. "We are meeting my uncle king at the smithies."

It was a relief that she would be able to get to work soon. Mordred led them through the crowds and stalls to the other end of the market. The smithies were kept at a distance because of the heat and smoke. Seeing Arthur waiting for them there, Guinevere felt her heart grow lighter. Everything she learned about him made her more sure she had made the right decision in coming here. Arthur was a protector, and it was a very fine thing to protect a protector. She smiled as she took his arm. The sun winked on his silver circlet crown, and the crowds gave him a respectful berth—aided, no doubt, by the knights orbiting around him.

"Did you enjoy the market?" he asked.

"It was . . . illuminating."

"You will never guess who we met," Mordred said.

"Who?" Arthur asked.

"I will give you a hint: they evaluated your perfect bride by commenting on her teeth, her hair, and the size of her—"

Arthur groaned, putting a hand over his face. "Sir Ector and Sir Kay are here."

Guinevere patted his arm. "It was informative."

"Please accept my apologies for anything they said, and anything they may say in the future. They mean well, but—" He paused. "Actually, I am not sure they mean well. But they are benign creatures. If they are not good, at least they are not bad."

Mordred tucked a handkerchief back into his vest. "Their smell, on the other hand . . ."

Brangien laughed. Then she ducked her head modestly. Mordred met Guinevere's eyes and grinned over the victory of making Brangien laugh. Guinevere matched his smile. She felt better now that she was back with Arthur and working on a problem she had a plan for.

Heat radiated from the smiths' shaded work areas. There were fewer people here—most could not afford what the smiths were offering. But Arthur and Mordred were both familiar with the best smiths, who had their spots closest to the main market.

"My queen would like iron metal as fine as thread," Arthur said to a smith with arms like tree trunks.

"Why?" Mordred asked.

"To weave through my hair," Guinevere said. "I cannot wear jewels in it anymore now that I am married"—a rule she had not known until Brangien told her—"but I thought the metal would sparkle nicely. It has to be very thin and supple, though, so I can twist it how I want."

"I do not understand women's fashions." Mordred frowned, examining a selection of daggers and swords.

The smith had no such qualms. He scratched his beard, his smoke-blackened face wrinkling in thought. His hair was cut as close to the scalp as Arthur's. Now that Guinevere thought about it, most everyone at the market had close-cropped hair. Only the obviously wealthy men had longer hair.

"I can do that," the smith said. "Give me an hour."

They spent the time examining other wares. Arthur bought Guinevere a pretty iron dagger. When she touched it, it was as though there were a note playing just a fraction too low for her ears to hear. It was unnerving. She sheathed it and the sensation stopped.

Brangien passed a bag to Arthur, then begged leave to pick up some supplies of her own, promising to meet up with them later.

"Go," Guinevere said. "Take the rest of the day for yourself. I will see you back at the castle." That way, she would be free to use the tunnel instead of the ferry. With a grateful, excited smile, Brangien curtseyed, then hurried back to the main market.

"Why not silver?" Mordred asked, testing the heft and balance of a sword. He might not join the knights in the arena, but there was no question he was skilled with a blade. It looked like an extension of his arm—deadly grace and ease in every movement.

"Silver?" Guinevere looked up from the horseshoes she was pretending to examine instead of watching Mordred and his sword. Arthur was nearby, speaking with the smith about something. But Mordred had not abandoned his charge to remain with Guinevere.

"For your hair. Silver shines better than iron."

"Oh. Yes. Well. I am not certain it will work. I want to try with a less precious metal before wasting King Arthur's funds on silver. It is frivolous already."

Mordred gave her a twist of a smile. "I thought ladies were encouraged to be frivolous. That it was a duty of your rank."

"If you think so little of us, perhaps that is why you have yet to marry."

Mordred laughed. "Oh, I think very highly of women. Fearsome and wondrous, every one. You, in particular, I find most fascinating. You are a puzzle."

"I am no such thing." Guinevere picked up a horseshoe as if she had any idea how to evaluate one for quality.

"Unlike most in the city, I have been to the southern reaches of the island. And you do not have a southern accent."

Guinevere startled. "I— My time in the convent must have softened it."

"Mmm. I have also never seen a lady of your standing so delighted by a market, or so willing to smile and engage with a dirty chicken-maid waif."

She scowled defensively. "Arthur loves all his people."

"Yes, but Arthur was not raised a king. He was raised a servant. He sees the world as no nobleman ever could. And you, I think, see it as no princess would." He raised his hands. "It is not a criticism. I am surprised, is all. You are nothing like what I expected."

She made her voice cold and low like the iron. "I am sorry for not meeting expectations, Sir Mordred."

He leaned close, picking up one of the horseshoes. She could feel the heat of him beside her. "I am *not* sorry, Lady Guinevere."

A bright burst of laughter drew her attention and she beamed with relief at the break from Mordred's intensity. A group of children had a leather ball and were kicking it around an open space of ground in the middle of the smithies. Arthur had joined in, and was just then balancing the ball atop his head. A boy slammed into him, knocking it free. Everyone watching held their breath. The boy had hit the king.

Arthur laughed even harder, grabbing the boy and lifting him in the air before he could kick the ball.

"Sometimes I forget how young he is," Mordred said, his voice soft.

"Guinevere!" Arthur called, setting down the boy and kicking the children's ball so they would have to scurry after it. Guinevere hurried to his side, feeling oddly chilled once she moved away from Mordred. And grateful to escape the conversation and his inconvenient observations. She flashed Arthur a falsely bright smile.

"Mordred pays a lot of attention to details." Her eyes widened, trying to convey more than she was saying. "Like my manner of speech."

Arthur frowned, then shook his head. "You have nothing to fear there. If he speaks to me of it, I will divert his suspicions." He tucked her hand into the crook of his elbow. "Come, the iron should be ready."

She examined the thin strands, this time with the careful eye of someone who knew exactly what she needed. The thread fulfilled every requirement. She showered the smith with praise for his work. He bowed stiffly, his thick leather apron creaking. "It is my pleasure. Anything for the king, which means anything for his queen."

Her work that night would be exhausting and difficult. She wanted to get started as soon as possible. "Can we return?" she whispered to Arthur as they strolled back to the market. She searched the crowd for the mysterious woman or more signs of rocks being distributed, but saw nothing. "I have much to do. And I would like to take the tunnel, if we can." She could not be as strong as she needed to be if she had to travel across water again. It made her feel foolish and weak, neither of which was a solid foundation for magic.

"Yes, of course, let me—"

"My lord king," one of Arthur's knights called, running up to them and bowing. She thought it was Sir Gawain, but she was not sure. He was young like Arthur, barely able to grow facial hair. "We have had another messenger." He held out a sheaf of paper, sealed with black wax.

"Sir Maleagant," Arthur whispered.

"What is it?" Guinevere asked.

Arthur smiled at her, but he was too honest to maintain a false smile. His face cracked around it, worry creasing his brow. "I am not certain. But I must speak with these men."

"I can wait," Guinevere said.

"You should not have to wait on my business. Mordred?"

Mordred moved closer from where he had been lingering on the edges of the group. "Yes, uncle king?"

"Will you escort Guinevere back to the castle? She is fatigued. Take my private boat."

Mordred nodded in understanding. "I know exactly the boat the lady prefers. I will see her back and then return."

"Thank you." Arthur grasped Mordred's shoulder and squeezed. "I will want your advice on this."

Mordred bowed, then held out his hand to direct Guinevere. He did not offer his arm, which she was glad for. "Is this proper?" she asked as they walked away from the market to their horses. She did not know whether it was permitted for her to be alone with Mordred. And after the way Sir Ector and Sir Kay had discussed her, she worried about perceptions.

"Surely if my uncle king trusts me to see you safely to the castle, you can as well."

"Oh, I do—that is not—I was not saying—"

Mordred laughed. "I like the way you blush beneath your freckles. More ladies should try to get freckles. They are very charming."

Guinevere scowled and Mordred shifted his face to be innocently apologetic. "Of course you were not saying that. And usually a lady would be accompanied by her maid. But Brangien is lost to the market, and you seemed to have an urgent need to return to the castle. I am your husband's nephew. If you cannot trust family, whom can you trust?"

Guinevere had no answer. She mounted her horse awkwardly while Mordred retrieved his mare.

"Tell me about your own family," he said as they rode around the edge of the lake. With everyone at the market, they were quite alone. The shore of the lake was made up of smooth black rocks. They contrasted with the lively green of the grassy plain. Guinevere looked out over the plain instead of over the lake.

"My father is King Leodegrance. My mother died several years ago. I have two half brothers and a sister. She is younger than I. We have not seen each other in three years, since I was sent to the convent to prepare to be a wife."

Did dead Guinevere's family miss her? Did her father ever think of her? He had agreed to the marriage alliance without meeting Arthur. He had not even come to the convent to see his *daughter* safely delivered to her husband's men.

Somewhere out there, dead Guinevere's sister still thought herself not alone. That was the cruelest part of the deception. Dead Guinevere had been a sister, a daughter. And those people had no idea the girl they had known, hopefully had loved, was gone. A changeling in her place.

Guinevere did not feel sorry for the deception in Camelot. It was necessary. But she felt very sorry for the girl whose death had made it possible.

"I apologize," Mordred said. "It has made you sad, thinking about your family. I should not have brought it up."

"No, it is fine." Guinevere hurried her horse so they were not level and he could not see her face with his eyes that saw too much, always. "I am happy here. I left nothing behind I long for."

Except the trees. The tiny cottage that she swept. And Merlin. It was odd, thinking of Guinevere's father, wondering what he was like. She never thought of Merlin as her own father. He had been her mentor, her teacher. When she thought of him as a father, it was like a tunic that was too tight, straining and tugging at her.

Merlin was not a man—not exactly. He was something between. She had never wondered what that might make her. It did not seem important when it was just the two of them. But now, surrounded by humanity, she felt herself separate. Was it because of the lies she robed herself in? Or was it because she had too much of Merlin in her to truly belong?

But she had nothing of his powers. Hers were a trickle to his torrent. She was planted firmly in the current of time, while Merlin existed somewhere outside it. As much as he was the sole figure of her past, he remained an enigma.

Perhaps that was another reason she felt so comfortable with Arthur. He was right—they both had complicated fathers. But she had by far the better.

When they arrived at the hidden passageway, Mordred dismounted.

"What about the horses?" Guinevere asked.

"They know where to go." He stroked his white mare's neck. "She always knows where to go." He whispered something to the horse, then held out a hand to Guinevere. She took it.

A spark. A moment that felt like one of her cleansing flames, burning away everything unclean and leaving only the truth. She gasped, sliding down too fast in her surprise. Mordred caught her. His heart raced to the same beat as her own. For one breath, two breaths, two breaths too many, she stayed pressed against him.

And then she backed away, bumping into her horse and fumbling to avoid stepping on its hoof or being stepped on.

Mordred calmed the horse, whispering to it. Then both horses ambled away. "You really are tired," he said. "You nearly fell."

"Yes. Tired." She followed him silently through the tunnel, still feeling the lightning static of him in her hand. Had it been her sense? Or had it been . . . just Mordred?

And why had Arthur's hand never felt like that?

It was a relief in many ways to bid Mordred goodbye and seal herself in her rooms. She leaned against the door, trying to calm her heart. She had work to do. Nothing else mattered.

A brief imagining of another day like today. A market, enjoyed without searching for threats. A visit to smithies for jewelry instead of weapons. A stolen moment behind a tent with—

With whom?

Nonsense and selfishness. She had no timeline on the threat. She could not afford to be complacent or dreamy. The danger to Arthur could be nearly here, or it could be years away. She would prepare for everything. Starting with the castle and spreading outward, forming circle after circle of protection around her king.

Arthur had been Merlin's life calling since before Arthur existed. Guinevere would view her time here the same way. It would last as long as Arthur needed it to.

She pulled the iron threads from the pouch she carried and went into Arthur's room. The smith had done his job well. The iron thread was thin and malleable. She busied herself with the easy task of shaping the basic knots. She had gotten an exact count of every door into the castle from Arthur. The windows did not open, and the panes of glass were held in place with metal, so they were not essential to protect. Which was fortunate, because she did not have enough blood in her for that.

Once the knots were all formed, she knelt on the floor and arranged the metal spells in a circle around herself. She held Arthur in her mind. Held the castle. Held everything that Camelot was. It was the hope of mankind. The promise of a future free from chaos, where humans could grow and learn and live as they should. She believed in Arthur. She believed in Camelot.

She drew the dagger Arthur had given her and sliced her bottom lip.

Bowing to the first iron knot, she pressed her bleeding lip to it and whispered what she was asking of the iron. The iron knot grew warm, and then the blood disappeared, accepted and sealed. She moved to the next. And the next. And the next. By the time the last iron knot glowed and sealed, she was light-headed and dizzy. She pulled out her kerchief and dabbed at her lip. The iron had asked for more blood than she had anticipated.

The door opened. Guinevere stood to greet Arthur, then swayed and fell to the floor.

He rushed to her side. "What happened?"

Her eyelids were heavy, her head light. "Just the magic. It takes more than breath and hair to seal a castle."

"Your lip is bleeding."

She touched her tongue to the blood. It tasted like iron. She shuddered, repulsed. That was why she had to use blood. It was the only bit of magic iron would accept. And it was evidence that, unlike Merlin, she was human. "It will heal. The knots are ready. But I cannot place them yet. It would not do to have the queen wandering the castle, bleeding and fainting."

Arthur laughed, though his laughter was strained. "No, that would not do at all." He lifted her and set her in the middle of his bed. "Can I finish it instead?"

"It has to be me. The iron will not listen to anyone else now."

"Well, tell the iron I am its king and it must obey me."

Guinevere sank into the feather mattress and covered her forehead with her arm. "Iron answers to no king. It only likes blood."

He sat next to her on the bed, leaning against the rock wall behind it. "I have built my entire reign on the bite of iron and the spill of blood."

Guinevere rolled to the side, looking up at him. His own eyes were closed. She wanted to reach out to him, to rest her hand on his arm. But he seemed so separate from her. "You have built your reign on justice. On peace. The cost has been high, but I have seen Camelot. I have seen your people. And I have seen what they fear." She remembered the forest, the house. The boy. All devoured. She knew the stories of the great war with the Dark Queen and her forest of blood.

Drawing Excalibur was only the beginning for Arthur. He was the bridge between man and magic. Between tyrants like Uther and chaos like the fairies' Dark Queen. Merlin was right. The world needed Arthur. He was the best chance mankind had.

Arthur pressed his thumb as lightly as a whisper against her bottom lip. Then he lifted it. "No more blood."

"Blood stops. Peace and protection last." She closed her eyes. But though she was weak everywhere, she could not sleep. It hurt too much. Her blood burned cold, tracing its way through her body with spikes of pain. "Tell me a story," she said. "Tell me how you defeated the Dark Queen. I have only heard it from Merlin, and you know how confusing his stories are. He starts in the middle and it only gets more jumbled from there."

Arthur sighed, shifting and sliding down so he lay next to her with his hands behind his head. The weight of him depressed the mattress and she slid closer. Neither of them moved.

"The wolves came first," he said.

The wolves came first.

Teeth and jaws coated in the sticky blood of the throats they had already torn. But men could fight wolves, and they did. The wolves melted back into the darkness, repulsed.

Then the insects came. Crawling, biting, swarming. A man cannot fight a thousand wasps with a sword. Merlin called down birds, flocks of starlings and murders of crows, so thick that the rushing of their wings was as a hurricane, the stretch of their wings blocking out the sun. The birds ate the insects.

Then the Dark Queen woke the trees. A forest where there had been none. Spirits ancient but fragile enough to fear men. To hate men. The trees separated the soldiers. Voices cried out in pain, in terror, and the wolves found them.

Merlin called forth fire. He lashed at the trees with terrible force.

The trees felt their brothers and sisters dying. They quaked and trembled. What was the love of a dark queen against the fire of a mad wizard? Better to live for a hundred years before tasting the ax of man than to burn away in a single moment. And so, when Merlin bade the trees sleep, they sank their spirits deep into the soil, away from where the Dark Queen could call them.

Merlin quelled the fire. The men stumbled from the trees. The wolves stayed in the shadows and the darkness. The Dark Queen emerged, ringed by her knights. They wore armor of stone, of roots, of skulls and bones. Snakes, fangs bared, encircled their arms. Bats clung to their backs—wings pulsing, ready to fly into battle.

Merlin told her to stop. She laughed, the sound like the wailing of infants, the cries of women, the dying gasps of men. *What will you do, old man, against the water?*

The men trembled. They fell to their knees in despair. They were on the shores of a great lake. Birds could not fight water. Fire could not drive it back. Swords could no more cut a deluge than they could grow if planted in the ground.

The Dark Queen raised her hand, calling out their destruction.

The water stayed cold and still. Unmoving.

The Dark Queen screamed in rage, demanding, pleading. But still the water did not join her. Forest and water, ever allies, ever companions, now divided.

Here, Arthur paused in his telling. The cadence slipped, the images he painted for Guinevere suddenly became less story and more . . . personal.

"The Lady of the Lake," he whispered, "chose my side. Just like Merlin. But the rest was up to me." Then he pulled the story back in place, like tucking a blanket around Guinevere as he told the rest.

The dread fairy knights charged. Alone, Arthur stood against them. Excalibur pierced them, unmade them. The Green Knight, ancient forest god and unbeatable foe, became dead leaves and branches. The bats released their hold on the Black Knight, flapping blindly away and dropping their liege to shatter like glass against the ground. The snakes fled, the skulls and bones of the Dead Knight becoming lifeless things once more. Where there had been a living nightmare menace, now there was nothing but the detritus of ages past.

The Dark Queen stood alone.

Merlin did not want to kill her. He did not want to see her ended. He bade her retreat as the trees had done. Send herself deep into the earth. Let chaos sleep.

A great stag bolted free from the trees, its eyes red with madness. It lowered its head and charged at the Dark Queen. It impaled her, lifting her high in the air. Her arms were outstretched, her face beatific. Then the stag turned and disappeared back into the trees, the forest claiming the Dark Queen forevermore.

CHAPTER NINE

"No," Guinevere said. The story matched what Merlin had told her in bits and pieces. He delivered stories the same way the grouchy falcon delivered food. A little here, a little there, dropped on the head when least expected. She struggled to sit up as certainty gripped her. "The Dark Queen is not dead. You saw the knights. They were not killed. They were *unmade*. She was not unmade."

Arthur turned on his side so they were face-to-face. "I followed her." He sighed. If the early story was blood-tinged horror, this part was the stage beyond horror. The weariness of unspeakable tasks. "Through the forest. Across plains. Finally, we came to a meadow. I shot the stag. Her body fell. And then . . . we destroyed it." He closed his eyes. "The Dark Queen is dead. There are traces of her magic still, the chaos that bites at my borders. Like the village you saw. That used to happen regularly. Now, it is so rare people forget to fear the trees. Soon they will walk and hunt in forests fearing only the things they should."

Guinevere felt oddly deflated. She should have been terrified to think she might face the Dark Queen, but at least there would have been a target. An opponent. "What should people fear? Other men? Like Sir Maleagant?" She wanted him to tell her what had been in the letter. If she could not define the threat she faced, she wanted to know about all the others.

Arthur sighed. "Yes. Other men. We do not need a dark queen when we have so much darkness within ourselves. But we will beat back the chaos and the darkness. I am glad you are here. I have been fighting this battle for so long. When I lost Merlin, I was alone."

"I am sorry you had to send him away."

"It was for the best. Magic and Camelot cannot exist in the same space. Magic—even good magic—thrives on sacrifice and chaos. Pain." He reached out and touched her lip once more. "I am sorry it must go. I have seen wonders and miracles. I have been given gifts unparalleled. The Lady of the Lake . . ." His voice went distant, and a spike of jealousy pierced Guinevere. Because here, finally, she saw what Arthur looked like when he longed for something. And she knew he would never long for her that way.

She did not need him to. Or even want him to. She was simply tired. That was all.

Arthur cleared his throat, back beside her instead of far away in a memory of magic and wonder beneath the waters of a lake. "She passed the mantle on to me. It is man's time. And I will do whatever it takes, no matter how difficult, to build the kingdom my people deserve. I will always choose what is best for Camelot, no matter the cost. Nothing comes before peace and order. Not even myself." He smiled fondly. "But you understand. Thank you for your service to my people."

She had only come here for him. But Arthur *was* his people.

Arthur was Camelot.

After a few fitful hours of rest, she was ready to finish it and be done. It was the middle of the night, the castle sleeping around them as Arthur took her from door to door. Where there were guards, he laughed about taking Guinevere on a midnight tour of their home.

When the last seal was affixed on the bottom of the last door where it brushed the floor and no one would ever see it, Guinevere was done. And she was *done*.

Fortunately, they had ended up back at the exterior door nearest their rooms. Guinevere could hardly stand. She was no longer connected to the iron the way she would have been with the lesser magic done with her hair or breath. The cost was paid up front. And it was steep. Arthur opened her door and lifted her into her bed, leaving her to the darkness with a whisper of thanks and the soft press of lips against her forehead.

It was late in the day when she finally pulled herself from the suffocating confines of sleep and sat up, bleary-eyed and light-headed.

"Good morning," she said to Brangien, who was sitting next to the bed, sewing.

Brangien dropped her embroidery and rushed to Guinevere's side. She pressed her hand to Guinevere's forehead, then held a goblet of watered wine to Guinevere's lips. Guinevere laughed but drank willingly and deeply. Her throat was dry, her stomach cramping from emptiness.

"I slept so long! The day is nearly over."

"You have been asleep for two whole days, my lady."

"What?" Guinevere lifted a hand. It trembled weakly. That would explain her hunger. She had felt so strong at Arthur's side, so inspired, that perhaps she had pushed it too far. Merlin would not have broken a sweat accomplishing something similar. It was unfair. She had mere child's tricks compared to the elements he commanded.

But her tricks could sneak beneath the notice of Camelot. His power never could.

Brangien placed pillows behind Guinevere's back, helping her sit up. She was fussing too much, but Guinevere let her. As she ate the plate of food Brangien had waiting, she asked what she had missed.

"Ever so much gossip. But it is all about you, so I suppose you did not miss anything anyone would have said to you."

Guinevere dropped her bread. "Gossip? What?" Had someone seen her alone with Mordred? She *knew* she should not have agreed to that!

"All about your purity. They are dreadfully impressed that you are so virtuous and delicate, one night entertaining the king in his bedroom requires two days of rest." Brangien lifted an eyebrow wryly.

"They are saying that? Arthur's bed is really the topic of so much discussion?"

"Everyone is very invested in the girl who finally found a place there. Many have tried over the years. This is pure vicious gossip, mind you, but I have heard from more than one source that Dindrane, Sir Percival's sister, once paid a servant to sneak her into Arthur's bedroom, where she waited . . . alone . . . in his bed . . . with only the clothes she was born in."

"No!"

"Yes!" Brangien's eyes twinkled in delight. "But our king is as virtuous as he is strong and kind. He asks nothing of others that he would not do himself. Thus, to wed a virgin, he himself was a virgin."

Guinevere knew very little of men. Merlin hardly counted as one.

She did not know what to make of this information about Arthur. She changed the subject. "I might love Dindrane now. Is that odd? How brave she must be, how bold to attempt such a direct attack!"

Brangien laughed, handing Guinevere another goblet of watered wine. "You are a surprising lady. But she has nothing and therefore nothing to lose. Be careful what you say or do around her. We will avoid her whenever possible."

"Thank you, Brangien. I would be lost without you."

Brangien waved away the compliment, but Guinevere could tell she was pleased. She let Brangien brush and braid her hair, chattering and filling her in on everything else. Arthur had been to visit her twice to check on her state. But he had left that morning on business.

When Guinevere used the chamber pot in private, though, she had a terrible shock. The magic must have broken her. She cried out in fear, needing Merlin. Needing anyone.

Brangien rushed in. "What is it?"

"Blood," Guinevere said, staring at her underclothes in horror.

"Well, that is no concern. The timing was not right to conceive anyhow."

"What do you mean?" Guinevere could not help the tears streaming down her face. She had broken herself. She would bleed to death from the inside. No one would be left to protect Arthur. No one would know where the real Guinevere was buried. And she herself would die unknown, unloved, unnamed.

Brangien's face shifted to shock and then pity. "Oh, my lady. You have not— This is your first time?"

"My first time what? I do not understand. I am dying, Brangien. Please tell Arthur—"

Brangien led her to the bed. She picked up the blood-stained underclothes and tucked them away with the wash, then busied herself getting new ones, along with several narrow lengths of cloth. "Your convent has a lot to answer for," she grumbled. "Imagine, sending a girl to be married who has not yet started her courses, and who does not understand her own body." Brangien layered the cloth into the underclothes, then slipped them both up Guinevere's trembling legs. "This is normal. Healthy, even. It will happen every month until Arthur's seed takes root in your womb."

"What?"

Brangien laughed. "It is not quite fair, is it? But it is the way of women's bodies. You may have some pain, exhaustion, even. That could explain the last couple of days. But it will pass in under a week, and then you will be clear as a summer morning. Until the next moon."

"This happens to you, too?"

"Yes."

"It is awful. Who ever designed this system?"

Brangien laughed. "I believe that would be God, so you are welcome to take it up with him. In the meantime, I will heat some towels for you to hold against your abdomen. It feels nice."

Guinevere was even more willing to let Brangien take care of her. She felt fragile and new, unnerved at this strange development in her own body. And betrayed that she had not known it was coming.

"Can you—" Her voice cracked. She knew that men and women had babies. All things did. But she had never considered the specifics of how, as it related to humans. And Merlin had certainly never told her about it. That was one lesson she would not have forgotten. "Can you explain the part about the seeds?" she asked.

Brangien tucked the warm towels around her. "I am going to give those nuns an earful if we ever see them again."

A couple of hours later, Guinevere felt much better physically, if a bit unsteady emotionally. "I would like to speak to Arthur. When will he return?"

"No one told me."

"Hmm." Guinevere wished she knew, but doubted anyone would tell her. She was not important in the workings of the castle or the business of knights. "Oh!" Guinevere remembered another task to be done, now that the castle was secure. "When will there be another aspirant tournament?"

"They increased them! Two a week. I think the king is trying to get the patchwork knight through. One is happening right now."

"No!" Guinevere would lose her chance to try and steal an item of the patchwork knight's.

"You are in no state to go to the arena, anyhow. You need to rest."

"I have been resting for two days."

"And you will rest until I decide you are well enough to stop."

Guinevere did not want to wait until the next week to spy out the patchwork knight. And if she could not get something of his, she had another idea.

"Actually, I am quite tired. I should sleep more. Would you please see to it that I am not disturbed until the morning? I think one night of deep sleep will set me right."

Brangien nodded. She took away Guinevere's empty plate and refilled the goblet, which she left on a table next to the bed. Then, after leaving more cloth should Guinevere need it, she slipped into Guinevere's sitting room.

Guinevere stood on shaky legs. She padded her underclothes, her feelings as unsteady as her body, which had become a stranger. She pulled out Brangien's dress and cloak, once against tugging a thread and knotting confusion into it. She would have to go slowly, which meant she needed to leave now to reach her destination in time.

As she slipped out the door to go outside, she gasped. The thread she had knotted popped and sizzled. The magic snapped back, slapping her and leaving her winded and stinging.

How could she have been so stupid? She had set up the magical barriers herself! The iron spell had done its work, dismantling her confusion knot as soon as it passed the threshold. At least she had evidence that her work had not been in vain. Any magic that tried to pass these doors would be undone. Even her own.

Laughing in pain, she hoped the deep hood itself was enough to hide her. She did not have enough left in her to redo the knot. She eased down the steps, walking as gingerly as an old woman. Her pace through Camelot was slower than leisurely as she navigated the maze of buildings to the very edge of the city.

She settled into the ruined foundation of the crumbled building next to where she had lost the patchwork knight before. A spider crawled over her and she blew on it, bidding it go its merry way. From this vantage point, she would remain unseen but have a view of the patchwork knight when he removed his mask. And she knew—she *knew*—he would not be as he seemed. Arthur was wrong. Perhaps the fair folk had figured out how to create a knight immune to the biting power of iron. Whatever the secret was, Guinevere would discover it.

She did not mind waiting in stillness as the sun drew lower and then began to set. Stillness suited her current physical state perfectly well. Though she did wish for one of Brangien's warm cloth compresses.

At last she heard the soft, sure steps of the patchwork knight. He paused right next to her. If he but turned to the left, he would see her in the shadows. Her patience was doubly rewarded. The woman in the shawl ran up, out of breath. "I almost missed you. Here. For the girls. Tell them—tell them our time will come." She passed another bundle. The knight tucked it into his bag. The woman shuffled back toward town.

As soon as she was gone, the knight pulled off his mask, shaking his wild black curls free. Disappointment skittered over Guinevere with far more menace than the spider.

The patchwork knight had full lips and expressive eyes. High cheekbones. A dimpled chin. His tan face was bare of any hair, hinting that he was far more youthful than his skill indicated.

But his face offered no proof he was fairy. It was entirely human. He slipped down the cliff, climbing as he had before.

Guinevere hunched, cold and miserable. She had been so sure that the patchwork knight was not what he seemed. That she would return triumphant, having discovered a magical menace before he ever got close enough to hurt Arthur. She *wanted* the knight to be dangerous. She *wanted* him to be a problem only she could solve. In doing so, she would have proven her worth to Arthur.

And to herself. She headed back toward the main street that would lead her to the castle. She was so caught in her misery that she did not see the woman until they collided.

"Mind yourself!" the woman snapped, pushing Guinevere away.

"You," Guinevere whispered. It was the woman in the shawl. From close up, the woman was not so old as her walk had suggested. She was in her thirties, with a face shaped by sorrow. Before she could think better of it, Guinevere stumbled once again, pretending to lose her balance as she grasped at the woman.

"Get home. You should not be out alone with that much drink in you. It is not safe." The woman steadied her with a frown. "Do you need help?"

"No, no," Guinevere said, shaking her head and straightening. The woman sighed, then walked away.

Guinevere smiled. In her hand, she had a rock. Stolen from the woman's own bag.

The patchwork knight had not been what she expected. But the rock sang to her in high, clear notes. Notes of wonder. Notes of *magic*. The knight was not a fairy, and neither was the woman. But they were meddling with magic.

Guinevere hurried back to the edge of Camelot, staring down at where the knight had disappeared. Relief and triumph swelled in her breast. At last she understood why she had been sent. Why she was suited to this where Merlin was not.

The magical threat to Arthur did not come from fairies, or from powerful creatures like Merlin. It came from ordinary humans. Humans who wanted to bring magic back, bring down Camelot from within. Who could move about in this city at will without being caught or suspected.

Until now. Who better to hunt them than their own kind?

Tucking the magic-touched rock into her tunic, she picked up an ordinary one and threw it over the side of the cliff. "I am coming for you!" she whispered.

The stone spins through the air, falling, falling, until it hits the water. It rolls, slowly, pushed by currents until finally it leaves the lake and hits the river.

And then it stops.

Held in place, not sinking. The river churns, bubbling and frothing. Boats break free from their ropes, pulled toward the whirlpool that has formed where the stone is.

Then the water releases the stone, dropping it to the riverbed. Every-thing becomes still. Silent.

Except the form of a lady that moves swift and deadly down the river, through a stream, beneath the ground, flowing, flowing, flowing.

The Lady will end him. Merlin will pay for what he has taken from the water.

CHAPTER TEN

She begged another day of rest from Brangien. In truth, the last thing she wanted was to be in bed, but if she admitted she was well, she would have to play queen. As soon as Brangien had left to go to the market, Guinevere made her way outside. She stealthily checked every door.

Odd. Each one had a small collection of dead spiders and moths outside. When she tried to pick them up, they crumbled to black dust in her fingers.

But she could see nothing else. Troubled, she climbed to puzzle it out and clear her mind. Her body was still weak from the iron magic, but it felt good to use it. Up and up the outside of the castle she went, to the very top part of the treacherous stairs.

The wind caressed her with greedy fingers, trying to pry her hood away from her face. She found shelter in an alcove buffered by a low wall. It was good she had not come when she was still so weak from blood loss. Even more recovered, she swayed and felt dizzy. The world unfurled beneath her. From this height, the lake was almost tolerable, one shining mass beyond the city. Surrounding that, the fields glowed golden and green. As long as she squinted out the lake, she had never seen a view so beautiful.

She leaned against the back wall of the alcove and closed her eyes. Camelot was a wonder. And there were people inside who wanted to bring it down. She fiddled with the rock, which she had left hidden outside the castle so her own protections would not undo the magic before she figured out what it was.

She knew a knot for seeing. Usually it was used to find an object or a person. She might be able to use it to discover the rock's purpose. A bigger thought occurred to her. If she were up here, she might be able to look out over the city and find any concentrated pools of magic. That could lead her to the woman. It would dull her vision for hours, but—

"Hello."

Guinevere startled and opened her eyes. Mordred stood in front of her. The sun was behind him, haloing his head but making it impossible to see his features. At least she had not started the knots yet! She would have been caught.

"I am sorry," he said. "I have never run into anyone here before. I can go."

"No." Guinevere shifted aside to allow him in. "I am the intruder. I wanted a quiet place to think." It was good she was interrupted. Doing magic out in the open was a *terrible* idea. She could be patient. She had to be.

"You found the best quiet place in the whole city." He joined her, resting his hand against the alcove. She had been so distracted by the height and the view that she had failed to notice the alcove itself. It was carved with a thousand images. They had been smoothed and worn with age, but she saw hints of people, of suns, of moons. Of dragons and trees and beasts. There was an odd grace to them. Almost as though they formed themselves from the rock. If there ever were chisel marks, she found no evidence of them now.

"I have tried to read it many times," Mordred said, running his fingers along the carvings. "Tried to puzzle out why they made Camelot. But the past holds her secrets dear, and try as I may, I cannot coax them out of her."

Guinevere touched the alcove.

For the briefest moment, she had a sense. Not the sense of the mountain, or the rocks. But the sense of the hands that had lovingly carved Camelot free from the stone. Purpose flowed through her, buoying her up. Determination. Promise.

And then it was gone, faded as much as these carvings. It left her feeling deflated and sad. Whoever had created Camelot had done it for a reason. Long before Uther Pendragon took it. Long before Arthur took it from him.

Whatever their purpose in making Camelot, it was lost to time.

Mordred sat on the floor of the alcove, stretching his legs in front of him and leaning against the back wall. It was so easy and casual a position that Guinevere felt out of place. He pulled out a cloth-wrapped bundle and revealed bread, cheese, and nuts.

"Stay as long as you like," he said. "I have only a little while before I have to be at the court."

"Why are you here?" Guinevere asked.

Mordred looked up at her. "I told you. This is the best spot in the whole city."

"No, I mean, why are you in the city? I thought Arthur and all his men were out doing . . ." She trailed off. She did not know what they were doing. And it bothered her. She had been unconscious when he left, but should he not have figured out a way to inform her?

Should he have, though?

Yes. If he was out there, he was vulnerable to magical attack. It was her job to protect him, and she could not do that if she was left behind, unaware of his location. She would have to craft some protections he could take with him.

"When my uncle king has to range wide afield, I am left in charge of the city. Everything cannot stop because he is gone."

"He trusts you." Guinevere sat next to Mordred, trying to arrange her skirts and legs in the least awkward configuration. Women's clothing was not made for sitting on the ground.

"He does." Mordred sounded unhappy about it.

"But . . . ," Guinevere prodded.

He leaned back, squinting at the sun. "But I do not like staying in the city. I would rather be out in the wilds, at my uncle king's side. I know it is an honor, a tremendous responsibility. But it still feels like being left behind."

Guinevere understood. She reached over and took some of Mordred's bread, breaking it into smaller pieces as she stared out over the landscape. "He did not even tell me where he is going."

"Do you *want* to know?" Mordred handed her cheese without being asked.

What would a real queen answer? "I do not know what my role here is supposed to be. It would help if I knew what was expected of me." She had a goal now. A target. But she still had to be queen in the meantime, and it was complicated.

"You should speak to your husband about that."

"My husband is rarely here!" She snapped her lips shut against the unexpected force of her exclamation.

Mordred laughed. "Perhaps if you dressed as a knight you could get more of his attention. Arthur is single-minded. It is what makes him a great king. And, I suspect, a challenging husband. If you are not a problem that needs to be solved or a battle that needs to be fought, it will be hard to keep his attention."

Guinevere did not want to be sad. She should do her best not to be a distraction. She was not Arthur's wife, not really. But she was sad nonetheless. It was not easy, revolving around someone who did not revolve around her.

She replaced her sadness with determination. If Arthur would not take her, she would figure out a way to send protection with him. And she would always be ready here, to defend Camelot. To defend Arthur. It had been Merlin's calling, and now it was hers.

"Come." Mordred stood and brushed the crumbs from his legs. "I have to preside at today's trials. It might be interesting for you to see some of how the city is run. And on our way down, I can tell you where your husband is. I do not think it is a secret."

Guinevere stood, too. She did need to know more about Camelot. And this would give her time to plan her attack against the patchwork knight and the mysterious woman. "Thank you."

Mordred paused, the wind running its invisible fingers through his black hair. She had the briefest impulse to fix it. He swept his arm out for her to leave the alcove first. "I am sorry that your husband is not what you were expecting him to be."

Guinevere stood at his side, her hand on the warm wall. No purpose was left to fill her. It was gone. "He is exactly what I was expecting him to be. It is myself that I worry will be found lacking." She hurried down the steps, Mordred's softer steps following.

Mordred explained that Arthur was away defending a conflicted border. There were several lords and kings whose land abutted the borders of Camelot's country. It was often required that he ride out and resolve disputes—through reason, gold, or the sword. Mordred could not tell her which solution this one would require.

"At least it is not Maleagant," Mordred said as he escorted Guinevere into a building close to the castle. The ceilings were low, which should have felt confining, but they were carved with flowers and birds and the most delightful images, so their height felt like a gift. It was obviously one of the original buildings of Camelot, not an addition. She felt better in the old ones, for some reason.

"Who *is* Maleagant?" she asked.

"A thorn in the side of Camelot. Ah, Conrad, thank you. What is on the schedule for today?" Mordred looked over a carefully written scroll given him by a round, friendly-faced young man. There were benches lining the walls, and each bench was filled with people. Some wore the nice clothes of merchants, a couple the fine clothes of nobles. But most the rough, serviceable wear of farmers and peasants.

In the front there was a cage made of iron. In it stood a woman, facing away from them. Her shoulders hunched, her head drooped. Guinevere did not understand what she was doing in there.

Mordred gestured for Guinevere to sit on one of three padded chairs on a platform apart from the crowd. She regretted coming. She was on display, and she had not been prepared for it. She left her hood up, knowing her hair was beneath Brangien's standards.

She sat as still and regal as she could, hands folded primly in her lap. The first few matters were business-related. A man applying for space to sell horses in the next market. A woman petitioning to buy a shop on Market Street. When the woman tripped over saying Market Street, Guinevere smiled, remembering what Brangien had said about how hard it was to get rid of the old names. Next were several fieldworkers and their masters. The fieldworkers had filled their terms of service and were being given their own plots of land. Guinevere could see their pride. And their masters did not seem upset. Several of them embraced afterward, or clasped hands warmly. Everything felt prosperous, hopeful.

Then Mordred turned to the woman in the cage. "What are the charges laid against Rhoslyn, daughter of Richard?"

The woman raised her head. Guinevere stifled a gasp. It was the woman from before—the one passing magical items to the patch-work knight.

Conrad bowed, pulling out another sheaf of paper. He cleared his throat, then read. "Witchcraft and magic, my lord."

"What evidence do we have?"

The woman, Rhoslyn, stood straight, her voice high and clear except around the edges, where it wavered, betraying her nerves. "I meant no harm or mischief. My niece was sick. I knew I could help her. I—"

"Her family is known to practice dark magic," Conrad said. "Her sister was banished three months ago. Rhoslyn was found with items required for working spells."

Rhoslyn shook her head angrily. "Tools of a trade, the same as a butcher or smith would have for theirs!"

Guinevere twitched, wishing she had some way to demand to see what Rhoslyn had been found with. If she could examine it, she might be able to tell what Rhoslyn had been planning to do. But she could not ask without admitting she would understand what she was seeing. And Arthur was not here to get the evidence for her.

Mordred's voice was soft. "Rhoslyn. You know the laws. If we allow magic into Camelot, we allow chaos in. If we allow chaos, everything we have built threatens to unravel. Do you understand?"

Rhoslyn clenched her jaw, her face white. But then something inside her relented, and she softened, nodding.

"You do not deny the charges?"

"No, my lord."

"Very well. Because you were forthright and honest, your punishment is banishment."

Her mouth was set, a single harsh line, as she looked out over the crowd. There were murmurs and whispers. At first Guinevere thought people were upset with the severity of the sentence. Then she realized they were upset with Mordred's leniency. She heard several hisses of *Drown her.*

Mordred apparently heard them as well. "Punishment to be carried out immediately. Conrad, see that she is escorted to the borders of Camelot. Rhoslyn, you will never again be welcome in this kingdom. God have mercy on you. Go."

"My niece?"

"She will be taken into the care of the castle. I promise you."

Rhoslyn nodded. Conrad and two liveried men retrieved her from the cage and hurried her out a back door. Guinevere stayed as still as a stone.

If the rule of law was that *any* magic—no matter the intention—was grounds for banishment or death, she did not want to think about what would happen if they suspected the queen herself was a witch. She would have to be much, much more careful. But not right now. Right now, she had a conspiracy to unmask.

She stood and and walked as regally as she could manage from the room, hoping no one wondered why she chose that moment to leave.

Guinevere did not have time to return to the castle and change into Brangien's clothing. She hurried down a side street, working her way into the more residential—and less wealthy—portion of the city. Hanging on a line to dry was a serviceable hooded cloak of sturdy brown cloth. With a twinge of guilt, she stole it. She could not leave her own in its place. And she doubted the owner would be able to afford to replace the cloak anytime soon.

It was for Arthur, though. She threw the cloak around herself, hastily tying knots of shadow and confusion. She could not risk being recognized. With that in place, she darted back to the main street. Her speed had worked. Just ahead of her at the docks she saw the woman Rhoslyn being loaded onto a ferry alongside several paying passengers. Guinevere took a deep breath and stepped aboard.

And immediately regretted it. The ferry dipped and lurched. Before she could turn around, they had pushed off.

"For Arthur," she whispered to herself, closing her eyes and hugging herself against the dread and panic. She was here to protect Arthur. This was how she could do it.

The ferry was crowded enough that Guinevere was bumped and jostled in the midst of others. It was oddly comforting. She had nothing to hold on to, but they were packed so tightly that she could not fall. And there were bodies—living, breathing, pungent bodies—between her and the water.

Rhoslyn and her guards were on the far end. Guinevere wanted to study the other woman, but it was all she could do to keep breathing in the midst of the existential dread that filled her with every creak of the ferry.

After an eternity, the ferry met the other side of the lake. She was pushed off in the press of bodies around her. At some point—she genuinely did not know when—she had latched on to the arm of an older man. He kept peering at her, his eyes narrowed in confusion, as he tried to figure out who she was. Her own head ached as her knots struggled to hold back his attempts to see past the magic.

She let go of his arm and walked in the opposite direction. As soon as she was out of his immediate sight, he turned the other way, a mildly baffled look on his face.

The soldiers loaded Rhoslyn, pale-faced and trembling, into a cart pulled by a solitary horse. Guinevere was relieved. She could not have kept up had they all been mounted. Stealing a horse from Arthur's stable was an option, but a risky one. And she could not very well demand one as the queen. She would not be allowed out on her own. The ruse that kept her close to Arthur also complicated things in such an aggravating manner.

The soldiers kept to a clear road. Guinevere maintained a cautious distance, passing the occasional traveler heading toward Camelot. All their eyes slid away from her. Her head was light, her vision slightly blurred, but she would not abandon her mission.

After two hours, the soldiers turned off the main road and took a less-traveled path through fields toward a looming forest. Arthur had not cut down all the forests in Camelot's realm. Some were still needed for wood and hunting. But this was the beginning of the end of his land. Guinevere's feet were sore, her throat parched. If she had known tracking a witch would be part of her day, she would have prepared differently.

At last the soldiers stopped. Rhoslyn was lifted out of the cart and set on the forest floor without ceremony.

"Good luck," one of the soldiers said. The rest shared a conspiratorial laugh. Guinevere thought it odd that none of them gave the witch a final warning to stay out of Camelot, or instructions, or anything of the sort. She tucked herself against an ancient, gnarled tree as the soldiers passed her.

Their casual attitude made much more sense when, as soon as they were gone, six men on horses melted from the trees.

"Hello, witch," one of the men said, baring his teeth in a sneer.

Guinevere's heart seized. Each of the men held a thick wooden club. Was this Arthur's justice, then?

"You cannot do this," Rhoslyn said, her voice small and frightened. "I was banished. Not sentenced to death."

"Ah, but this is not Camelot, is it?" The leader looked around the trees, holding his arms wide. "I see no king here. Which means you are no longer under his protection. And we do not look as kindly on witches as the benevolent king does."

Guinevere was frozen in the shadows. Violence simmered, ready to boil forth. She had come here to hunt Rhoslyn and find out how she was a threat to Arthur. Would she stand hidden while the woman was beaten to death?

The leader raised his club. Guinevere stepped out onto the path. She did not know what to do—what she should do—but surely this was not right.

An arrow whistled through the air, landing with perfect precision in the center of the leader's hand, pinning it to the club. He screamed in agony and surprise. Two more arrows found targets, one in a leg and the other squarely in a chest. That man slumped and fell from his horse. Several more arrows flew through the air as the leader shouted and the survivors turned their horses and galloped away into the cover of the trees.

Not defenseless, then. Or at least not undefended. Guinevere slipped back into the embrace of the tree as a man on a brown horse rode up and dismounted.

Rhoslyn let out a sob and threw her arms around his neck. He lifted her onto the horse, revealing a familiar face.

The patchwork knight.

Just as the men had been waiting to ambush Rhoslyn, the patchwork knight had been waiting to save her. He and Rhoslyn were working together. Guinevere had been right. She waited until they had disappeared, then left the shelter of her tree. Even if she could follow the trail, she could not say how long it would take. They were mounted; she was not. And she could not stay away from Camelot any longer. She had lingered too long already.

Her knots did not make her unnoticeable to insects, and she wearily swatted them away. The cloak was too heavy for the sullen summer heat. She was sticky and exhausted and more determined than ever. She would return and face this threat as soon as she could.

It would be a long walk back to Camelot. She would not get there before dark, which was going to make everything a lot more difficult to explain. Particularly to Brangien, who would not miss the fact that her queen had not spent the night in the castle. Would Brangien alert the guards? Guinevere puzzled through possible excuses and solutions.

Her other line of thought concerned what to do about Rhoslyn and the knight. What were they plotting?

Arthur's laws and rules were better for the kingdom, but that did not mean they were better for everyone. Rhoslyn could be angry and powerful enough to pose a threat. Especially when conspiring with the patchwork knight. Guinevere cracked her knuckles, anticipating the knots she would tie to meet that threat.

A snapping twig to her right startled her. She drew the dagger Arthur had bought her and raised it against—

The horse of the man who had died. It took a hesitant step toward her. Closing her eyes and releasing a breath of gratitude and relief, Guinevere sheathed her knife and mounted the horse.

"Good girl," she said, then raced the horse back to Camelot.

CHAPTER ELEVEN

Arthur was still away when Guinevere slipped into the castle just before curfew. If Brangien had noted her absence, she said nothing while preparing her queen for bed.

Brangien's preparations were for naught. Guinevere lay awake all night, plotting. Thinking. What was her best course of attack? Confront the patchwork knight directly, or try to find any other of Rhoslyn's allies within the city? Alert Arthur so he and his men could hunt her down?

The whispers of *Drown her* haunted Guinevere. The callous abandonment of the soldiers, knowing what awaited the woman, whose only punishment was supposed to be banishment.

But this was the threat. These were the stakes. Arthur made difficult decisions every day as king; she would do the same. Besides, this was her fight. Her duty. Not the soldiers'. So she would deal with it herself rather than send armed men against something they might not be able to face. She sat up the next morning, eager to get started.

It was a mistake. Brangien noticed her vigor and seized upon it.

"It is time to begin your visits."

"My what?"

"Your visits. To the other ladies."

Guinevere slumped. "Must we?"

"It is a duty of the queen."

Once again Guinevere cursed Merlin and Arthur's idea to have her be queen. She should have come here as a maid! The business of being queen demanded so much, and took her away from her duties of protecting Arthur.

As Guinevere and Brangien stood outside the castle gates, gazing down at the manors, Guinevere felt nearly as much fear as she had going on the ferry. She was not ready. "I do not want to do this," she whispered.

Brangien shrugged. "Could be buckets. Sir Bors has no wife, so we are in luck there. We never have to visit him. I would recommend visiting Sir Percival's wife and Sir Caradoc's wife on the same day. They will of course be offended no matter what the order, but at least that will keep them in close enough proximity that we can maintain the illusion of neutrality. Then—"

"Can we start with Dindrane?"

"Dindrane?" Brangien, aghast, looked at Guinevere. "Dindrane is the spinster sister of Sir Percival. She can be included in our visit to Blanchefleur. You will have to take a meal with her eventually, but next month. Or the month after. Dindrane does not matter at all."

"Exactly. No one can be offended if we visit her first. The ladies will be too surprised and confused. And it will be nice to cut my teeth on visits by starting with someone who 'does not matter at all.'"

Brangien's frown shifted as she considered it. Finally, she nodded. "It might be a brilliant opening gambit. *Or* it is the worst decision you have made so far as queen."

"Thank you for your vote of confidence."

Brangien grinned mischievously. "I just want to cover all possible outcomes so no matter how this plays out, I can say I did warn you."

"What *would* I do without you?" Guinevere linked her arm through Brangien's and they headed down the street to Sir Percival's manor. Brangien knocked on the front door, but was informed by a servant that Dindrane entertained in her own room. She promised she would let Dindrane know they were there, then directed them around the side of the house to an alley so narrow it only received light a handful of hours every day.

They entered through a side door. The room was tiny and dim. The main light came through a door left open to the rest of the house. From the looks of it, the next room was her sister-in-law's bedroom. Which meant Dindrane's only options for coming in and out were to go around outside or to go through Blanchefleur's room.

The manor was large enough to accommodate giving Dindrane her own set of rooms. Even Guinevere, uneducated in the subtle arts at play here, understood the power Blanchefleur was wielding. She used her social status as a spell to keep Dindrane in place.

Dindrane burst in from the outside door. Her face was flushed and her hands red and raw. It looked as though she had been cleaning. But she held her head high and greeted Guinevere with a polished curtsy—that doubled as cover as she kicked the door to Blanchefleur's bedroom shut. "Apologies, my queen. I did not expect you. Usually when I have callers, they send word ahead of time to make certain I am available. You are fortunate. My schedule is quite full."

"Thank you for making time to see us." Guinevere sat in one of the two worn chairs that Dindrane gestured toward. Brangien stood against the wall as Dindrane took the other chair. Dindrane's clothing was nice—it would have reflected poorly on Sir Percival if it were not. But her hair held no jewels and something about the way her sleeves strained made it clear they had been sewn for another body.

Her eyes were clever and sharp, a pleasant warm brown, and her hair shone chestnut, well cared-for.

"I am afraid I have no refreshment to offer. I have just finished entertaining."

Guinevere allowed her the lie. "Oh, we have already eaten. But it is kind of you to worry about us. I did not get a chance to speak with you at the wedding celebration and wanted to get to know you."

"Mmm." Dindrane smiled tightly. The silence was as close and confining as the room. Finally, she leaned forward. "Your hair is lovely. Is that the style in the south? It certainly is not the style here. But it suits you. I could never be so brave as to wear my hair like that." Dindrane's smile stayed firmly in place. Guinevere was positive she was being insulted. It was *delightful*. Everyone else was so careful with her, but Dindrane came prepared for battle.

"Have you always been so pale?" Dindrane asked, tilting her head to the side. "It does make your freckles stick out so. But the only solution is to spend more time in the sun, which will cause more freckles."

Guinevere laughed. She could not help it. She had no desire for an enemy, and no need to feel insulted. She suspected Dindrane could use a friend even more than she herself could. At least she had Arthur. What must it be like, owing everything to your brother and the sister-in-law who obviously hated you? If Guinevere was out of place and struggling, Dindrane was, too. "I like you very much, Dindrane. I hope you will let me visit you often. And I would love to have you visit me, as well."

Dindrane wilted, disarmed. "You would?"

"I have had no company but nuns for several years. I should very much like to consider you a friend. Or a sister, even."

Dindrane's smile was hesitant but genuine. "I have always wanted a sister."

"You have a sister," Brangien muttered, eyes on her ever-present sewing.

"My brother has a wife. That woman is not my sister."

Guinevere reached out and took her hand. Dindrane gave no strong impression. It was reassuring. If she were a threat, Guinevere would feel it. Dindrane felt as Dindrane looked: tired and stubborn and the tiniest bit hopeful. "Allow me to be your sister, then. Would you accompany us to the chapel today? I need someone to sit by, since the king is away."

Dindrane pretended to consider it, as though it were not a tremendous honor that could not be passed up. Guinevere knew whoever she sat by would be remarked on and noticed. Guinevere had wanted to sit by Mordred, but this was a better option. It would cause gossip, but no damage. Finally, Dindrane nodded. "I would be happy to assist you." She smiled as though she were doing Guinevere a favor. "Your maid can help me dress before we go."

Brangien's expression indicated this was not an option. Guinevere stood. "Oh, I am very sorry, but we needed to pick up . . . a . . . ."

"New thread," Brangien finished, tucking away her sewing. "We will meet you in front of the manor when you are ready."

It was a relief to escape Dindrane's cramped room. They walked a fair distance in silence. Guinevere wondered if they really were going to get thread to complete the charade. Finally, Brangien spoke.

"Dindrane? Really? You choose Dindrane?"

"She is harmless."

"I would not have been harmless had I been forced to dress her."

Guinevere laughed, tugging Brangien to a stop in a glorious shaft of sunlight. "I promise you will never have to help her."

"You are helping her enough for both of us." But Brangien softened, tipping her face up to the light and closing her eyes. "You are like the king."

"How so?"

"He sees value in everyone. You are a good match."

The warmth in Guinevere came from more than the sun. She wanted to be like Arthur. But the warmth was pierced with a nagging worry. Rhoslyn was still out there. Even now, she could have agents within the city. Guinevere was not here to be a good match for Arthur. She was here to save him.

But first, church. Being queen was absurd. The last thing she should be worried about was making an appearance to support a religion she neither understood nor cared about. But it was Arthur's religion, and thus had to be hers. She rubbed unconsciously at her wrists, tracing the lines where Rhoslyn had been bound. Appearances had to be kept. She had to be above suspicion.

They wandered back to Sir Percival's manor just as Dindrane hurried out to meet them.

Arthur had built the church in the center of Camelot. It was the one new thing he had constructed in his three years as king. They walked there together, Brangien on one side of Guinevere, Dindrane on the other. "You know," the older woman said, "he was in love with me for a while. The king. Such advances he made! But I thought it best for the kingdom that he find a young wife. One who could bear him many children."

"You are as noble as you are kind." Guinevere smiled, grateful for the distraction from her far more real worries. "I am grateful you did not snatch him up when you had the chance."

Dindrane sniffed dismissively. "He is not really my type. Awful hair. You should make him grow it." She sat next to Guinevere on the bench nearest the altar. It did not go unnoticed by those already gathered. Dindrane glowed with pleasure at the whispers.

Guinevere had never actually attended a Christian church service before. Merlin had no use for the Romans' castoffs. But Arthur had taken to it, and Guinevere could see why. Everyone was gathered in the same large wooden building. The ceiling soared overhead. It was simple but elegant. Clean. They all sat on the same level. Everyone listened to the same prayers, performed the same actions. It was an equalizer. And it gave the people something in common with each other. Something to unify them.

Once the service was done—a relief, as Guinevere had had to pretend to understand Latin, which she most certainly did not— she sat through a meal with another knight's wife. And then called on another. And another. She saved Blanchefleur for last, and made certain that Dindrane was invited. Blanchefleur positively seethed with resentment.

By the end of the day, Guinevere's head ached as much as her feet did. Performing queenly duties was almost as exhausting as performing magic. Women truly were the stronger gender. All the subtle games they had to play, the ways they teased power from those around them! She had much to learn there.

But no time. She had a far greater first duty. When the day was at last finished, her real work began.

CHAPTER TWELVE

During the droning conversations of the day, Guinevere had imagined knots, in infinite combinations and possibilities. It had been a useful exercise, making her realize a simple sight knot to see magic would not have worked. Sight knots could work with a specific target, but asking her eyes to see something unknown would be too taxing for such a delicate sense. She could have blinded herself.

Knots could enhance and direct what already existed; they could stop things. But they could not make her senses do something new. Knot magic was pedestrian. It was about *binding* magic to a task, not discovering new things. But surely she could find a way. Her fingers twitched, tying imaginary knots.

And then she realized the solution. It was not her eyes that needed to see better. Her eyes took in only what the world presented to them. Her *hands* were what could take information not readily given. Her hands sensed things her eyes never could. If she could enhance that sense, extend it, then she would have what she needed.

She wrapped herself in a robe and hurried outside, up and up and up the castle to the alcove. It was the middle of the night. If she were caught, no one could see what she had been doing. And she could claim difficulty sleeping while Arthur was away. Once she was tucked in away from the wind and any eyes that might spy her, she got to work.

She used hair, not thread, since she needed as much of herself as she could afford. She looped the strands around her fingers, tying an altered version of a knot for extending sight. Her fingers tingled with the rush of her pulse. The blood was caught there, pooling, throbbing. Guinevere stumbled, leaning against the outer wall of the alcove. Everything else in her body was light and distant, her whole self seeming to dwell in her fingers alone.

So she held out her hands and she *felt*.

She started with the city. There were tiny warm spots scattered throughout, and she noted the location of each. She let her hands roam over Camelot. A few pinpricks of darkness, but they vanished like smoke beneath her hands before she could determine what they were.

She took a deep breath. The next one she wanted to avoid, but she would not turn away from her duty. She pushed her hands to the lake. And she felt . . .

Nothing.

She shuddered, chilled straight through. There was an absolute absence of magic. This was the lake that had held the Lady. This was the lake that had delivered Excalibur to Arthur. And now? A still void.

Trembling, the demands of the magic already draining her, she hurried past it, pushing her hands out, out, out among the fields, among the regions surrounding Camelot. They were not as lifeless as the lake, but they were dormant. Nothing sparked or seethed until she got to the area where she had lost Rhoslyn and the knight. It crackled like a campfire, warming her hands.

She collapsed. The strands of hair around her fingers snapped. The blood returned to its normal flow. She wondered when feeling would return to her hands, and suspected this awful pins-and-needles feeling would continue for some time.

She had found some leads, but it was the absence she discovered that bothered her more than anything. A lake that size, with that history, should have had *some* magic. As she stumbled back down the stairs, her hands throbbing and agonizingly numb at the same time, she tried to understand what it could mean.

A dark possibility seized her. If she could channel herself into her hands to make them more powerful than ever, who was to say that the dark magic of the world could not be made to do the same?

What if someone was siphoning all the magic of the lake, all the magic of the land? And what would happen when they amassed enough?

She had to get to Rhoslyn. She had to stop her.

For the first time in her life, Guinevere wished for a sword.

She had anticipated fighting magic, not people. But this was why she was here. Whatever it took, she would face Rhoslyn and her knight, and she would come out triumphant.

She slipped into the darkness of sleeping Camelot. The streets hummed and whistled with the wind from the lake. She shivered, remembering the cold void. But that was not her mystery. In her mind, the warm spots of magic burned like the afterimage of the sun. Sliding from pool of darkness to pool of darkness, feeling more like the night than like a person, Guinevere found the first location. It had been the most familiar to her, after all. The edge of the cliff where the patchwork knight had twice eluded her.

Her hands were numb and useless, but she had her eyes. She searched and searched for something amiss, something that did not belong.

After several frustrating minutes searching the rubble and detritus of crumbling foundations, she realized her mistake. The magic was hidden in something that *did* belong. Almost. She reached down and picked up a perfectly smooth, rounded rock. Like the one Rhoslyn had dropped. This time, she saw what she had missed before. Someone had knotted magic into the rock itself. It held something. A spell, a memory, a curse—she could not tell. But she knew what she was looking for now.

She hurried through the night. Seven rocks at seven separate points in the city. Seven anchors of magic. She could not bring them into the castle—it would break their magic before she discovered what it was.

It was nearly dawn. If she left now, she could reach Rhoslyn within hours. But she would not be able to explain her absence or her actions. It would mean defeating the threat but destroying her role as queen. She could not easily come back to it.

The darkness enveloped her, bade her keep moving.

If she did this for Arthur, she would be fulfilling her purpose but losing her place at his side. She closed her eyes. She would prepare today, then leave tonight. It would keep until then. Sagging under the weight of the coming dawn, she hid the magic rocks and then hurried back to her room.

She only just beat the sun. As soon as night fell, she would hunt. She crawled into bed, planning her attack.

Brangien opened the door as soon as Guinevere closed her weary eyes.

"Happiest news, my queen!"

Guinevere sat up, her hands alternately freezing and burning, pricked with pins and somehow still numb. Her eyes could barely handle the dim light of her room after attuning themselves so thoroughly to shadows. "Yes?" she asked, forcing a smile.

"The king has sent for you! We must pack and leave immediately."

"Oh no," Guinevere said, sighing. Brangien paused, her arms full of cloaks. She lifted an eyebrow in surprise and alarm. Guinevere flinched, trying to cover. "I do not know what to wear."

Brangien laughed and went back to gathering. "That is not for you to fret over. That is my job."

Guinevere flopped back onto her bed, throwing an arm over her face to hide her expression. She had work to do, and no way of letting Arthur know she was needed here. She could feign illness, but maybe Arthur was asking for her for a reason. Maybe he needed her help, specifically. Why else would he send for her?

As long as she was by Arthur's side, she could be certain he was safe. But it was aggravating. They were going to have to figure out better ways to communicate so Arthur would be able to help her efforts instead of interrupting them.

Arthur. The thought of seeing him again—it had been only days, but they felt an eternity—returned feeling to her heart, if not her hands. Very well. She would be queen today, and avenging protector as soon as she returned.

The wind whipped Guinevere's hair, tugging it free from its plait with callous disregard for all the time Brangien had spent wrangling it into submission. If she could not be staging her attack against Rhoslyn and the patchwork knight, at least she was outside the city, with the wind and the wild and a horse. It felt almost like freedom.

"Whoa!" a guard shouted. To her dismay, her horse responded, slowing from a gallop to a trot and then an easy walk. Brangien had been left far behind. She was not very comfortable on horses, and it would take her some time to catch up. Guinevere wished the guard were in the same position.

The guard rode to her side, his expression horrified. "Did you lose control of your horse, my lady?"

"Yes," Mordred interrupted, veering his own horse toward hers. "That mare often breaks into a gallop. I will ride next to the queen to see that it does not happen again."

The guard nodded, satisfied, and gave Guinevere a polite distance again. Mordred leaned precariously far and put a hand on Guinevere's mare's neck. "Your horse is the most obedient and well-trained of our stable."

Guinevere's smile, much like her hair in the wind, could not be restrained. "I am sorry. But riding is—" She took a deep breath.

"Freedom," Mordred said.

"Yes." She had not realized quite how constraining being queen was. It was a weight that became unnoticeable until shrugged off. But putting it back on made it nearly unbearable. She should not have prowled through the night on her own. Darkness was a seductive freedom, and she had to stay focused.

Or she should have followed the shadows and gone straight to where Rhoslyn was hiding. She would have finished with it by now.

"You are a different person when you are outside," Mordred said.

Guinevere reached up, trying to tame her hair again. Her hands fumbled the action. They still stung, numb and clumsy. She could feel nothing with them. "What do you mean?"

"You stop pretending."

She froze.

"Ah, there it is again. You are trying to decide which expression to give me to deflect notice or conversation." Mordred tapped the side of his nose. "It is easier for you when you are behind walls, trapped by stone and expectations. But out here in the wild you have a harder time."

Guinevere needed some excuse, some reason why she would behave this way.

"You treat the world with the wonder of a child," Mordred said, filling in the empty space between them. He looked nothing like Arthur. Arthur was carved from the same stuff as Camelot—regal and majestic. But Mordred belonged out here, with her.

She shook her head, correcting herself. This was not where she belonged.

She needed to choose her words carefully. How to explain that the whole world *was* a wonder in a way that would not be suspect? She loved the way it smelled, the way it felt. The movement of the horse beneath her. The simple food they would eat when they stopped for a meal. Seeing a new place—seeing any place at all! Of course she could not hide the way she felt. "It was a long time to spend in a convent. Everything feels new outside those walls."

"Except you traded those walls for different ones."

"Camelot is incredible!"

Mordred laughed, raising his hands in innocence. "It is. But it is tame. Structured. Sometimes we need a break from that."

She had planned a far more dangerous break. But he was right. She loved it out here. She would not let the tasks ahead of her steal away the joy of travel and the anticipation of meeting Arthur at the end. The warmth of his smile flashed through her like the sun through parting clouds, and she admitted it was not only the honesty they shared that she missed.

Mordred kept close. Their party was stretched out, the open plain offering no threats, but he always rode next to her. Guinevere had been surprised that he had joined them at all. Bored with the slower pace, she brought it up. "I thought you were the one left behind to take care of Camelot in Arthur's absence. Why are you coming with us?"

Mordred scanned the horizon. "Your husband would not trust you to travel to him with anyone but his family. And he wants all his best knights with him for this meeting. Camelot can be held against enemies for months with the men in it now. It will keep."

"What is the meeting?"

"Something with the Picts. Arthur has been active on the northern borders. He will have to play nice and reassure them he is not expanding, merely maintaining."

"Why does he need me, then?" This sounded like politics and military issues, not magical threats. She wanted to help Arthur however he needed, but if she was not essential, she was wasting her time and risking Arthur's safety. She could almost feel Rhoslyn getting farther and farther away. Having more time to plot wickedness with the patchwork knight.

"What better way to show peaceful intentions than to bring his new bride? It demonstrates that he trusts them and is treating this as a pleasant meeting between friendly allies."

"So I am a decoration?" Her heart sank, and she gritted her teeth.

"You are a vital piece in a complicated game."

"Mmm."

"You do not sound happy with that answer."

"I am happy to help the king in whatever way I can." But her face would not give up its frown. Maybe there was more to it. There could be something magic in play, and Arthur was bringing her under false pretenses.

"Well," Mordred said, "I am afraid your disobedient horse is about to break into a gallop again and I will have to follow. It may be a while before we can get the horse to slow down."

Her horse was walking calmly. Mordred's mossy-green eyes twinkled expectantly. She clicked her tongue and tapped the horse's sides. It broke into a gallop, the wind greeting her once more.

After a tongue-lashing from Brangien—who apparently felt freer outside the walls, as well, and had no qualms about shouting at the queen for risking her neck and riding too fast—Guinevere was forced to keep her horse at a reasonable walk.

To further emphasize her point, Brangien planted her horse twenty feet ahead of Guinevere's and kept it there. Mordred grew ever more focused on their surroundings.

The countryside offered no threats, though. In their daylong ride, they passed field after field. The vista of green and gold was broken only by the occasional small town or hamlet. There were not many people in the towns—they were out in the fields, working. But a few children were around, playing happily or watching the mounted procession with open curiosity. Horses were not a common sight out here.

As afternoon stretched out warm and content like a cat, they passed through another small village. A woman and her son sold them fresh bread. It reminded Guinevere of what Brangien had said about the little boy in the village claimed by the forest. When the whitewashed cob houses faded in the distance, Guinevere turned to Mordred.

"Have any forests grown here? Do you have to fight them back often?"

"No." Mordred looked past her. On the far horizon there was a dark smudge, but that was the only evidence of forestland she could see. Her hand-knotted magic had not reached that far north—she had focused it all in Rhoslyn's direction. "Magic thrives on blood and wonder and chaos. Camelot is so well ordered, so structured, that magic can find no hold. Arthur strangled it, starved it, and cut it out. He allows no seeds within his borders."

Well. Except her. But what Mordred said made her curious. Maybe Arthur had done something to the lake, and that was why it was so dead. She would have to ask him. "And that is why he banished Merlin, even though Merlin had always helped."

Mordred ran his fingers along his jaw, where dark stubble was beginning to peer through his pale skin. "Not all of us agreed that was necessary. But yes. Merlin himself is chaos in mortal form."

Guinevere snorted. Then she tried to cover it with a cough. *Chaotic* was an excellent way to describe Merlin. Was it any wonder her memories were confusing jumbles of images and lessons, with gaping holes between?

She closed her eyes at the sudden flare of discomfort, the suspicion that there was more to her missing memories than she was allowing herself to see.

She had to focus, though. She was not here for herself. She was here for Arthur and Camelot. Merlin was a risk to associate with, certainly. But surely Camelot could understand the necessity of keeping certain weapons. Most of the city was stone, but the inhabitants still kept barrels of water everywhere in case of fire. They did not want fire, did not set it, but they were prepared to fight it the only way they could. Magic was the same. Keeping someone capable of recognizing and combating it was not the same as inviting magic to take hold within the city.

Was it?

"What if someone attacks using magic?" she asked, keeping her tone as light and innocent as possible. "Who will defend you with Merlin gone?"

"Keeping Merlin in the city was too risky. Like calls to like." He glanced over at her, then looked quickly away. "Besides, people did not trust the wizard."

"Why not? He always fought for Arthur."

"In his own ways, when he chose to, how he chose to. He was bound by no laws, not even Arthur's. And then there was the matter of Arthur's birth."

She wanted Mordred to keep talking, but she had to be careful what she revealed. How much would the real Guinevere have known? "I have heard the rumors. That Uther Pendragon used a wizard to trick Igraine so he could lie with her." Guinevere shuddered. It was a violent, terrible magic. It could breed only evil. How had it produced Arthur? "I can understand why they would not want another wizard in Camelot."

"Another wizard? What do you mean?"

Guinevere turned her face to him. "What do *you* mean?"

"It was Merlin."

"No." Guinevere shook her head. The information did not fit. It could not fit. Her chest squeezed, like she had been laced too tightly. "No, it was a dark sorcerer."

Mordred's smile was as soft and blue as the twilight falling around them. "Yes. Merlin. That is the nature of magic. When you bend the world to your will, when you twist nature around yourself, where does the power stop? Who tells you to stop?"

Had Guinevere not been on a horse, she would have stopped in shock. As it was, she was grateful for the cloak of evening to hide the horror claiming her. Merlin. Merlin had done that. It was the most violent act possible, the taking of someone's will. She would never have made knots for it, would never have participated in such a deception. Such depravity. But Merlin—her protector, her teacher, her father—had. "How could he?" she whispered.

"Merlin saw that the world needed a new kind of king. So he made it happen." Mordred sighed, patting his horse's neck. "I do not agree with what he did. It was my grandmother who was violated by a man she thought was her husband. But without it, Arthur would not be here." He held out his arms to the peaceful, rolling countryside. "We cannot deny the end result. Merlin saw what Camelot demanded, and he created the means for it. He engineered his own banishment, in a way. The wizard is a puzzle. But Camelot is a success."

"And all the suffering and loss it took to get here?" Guinevere asked, devastated and heartbroken for herself. For Igraine. For Arthur. For Mordred. For all the lives that had been stained by the darkness of Merlin's choice.

"Such is the cost of progress." Mordred glanced at her. Apparently some of her emotion was evident even in the near-darkness. His voice went soft. "I am sorry. I should not speak of such things to a lady. It was indelicate of me."

"No, I am glad. I would rather know the truth. I do not like being behind walls, either in the castle or in Arthur's life." Or her own.

Merlin had done that. He had done that, and not told her.

What else did he keep from her? How could she trust him? And if she could not trust the wizard who chose her to protect Arthur, how could she trust herself?

It was fully dark when they reached Arthur's camp. He stood at the edge, waiting. Her anticipation of seeing him had turned tense and sour in light of Mordred's revelations. They had much to discuss. Too much. Arthur helped Guinevere down from her horse, then surprised her by giving her a quick but fierce embrace.

"Thank you for coming," he whispered against her ear.

"Of course." She could feel the heat in her cheeks at his nearness. "We need to talk. Alone."

He put her hand on his elbow and walked her into the camp. "I am sorry to bring you here. It will be unpleasant. And dangerous."

She squeezed his elbow. "I am here to protect you. However that happens." Some of her anxiety loosened at his words. It was irrational to be relieved at being put in danger, but at least she had not been pulled from her campaign against Rhoslyn and the patchwork knight for nothing.

The camp was bigger than she had expected. Not only did Arthur have all his knights with him, he also had a hundred fighting men.

"Do you expect a fight?" she asked.

"What?" Arthur lifted a tent flap, bringing her into a dim, enclosed space. The ground was covered in furs. Though it was summer, the nights still had teeth.

"So many men."

"Oh. No. The fight did not happen. Gildas and Geoffrey, two lords, were feuding, and it was spilling over my borders. I had to remind them to keep their quarrels to themselves." He paused, and his smile was weary. "They do not want me to become one of their problems. Showing up on their doorstep with this many men was a good reminder. For the meeting with the Pictish king, most of the men will stay here. I will take only my best knights. Enough to appear powerful without outright challenging King Nechtan. Gildas and Geoffrey will come, too, to show that everything here is stable and there is no room for the Picts to move down. And I had to bring you as a show of trust and friendship. I tried to think of another way, but your absence would have been an insult."

"It sounds complicated."

He flopped onto the furs and put his forearm over his eyes. "It is. Why do people get bored with peace? Why is a border seen as a challenge rather than a barrier?"

"But even you fight battles that are not your own."

He lowered his arm and peered at her. "What do you mean?"

She settled next to him, sitting with her skirts tucked under her. "You fought back a forest that did not threaten any of your land."

He grinned sheepishly, caught. "Perhaps even I can get bored with peace sometimes."

"That is not it." She poked him in the side. "You see all men as your responsibility. You cannot deny anyone who needs your help."

He closed his eyes. Though he had been fighting and working nonstop, he did not look exhausted. He looked . . . ready. As though at any moment he could leap up and storm a forest, fight back fairy knights, or negotiate peace with human ones.

She did not feel the same. She was tired and sore after a long day's riding, not to mention heartsick and confused over Mordred's revelations about Merlin. Her hands still tingled, but now they ached, as well. She needed to rest. Especially if she had to draw on strength reserves for magic tomorrow. She shook out her hands, for all the good it did in dispelling the remaining pins and needles. "We need a better way to communicate. I was in the middle of something in Camelot."

Arthur sat up, alarmed. "What?"

"There is a woman. Rhoslyn. I have seen her before, talking to the patchwork knight. She was caught practicing magic and banished."

Arthur nodded; he looked sad but not surprised. "It is against the law."

"I followed her. When your soldiers left her on the southern border, men were waiting to kill her."

At this he did look surprised, and angry. "*My* men?"

"No. I do not think so. But I am fairly certain your soldiers knew about it and left Rhoslyn to die."

Arthur rubbed his face. "I do not want those who are banished to be killed, or even harmed. They cannot be in Camelot, but that does not mean they cannot live freely elsewhere. Thank you for telling me. I will see to it that things change."

"That is not the point of my story. She was not killed. The patchwork knight saved her."

"He did? You saw him fight?"

"It was barely a fight."

Arthur's eyes shone brightly. "I wish I had seen it!"

"Arthur! Please focus." Guinevere shook her head at his sheepish expression. "The knight obviously knew where she would be left, as well. After he fought off the attackers, they both went deeper into the forest. Together."

Arthur frowned. "I do not understand. Where is the problem?"

"They are your enemies! Camelot's enemies. I found remnants of her magic in Camelot, and sensed far more of it in the forest on your border. They are plotting something. And I think we cannot wait to find out what it is."

Arthur shifted, humming low in his throat. "She was banished. If she is not within my borders, I have no claim. Who am I to tell her she cannot do as she will outside my lands?"

"This is a *threat*."

"Then when it comes within Camelot's boundaries, we will face it."

"Why wait, when we know where she is? When we know she works with the patchwork knight?"

Finally, the exhaustion showed in Arthur's face. His smile lines disappeared, and his eyelids drew lower. "Because I refuse to be a warlord king. Not like my father. I will leave my borders to defend innocents, but never to attack."

Guinevere hung her head. She could not argue with him on this. But she did not agree with allowing his enemies the time they needed to build an attack. Arthur was generous and noble.

She could not afford to be. She would take care of it alone. She would fortify Camelot, and, when she got the opportunity, she would do what Arthur could not and would not.

Was this how Merlin made his decision? She cringed at the thought.

"Did you hurt your hands?" Arthur asked.

"Oh." She looked down where she had been unconsciously kneading them, trying to counterbalance the fierce ache. "No. Well, yes. But for a good cause. Magic always has a price."

Arthur took her right hand between his. His hands were big and calloused, but his fingers worked with precision as he began massaging her palm in circles. Guinevere stifled a small gasp.

Arthur froze. "Did I hurt you?"

"No, it feels—it feels nice." It felt more than nice.

Arthur tugged her hand, gently guiding her to his side. She leaned against him and he worked the numbness and pain out of both her hands. His skin on hers was like magic.

She wondered what the price would be.

"It is such a relief to be able to touch you," Arthur said, startling Guinevere from where she had almost dozed off against his shoulder. "I have to be so careful with women. There are a lot of rules. And people are always watching."

"Yes, I have noticed that. And I have missed you. Every day is filled with lying about my very self. When I am with you, I do not have to."

Arthur's motions paused, then became softer as he massaged

down each of her delicate fingers. "Keeping secrets is like a thorn beneath the skin. You can get used to it, but it is always there, festering."

She opened her mouth to ask him about Merlin, about what he had done to Igraine. But she did not want to bring that much darkness and violence into this fragile, safe space they had.

Besides, it was Merlin who had kept the truth from her. Arthur had no blame in this.

With the pain in her hands lessened, Guinevere felt heavy and dull with exhaustion. She wanted to curl up right here. "Where should I— Where am I sleeping?"

Arthur sat up straight, dislodging her from his shoulder. "I am sorry. I have kept you too long. You could—" He paused, and she leaned forward, wanting him to invite her to stay. But something closed off in his face and he cleared his throat. "Tonight there is a tent for you and Brangien."

She had half thought—perhaps even half hoped—that she would be sharing Arthur's tent. But she needed to rest. And so did Arthur, of course. The price of the magic of his touch was revealed: it left her wanting more, craving something she had not known she needed until she had it.

He stood. "Brangien can help you tonight and tomorrow morning, but she cannot accompany us past this point. I will not risk her."

Guinevere smiled that she herself was not considered something to be risked—she was a strength, not a weakness. "I can manage fine on my own. I am not so spoiled that I cannot live without a maid."

Arthur laughed. "You may yet get there." He led her to the tent next to his. Brangien was already inside, bustling about. Guinevere entered and Arthur closed the flap.

Unfortunately, the tent was not thick enough to block out several low laughs and whistles, and one shout of "How was your reunion with your queen?"

"Get some sleep," Arthur shouted back. "That is a command!" But he did not sound angry or upset. He sounded playful. He was not going to discourage them from thinking that he had a normal relationship with his wife. After all, the legality of their union depended on it. She shoved away the dangerous thought that she would have preferred to stay in Arthur's tent, and not just to bolster their ruse.

She was curious, was all. Increasingly so.

Brangien scowled. "They are distasteful *and* stupid. Obviously nothing happened because Arthur could not have done your laces back up by himself. Idiots."

"Oh, that reminds me!" Guinevere rushed to cover up her embarrassment at both the men's assumption and Brangien's insight. "Can you teach me how to do it on this dress? You are not coming with us tomorrow."

"What? Why?"

"Arthur is afraid it will be dangerous."

Brangien scoffed. "No more dangerous than riding across the entire country with these fools."

"I could not live with myself if something happened to you."

"But it is my job to serve you."

Guinevere turned, interrupting Brangien's progress and forcing her to meet her gaze. "But you are also my friend. If Arthur thinks it is too dangerous to bring you, I trust him. He takes care of his people. I will be fine. Better than fine, because I will know you are safe."

Brangien's eyes lowered. A flash of some emotion Guinevere could not place went over her maid's face. Then Brangien got back to work, unlacing Guinevere's sleeves and helping her remove her outer clothes. "Very well. But if you mess up your plaits by riding too fast, I will not be there to fix them, and all the Picts will blame me for your state. My reputation will be ruined."

Guinevere dutifully turned around so Brangien could undo her braids and comb out the decidedly unmagical knots. "I promise I will do right by you."

"And stay safe," Brangien whispered.

"And stay safe," Guinevere agreed. She hoped it was a promise she could keep.

There is nothing to hold on to in Camelot. Wings flutter, legs skitter, but the little bodies have nothing to pull them, no source of light to be drawn toward.

Magic has left Camelot.

She will have to wait until it returns. But she is hungry. And more than hungry, she is bored. A child has wandered from her parents. The dark queen winks with insects, flashes butterfly wings. Lures the child deeper and deeper into the woods.

Devours.

Never sated but not starving, she moves on. She ripples through the earth, nudging against the borders of Camelot. Trying to find a weak spot. Trying to find a place that will allow her, make room for her, feed her.

A river stops her. It is not any normal river, eternal, rushing, uncaring.

This river is livid.

She forgets her hunger. She forgets her boredom. A hundred bats flap into the sky, a colony of darkness against the blue, and if anyone were looking, it would look like a smile. With very sharp teeth.

CHAPTER THIRTEEN

Arthur rode with his knights. At the front, at the back, ranging to the outer reaches of their company. He was everywhere except at Guinevere's side. Even Mordred did not talk to her. No one did. Not as a rejection of her, but as a response to their new situation.

They were not in Camelot anymore.

Guinevere had not expected the change to be so sudden and stark, but she could *feel* when they crossed the border. The fields fell apart, becoming patchy and disorganized. A few shabby villages clung to the borders, but there were no children playing there. The people who watched them pass did so with narrowed eyes and hands on weapons.

They also skirted around great stretches of forest. Part of Guinevere longed to go through them—she missed the cool green spaces more fiercely than she knew was possible—but the white-knuckled grips the knights kept on their swords reminded Guinevere that these were not Merlin's trees.

Their company was twenty-five men strong. All of Arthur's best knights, plus five servants with packhorses carrying their supplies.

They were meeting on the edges of Pict land. Guinevere drew deeper into the shade of her hood as they passed the burned-out shells of an old settlement. The sooner they met the Picts, the sooner they could leave.

Glad as she was that they had left Brangien behind, she missed her maid and friend. It would have been comforting to share this with someone. Though she was in the center of the men, constantly surrounded, she felt very alone.

"Not long now," Mordred murmured, once again at her side. Guinevere had not noticed him. Her hands were busy beneath a shawl she had draped over them. She finally had enough feeling in her fingers to work with the strands of thread she had stolen from Brangien's things. Her knots were all about confusion, blindness, disguise. If things got bad, she could throw the knots at their enemies and buy some time. But it cost her her own vision. Everything was blurry and indistinct.

She did not mind a veil being drawn over her eyes to hide the state of the world they rode through. If her journey from the convent had been punctuated by the one strike of terror in the new forest, this one was drawn low with an undercurrent of bleak dread, constantly tugging at them. How did people live out here? How could anything survive this unending stress and fear?

Arthur called something out and his men stopped as one. Mordred took Guinevere's horse's reins. The horses snorted and stamped, impatient.

"A party is coming to meet us," Mordred whispered.

"What should I do?"

"Exactly what you are."

"And what is that?"

"Look beautiful."

Guinevere snorted like her horse. Mordred's laugh was low and pleased. "No one expects you to speak or understand Pictish. Stay by Arthur's side or by mine. Do not ever step out anywhere alone, and never let one of their servants or men lead you anywhere. This should be painless."

Guinevere relaxed and let her features settle into pleasant, cool detachment. They thought her a decoration. That was good. If she had to attack, no one would expect it.

She watched as Arthur greeted the man-and-horse-shaped blur that rode up to them. Arthur gestured toward her. Mordred urged their horses forward and she was delivered to her husband's side.

Arthur said something in a musical language. She heard her name and inclined her head. The Pictish king, Nechtan, was a bulk of beard and fur and menace as he leaned toward her. He reached out a hand, so she lifted her own. His engulfed hers. He lowered his forehead to the back of her hand, then released her.

The impression she got from his touch was far sharper than her vision. He was like a falcon. Circling. Watchful. Predatory. But not immediately threatening.

They were led into camp. Arthur lifted her down from her horse and tucked her hand against his elbow. She was grateful. He did not know how poorly she saw right then. He guided her to a large table set up in the middle of a field. Beneath it they had laid bright rugs. Who had brought it all out here or who would be responsible for taking it back, she could not say. The table gleamed with candles in the fading afternoon light. Bonfires burned in orange blurs around them.

Arthur pulled out a seat for Guinevere, then sat next to her. She lowered her hood. Her smile felt vacant and disconnected. It was not feigned. She could understand none of the chatter around her. King Nechtan sat next to Arthur, Mordred sat on Guinevere's other side, and as far as Guinevere could make out, she was the only woman present.

She wondered where the Pictish queen was. If Guinevere was there to show trust, why did the Picts not do the same? She hoped it was because Arthur came from such a place of strength he could afford to be generous, whereas the Picts needed to appear strong.

Food was brought. She reached for her goblet, parched.

"It has all been tasted," Mordred whispered into his cup so his mouth was hidden. "Nothing is poisoned."

Guinevere froze with the wine halfway to her lips. She had not even considered it. There were so many ways for men to hurt each other, so many methods of ending one another. No wonder Arthur's knights did not worry about magical threats. They had a world full of other menaces to consider.

Her appetite considerably diminished, Guinevere picked at her food enough to be polite. Arthur and King Nechtan kept up a steady stream of talk. It sounded friendly.

"We have peace with the Picts," Mordred said, his voice so low she could barely hear it. "But it is tenuous. They are renowned fighters."

"Why have they not come against Arthur, then?"

"They have. We bought peace with five thousand Picts dead by our swords."

"That is a steep price." Guinevere had never seen five thousand people together. The enormity of imagining five thousand dead was more than she could hold. Her head swam.

"Arthur is here to remind them that we are friends, because we have not always been so."

"How am I doing with my part?"

"You are exceptional at sitting and being lovely."

Guinevere wanted to roll her eyes, but it was not queenly. Arthur leaned close to her, a smile on his face. But he spoke to Mordred through gritted teeth. "Where are Geoffrey and Gildas? They agreed

to come. Their presence here—and their apologies and assurances
of peace—was the whole point."

"I will find out what I can." Mordred moved to stand, but froze.
The conversation at the table, a low constant hum, snapped shut like
it was caught in a trap.

A man stood across from them. He pulled out a chair and sat,
leaning back. "No, do not get up." He gestured for everyone to sit.
All the men around Guinevere were half-standing, hands on swords.
"I came for a meal, not a fight. Though rumor has it the Picts' food is
not nearly as good as their fighting."

"Maleagant," Arthur said.

Guinevere felt a chill down her spine. Sir Maleagant. The one
Arthur had been receiving messages about.

"What luck this is. I wanted to visit King Nechtan, and here he is
on my own borders, waiting for me."

"These are not your borders," Arthur said, his voice terribly still
and calm.

Maleagant ripped off the leg of a roasted fowl. "Are you waiting
for Geoffrey and Gildas? I am afraid they will not be coming. Our
land negotiations went well. For me." He tore a hunk of meat from
the bone, then reached out, snagging Arthur's own goblet and taking
a long draught from it. "These are *my* borders," he said, setting the
goblet down. "And, King Nechtan, you are most welcome."

"Thank you for your hospitality," King Nechtan said. Guinevere
had not known he spoke their language. Arthur communicated with
him in Pictish. Maleagant offered no such courtesy. "I am very . . .
curious about this new development."

"Time for that later. Tonight we should celebrate! We three happy
kings, sharing borders and a meal!" Maleagant turned toward Guinevere. She did not need perfect sight to be unnerved. If the leaf in

the devouring forest had teeth, Maleagant's gaze had tentacles. She could feel it crawling over her. "Arthur, you brought a pet. Younger than I remember you liking them. Introduce us."

Arthur did not respond to Maleagant's command. He turned back to King Nechtan and resumed speaking in Pictish.

Guinevere felt Maleagant's eyes like a burden. He was angled to watch her as he ate, as he drank, as he laughed and interrupted Arthur and King Nechtan's conversation. Guinevere's hands twitched beneath the table, longing to cast her blindness knots at him if only to force him to stop staring. She startled as another hand found hers under the table.

Arthur squeezed her fingers. He did not turn toward her or react to Maleagant, but he noticed. His steady warmth and strength coursed through her. Rather than looking away from Maleagant, she stared—unsmiling, unblinking—at his silhouette. She did not turn away or blush or do anything that a girl would be expected to do. She was no pet. She was no queen, even. She was a secret weapon.

Maleagant laughed. He raised his goblet in a toast to her.

"Best not to draw his attention," Mordred whispered at her shoulder, pretending to lean closer to hear something Arthur was saying.

"And how do you recommend I avoid it as the only woman at this table?" She turned toward Mordred with a smile. "What should I do instead?"

"You are tired. You wish to retire for the evening."

She was and she did. She hated the idea that Maleagant would think he had driven her off, but she trusted that Mordred would advise her well.

"King Nechtan," she said, "it has been an honor to dine with you. But I am afraid the journey here was wearying. I should like to retire for the evening."

Arthur stood. King Nechtan did as well. Maleagant leaned back, stretching his long legs. "I can escort her if you would like, Arthur."

Arthur took Guinevere's hand and pressed his lips to it. His kiss felt like a shield. "Sir Mordred, would you see my queen to our tent? I still have much to discuss with King Nechtan."

Mordred bowed. King Nechtan nodded at Guinevere in farewell. She had not taken two steps when Sir Tristan was at her other side. Sir Gawain and Sir Bors both fell in step, as well.

It had the opposite effect of making her feel safe.

She wanted an excuse to visit the horses. If she could get to Maleagant's horses, she could knot weakness and sleepiness into their manes. But surrounded by knights, she could do nothing. Cross and nervous, she was taken directly to a tent.

Arthur did not join her until the middle of the night. The tent was small, the ground covered with furs. Guinevere had been sitting in there, alone. She had not undressed for fear she would have to run or fight at a moment's notice. Several times, she had peered out to find Mordred, Sir Gawain, Sir Bors, and Sir Tristan all still outside the tent.

"Is he gone?" she asked as Arthur sat next to her and rubbed his face wearily.

"Yes. An hour ago. Then I had to spend time making certain King Nechtan would remain on my side should Maleagant get aggressive."

"Will he?"

He lay back. "I do not know."

"Maleagant was one of your father's knights?"

"One of my own, too."

"*What?*"

Arthur closed his eyes. "He was my earliest supporter. Besides Merlin. He helped me plan the campaign against my father. I did not see then that he was using me to get Uther out. He thought me young and naïve enough that I would be an easier opponent. And in a way he was right. I banished him when I should have had him killed. It has haunted me ever since."

"You cannot blame yourself for his actions."

"I can, and I must. If he threatens Camelot, it is because I allowed it. Oh, I wanted to *strangle* him tonight."

"Was he difficult during the discussions?"

"No, I mean when he would not stop staring at you."

A flush of surprise and pleasure coursed through Guinevere. She knew Arthur had noticed. But she was oddly delighted that it had bothered him on a personal level. "What did he mean, that I am younger than I should be? I am only two years younger than you."

Arthur's face twitched. He did not open his eyes. "Maleagant . . . knows more of my history than I would like. There is a reason I banished him instead of killing him." His pause stretched so long that Guinevere wondered if he had fallen asleep. "Her name was Elaine. She was his sister. I thought she loved me. She told me she was with child, and I was ready to marry her."

Guinevere could not manage to draw a breath. The rumors that Arthur was a virgin king were . . . rumors. He had loved and been in love before. Somehow this felt almost as painful a revelation as Merlin's role in Arthur's birth. But Arthur had never lied to her. She had simply chosen to believe gossip because she wanted to. She wanted him to be as new to all this as she was, because it made her uncertainty feel less humiliating.

"When I discovered Maleagant's plans and misdeeds, I banished him, and in my rage sent Elaine to the south. She died giving birth. The baby, a boy, survived only a few hours. And I was not there."

Guinevere lowered herself to the furs next to him. She took his hand in her own. "I am sorry."

"Even when I knew she had deliberately trapped me—that Maleagant planned to assassinate me and use my child as a means to the throne—I still loved her."

Guinevere flinched. Maleagant's plan was not so different from Merlin's. At least Elaine seemed a willing participant, unlike Arthur's mother.

"Elaine begged me to be merciful. And because I put my own feelings before the good of Camelot, I did not kill Maleagant. My people will suffer—some may even die—because I acted as a man instead of a king."

"You were a boy still."

He brought their hands to his mouth and brushed his lips across the back of her hand. His lips were soft and cool, and she felt it through her whole body. "You are generous. Thank you for letting me tell you. All these long years, it has been a secret shared only by myself, Mordred, and Maleagant."

She moved closer to him. Knowing this secret made her feel important, like she mattered in his life. But it also made her worry even more. If Arthur was not a virgin king, was their false marriage holding him back from things he wanted? She had worried about him missing alliances and politics. She had not considered that they were both missing . . . physical alliances.

"I do not mind," she said, her voice as soft and quiet as the darkness cocooning them in the tent. "If you . . . pursue other women. I understand. I do not want you to think that our arrangement prevents you from that."

He shifted closer to her, his body solid and radiating heat. "I would never give people a reason to talk about us, or to scorn you. I know we do not have a normal marriage, but I am happy with you by my side. Are you?"

"Yes." She did not hesitate. In this moment, the heat of him warming her through, she was perfectly happy.

"Good. I want—" He paused.

She strained closer, the pause after *want* hinged with unknown promise. Finally, he spoke again. "I want to get to know you. The real you. We are both here because Merlin wanted it so, but it is time he is no longer between us. We are in this together, Guinevere. I like that."

She turned so her smile pressed into Arthur's shoulder. She did not know whether she was hiding the full effect he had on her, or whether she was pressing her joy into his shoulder as a kiss. "I like it, too."

"So tell me something no one else knows about you."

She laughed. "Arthur, no one else knows anything about me. Only you do."

His laugh was embarrassed. "I suppose that is true. I gave you one secret; you gave me all of yours. Except . . . your name."

A cold rush of emptiness descended on her. She wanted to tell him. To give it to him. But when she reached for it, it was gone. She had given it to the flame, and it had been devoured. The loss hit her anew.

"How about I tell you a story instead. About the stars. I named them all."

Arthur nodded, slipping his arm around her and stroking her hair with a movement so soft she wondered if he realized he was doing it. She wove the story for him, tying it around him like knots until he fell asleep.

This journey had brought so many new revelations, so many new threats. Maleagant was not one she could fight. Neither was the ghost of Elaine and Arthur's failure. Her heart broke for him, carrying that alone all these years. And somehow he had taken that pain and forged it into something powerful and sharp. Something to wear as naturally as he wore his crown.

She rested a hand against his heart, her own beating like a bird startled from a bush. She wanted to give him her name. She wanted to give him *everything*.

And it terrified her.

CHAPTER FOURTEEN

Guinevere awoke to an argument.

"How could you?" Sir Tristan demanded.

Guinevere sat up. She tried to rub her bleary eyes clear, but nothing worked. If she did not end up using the knots she had tied that cost her this, she would be furious. She checked that her hair was still more or less in order, then crept to the tent opening and listened.

"Maleagant knows I am here," Arthur answered. "That means Camelot is vulnerable. I did not want our waiting men cut off."

"But now we have no men to bolster our forces! Maleagant knows you are here, which means *you* are vulnerable."

"Better I fall than Camelot."

"If you fall," Mordred said, his voice softer than Sir Tristan's, "so does Camelot."

"Camelot will live on. And so will we. I know Maleagant. He will lie in wait for us along the roads or set a trap in a village. We will ride through the forests."

Sir Bors sounded like gravel crunching underfoot. "Of course he will wait on the road, because riding through that much forest is madness."

"I like our chances."

Guinevere could hear the smile in Arthur's voice. He sounded as though he was looking forward to the challenge. She sided with Tristan, though. Better to protect Arthur than to send the waiting camp back without them.

She steeled herself. If they were all he had, they would be enough.

She gathered her knots, checking each one to make certain they were still tight. There was no time for the weakness that making new ones would induce. She had to be her best for the forest.

Lifting a tent flap, she emerged into the brilliant sunshine.

"What about the queen?" Sir Tristan asked, challenge in his voice as he used her as a reason not to follow Arthur's plan.

"The queen," Guinevere said, pulling up her hood, "is ready to ride at her king's side, wherever that takes her." She strode to her waiting horse. Arthur lifted her to mount.

"Are you ready?" he whispered.

Confident and afraid in equal measure, she smiled down at him. "I am."

She maneuvered so she would be the last to enter the trees. A branch brushed her arm; she draped a single knot of confusion and blindness there. Anyone pursuing them would be unable to find the trail.

Once under the trees, everything changed. Even the air was different. Warmer. Closer. As though the trees were breathing, wrapping them all in the steam of their exhalations. They had to slow their pace as the horses picked careful paths through the undergrowth.

There was no discernable trail. No one was stupid enough to go through the forest if they did not have to.

Still, it was boredom and heat that oppressed Guinevere more than fear. After several hours of slow progress, she had removed her hood and longed to unlace her sleeves. The knights around her had not shed any of their metal-plated leather armor, and they all sweated in silent misery.

Mordred rejoined them from scouting ahead. "More of the same. Trees and leaves and insects. If we continue south, we should break free on the borders of Camelot within two days. Tonight when we make camp, I will set traps for—"

A howl sliced through the thick air.

"We have daylight yet!" Sir Bors said as the horses jostled, ears alert, nostrils wide. "They cannot be hunting."

Another howl answered. Then another. And another.

"They are hunting," Arthur said, his expression grim. "And we are surrounded."

Guinevere's horse stamped its feet, tossing its head and jostling sideways. She looked down to see a fine mist creeping upward from the soil. It tugged at her horse's hooves and wrapped lovingly around them.

"The ground!" Guinevere shouted.

"I see it, too!" Mordred drew his sword. "Ride!"

He slapped her horse's rump, sending it careening through the trees. All around her the knights did the same. She held tight to her reins, ducking branches that swooped down like grasping claws. The trees seemed to lean closer together, giving them a dozen separate paths for their horses. Separating them.

"Guinevere!" Arthur shouted. She tugged on the reins, forcing her horse from its determined course and toward Arthur.

A gray flash leaped in front of her. The horse reared back, kicking its front legs. Guinevere fell hard to the ground and rolled free of the hooves. Her horse screamed, then disappeared into the trees with the wolf snapping at it.

But there was more than one wolf. She stared into the yellow eyes and bared teeth of the one padding closer to her. It opened its jaws and jumped. A man dove in front of her, tackling the wolf and rolling with it. Sir Tristan. The wolf clamped down on his forearm, breaking through the leather. Sir Tristan shouted with as much fury as the wolf's growls. He threw it free. Then he ran to Guinevere, picked her up, and tossed her into Arthur's waiting arms.

She clung to him, her seat on the horse terrifyingly precarious. Arthur had one hand around her waist, the other wielding Excalibur. Her head swam. Cold sweat broke out, and she had the sudden urge to throw herself back to the wolves rather than stay on the horse.

But the howling had faded. Arthur pushed his horse dangerously fast until they came to a clearing. He stopped and Guinevere dropped down, crawling away, trying desperately not to vomit. Her whole body shook.

"Form a circle," Arthur commanded. "Bors, Gawain, gather wood for a fire. It will be dark soon and we cannot be in the trees."

"Guinevere." Mordred crouched next to her. His hand hovered over her back, but he did not touch her. "Are you all right?"

"Yes," she whispered. It was a lie. She could not stop shaking. Something had affected her more than the fear. Perhaps she had breathed in some of the mist. "Is Sir Tristan here?"

"I am." Sir Tristan sat heavily beside her. His arm was wrapped in a piece of cloth. It was not bleeding too much.

"Thank you." Guinevere rolled to her side, then sat up. "You saved me."

"You are my queen," he said in answer. Then his face softened. "And you are Brangien's friend."

She stayed where she was next to Sir Tristan, with Mordred standing near, as the men organized a defensive circle and got a fire going. When she had recovered enough, she stood and found Arthur.

"I can help," she said.

He shook his head. "No. I need you safe. Please."

The pleading in his voice softened her. But she *had* to help. "I already have knots made. They are for blindness and confusion. If we place them around the meadow, it might slow or deter any wolves. Or other predators." She could only imagine what else might be in the trees. She certainly counted Maleagant's men as predators.

"Does it have to be you who places them? Like the door knots?"

"No. Anyone could."

He unbuckled his sword belt and set Excalibur, now sheathed, gently on the ground. "Give them to me. I will do it."

She reached into the pouch secured around her waist and withdrew the knots. "Leave them at even intervals. Circle the whole camp."

Arthur disappeared into the trees. She rejoined Sir Tristan. Even in the waning light, his color did not look good. "Let me look at your wound," she said.

He held out his arm obediently. She unwrapped it. The blood was trickling out, but not at a pace that was worrisome.

Worrisome, however, was the heat of his skin around it. He was burning up. Guinevere put the back of her hand against his forehead. It radiated heat. But there was something . . . different there. Something that was not Sir Tristan. Like mold growing on bread. "Why is he so hot?" she asked, her voice high and tight.

Mordred heard her and knelt by Sir Tristan. He examined the wound. "This is too soon for infection to set in."

"What is infection?"

He frowned at her. "You have never seen? It is blood poisoning.

Something gets in through the wound that should not be there. It . . ." He trailed off. He would not meet her eyes. Sir Tristan leaned back, lying on the ground. "I will get him some water." Mordred hurried away.

"Cold," Sir Tristan said, his teeth chattering.

Guinevere took off her cloak and draped it over him. He shivered and shook. Then, worse, he went still.

"Arthur!" she shouted. Sir Tristan did not stir. After a few moments Arthur rejoined them. The look on his face confirmed her worst fears.

"There is nothing we can do," he said. "The infection spread too fast."

Guinevere shook her head. She could not accept that. She would not. Sir Tristan had been hurt protecting her. But how could she fight poison in his blood? She could not clean it, could not—

An idea took hold of her with as much force as any wolf's jaws. The rest of the knights were far enough away, and Sir Tristan was in no position to hear or understand her. "I think I can help him."

"How?"

"Cleansing. I have only ever done it on myself, and only on the outside of my body. But if I focus it on his wound, I might be able to burn out the parts that are not him. The parts that are killing him."

Arthur looked down at his knight. He stroked a hand down Sir Tristan's cheek. Then he stood. "No."

"I have to try! It might not work, but—"

"It is not about that. You cannot do magic here, in the middle of my men. You could be discovered."

"But Sir Tristan—"

"Sir Tristan knew the risks of fighting at my side."

"As do I!"

"Guinevere. Please. If what you are were known within the

kingdom, at best you would be banished. At worst? It would disrupt everything I have built. People would suspect that I knew, that I allowed it. How could I justify all the people who have been banished or killed for using magic? Sir Tristan lived with honor. If he dies, it will be the same way, and he will always be remembered. I will *not* lose both of you."

"Arthur, I—"

"*No.*"

She shrank from his voice. This was the first time he had spoken to her not as Arthur, but as a king. The power and weight of his command had a physical aspect to it that left her cowed.

"I have to keep you safe," he whispered, Arthur once again.

"King Arthur!" one of the knights shouted. "Wolf!"

"Form a circle around the clearing!" Arthur strode away, picking up his sword from the ground and unsheathing it. Guinevere shuddered. "Face out! Let nothing through!"

Mist was curling around the clearing, sending tendrils in as though probing for weaknesses. There was no howling, no noise. Which made it worse, in a way. Then Sir Gawain shouted, and there was a snarling yelp. Guinevere could do nothing.

But . . . no one was watching her. They were all occupied with staying alive.

She hurried to the fire and took a single twig from the edge. The tip of it glowed with a spark. Back at Sir Tristan's side, she knelt and closed her eyes. She needed to change the way the magic flowed, change what she wanted it to do. She risked the fire taking control and burning Sir Tristan from the inside out. Either way she would be responsible for his death. She would not let it happen without a fight.

She put her finger against the spark, let it jump to her. Fed it her breath. Then she held it in front of Sir Tristan's mouth and let it taste his breath. She brought it to his wound and coaxed it from her finger to his skin. Sir Tristan flinched, but did not wake up.

"Burn all that is not him," she whispered, focusing on the flame, focusing on bending it to her will. It danced, a shimmering light, along the marks of the wolf's teeth. And then it disappeared.

Sir Tristan twitched. Sweat broke out on his skin and then evaporated as quickly as it appeared. She kept her hand on his arm, kept herself attuned to the spark running through him. It was greedy, starving. She commanded it to only feed on what was not Sir Tristan. There was so much there. She could feel the infection, a creeping darkness trying to take him. It felt menacing and angry and . . . sentient.

She pushed the fire harder. It ate, and ate, and just when she thought it would not work fast enough to save Sir Tristan, the fire paused. There was nothing left for it. Nothing that it had been commanded to eat. It turned outward, ready to devour Sir Tristan.

She called it back. It hesitated. She was going to lose control. Panic flared, but she met it with determination and instinctive desperation.

She *would not* lose him.

Something inside her, something unknown in the midst of all the knots and spells, surrounded the fire, drawing it back. Chasing it and channeling it away from Sir Tristan. It rushed back to her hand, burning her. She cried out in pain, smothering the flames with her hood. Her fingers were blistered. But the fire was out.

She looked up to search for a canteen but froze like a deer before a hunter. Mordred was watching her. He was half-turned to the forest, but his eyes, ever attuned to her, had seen everything.

She was caught.

It was over.

Then Mordred looked back toward the forest without a word.

Shaking, her hand in searing pain, she grabbed a canteen and helped Sir Tristan drink. His skin had lost the killing heat of the infection. His eyelids fluttered open. "My queen?" he asked.

"Rest." She cradled his head in her lap. She tipped the water into his mouth, little by little, too frightened to look up lest the wolves of men descend on her for her transgression.

They battled the pack all night. When morning finally pushed back the darkness, the knights were weary, but none bloodied.

"The way they moved," Sir Bors said. "It was as though they were drunk. They could never figure out where we were. God has protected us."

"Yes," Arthur said, his voice firm and bright. "God has protected us."

Guinevere said nothing. Her knots had done their work. She had felt it as each one wore out, her vision finally back to normal. Her eyes ached and stung, but the pain was nothing compared to that of her burned hand.

Sir Tristan was checking the horses. Arthur embraced him quickly. "You are well?"

Sir Tristan flexed his arm, looking down at it. "It is sore, but the fever has passed."

Arthur clasped his shoulder. "You scared us."

Sir Tristan smiled, his full lips blooming like a spring flower. "I shall endeavor to never scare my king again."

"See that you do," Arthur said with a laugh. But when he turned and caught Guinevere's eyes, his smile disappeared and his face darkened. He knew what she had done.

He did not speak to her. Neither, for that matter, did Mordred.

Now that things were calmer, she stood, tense and ready for the accusations. But all the knights prepared their horses with efficient and practiced focus.

"Guinevere needs a horse," Mordred said.

"She can ride with me, if that is acceptable to my king," Sir Tristan said. "I cannot wield a sword well on horseback with this wound, but I can protect her."

"Thank you." Arthur inclined his head, giving permission. She wanted to speak with him, but there was no privacy, no opportunity.

Guinevere joined Sir Tristan on his horse. They rode for hours, their passage swift but cautious. There was no sign of the wolves. No hint of pursuit. The nature of the forest changed, as well. The trees loomed less, the air cleared out. It was still a wild and untamed place, but it felt less threatening.

Late afternoon, they broke to rest. A creek babbled nearby, and the men led the horses there to refill their canteens. Guinevere walked in the opposite direction. She kept everyone in sight, but her head ached with the strain of the night before coupled with the stress and fear of discovery. She wished Arthur would join her so they could talk about what she had done, but he remained with his men.

Sir Tristan walked among them. Healthy. Alive. She had done that. And she did not regret it. Even if she had been caught, she could not have regretted it. It had been the right thing to do.

Arthur had told her once that he would never put anything above Camelot. Remembering this, she cringed, guilty. She had put Sir Tristan above Camelot. If she had been caught, it could very well have threatened Arthur's rule. She understood why he had forbidden her. But she could not bring herself to accept that Sir Tristan should have died to keep her secret safe. She would have lied, said she was sent to trick Arthur. Said she had bewitched him and he never knew. Done whatever she had to in order to protect him.

She rested between the roots of a massive tree. A hand against its bark revealed no bite, no malice. Just the deep, peaceful slumber of soil and sun and water. She closed her eyes, relishing the feeling of the sun on her. A brief, silly wish for leaves and roots filled her. How peaceful to be a tree! Trees had only to grow. Trees had no hearts to confuse and complicate things. Trees could not love kings and still disobey them.

A shadow blocked the sun from her imaginings. She opened her eyes to find Mordred standing over her.

She stood to meet his accusation. He gestured for her to hold out her burned hand. The evidence of her forbidden magic use. It had been agonizing all morning, but she had kept it covered beneath her clothes. She held out the proof with a defiant gaze.

"Your eyes are green today," he said. He crushed several leaves and then pressed them gently against her blistered skin. The sensation was instantly cooling. She let out a soft sigh of relief. Mordred wrapped a band of torn fabric around her hand to hold the leaves in place. Their skin never touched. She was glad. She did not want another spark right now, and Mordred ever seemed to burn. "They are not always green, your eyes. Sometimes they are blue like the sky. In Camelot, they are gray like the stones. I like green and blue better."

Guinevere did not understand what he was saying. She had never thought about her own eyes. But she *did* understand that he was not accusing her or announcing her guilt. He was protecting her.

"How do you know how to do this?" she asked, wanting to talk but not about what she had done. She lifted her soothed hand.

"Not everything in the forest is destruction. The forest is also life." He pulled a delicate purple-and-yellow blossom free from his leather vest. "Can you feel it?"

"I can," she said, tentative.

"Some things only grow outside of walls." He held out the flower with a secret smile. He was not going to tell the other knights. He was going to protect her. "Keep it outside the walls and no one needs know."

She took the flower. "Thank you," she whispered. Relief and gratitude swelled in her. Mordred was on her side. Guinevere tucked the flower beneath her dress, against her heart, where it would be both secret and safe.

Her wolves had almost tasted her. They came so close to knowing what the queen-not-queen was hiding.

They failed.

But they had succeeded, too. The queen-not-queen spoke to fire, and fire listened. And that is worth knowing.

She brushes against the tree that cradled the queen-not-queen, feels the longing left behind in her wake. The queen-not-queen is not a creature of stones and walls, of rules and laws.

The queen-not-queen is chaos.

And Arthur brought her into his heart.

CHAPTER FIFTEEN

At last they left the forest behind and were delivered safely to the borders of Camelot. The rest of Arthur's men were waiting for them there.

Arthur still had not spoken to Guinevere alone. Nerves and relief in equal measure seized her as he drew her away from the group. They stood together in the sun, out of earshot of anyone else. But Arthur's face was clouded with an emotion Guinevere could not place.

Ready to burst, she spoke first. "You cannot be angry with me for saving him."

Arthur sighed. "I can, and I am. And I am not. I am glad Sir Tristan is alive. He is very precious to me. But I cannot risk you."

She threw her arms in the air, exasperated. "I am not a fragile princess! I am here to be risked!"

He opened his mouth to answer her, then deliberately drew his lips together and closed his eyes. He was holding something back, holding something in. She could see the strain of it on his face. Finally, he opened his eyes once more. "I have go to back out and see to the northern borders. We will speak more when I get back. Please do not do anything in my absence." As though he could read her thoughts, he grabbed her hands in his. "Guinevere. Please. The banished woman will wait. When I get back, we will discuss it and come up with a plan. Together. Promise me you will wait for me."

She wanted to be defiant, but it was not anger or command in his face. It was genuine worry pulling his features tight with strain. She sighed, the fight leaving her. "Oh, very well."

"Thank you," he said. Then, to her surprise, he pulled her close and brushed his warm lips against her cheek. The heat of him lingered as she watched him ride away once more.

The heat did not linger long enough to comfort her upon finding herself again on the barge to Camelot. Brangien held her as she cowered in the center. Even Mordred had gone with Arthur, so no one was there who could take her through the tunnel.

Sir Tristan had been left behind in Camelot to heal, and along with Sir Bors he was in charge of running the city in Arthur's absence. Guinevere had nothing to do but be queen. Exhausted, she let Brangien fuss over her once they were back in the castle. Her burn she excused as a hazard of tending to the bonfire in the forest. But thanks to Mordred's ministrations, it was no longer painful.

When it was finally time for bed, she planned to wait until Brangien fell asleep and then see to the magic-soaked rocks she had left hidden outside the alcove. They had given her an idea for something she could do during the intolerable wait. Instead, sleep fell as heavy and thick as a blanket over her.

The next three days were much the same. There was no Arthur, no Mordred. No patchwork knight to chase, no Rhoslyn-witch to conquer. Guinevere had made her own magic-bound rocks and placed them as sentinels throughout Camelot so any magic done within the city—not just the castle—would alert her. But as with the castle, all her knots were intact. Nothing had triggered an alarm.

For the time being, she was simply a queen. It was tediously busy. Now that she had made it known she was available, she had callers all day. She made an effort to walk in the afternoons with Brangien and a guard, to visit merchants and be seen about the city. She did not want to be an invisible queen in the castle. Arthur did not rule that way. And she wanted to be his match. His equal.

His partner.

She could no longer deny it. She wanted to be more than a protector to him.

A small part of her feared she had agreed to his delay so that she could draw out her time here. Because if she was right, and Rhoslyn was the reason Guinevere had been sent here, what did that mean after? What purpose could she serve once her mission had been accomplished?

The idea of going back to the shack in the woods filled her with that same nagging emptiness she felt when trying to find so many of her memories.

Arthur still had not returned. It worried at her. For three nights, she had intended to stay up and try some small magic to locate him. And each night, sleep claimed her with brutal efficiency. When she awoke the fourth morning, her bed curtains drawn closed again though she had not done it, she knew something was amiss. She would have awoken to Brangien drawing her curtains. She checked all the doors, even put knots on the windows again, but nothing had gotten through.

That night, before she slipped into bed, she tied a knot in her hair and placed it over her eyes. After a few minutes, she felt the weight of magic push down on her, trying to slip past her own guard. Someone had been forcing her to sleep! She pretended it had worked, keeping her breathing even and deep. But no foe appeared. She was alone in her bedroom. What was the attack? What was the point of forcing her into enchanted sleep if Arthur was gone? She had been unprepared to be a target herself.

And the attack had to have come from within the room. Any magic would have been undone passing the threshold.

Her heart broke. *Brangien.*

She heard soft voices from her sitting room and sat up. A piece of cloth fell from where it had been dropped on her chest. She knew that red thread. The embroidery Brangien was always fiddling with. How had Guinevere not seen it? Brangien knew knot magic. And she had used it on Guinevere.

Surely her maid would not risk being banished or executed just to steal a few nights with a lover. Brangien seemed too smart, too practical for that. The sitting room was always empty at night. Brangien could have snuck in a man under cover of darkness.

There had to be something sinister at play. It made Guinevere sick. Brangien had been her guide. Her friend. And she had been blind to magic being done right under her own nose. What if Brangien had struck? What if she had hurt Arthur?

Guinevere was a fool for trusting anyone. Everything about herself was a lie; she should assume the same of everyone around her.

The sitting room door was open just a crack. Guinevere put her eye to it and peered through. Brangien was inside with . . . Sir Tristan. Guinevere had risked everything to save him. Was he, too, against her and the king?

Brangien was in his arms. Maybe it really was that simple. A maid and a knight in a relationship that would be gossiped about. Brangien was not socially inferior to Sir Tristan, though. And Guinevere and Arthur both would have celebrated it.

The way her shoulders were moving. She was not being embraced with amorous intentions. She was being held as she wept. The bath was full, nearly brimming over with water. Guinevere watched as Brangien pulled herself together, sniffling.

"I will try again. You are right. We cannot give up."

She leaned over the bath and pulled a lock of hair from her bag. She dipped it into the water, using it to create ripples and movement. Brangien was scrying—looking for something or someone through the water.

"You are doing it wrong," Guinevere said, stepping into the room. She held the dagger Arthur had given her. There was a killing knot—a simple, brutal movement—that she could tie on skin with the point of the metal. Far more effective than a stabbing Sir Tristan might survive. Her stomach turned, but her resolve tightened. She would do it. If she had to.

Brangien cried out in fear and dropped the hair on the floor. Sir Tristan spun, hand on the pommel of his sword. Then his eyes widened in surprise, and he bowed. "My queen. I am sorry. We were—"

"You were scrying."

Brangien picked up the hair and clutched it to her chest. "Please, my lady, let me explain."

"Explain why you were using magic to force me to sleep?"

Brangien hung her head in shame. "Please, I beg mercy. Banishment, not death. If I have done anything to help you, anything to—"

"It was well done. The knot magic, I mean. I have not seen those patterns before, but they make sense. You combined sleep with . . ." Guinevere waited. Neither had moved toward her. The promise of violence made the dagger feel heavier than it should.

Flinching, Brangien filled in the details. "Weight. It holds the sleeper down so nothing disturbs their rest. I used it once before when you were so tired but your sleep was restless. I wanted you to get better. And it worked so well, I thought . . . I thought I could use it so we would have enough time to scry without being caught." Brangien lifted her chin, strong and defiant. "Sir Tristan did not use magic. He does not know how. I bewitched him."

"Brangien," he said, shaking his head.

"See? He is still under my control."

Guinevere had planned on the same lie should she be caught and Arthur implicated. "Not if he has been through the doors in the castle in the last few days. Any spell would be broken."

"That was you?" Brangien gasped. "I had to redo my work so many times! I thought I was losing my skills!"

"You do not seem surprised I know magic, though."

Brangien shook her head, wringing her hands nervously, the hair still clutched there. "I saw the knots in your hair. A few other things. I know things are different in the south. I thought— Well, I thought you might understand."

Brangien had been revealed, but Guinevere had, as well. She could see the realization dawning on Sir Tristan. His hand drifted to his arm, the wound still wrapped but healing nicely. "Did you—"

"I was not about to lose such a good man. I thought you were a good man. I need you to be, still. Brangien, you are my only friend here. I have never felt a threat from you." She would have known. Surely she would have known. She would have felt it in Brangien's touch. This was a betrayal, but perhaps not as dangerous as Guinevere had feared. "Both of you, tell me truthfully: Are you a threat to Arthur?"

"No!" Sir Tristan exclaimed. He dropped to one knee and shook his head, his beautiful brown eyes hurt at the very suggestion. "I would die for my king."

"And for your queen." Guinevere had not forgotten, would never forget. Sir Tristan had not hesitated to put himself between her and the wolf. That was not the action of a man who was conspiring against them.

"I believe in everything King Arthur is doing here," Brangien said. "Surely in our time together you have seen that. I believe in Camelot. I would never harm the king."

Guinevere noticed the way Brangien held the hair, how unconsciously she stroked it. It was not Arthur's hair, which was always cut short. Or Guinevere's, for that matter. It was rich auburn in the candlelight, long and soft.

"Give me your hand," Guinevere said. Brangien complied, raising one trembling hand to Guinevere's.

Normally Guinevere only took whatever the touch magic forced her to experience. But this time she actively used it, pushing out, searching. Brangien was there. All of her. Wit and cleverness, resourcefulness. A well of sorrow so deep and pure Guinevere gasped as she touched only the edge of it. Anger and fear, as well, but nowhere did she find malice or vengeance. Nowhere did she feel a threat. Only yearning.

Satisfied, she withdrew her hand. The absence of Brangien was a relief. Bearing another person's emotions was overwhelming. Guinevere felt light-headed and distant from herself.

She sat heavily in the chair. Brangien was not malicious. And now they knew each other's secrets. Or at least Brangien knew *one* of Guinevere's. "Very well. Tell me what was worth risking everything for."

"I am trying to find her. Isolde." Brangien's eyes brimmed with tears. "It has been so long. There were a few letters at first that she managed to smuggle out. But I have heard nothing of her and I am afraid—I am so afraid—" The tears spilled over. Guinevere wanted to comfort her, but that meant stepping close to the full bath, which she was not willing to do.

The tremendous sorrow. The overpowering yearning. "Sir Tristan is not the one who loves Isolde, is he?" Guinevere asked.

Sir Tristan shook his head slowly. "I would do anything to see her happy. Brangien, too. Both of them together."

Isolde and *Brangien*. No wonder she had been banished along with Tristan.

Guinevere did not envy the pain on Brangien's face. But how would it feel to love so deeply she could hurt that much? The overwhelming sorrow seemed precious, almost holy. Brangien carried that within herself always, a dedicated portion of her soul. And if the sorrow was that deep, how much deeper must be the love that formed it?

Envy stirred in Guinevere. She wanted that. And she wanted Brangien to have it back. "You are trying to see Isolde?"

Brangien nodded, warily hopeful.

"One hair," Guinevere said. She had seen Merlin do this. She could not remember when or how, but she distinctly remembered looking up at Merlin as he peered into a tub of water and made a circle out of a hair, framing the water and guiding it toward what he wanted to see. "Take one hair, and make a circle on top of the water with it. Then reach through, holding on to Isolde in your mind. Pull your hand back up and you should have what you wish. Wait. No." Guinevere was missing something. What was she missing? Blood fed iron magic. Fuel fed fire magic. What fed water magic? Why could she not remember?

Because she *hated* water. Forcing her mind to think of it felt like pushing against the barrier between sleeping and waking.

A face in the water. Bubbles. And then nothing.

Guinevere shuddered, angling her body in the chair so she could not see the bath at all. "I remember. You do not want to do what it takes to do water magic."

"I do. I will do anything."

"Water wants to fill. To take the shape of whatever it finds. To be able to do water magic requires a sacrifice up front. Once the water has breath as payment, it will do what you want. But you have to drown someone."

Brangien sank to the floor, defeated. "Then she is lost to me."

"No. I have another way. And this way, Isolde will see you, too." Guinevere smiled, but her smile was forced around the discomfiting dread of the memory. Of Merlin and the water. When had that happened? Whom had he drowned? And why?

Why had she not thought of it until now?

They went back into the bedroom. Guinevere knew she should wait and investigate this further. But she desperately needed a distraction. Guinevere took Isolde's hair and knotted it into Brangien's. Brangien lay on her cot, and Guinevere checked over her work. She would sacrifice her own dreams for a week with this magic. But it was worth it. Her dreams had shown her nothing useful. She barely remembered them.

She placed Brangien's own sleep knots on her chest, and Brangien's mind was gone.

Guinevere sat back, satisfied. Sir Tristan shifted uncomfortably next to the door. He should not be there. If he were caught, he would be in tremendous trouble. They both would be.

Now she had not one but two more allies within Camelot, though.

She did not know whether she would tell Arthur about them. Arthur had been so rigid about the rules in the forest, and she could not be certain he would let them stay.

Her secret for now, then. She waved for Sir Tristan to leave. "I will watch over her. Go and rest, good knight."

He gratefully exited. Guinevere sat at Brangien's side, hoping that the smile that flitted across Brangien's dreaming face meant their magic had worked. Kindness through magic was not something she had been able to offer before. It did not solve her problems, but it felt nice, and she would take it.

"Who are you really, Merlin?" she whispered. She wished she could visit him, speak to him. Demand answers for all he had done.

And then she realized her answer was lying right in front of her. She cursed her lack of foresight in denying herself dreams for a week. Maybe she had done it on purpose. She knew she had been rushing to help instead of thinking things through. It was because she had not wanted to face the difficult questions. To risk getting answers.

No more. In seven nights, she would have her own dreams back. She would walk them to Merlin.

CHAPTER SIXTEEN

Guinevere was already awake when Brangien sat up. It was the first time she had managed to rise before Brangien in the morning. "Oh no," Guinevere said, covering her mouth. Brangien's eyes were filled with tears. "What happened?"

Brangien shook her head, beaming. "I saw her. We were together. Thank you. Thank you forever, my queen." She burst from her cot and threw her arms around Guinevere. Guinevere was shocked at the contact—though Brangien dressed her, she had never been affectionate. Guinevere relaxed into the hug, appreciating it. She and Brangien shared the bond of secrets now. Slowly but surely Guinevere was carving out her place in Camelot. Brangien and Sir Tristan. Mordred. And Arthur, of course. It was nice to have more friends and allies than just Arthur.

But it was also dangerous. The more people who knew some of her secrets, the more likely it was that they would discover too many of them.

Brangien released her, then went bustling about her morning chores and chatting happily about her dream time with Isolde.

Guinevere released some of the worries and fears she kept clutched in her own chest. This act had done nothing to protect Arthur, but she had made Brangien happy. With all the darkness swirling around what she knew of Merlin now, it was a comfort knowing her own magic could be used for gentleness, kindness, love.

"Will you come to the market today?" Brangien asked, laying out clothing options.

Guinevere recoiled from the idea. With both Arthur and Mordred gone, she would have to do the lake passage twice. She had no desire to, and no need for the market. "I would like a day of rest. But you go. Besides, I am to walk this afternoon with Dindrane, and this way you are spared."

"Kindnesses upon kindnesses, my queen." Brangien laughed, her cheeks flushed and her eyes bright. Guinevere had never seen her so happy, and it was a balm to her own soul. Doubtless it would disappoint Brangien when, in a week, Guinevere would need to reclaim her ability to dream, but in the meantime her happiness was contagious.

"Get some thread. I want you to teach me the knots you know."

Brangien nodded. "My mother taught me. Where did you learn?"

"My—" Guinevere caught herself. Only some truth with Brangien, not all. "My nurse. It is not so uncommon in the south. But we must be careful." Guinevere wanted to defeat Rhoslyn. Not join her in banishment.

"Of course. Always." With a pretty curtsey, Brangien left.

Guinevere considered taking a leisurely morning, lying abed, but she was itching with impatience and boredom. She should have gone to the market, after all. The alcove was empty save for the rocks she had brought in, and they kept their silence. No matter how she poked and prodded them, she could not determine their purpose. She was probably best off taking them and dropping them over the side of Camelot into the lake. But then she would always wonder what she had missed.

She put one in a pouch and carried it with her to meet Dindrane that afternoon. As they strolled the streets of Camelot—one guard accompanying them in Brangien's absence—Guinevere idly toyed with the rock. Dindrane gossiped cheerily, though she remarked several times how disappointing it was that the city was so empty with most of the citizens at the market. Dindrane liked being seen with Guinevere. It was social currency, and Dindrane had had precious little to spend before gaining the favor of the queen.

For her part, Guinevere found Dindrane relaxing. There was never any pressure to speak or risk of saying the wrong thing. Dindrane steered the conversation the way an expert rider guided a horse.

They turned down a side street and walked toward a merchant's shop Dindrane wanted to look at. In Guinevere's hand, the rock was as warm as the day around them.

The rock grew warmer.

Guinevere stopped, the rock clutched in her hand.

"Is something the matter?" Dindrane asked.

"No. Nothing." As they walked farther that direction, the rock grew warmer and warmer. They passed several homes and shops. And then the rock began to cool.

"I saw something I wanted to look at," Guinevere said, abruptly turning around. She worked her way back, Dindrane grumbling, until the rock was once again almost too hot to hold. She was standing in front of an unremarkable home.

"Who lives here?" Guinevere asked.

"How should I know?" Dindrane looked longingly toward the shop she had wanted to visit.

The guard surprised Guinevere by speaking up. "We caught a witch here not a week ago."

"Really?" Guinevere clutched the rock. *Rhoslyn.* This was Rhoslyn's home. And the rock had led her straight here.

The rocks were guides, allowing those who knew about magic to find each other. But now they led only to an empty house. Fortunately, Guinevere already knew where Rhoslyn was. And now she knew that Rhoslyn *had* been organizing others within Camelot.

Flush with triumph, Guinevere let Dindrane drag her back to the shop, and then to another, and then another. When they got to the main street leading to the castle, Brangien rushed up to meet them from the direction of the docks. Sir Tristan followed respectfully behind. He nodded to Guinevere's guard, who left them, with a bow.

"Sir Bors is hunting a dragon!" Brangien said, out of breath from the climb. "A *dragon*! Not four hours' ride from here!"

Guinevere frowned. "There has not been a dragon in a hundred years."

"And yet! Sir Bors is determined to kill it, if it exists."

"Sir Bors is a canny hunter," Dindrane said. "My brother could never do such a thing."

"What proof does Sir Bors have that the creature exists?" Guinevere asked.

As they resumed walking toward the castle, Brangien resettled the parcels she was carrying. "Rumors. A reliable woodsman with a burned arm, screaming about a demon in the forest. Some evidence of scorching. If it is a dragon, Sir Bors will find it."

"I cannot wait to tell my sister-in-law," Dindrane said, smiling wickedly. "A dragon! And her husband will not be the one to face it." She hurried away from them.

It was news indeed. Terrible news. Dragons had been the favored creatures of the Dark Queen. For centuries she had wielded them, sending them to attack farmsteads, to ruin settlements. They had been hunted with ruthless efficiency by the Romans. Even Merlin did not think any still lived. Guinevere had asked during one of their lessons. Merlin had rambled about the old making way for the new, bones buried deep in the earth to grow the seeds of new life.

But if a dragon was on the prowl, that meant Arthur was vulnerable. Even Camelot was. A dragon in flight could lay siege to the city the way men could not. If the dragon had any alliance to dark magic—or was under the control of someone like Rhoslyn—it had to be stopped.

"I must go," Guinevere said, her mind already made up.

"Go where? The market is over."

"Go to the dragon." If there really was one, she did not trust Sir Bors to take care of it himself, canny hunter or not.

Brangien stopped walking, stunned. "My lady, that is a job for knights. Not for queens."

Guinevere had not told Brangien the truth of her identity. It was one thing for them to share a secret of magic; it was another entirely for Guinevere to reveal her whole self. Guinevere pulled her hood on. "King Arthur is my husband. I will do whatever it takes to protect him. And no one else in this kingdom will be able to know if the dragon is doing the bidding of some dark force. I can. But I will need Sir Tristan to help me." She turned to the knight.

His brown face had gone pale. But he nodded, hand on the hilt of his sword and jaw clenched with resolve. "I will need to get my cloak and more weapons."

Brangien smoothed her skirts nervously. "I think this is a bad idea."

"Meet me where the horses are kept, Sir Tristan."

"But you will need a boat!" Brangien exclaimed.

"I have one." Guinevere hurried to the castle, leaving them at the gate. She made her way out to the walkway that led to the secret passage's storage room. She stopped outside the doorway. This one, fortunately, they had not magically protected, since it did not lead directly into the castle. She pulled an extra thread of iron from her pouch, pricked her lip with it, and then fashioned it into a knot that would pull apart at the slightest tug. She inserted it into the keyhole, then pulled, releasing the unlocking magic.

The door swung open. Relieved and only slightly dizzy, she hurried inside and closed the door behind her. The barrel was a bigger problem, quite literally. It took her nearly ten minutes to shift it enough that she could squeeze through.

She hurried through the dark, slick tunnel. When she came out the other side, she rushed to the horses' pen. To her surprise, it was not only Sir Tristan, mounted, waiting for her.

"What are you doing here?" Guinevere asked Brangien, who was holding the reins of two other horses.

"No lady's maid would allow her lady to go on an unaccompanied trip with a knight!"

"But they would allow their lady to seek a dragon?" Guinevere mounted her horse, laughing.

"Well, no. But I can only control one of those things." Brangien stuck out her tongue at Guinevere.

Sir Tristan led the way, and they pushed the horses as fast as they dared. If Sir Bors killed the dragon before she arrived, she would not be able to determine if it was under the sway of the dark magic. The dragon problem would be solved, but no answers would be obtained. As they rode, Guinevere asked Brangien to show her the knotting method she used. It was a good distraction.

They were heading in the same general direction as the forest where she had seen Rhoslyn's magic sparking. What if Rhoslyn *had* figured out a way to control the dragon? Arthur had made Guinevere promise not to go against the witch, but she had not promised not to go against a dragon. And if she found a link between the two, she would break her promise.

The lush and well-tended fields gave way to scraggly trees, and then to dense and gnarled old growth clinging to a low mountain. Rhoslyn's location was farther south, but that did not mean she and the patchwork knight were not involved.

Sir Tristan rode with one hand on the pommel of his sword and a wary eye on their surroundings. "The dragon is supposed to be in this region. But it could be hours—or even days—before we find anything. Sir Bors is the tracker."

They did not have time for that. She had to be back in Camelot before nightfall. "Then we need to find Sir Bors." Guinevere frowned. An idea took shape. "Brangien, do you have cloth, a needle, and thread?"

"Yes." Brangien sounded wary, but handed the supplies over. Guinevere tugged several eyelashes free, then sewed them onto a strip of cloth. How clever of Brangien to anchor the knot magic! It made everything so much easier to manage. It would have been a nightmare trying to knot the eyelashes with only thread.

She held the cloth up to her right eye, peering through.

"How can she see anything through that?" Sir Tristan asked.

"Hush," Brangien chided.

Guinevere's eye pierced the knot, went through cloth, tree, stone. She fought the wash of spinning disorientation as her sight left her and found her target. Sir Bors was paused next to a stream, refilling his leather canteen.

"He is by water," she said. "A stream. And—oh, he is standing. Smoke! He sees smoke!"

"There." Sir Tristan pointed. "Where the trees are thickest. That is where the stream will be." It was around a curving hill. When they got closer, Guinevere looked up and she, too, saw the smoke. Though only with her left eye. Her right eye she had to keep closed against the blinding aftereffects of the magic.

"Wait here," she said.

"My queen." Sir Tristan drew his sword, staring at the smoke. "I can do no such thing."

"I *am* your queen, and I command you both to wait here. I will be perfectly safe." Guinevere turned, having delivered her lie with enough cold confidence that she hoped they believed it. Then she hurried her horse in the direction of the smoke. A maiden desperately hoping to run into a dragon—that had to be a first.

She did not have long to search. The sounds of battle between man and beast were terrible. Guinevere jumped from her spooked horse, tied it to a tree, then ran over to a low ridge.

Down in the stream valley, Sir Bors had the dragon cornered against a boulder and a thick stand of trees. The dragon's wing had been sliced open, so it could not fly away. It blew fire, but Sir Bors ducked behind a shield lashed to his bad arm. The fire was weak, barely flickering where it hit the shield. The dragon drew another breath. Sir Bors lifted his great sword to strike.

Guinevere decided to do something tremendously stupid.

She threw down a scrap of cloth so that it landed on Sir Bors's head—and immediately dropped him into sleep. He fell hard to the ground, brought down by the sleep knots Brangien had made while showing Guinevere how to tie them.

The dragon, already braced for a killing blow, froze. It tilted its head.

Guinevere slid down the embankment and scrambled to get between the dragon and Sir Bors. The dragon swung its huge head, following her. It was the color of mossy rocks, with two great, curling horns and fur like whiskers drooping over its mouth. Its eyelids, too, drooped low, making it look as sleepy and cross as . . . Sir Bors. Actually, now that she thought about it, the dragon looked like nothing so much as Sir Bors in beast form. It even had one leg it held against its body, curled and withered from an old, poorly healed wound. Its tail was stunted, its right wing split open, and several spears protruded like spikes from lumpy, scarred tissue along its back.

Guinevere stumbled, her depth perception off with one eye closed. "Please." She held out her hands to show she had no weapons. "I have a question. Can you understand me?"

Dragons were rumored to be terribly clever, capable of understanding human speech. But that was the myth. She did not know the reality. It leaned its head close to her—so close she could see the fine detail of its scales, the faint hint of pearlescence. It took a deep breath, smelling her.

And then it tilted its head. A huff of air like that from opening a stove blew over her, and then the dragon stuck out its long, elegant purple tongue . . . and licked her face.

She had miscalculated terribly. She was going to be eaten.

But the dragon sat back on its haunches, lowering its head so they remained eye-level. It nudged her once, gently. She reached out to balance and put her hand on top of its head, and then—

"Oh," she whispered.

The freedom of night, of sky. No up or down, no ground, only flight. The wind caressing, buffeting, helping and hindering. Looping lazy circles for the sheer joy of it, surrounded by mother, sister, brother.

The sharp thrill of pleasure catching sheep between claws, the promising weight of them, the satisfaction of hot blood and torn meat.

Burrowing beneath the earth, deep, deep, sleeping away the cold months with the heat of mother, brother, sister, curled around each other.

And then—

Arrows in the sky. Spears. Sharp points of terrible pain, teeth no animal as small as man should have. Mother. Gone.

Brother.

Gone.

Sister.

Gone.

Wandering, lonely. Flight lost to the threat of arrows. Crawling on its belly, looking, searching, finding . . . nothing. No one. Curling around itself, alone.

The sky lost. The family lost. The joy and power of existing. Lost.

Guinevere's throat burned. Tears streamed down her face. "I am sorry," she whispered. She looked for darkness, for influence of angry magic, for any connection to Rhoslyn, and found only sorrow and loss and unbearable weariness. This beast was not under any spell.

It nudged her hand again. This time, in the emptiness of the dragon's future, she saw it curled around itself, slowly fading. And then she saw . . . herself. Alone. Slowly fading.

Why was the dragon showing her that?

"What do you need?" she asked. She had been ready to fight. Instead, she wanted to weep and comfort this creature. But how could she comfort it against the relentless destruction of time?

The dragon glanced at Sir Bors, still asleep. Guinevere sensed the fear of pain, of the cruel bite of iron. The dragon crawling, pursued. It was right. Sir Bors would never stop hunting it. And she did not know if she *should* stop him. As much as it pained her, the dragon was still a threat.

"What would you do if I could stop him from hunting you?"

The images changed. The dragon stayed in the wilds, basking in the sun, rolling in the autumn leaves, relishing the snow for one more year. Then it crawled into the earth and went to sleep. And it did not come out again.

"You want one last year to say goodbye," Guinevere said.

The dragon dipped its head once in acknowledgment.

Dragons had been terrible menaces, but . . . to be the last of one's own kind, alone, knowing that your time was ending and there was no way to return to how the world had been. Merlin was right. The old was buried to give life to the new. Even though it was for the best for men, for Camelot, for Arthur, she could still mourn what it cost this ancient creature.

She could give it the gift of a year for farewells.

"If you stay far away from men, I can promise this one will not come after you. He will think you dead. But first, I must know. Have you been called by darkness? Is anything stirring?" They had met with darkness twice now. The forest that swallowed the village, and the mist and wolves while fleeing Maleagant. Neither seemed tied to Rhoslyn. Guinevere hoped they were like weeds of leftover magic, clinging to life.

The dragon's eyelids slid half-closed. A low hiss sounded in its throat. *Demands. Sharp tugs. The trees and the men screaming. The dragon turning its back, leaving the Dark Queen to her fate.* The dragon had abandoned the Dark Queen during the great battle. That was a relief.

But then . . . *Tendrils. Something small, something searching. Darkness looking for something to hold.*

The dragon huffed, making it clear it had no interest in being held. It was enough. Guinevere believed that the dragon was not under dark sway. But something had searched for it, or tried to call it. Something powerful enough to guide darkness, but not command it as the Dark Queen had. Rhoslyn's rock was heavy in her pouch. The witch needed to be dealt with.

But not today. Today, she had terrible work to finish. Guinevere knelt next to Bors. There was an old magic that blurred more lines than

she cared to. It was one thing to influence objects or events. It was another thing entirely to reach into minds and change things. Merlin had
done it to the nuns at the convent so they would not realize Guinevere
was a stranger to them. With a sick twist, she suspected he had also
used it on Igraine the wretched night that Arthur was conceived.

She knew how to do it. She was not entirely human, after all.
Her hands already brought information in. They could send it out,
as well. But she had only ever used them to see. Never to show. And
never to force a change.

It was a violent act. Magic of conquest and force. Was it justifi-
able when being used to protect a vulnerable creature? Her hands
shook as she lifted them to Sir Bors's temple, and she *pushed*.

The trick to changing a memory, Merlin had said, carefully setting
seven white stones in a row, *is to make the replacement memory so
unpleasant, so viscerally awful, that they will never poke too hard at
it. Make them flee from the memory. It is the skin on old milk. If they
force it, it will break and the truth will spill free. So make the milk
rancid. Who would ever touch rancid milk?* He had looked up then.
You should not have told him. You should never have told him.

Shaking off the terrible weight of Merlin's gaze in the memory,
still unsure what he had meant by the last part, she got to work. She
let her hands sink into Sir Bors's memories. She did not have to go
far, nor did she want to. Once at the dragon, she whispered the story
to the knight with her mouth, and put it in place with her hands.

"The dragon blew fire, but you shielded yourself. Then, as it drew
a breath that would end you forever, you plunged your sword deep
in its belly. Your moment of triumph turned sour. Its belly split open,
spilling a week's worth of rotting sheep and stinking, half-digested
offal all over you. You stumbled away, vomiting on yourself. You vom-
ited so hard, you also soiled yourself. The dragon is dead. That is all
you will tell anyone, and all you ever need think of again."

She smoothed his forehead, feeling the memory settle. Bors's mind was a simple, determined thing. He was a creature of pride. He would never want to remember the shame of the memory she had crafted.

She sat back, exhausted. She could feel something was missing. She was forgetting something. A memory, lost, as she pushed the new one on Sir Bors. What had she given up? She would never know.

She felt as dirty as the memory she had created for Bors. He was a good man, and she had violated his mind.

Something dropped in her lap. She stared down at a large, worn tooth. Like the scales, it had a pearl sheen, oddly lovely. A gift.

The dragon nudged insistently at her. She put her hand on its head once again. It fixed one sorrowful golden eye on her. One last message pulsed through to her:

Familiarity. The dragon saw her, and felt they were the same. She shook her head, confused. *A lake. The dragon's reflection in it as it flew overhead, terrible and glorious.*

Huffing a last puff of scorching air, the dragon ambled away, free to see one last year of solitary decline.

Guinevere did not know if she had truly done it a kindness. She hoped so. At least it would be free, now, to choose its own death. Was everything old and magical doing the same? Finding holes to crawl into, to slowly fade in peace? She prayed her mercy would not come back to haunt her. An old, battered dragon was still a dragon, and the darkness had always loved them.

But the dragon was not fighting or plotting. It was barely existing. Lonely and weary, she wanted nothing more than to rejoin Brangien and Sir Tristan. Tell them that she had been too late, the dragon already dead.

No. She wanted nothing more than someone she could talk to about *everything* she had done today. But Arthur was gone, and she did not know if he would want to hear this. She had not sought out Rhoslyn, but this was just as dangerous.

She would tell Arthur. He was the only person she could be honest with. She would not give that up. And it was another reason to go after Rhoslyn and the patchwork knight. Something was creeping in the dark and hidden places surrounding Camelot.

She had one more odious task to complete here, though. Bors could not wake up to clean clothes—they were evidence that contradicted his memory. She began to undress the battered old knight.

*The dragon feels the tug. Feels her sending out her dark tendrils
again, calling for aid.*

It sighs, a slight hiss around its missing tooth.

She tugs harder.

*It has the gift of winter to look forward to, now. Magic can offer it
nothing but death, and that is already its constant companion, having
taken all its kind and waiting ever-present for the last dragon. The poor
lost girl should have stayed. They could have curled together against the
night, against the darkness, against time.*

The magic tugs.

The dragon goes back to sleep.

CHAPTER SEVENTEEN

Guinevere stood on an exterior walkway, her red cloak whipping in the wind, as Arthur and his knights walked up the long hill. He saw her there and lifted a hand in greeting. She matched his gesture.

She waited in his room for him. It was still several hours before he returned. The stone floors bore her pacing with ancient patience she could not feel herself. When Arthur came in, his armor was already left behind. He wore only a thin white tunic. He set Excalibur against the wall, then sat heavily on the end of his bed to remove his worn boots.

"It is good to be home," he said. Then he moved straight back to their last conversation, not dancing around the questions and tension between them. "And I am sorry for how we left things. I have thought on it every free moment. I *am* glad Sir Tristan is alive. His loss would have been hard to bear. But please trust that when I make those decisions, I make them knowing the consequences on both ends. I have lost men. Good men, true men. Men who cannot be replaced. I never give up a life lightly."

Guinevere was drawn to the sorrow in Arthur's voice. She had been worried he would still be angry with her. But she saw how sad it made him to have to weigh the lives of those he loved against the burden of an entire kingdom. She had made it harder for him, forced him to protect her at the cost of Sir Tristan. How could he live with such decisions?

Though *she* had done a terrible thing to Sir Bors, changing his memories. She did not know if she would be able to look him in the eyes ever again. Being in power required sacrifices both physical and emotional. And being adjacent to that power did, as well. She did not want to understand why Merlin did what he did. But if her actions with Sir Bors were any indication, she might eventually get there.

There was good, and there was evil, but there was so much space between the two.

She shuddered and paced, tugging at her sleeves. She longed to have bare arms. To sit in the winking sunlight, watching as the rays filtered down to her. "There was a dragon."

Arthur lay back on his bed, rubbing his face. His legs still hung over the side, his feet on the floor. "I heard. Sir Bors killed it."

"Well. He—" She stopped. Arthur looked so tired. Her heart broke a little, seeing the wear of the last few days. Protecting him from magic was her job. He should not have to make those decisions, nor bear the cost. "Yes. The dragon is gone. Are you well?"

"Tired. But you have been waiting a long time here to speak with me. I am sorry I leave you alone so often. Tell me, what do you need? What can I do for you?"

Her voice betrayed her. She could say so many things. She wanted to move to his side. To rub his weary forehead for him. To curl into him. To tell him about the dragon and how lonely thinking of it made her feel.

She wanted to run her finger along the fullness of his lower lip. To feel his smile against her own. And that was dangerous. As dangerous as what she had done to Sir Tristan in the forest. Because if she lost herself in this pretending, how would she ever be able to protect him?

It hit her with the force of a blow. She sat heavily in a chair, winded. She had already created more problems for Arthur than she had solved. If she truly wanted to serve him, to protect Camelot, she could not do it as his queen.

Arthur could not go against a witch outside his borders. Neither could the queen. But the daughter of Merlin could.

It was time to follow the tendrils of darkness and see where they led. Arthur was safe in Camelot. Whatever was threatening him, it was not here. She would stop it before it arrived.

It would be dangerous and solitary, and now that it was time, she found she did not want to. She wanted to stay here with Arthur, with Brangien, with Mordred and Dindrane and Sir Tristan. She did not want to go back to her life in the forest, with only the animals and the increasingly unfamiliar Merlin. But once she left, there would be no returning. She had become Guinevere to protect Arthur; she would give up Guinevere to do the same.

Perhaps that was what the dragon had been trying to show her. It was time to be alone. Arthur always made the hard choices. She could, too. "I need you to get rid of me."

Arthur sat up, alarmed. "Has something happened? Did someone see what you did for Sir Tristan?"

Only Mordred. He would not betray her. The thought of not seeing him again made something tight and painful clench in her chest. She shook her head. "I am no use in Camelot. My work threatens your rule. You said as much in the forest. I know where the threat is, who it is. I need to stop it. And I cannot do that as queen."

Something shifted around Arthur's warm brown eyes. Gone was

the weariness, the sorrow, replaced with . . . hurt. "Do you *want* to leave?"

"No! No." The thought of leaving Arthur behind made tears burn in her eyes. How quickly she had grown to be Guinevere!

Arthur crossed the room to her, kneeling in front of her chair and putting his hands on top of hers. "You are useful to me."

"My strengths are a liability here. You know it is true."

His hands tightened around hers. Her breath caught, waiting for what he would say next. "Merlin sent you here. That is reason enough to stay."

"But—"

He pulled her suddenly close, wrapping his arms around her. Her chin was on his shoulder, the side of his face against hers. "Guinevere. Please. I want you in Camelot. Do not leave. Promise you will not leave."

She closed her eyes. The heat of his cheek against hers, the slight roughness of his skin. It made her feel real. She had only just learned how to be Guinevere. She worried that alone in the forest, hunting, she would become something new. Darker. Maybe that was how Merlin could justify hurting others; when you lived your life apart, it was easy to forget how real other people were. He had done terrible things to create Arthur, to protect him. What would she be willing to do?

"What if the darkness comes here?" she asked.

"It will. It always does. It will come tomorrow or in a year or in fifty years." He released her, slyness in his normally clear, direct eyes. He smiled. "And you will only know when it is here if you are still here, too. So you cannot leave. As king, I forbid it." His tone had shifted from serious to teasing.

A part of her wilted in disappointment. She had wanted him to say something else. The hope lurked, nebulous and hungry. She wanted him to want her to stay because he wanted . . . her. She wanted to stay for him. Not for King Arthur. For *her* Arthur. It was why she should leave.

It was why she would not.

"I will stay for as long as you want me to," Guinevere said. "But you must let me spy on Rhoslyn and the patchwork knight."

She had not expected the sheer relief on his face as he nodded. "We will make plans. But not tonight. We are going on a hunt tomorrow, and you will accompany me." He stopped, then smiled hopefully. In his tunic, in the dim light, without his crown and sword and armor, he was so *young*. Her heart gave a painful squeeze as he said, "If you want to come. I want you to."

If she could only be herself around him, perhaps it was true that he could only be himself around her. And she suspected Arthur desperately needed to be an eighteen-year-old boy sometimes, instead of the hope of all Camelot. This was a different type of protection she could offer him. It was certainly not what Merlin had in mind. But, oh, she wanted it. Because if Arthur was eighteen, she was only sixteen. She was not a weary, ancient dragon, ready to fade, or a gnarled old wizard content to retreat to his forest shack and mutter inscrutable prophecies.

She wanted to live. She wanted to live *here*. She leaned forward, batting her eyelashes. "Will it be *terribly* dangerous?"

"Oh, very much so. You will have to talk to Sir Percival's wife."

"Save me!" She threw a hand over her forehead and pretended to swoon. He laughed, catching her against himself. He pressed her to his chest and she felt and heard as his steady heart began to beat faster. Her own matched its pace. He stood, slowly, pulling her up with himself. "Guinevere," he said, his voice as soft as the night around them. She wanted to touch his hand, to feel him. To feel if what was sparking in her like flint trying to catch a torch was also inside him.

They stumbled a bit as she rose, and she knocked into Excalibur leaning against the wall. Her fingers brushed the hilt and—

Oh

Oh

No

Darkness and void and nothing

Nothing, so much nothing she spun in it, she fell in it.

But falling is something falling has a destination falling stops and this this would never stop could never stop—

Her fingers left the sword. She ran from the room and into hers, emptying her stomach into the washbowl. Over and over, her body spasming, until at last her head stopped spinning and her heart stopped twitching. She ran her hands over her body. She was here. She was here. She was real.

"What is wrong?" Arthur asked, concern tightening his voice.

"I do not know," Brangien answered. Guinevere had not even realized Brangien was there holding her hair back. "Maybe something she ate."

Guinevere sank weakly to the floor. It had not been magic. She would have recognized a magical attack. This had been . . . the opposite of magic. If magic was chaos and life, this was a void.

And she had felt it when she touched Excalibur.

What was the sword?

Guinevere had imagined riding next to Arthur, her cloak streaming in the wind.

Instead, she rode beside the ladies. They did not even trot. Their horses plodded along at the same pace as the conversation. Guinevere kept Brangien by her side. She was still not feeling entirely herself after last night's brush with Excalibur. When they had set out this morning, she could barely look at Arthur, knowing he carried the sword.

She remembered, now, how she had felt on his horse in the forest when he was wielding it. How throwing herself to the wolves had briefly seemed preferable. At the time, she had dismissed it as the panic of the moment. But now she knew it had been the sword.

Fortunately, the men—and the sword with them—were allowed to gallop. They quickly outpaced the women, riding ahead to set up the day's camp. Around the women were several soldiers, and behind them, the carts with the supplies. A few carts and servants had been sent the night before so that they would not arrive to an empty field.

For a few sullen minutes she wished she had not promised Arthur she would stay. That she were riding away, alone, to do what needed to be done. She longed to prowl barefoot through the trees. Canopies and cushions and company were not something she required or wanted.

And maybe Arthur could meet her there, in the secret embrace of the forest. And maybe if they were not king and pretend-queen, maybe things would not be so complicated. . . .

But he would leave. She could not keep him that way. She could not keep anyone. She wrapped her arms around herself, feeling the realness of her, her ribs and her breasts and her heart beneath it all. She did not want to be alone. She wanted to be *real*. And seeing herself reflected in the eyes of those she loved made her feel more real than anything.

"My lady?" Brangien asked.

Guinevere sat up straight. "Yes?"

"I said, are you feeling better?"

"Our queen was ill?" Dindrane perked up and shifted her horse closer so as not to miss any of the conversation. She was trimmed in scarlet and blue. Since Guinevere had worn the colors at the wedding, most of the women had begun wearing them with greater frequency. Guinevere wore green and brown. Her hood was yellow, shading her face from the sun. Brangien, next to her, wore all brown.

Dindrane was counting on her fingers. "You were wed on the evening of the festival, which was not three weeks ago, so—" Dindrane leaned past Brangien to see Guinevere. "Has she had her courses yet?"

"*She* thinks her courses are none of your concern!" Guinevere said, leaning forward to block Dindrane's view.

Dindrane just laughed—a bright, brassy sound. "My sweet queen. Your courses are all of Camelot's business. People are placing bets on how soon you will provide an heir. Most think within a year. But a few worry you are too delicate."

Guinevere slumped, the weight of a nation on her shoulders. A queen *should* provide an heir. Arthur had said he did not care about alliances, did not need a queen for that. But what about for securing the future of Camelot? A kingdom without heirs was a kingdom without permanent stability. He had to know that. Had to see it. He was young, yes. But so many children died in infancy, and he himself was a warrior king. Nothing was certain.

He had chosen to marry her, though. And last night she had thought, hoped . . . She tried to imagine herself a mother. Instead, she remembered Elaine and her fate. Igraine, too. And her own mother. She had never known one. Merlin had never spoken of her. Who had she been? What had happened to her?

Was there not enough peril in the world already without the dangers of simply being a woman?

"I am sorry," Dindrane said, her voice soft. "I did not think. I am so used to hearing constant talk of wombs that I forget myself." Her own hand drifted to her waist. Her shoulders straightened and she lifted her chin, the picture of feminine strength. "I will stop anyone I hear speculating about you. It will be easy. I will tell them Blanche-fleur sleeps in the nude and that will shift every thought away from you in an instant."

Guinevere forced a laugh. "You are a fearsome friend."

"Yes, I am." Dindrane filled the rest of the hours of their ride with happy chatter. Guinevere was grateful. She had nothing she wished to say on any of the topics.

When they arrived at camp, they found the men testing spears, pulling back the strings on longbows, and in the case of a couple of the younger knights, wrestling. Arthur helped her dismount and sat close to her. She appreciated his quiet strength, as her own strength was still lacking.

They were in a meadow bordered by gnarled green-and-gray trees. It was far north of the dragon's territory, which was a relief.

But it was not more than a few hours' ride from where Merlin lived. Guinevere could sense it. She turned in that direction, longing to keep going. To demand to know how Merlin could do such terrible things and still live with himself. She had not yet tried to visit him in dreams, and she dreaded the confrontation. Already the Merlin she remembered was fading, twisting into something shadowy and unknown. What would be worse—to see him and have him revealed to be a monster, or to see him and have him revealed to be the same kindly, baffling old man who had taught her everything? How could she reconcile that?

"Sir Bors!" Dindrane called, sitting on a cushion in the shade of the canopies. "Tell us of the dragon! Tell us how you defeated it!"

As soon as Dindrane mentioned the dragon, Sir Bors's face went pale and he physically recoiled. He cleared his throat. "It tried to kill me. I killed it instead."

Guinevere did not want him to dwell on it, or others to press him to give more details. "Three cheers for Sir Bors, the dragonslayer!" she called. Everyone around her cheered and he seemed to relax, nodding and waving away their praise.

"I must see to the preparations. Will you be all right?" Arthur asked, his mouth close to her ear.

"Of course."

He took her hand and pressed it to his lips. A thrill coursed through her. He could be doing it for show—obviously they were being watched in this setting—but it felt joyful, sincere.

He rejoined his men, jumping in on several wrestling matches. He truly loved his knights. Sir Tristan, in particular, seemed a favorite, reminding her yet again of how much Arthur was willing to sacrifice for his kingdom.

Mordred slipped into the shade, finding a cushion near Guinevere and lying idly on his side. "Did you miss me?" His voice slid beneath the chatter so no one else heard.

"Were you gone?" Guinevere asked.

Mordred put his hands to his heart, feigning being pierced by an arrow. He fell onto his back and closed his eyes.

"Are you going to nap instead of hunt?" Brangien asked, cross.

"Yes." Mordred shifted around until he got comfortable. Guinevere envied him. No woman could lie at ease on the ground without bringing censure and judgment down on herself.

Guinevere stood, pulling her hood back on. "What do the ladies do during the hunt?" She wanted to stay close to Arthur. She should be by his side whenever possible, especially outside of Camelot.

Dindrane held out a plate of fruit and cheese. "We do this." She laughed as Guinevere's face fell. "Did you want to prowl through the trees, hunting alongside the men?"

"No, not precisely that, but . . . could we not have sat more comfortably at Camelot?" Every time she left the city it was complicated. Until she could get over her damnable fear of water, Arthur had to make up some excuse as to why they could not ride on the barge like everyone else. It was humiliating and inconvenient. And she would worry the whole time he was in the forest. This one was tame, within the bounds of Camelot, but still. She should be with him.

The servants around the knights and the king loaded themselves with quivers and extra spears. Then one of the heralds blew a bright note from his instrument, and the men rode into the trees. Arthur waved to her, but he was surrounded by his men. His friends. His protectors who did not have to hide what they were.

"You seem upset." Mordred cracked an eye open and stared at Guinevere. He alone of the knights had stayed behind. There were also a dozen servants and several armed guards.

Dindrane eyed Mordred appraisingly. "You seem unmarried."

Mordred laughed. "My heart ever wants only what it cannot have." But he did not look at Dindrane when he said it.

He looked at Guinevere.

Guinevere stood abruptly. She could not sit with these flutters of nervous energy going through her. She needed and she wanted and she did not know the source of or the solution to either desire.

The borders of the woodlands had been pushed back. This forest was an hour's ride from Camelot. Men had contracts to gather wood and bring it back to the city. They also bought rights to hunt there. The once-wild woods, now taxed and regulated. Used for sport. It made her proud of Arthur, and also unaccountably sad.

"Brangien," she said. "Would you accompany me on a walk? I

want to gather flowers." One of the benefits of Brangien's knowing about magic was that Guinevere did not have to engineer an elaborate way to avoid her gaze as she gathered some supplies. Brangien could help. And Guinevere wanted to feel out this forest, make certain it was safe from threats Arthur and his knights could not sense.

They skirted along the edge of the trees. They were still in plain view of the canopies. Guinevere glanced back, but she could not pierce the shade to see if anyone was watching them. She picked a few flowers to maintain the charade as they leisurely ambled away.

"Here," Brangien said. "We can turn into the woods. No one will see."

Guinevere entered the cool shade of the trees. She let out a long breath of relief. Then she remembered their ride from the convent. "But you do not like the forest."

"I do not like forests that spring up overnight and devour villages," Brangien corrected, leaning down to inspect a smooth white rock. She put it in her pouch. "This is one of the sleeping forests, commanded by Merlin himself. It is only trees." She walked confidently forward. Guinevere trailed in her wake, watchful, listening.

"Is it— Do you mind if I get supplies?" Brangien asked, hesitant.

"Please. And tell me what you are getting, and why." Guinevere wanted more knowledge that did not come from Merlin. Everything he had taught her seemed tainted now.

"These are good for sleeping. A gentler sleep than my knots." Brangien tucked some pale violet flowers into her pouch. She spotted a white oak tree deeper in and aimed for it. Guinevere followed, staring up at the way the sunlight shimmered through the leaves. It reminded her of looking up at the sun from a great depth, the cold—

She shuddered and hurried to Brangien's side. She helped her peel back several pieces of bark. Brangien wanted a certain type of beetle as well.

"I am not familiar with any of these supplies," Guinevere said. She had intended to gather young stones that she could place around Camelot to absorb things. Then she could get information from them. But she was not certain there was a need. She already had the sentry spells. Besides, nothing happened in Camelot that Arthur did not know about. Even the trees were taxed and accounted for.

Though he had not known about Brangien. Or Rhoslyn. And he did not know anything about the patchwork knight other than the knight's fighting skills.

Nothing had directly attacked Arthur yet, though. How long would she wait? How long could she wait without letting her guard slowly slip? Without becoming more queen than witch?

"I will teach you," Brangien said. "I used to specialize in draughts. Sleeping. Love. Confusion. My mother was a witch. My father loved her for it, since he did not carry the prejudices of Camelot or Christianity. Did your mother practice any magic?"

How had she never asked Merlin about her mother? In the forest, life was simply what it was. She had never thought to ask. But who had she been with while Merlin was helping Arthur all those years? Why could she not remember?

A terrible realization gripped her. As she had pushed Sir Bors's memories out and replaced them, she had felt some of her own slipping away.

Had she forgotten so much because that was not the first time she had done that magic? Who else had she hurt?

Another possibility struck her. Merlin had pushed the knowledge of knot magic straight into her mind. Perhaps he had carelessly pushed other things out. He only ever sought results, never worrying about the things lost along the way.

Or maybe he had pushed things out on purpose. Maybe the things she was learning about Merlin were things she had once known.

Things that had been taken from her so she would trust him. So she would do as he asked.

"Guinevere?"

"I remember nothing about my mother."

Brangien dropped the subject. She went from treasure to treasure, pulling them deeper into the forest. They moved at an angle, though, away from where the men had entered. Neither particularly relished the thought of a spear in her back. Guinevere paused beneath a soaring oak and put her hand against it.

"Brangien," she said, staring up at the tree. "Brangien, come feel this."

Brangien joined her, resting her hand on the trunk. "Feel what?"

"Can you not feel it?"

Brangien shook her head. Guinevere had hoped that maybe Brangien, too, had the touch sense. But she was alone.

And she was not alone, because the tree was there. Merlin had sent the trees into a deep sleep, past where the Dark Queen could call to them. Guinevere could feel the sleep, her sense pushed straight down into the roots, the soil.

But it was not a peaceful sleep. It shivered beneath her hand, dreaming. The dream had fire. The dream had teeth. And beneath the roots, darkness. Guinevere yanked her hand away, shaking it to free it from the sensation.

"What is it?" Brangien asked.

"Something—something is trying to wake the trees."

"Are you sure?" Brangien backed away, staring up in fear.

"No. I am not sure." Guinevere rubbed her eyes. "But something is giving the trees nightmares. And I have felt it elsewhere." In the other forest, with the wolves. She should never have left Rhoslyn to her own devices. This felt far bigger than the stones in Camelot. They had underestimated the woman terribly.

"We should go back." Brangien was already stepping in the direction they had come.

A crashing noise from deeper in the woods startled them. Guinevere turned, expecting to see the knights. She opened her mouth to shout a warning that she and Brangien were there.

But it was no knight.

A boar as high as her shoulders, tusks jagged, eyes red—not with frenzy but with terrifying focus—charged straight toward her.

CHAPTER EIGHTEEN

"Run!" Guinevere screamed. Brangien held up her skirts, sprinting. Guinevere followed. She veered to the right, avoiding a fallen log. The boar copied her.

She moved farther to the right, still running as fast as she could. She was changing her course from Brangien's. The boar followed.

If Guinevere chased Brangien, the boar would, too. But if she led it away, Brangien would get out.

Guinevere turned sharply away from Brangien and the camp, drawing the beast after her. She ran with all her might. She ran with the strength of a forest girl. Her hood fell as she leapt over roots. Her trailing cape caught on a branch and she tore it off, hair streaming behind her as she pushed herself faster than she ever knew she could go.

The boar did not stop, did not even slow. Her own breathing was so heavy and sharp in her ears she could barely hear the beast tearing through the forest behind her. She weaved through the trees, looking for an escape. Any escape. No trees had branches low enough for her to grab. The boar was too close for her to take the time to climb a tree. She could only run. And soon she would not be able to run much longer.

There was movement ahead. Her heart squeezed, fearing she would see another boar. But no. It was—

"Duck!" a voice shouted. Guinevere dropped to the forest floor. A spear flew over her, meeting its target with a sickening *thud*. But she could still hear the beast behind her. She pushed up, running to the man. Stunned as she recognized the face of the patchwork knight, she hurried past him. He crouched low, a sword in his hand. She could run no farther. Turning, she watched with horror as the boar, a spear jutting from its chest, stamped determinedly forward.

The patchwork knight angled to the side, trying to draw the boar away. The boar never so much as looked at him. It stared only at Guinevere.

The patchwork knight rushed it. Finally, the boar reacted, lunging its head and great tusks toward the knight. The knight leapt over the blow, rolling once on the ground before jumping to his feet and plunging his sword into the boar's neck. It let out a horrible squealing scream, then swiped its tusks against the patchwork knight, throwing him.

Its focus was immediately back on Guinevere. It no longer ran. It stepped purposefully and measuredly toward her. It moved not like a beast, but like a hunter.

Like a person.

"Who are you?" Guinevere asked.

The boar lifted its head, turning so it could fix one red eye firmly on her. And then it stopped as the knight's sword drove straight through its neck, severing the connection between head and body. The gleaming red light in its eye dimmed, and the boar fell, twitching. Then it went still.

The patchwork knight yanked his sword from the creature.

Guinevere stumbled backward, tripping on a root and sitting down hard on the ground. She stayed there, staring at the dead creature. Not wanting to touch it. Needing to touch it. She crawled to it, resting a hand on its now-still flank.

Berries. Mushrooms. Sunlight. Mates. Wary avoidance of predators. But then—there—something older. Something darker.

Something foreign.

She felt it curling beneath what the boar had been, seeping through it, poisoning it. Taking control. It was the same thing that had nearly killed Sir Tristan. And then it turned, focusing, toward—

Guinevere yanked her hand free, scrambling back. Whatever had taken the boar was still there. It had seen her. It knew her.

The patchwork knight wiped his sword clean on the boar's flank, then sheathed it. He grimaced, holding his side. The boar had hit him hard and he wore no armor. Guinevere could not quite make sense of the knight. He was different. Without his armor, he—

"You are a woman," Guinevere gasped. *That* was the secret. Not a fairy. A woman.

"And I am bleeding," the patchwork knight said. She lifted her red-coated hands from her side. Guinevere rushed to the knight and peeled back her tunic. The knight hissed in pain.

There was the faintest tickle against Guinevere's arm, and then a sting. She looked down to see an elegantly sinister black spider with its fangs embedded in her arm. She brushed it away, leaving two tiny pinpricks of red circled by white. The white spread, and turned purple as she watched.

"Oh," she said, and then darkness claimed her.

"She should have woken up by now."

"Keep going. There, not too much. Ailith, you next. If you start feeling dizzy, stop."

"What did this?"

"I have never tasted such darkness. And I kissed your brother once."

"*Girls.* We need to focus."

"Can I help?"

"No. Save your strength."

The voices pulsed in and out as though heard from a great distance. Everything hurt, but the pain was dulling from a lightning-bright tempest to a punishing rainstorm. Guinevere felt fingertips at her hairline, smoothing stray hairs back from her forehead. And she felt something else—soft but insistent—on her arm.

"Spider," Guinevere whimpered.

"No, dear. The spider is gone. We are taking care of you."

Her eyelids protested, but she cracked them open. The room was dark, her vision blurry. Someone was sitting next to where she lay on a cot. And someone else was—

"Sucking on my arm?" Guinevere tried to sit in shock but was unable to move.

"It was infecting you. Nasty and very fast. But we almost have it all out."

"You—you will be poisoned." The spider and the pain and the darkness. The boar had failed, but something much smaller had succeeded. Guinevere remembered the poison from the wolf's attack, how fast it raged through Tristan. These women did not know what they were doing. They would be killed.

"Women are strongest when bearing one another's pain. We each take a little on ourselves. No one dies, and we all heal together."

"Thank you," Guinevere whispered, closing her eyes.

"Rest, and let us help you."

"And be grateful you never have to kiss Gunild's brother," another voice said. Guinevere let the bright laughter and long-suffering *shush* push her back into sleep.

When she awoke again, only her arm hurt. Two points of agony, but to her relief, they were *just* pain. There was no darkness, nothing in her that was other.

She sat up, groaning. She was in a shack, a small, dim space with a low ceiling. But the packed-dirt floors were covered with fresh straw and the cot she lay on felt clean. Sitting against the wall was the patchwork knight. She held a blood-soaked cloth to her side, her eyes closed.

Guinevere crossed the room to the other woman. "Did you bring me here?"

The knight nodded.

"Thank you for saving me again, then," she said, kneeling. "May I?" When the knight nodded, Guinevere gently pulled the cloth back. The wound was deep and still seeping blood.

Guinevere gazed up at the knight. Her eyes were a warm, lively hazel, large and gentle. "You helped me, and I can help you. But first, tell me why you were there. In the forest."

The knight grimaced. "I wanted to see the king."

"To hurt him?"

The knight's eyes widened. "I wanted to see the hunt. Why would I hurt him?"

"I have seen you with Rhoslyn."

Light flooded the room as a woman entered, backlit by the sun. "How do you know my name?"

Guinevere stood so fast she nearly fell over. "You!"

"Have we met?" Rhoslyn let the mat covering the entrance fall back into place and Guinevere blinked as her eyes readjusted to the dim interior.

"I was at your trial."

"Oh. That." Rhoslyn took Guinevere's place next to the knight, looking at the wound with concern knitting her brow.

Guinevere scanned the room for a threat. There was nothing. "This was all you. The boar! The knight waiting for me!"

"Child, I cannot even control my own daughters. Controlling a wild boar is far beyond my skill."

"But you were banished from Camelot for magic! And now you seek revenge."

Rhoslyn sighed, turning her attention back to the knight's wound. "This does not look good. I have sent for my sister, but it will be a few hours. Stay still." She stood, wiping her hands on her skirts and eying Guinevere appraisingly. "I have no thirst for vengeance, and no energy to pursue it even if I did. It takes all my strength just to keep my family alive. Not to mention the occasional lost noblewoman who has gotten herself infected with dark magic."

Guinevere bristled, grateful at least Rhoslyn did not seem to know who she was, only that she was nobility. "How do I know that it was not you?"

"Why would I have saved you if it had been my poison?"

It was a fair point. "But surely you hate Camelot and everyone who lives there."

"It seems to me," Rhoslyn said, sitting with a weary grunt, "that it is man's work to hate and want to destroy what he cannot possess. I was sad to leave Camelot, yes. But it has its rules, and I did not follow them. In the end, we did not fit with each other anymore. Would I like the protection of walls and soldiers and law? Yes. But not so much that I was willing to give up the power my mother learned from her mother, who learned it from her mother. Camelot asked more than I was willing to give. I overstayed my welcome. I harbor no ill will. None of us do." She paused. "Except maybe Ailith, who mentions Gunild's soldier brother's shortcomings so often I suspect she is still in love with him."

"What about your knight?" Guinevere gestured toward the woman, whose face was going ever paler.

The knight answered, her voice tight with strain, "They have no one to protect them. And it is good practice for me."

Rhoslyn nodded. "She does not live here. We do not even know her name. But she protects those who need it out here in the wild."

"Will you heal her like you did me?"

Rhoslyn shook her head, letting out a long breath. "We did not heal you. We drew out the poison because it was magic, and we could call it and bind it. When it comes to the business of broken bodies, we are limited. My sister has some experience, mostly birthing babies, but she might be able to help. I will go see if Gunild is back with news yet." Rhoslyn patted her warm, dry hand against Guinevere's hand. Then she stood and walked out of the shack. Guinevere followed, peeking her head out. No one was watching. She could run.

But she felt none of the menace from the forest. If Rhoslyn wanted her dead, she would be. And they had made no demands, asked nothing of her. There had been no malice in Rhoslyn's touch. Surely if Rhoslyn could possess and control the same darkness Guinevere had felt from the boar, it would have come through when she touched Guinevere.

Guinevere took her position at the knight's side once more. "Can we trust Rhoslyn?"

The knight nodded.

"If you are lying and they are plotting against the king, I will kill you."

The knight opened her eyes. "If I had aided in a plot against the king, I would want to die. I swear to you on my sword, I am loyal to Camelot. I am loyal to King Arthur."

Guinevere felt the truth of it pierce her. "Very well. You saved me. I will return the favor in exchange for your silence."

The knight looked puzzled, but she nodded.

Guinevere allowed the flame to surround her hand. She closed her eyes, giving her breath to the flame and summoning it. The knight gasped, but did not cry out. Guinevere let the flame surround her hand. She did not have time to be afraid of being burned again. "Trust me," she whispered. Then she put her hand against the knight's wound and let the fire go.

The knight cried out in surprise, but she did not move. Guinevere pulled the purifying flames back before they could turn into devouring flames. It was easier than it had been with Sir Tristan, because she did not have to send it into the blood. Only the wound. The knight was sweating, her dark curls plastered to her forehead. She looked down in wonder. The wound was smaller. The blood on her side gone, consumed.

"One more step." Guinevere tugged up a sleeve. She pulled out her knife—the women had not taken it, or anything else—and, cringing, took a slice of her own skin as though peeling the top layer of an apple. She used the blood welling on the wound to write a knot into the skin, commanding it to bind to another. Then she placed it over the knight's wound. The skin stretched, grasping at its new body, finding the open edges and pulling them taut.

Where there had been a gaping hole, now there was a smooth patch of skin several shades lighter than the knight's own.

"What are you?" the knight whispered.

Guinevere smiled wryly. "What are you?"

"I am a knight."

"I am . . ." The daughter of Merlin? A forest witch? If the knight came to Camelot often enough, she would discover the truth anyway. "I am Guinevere. The queen."

The knight hung her head, her face falling. "Then my hopes are over."

"Why?"

"Because the truth of my body will keep me from being an aspirant." The knight pulled her bloody tunic down over the sealed wound. "I have known—*always* known—that I am a knight. And with King Arthur, I had a chance. If I could get to the tournament, if I could defeat them all, if I could fight the greatest king in the world, he would see my value. He would knight me. And then it would be too late for them to forbid me."

Guinevere sat and tucked her legs beneath her. The knight had saved her life from the boar, and then brought her to the only women who could save her from the spider's bite. She owed her far more than a little patch of skin. "What does my being the queen have to do with any of that?"

The knight frowned at her. "You will tell them."

"Why should I tell them? I have seen you fight. You fought for my life today. If you earn a place in Arthur's court, then it is yours. You have me on your side. Provided you keep my secret as well." She gestured toward the knight's missing wound. "Keep it from Rhoslyn, too. No one can know."

The knight's smooth face shifted with wonder and hope. "You will let me continue?"

"I would drag you to the city myself and force you to."

The knight bowed her head, closing her eyes. A smile parted her lips. She had dimples in her cheeks to match the permanent dimple

in her chin. "Thank you. We have saved each other today, I think."
She stood, holding out her hand. "Come. I will see you safely back
to your camp."

Extended was the final test Guinevere needed of the knight's
honesty. Guinevere took the offered hand. It was calloused and
rough like Arthur's, but narrower. It seemed to fit hers much better.
The sense she got of the knight was less a pulse or a spark, and more
a . . . settling. Rightness. Belonging. The tight, anxious knot inside
her that had grown since she arrived in Camelot seemed to loosen.

She let out a long, relieved breath. There was no malice, no lies.

Guinevere knew she should return to the camp. That Brangien
would be frantic.

But there had been so much darkness in the boar, in the trees, in
the spider. And she knew now her suspicions of Rhoslyn were wrong.
Guinevere's focus had been misplaced.

She could waste no more time. She was not enough to protect
Arthur from whatever was coming if she had not even been able to
withstand the spider's poison. She no longer trusted Merlin, but she
needed him. Arthur needed him. Maybe her role in protecting Arthur
was always meant to create a way back to Camelot for Merlin.

She squeezed the knight's hand. "Will you help me on a quest to
fetch a wizard and save the kingdom?"

The knight's eyes sparkled. She laughed, her low voice surpris-
ingly sweet with happiness. "You could do me no greater kindness
than to ask that. Let me get my armor and my horse. I will defend
you to whatever end." She paused, lowering her eyes. "Always, my
queen. I will defend you forever."

Guinevere felt a rush of pleasure, a warmth that suffused her.
Was this how Arthur felt all the time, having the loyalty of worthy
men?

She followed the knight out of the shack. Rhoslyn seemed

surprised but pleased at the knight's dramatic recovery. The small village was orderly. Several children were playing a game with sticks, laughing. Everywhere, Guinevere saw evidence of benign magic. Bundles of plants, knots at doorways, stones lining the borders. Thank goodness she had not sent Arthur's men against Rhoslyn. The idea of knights riding in and terrorizing what Rhoslyn had built made Guinevere feel sick.

"We must go," Guinevere said, offering no explanation. "You have my gratitude, and your aid will not be forgotten." She would find a way to help these women however she could in the future. But looking at their clean, happy camp, she wondered if they would need help.

Rhoslyn bent over a pot bubbling above the fire pit. "Keep our location a secret, and that is payment enough. And please avoid spiders from now on."

Guinevere firmly intended to. She had two tiny holes in her arm as a reminder not to let her guard down. The knight whistled and a chestnut horse ambled up to them. The knight's armor was draped across the horse's back, and she pulled it free to fasten it on. Guinevere lifted her hand to the horse, but stopped. The horse's eyes were scarred white.

"Your horse is blind?" Guinevere asked, shocked.

The knight nodded. "Thieves do it so the horse cannot find its way back home. I found her wandering, lost and alone." The knight reached up and stroked the horse. The horse huffed, nuzzling the knight. "We were alike that way. She is the best horse I have ever known. Do not worry."

Guinevere stroked the horse's neck. It shivered once, then lowered its head, stamping its front foot.

"She likes you. She is ready to go." The knight boosted Guinevere onto the horse's back, then climbed on behind her. They waved to the camp. A few women waved back, but most ignored them, as though a lady and a knight in need of magical intervention were nothing to be remarked upon.

Guinevere pointed out the direction that would take them to Merlin, and the knight guided the horse. It was early afternoon. If they made good time, they could get to Merlin by nightfall.

And so she rode away from Camelot, from Arthur and the others, knowing they would fear her lost or dead, but knowing that getting to Merlin was more important than she could ever be. It hurt her pride, but that was a small sacrifice for keeping Arthur safe. She had wanted to be the great protector. Instead, her role was errand girl. So be it.

She was glad not to be alone, though. "What is your name?" she asked the knight.

The knight deftly guided her blind horse around an obstacle, her legs pressing against Guinevere's. "Lancelot, my queen."

The dark queen waits for the beast to bring her prey.

And then her prey bests her beast.

But often the subtlest attacks are the most effective. Two tiny fangs in place of two great tusks. She senses her poison seeping in, spreading. She rushes toward it, needing to be close enough to understand what she is possessing, and then—

Gone. It is all gone.

She stops, the earth churning in rage. Someone has taken her poison and spread it so thin she cannot feel its borders. But she had a taste. This queen-not-queen is something different. Something new. Someone has changed the rules, and she knows only one who is capable of that.

Merlin.

She laughs and laughs, the trees around her trembling, the dark creeping things of the earth burrowing upward, drawn by the tremors of her rage and amusement. Because Merlin knows what is coming. And, fool that he is, it will still happen.

But there is work to be done now. She will have to put her trust not in beasts, but in man. There is so very little difference between the two, after all.

CHAPTER NINETEEN

She knew the trees as they got closer. The trees knew her, too, the leaves trembling. Home was close, home was—

A pulse deep within her tugged from the north, like she had forgotten something.

Lancelot guided her horse, the animal as capable as promised, through the lowering light. No smoke drifted from the cottage. Guinevere slid down. Lancelot followed, tying the horse to a tree.

"Merlin?" Guinevere called. The cottage was cold. Not just cold. *Abandoned.* It looked as though no one had lived there in years. She reached for the broom she knew was by the door, but there was only a rotted length of wood. The door swung open, revealing a crumbling interior. How had she swept floors that no longer existed? How had she slept on a bedroll that was not there?

"Something is very wrong." Guinevere backed away. Her stomach twisted, sick. What had happened?

A bird flitted to a nearby tree. Guinevere ripped out several strands of her hair, knotting and looping them. She threw the knot at the bird. The knot circled, then tightened. The bird chirped once in protest, then went still.

"Take me to Merlin," Guinevere commanded. Her head throbbed where she had pulled out the hair, the pain disproportionate to the action. But taking the free will of another creature was a violent act, and violence always left pain in its wake.

The bird hopped dutifully into the air, flying from tree to tree. Guinevere hurried after it, Lancelot behind her. But there was something in her way. She pushed against the air as it thickened around her, preventing her from moving.

"What is this?" Lancelot asked.

Guinevere would not be deterred. She pulled out her iron dagger and carved a knot of unmaking into the air. It gave with a soundless *pop* that made her ears ache. At last she and Lancelot came to a cave. The opening yawned before them. It was black. Black with dread. Black with . . .

Guinevere had been to this cave. She knew she had. But she could not remember when, or why. She was so intent on the blackness of the cave, she did not even notice the wizened, bearded old man standing in its entrance.

He waved his arms frantically. "You cannot be here! You are not here. You were never here."

Guinevere shook her head, tearing her eyes away from the blackness. "Merlin! Dark magic. I felt it. There was a boar, and—"

"You cannot be here," Merlin repeated, still waving his spindly arms at her.

"Do not tell me what to do! You are a *liar!*" She took a deep breath, forcing herself to calm. Now was not the time for her personal grievances. "You sent me to Camelot to protect Arthur, but I cannot protect him against what I felt. It was—"

Merlin trembled, and then his shoulders stooped. He looked . . .

old. So much older than she had remembered. "Please," he said, but he was not speaking to her. "Please, Lancelot. If you love your queen, *hide*. Now."

Lancelot grabbed her around the waist and dragged her away from the cave. She stumbled along, wanting to protest but infected by Merlin's fear. They crouched down behind a jumble of rocks and boulders. Lancelot put herself behind Guinevere, shielding her. A scrubby bush hid them from view, but Guinevere could still see the cave entrance through a gap in the leaves.

"You know him?" Guinevere hissed.

"I have never met him before. I do not know how he knew my name." Lancelot sounded as shaken as Guinevere felt.

A trickle of water rolled past them. Guinevere watched in horror as it grew from a trickle to a stream, to a narrow, rushing river. She cowered deeper into the rocks, pulling her feet up so none of the water would touch her. Lancelot climbed, peering over the top of their cover. Guinevere copied her, not wanting to be by the water alone.

The river stopped midair in front of Merlin. He waited patiently as the river fed itself, growing and growing until it formed into the shape of a woman. Her hair flowed down her back and into the river still behind her, her dress trailing into a pond at her feet. She shimmered and shifted, her form constantly changing. Now she was a woman terrible and tall. Now she was a young girl. Now she was neither and both. She lifted a hand and pointed it at Merlin.

"The Lady of the Lake," Lancelot whispered, awed.

You should have kept your barriers up, betrayer. You let me in.

Guinevere put her hands over her mouth in horror. The barrier she had undone. She had let this thing in.

You have stolen from me, the water murmured. It was a soft sound, but it was everywhere, surrounding them. A babbling brook turned shouting waterfall. *You have stolen from me.*

Merlin nodded, his face solemn and sad. He tugged on his beard, several strands coming loose. He dropped them to the side, distracted. "Yes. I did."

Why did you take something so precious? What have you done?

"I am sorry, Nynaeve, my love, my lady."

I will unmake you.

"If you must."

I will—

The water trembled, losing form, reforming, a hundred times so that Guinevere's eyes ached as though she had been staring at the sun rippling on a lake.

Why? the water asked, and in the single word Guinevere felt the sorrow of the ageless, the sorrow of the infinite passing of days. The sorrow of change.

"Because it was time."

I will reclaim what was mine. The boy cannot take everything. He does not deserve this.

The Lady of the Lake gave Excalibur to Arthur, after it had been dropped into her depths. Did she want it back now? Had Guinevere been lied to about this, as well? Maybe the Lady never gave them the sword. Maybe Merlin took it, the way he took so many other things.

"You are right," Merlin said. "He does not deserve this. But he might someday. And that is not your decision to make. The decision has already been made."

The water roared up behind the Lady, pushing her higher and higher until she towered over Merlin. *I cannot end what should be eternal. I am not like you. But I cannot allow you to continue. You have betrayed me. You have betrayed us.*

"I know." Merlin turned once toward their rocks and wiggled his fingers in a silly wave. Guinevere's throat tightened. This was her fault. Then Merlin backed slowly into the cave. "I am tired," he said. "And I am not innocent. This is just. Until we meet again, my love, my Nynaeve."

The water roared past the Lady, up the sides of the cave. A thousand years' damage was done in seconds, eroding and eating, carving away.

The cave mouth collapsed, sealing the entrance shut. The water carried silt, working between each rock until it finally receded, leaving only solid stone where once had been a cave. Guinevere bit her thumb so she would not cry out in horror. Lancelot was still and silent beside her.

The water did not re-form into the woman. It flowed back the way it had come, with a noise like weeping.

Guinevere pounded at the rocks, but she could not shift so much as a pebble. The cave was sealed. Lancelot stared at the solid stone in wonder.

Guinevere turned and slid down, her back against the seal between herself and Merlin. Silver strands winked in the twilight to catch the very last rays of the sun. The hairs from Merlin's beard, caught on a rock. She wrapped them around her fingers so tightly it hurt.

"What did she want?" Lancelot asked.

Guinevere hung her head. The Lady wanted what had been taken. What had been given to Arthur. Guinevere could think of only one thing that could be. "Excalibur."

"But I thought she gave it to King Arthur!"

"Perhaps we have been misled." Merlin had never given her the full story, the true story. And what she had felt when she touched Excalibur made her certain it was far more than a sword. Maybe it could even threaten the Lady of the Lake. "How could Merlin let this happen?" Guinevere slammed her fists into the rock. She had undone the barrier herself. But if Merlin had ever been honest with her, even once, she would not have had to do this! She stood, determined.

"Take me to Arthur." He had the sword. Guinevere had magic. Between the two of them, they would rescue Merlin. And then she would get answers.

It was the darkest part of the night by the time they reached the hunting grounds. But darkness mattered nothing to a blind horse, and Lancelot navigated confidently. Guinevere longed for wings, for speed.

They heard voices frantically shouting her name long before they saw anyone. Lancelot stiffened behind her. "I should—"

"Pull on your mask. Stay with me. They should know who saved me."

Lancelot did as instructed. As soon as they got close, Guinevere shouted. "I am here! Here!"

This time the crashing through the trees was not beast, but beloved. Arthur rushed toward them. He grabbed Guinevere from the horse and crushed her to his chest. "We found your hood, your cloak. The boar. There were more tracks, more boar prints. We thought— I thought you were taken. Dead."

Guinevere held on to him just as tightly. Something inside her broke and healed at the same time, as she felt how much she mattered to him by the strength of his embrace. She allowed herself one moment to cherish it. And then she spoke. "Arthur, it is Merlin. He has been attacked. He is trapped. We have to go help him."

Arthur drew a breath, but it was not a sharp breath of surprise. It was a long, slow breath of reluctance and resignation. Several other bodies crashed through the trees, surrounding them. Sir Bors, Sir Tristan. Mordred, pale and drawn in the torchlight as he searched her face.

They could not speak of Merlin now.

"Good sir," Arthur said, looking up at Lancelot, who was still on her horse. "How did you come upon our queen?"

"Lancelot slew the boar and saved me." Guinevere released Arthur. He did not do the same, still holding her. "But there were more of the beasts. Lancelot had no more spears. We ran from them until we found Lancelot's horse and could ride fast enough to escape them. We went too deep into the forest. We have only now found our way out."

"Camelot owes you our most profound thanks, Lancelot." Arthur's hand was at the back of Guinevere's head, stroking her hair.

"It was my honor, my lord king." Lancelot dismounted and dropped to one knee, bowing her head. She pitched her voice low and soft, so that if Guinevere had not known the truth of her sex, she would have assumed Lancelot was a young man.

"You are the patchwork knight, are you not?"

"I am called that, yes."

"Then I think it is high time you had your tournament. You have earned it."

The knights around Arthur cheered, clapping Lancelot on the back as she stood. Guinevere smiled at her, pleased for Lancelot's well-deserved good fortune. But she could not be happy, not truly. There was so much that needed to be done.

"Arthur," she whispered. "We need to—"

"I know," he answered. "We need to talk."

"But Merlin—"

"Is not going anywhere." Arthur released her, finally, putting a hand at the small of her back as he led her out of the trees. A huge bonfire had been built in the meadow. Brangien ran to them, nearly tripping in her haste. She dropped to her knees at Guinevere's feet.

"My lady, I am so sorry. I thought you were behind me. I would never have run if—"

Guinevere reached down and lifted her, then pulled her close in an embrace. "I know. I know, dear Brangien. But seeing you safe is all I need. I could not have lived with it if you had been hurt." She could not say that the boar had been after her alone, that if Brangien had been killed, it would have been Guinevere's fault.

Brangien nodded, tears streaming down her face. She wiped them away. Then she took stock of Guinevere. "Here," she said, taking off her own cloak and wrapping it around Guinevere. "Your sleeve! You have been hurt!" The shallow slice where Guinevere had taken the skin for Lancelot was already scabbed over. "And your wrists!" Brangien removed a length of cloth from her bag, wrapping it hastily around Guinevere's arm down to her hand. As though exposed wrists were anything compared to the troubles they now faced. But Brangien could fix only the problems she saw, and Guinevere appreciated it.

Arthur took her directly to a tent, making it clear no one else was invited. He drew the tent shut. Guinevere paced in the tight confines.

"Between my magic and Excalibur, I am confident we will find a way to free Merlin. The Lady of the Lake wants the sword back. We may have to fight her."

Arthur sighed. "Please sit down."

"I am not tired! We need to move quickly. I felt something dark in the boar. I thought it was from Rhoslyn, but I was wrong. What if it was the Lady of the Lake? The lake at Camelot is dead. No magic. She must have pulled it all to herself to amass power. We need Merlin. I am no match for that kind of magic. I cannot protect you from this."

"Please, listen," Arthur said, his voice firm but pleading as he pulled her hands until she sat on a cushion. He knelt in front of her. "We cannot go save Merlin."

"We can! I know we can." She doubted herself, yes, but she had Arthur, and he had the sword. They could do it. They *had* to do it. They needed Merlin.

"He does not want us to."

Guinevere shook her head. She looked down at her hands, where Merlin's beard strands were still wound around two of her fingers. "How can you know that?"

"He told me." Arthur reached into his tunic and pulled free a well-worn sheaf of papers. He unfolded it to reveal spidery handwriting that crawled up and down the pages, sometimes going left to right, sometimes top to bottom, sometimes writing over itself. "He knew it would happen."

Guinevere stood, furious. Merlin saw time out of order. He had *known* this was coming? "If he knew it would happen, why did he not tell me? I broke his barrier myself, fool that I am! Why did he not run, or hide?"

Arthur's expression was frustrated but resigned. "I do not know his reasons. Only that he had them. And I trust Merlin. If he says something must be done, then it must be done. We will understand someday." He looked down at the letter and frowned. "Perhaps."

"No! I refuse to accept this. He saw a threat coming for you. He sent me to Camelot because of it. I cannot face it alone!"

Arthur refolded the letter and tucked it away. He wiped a hand down his face as though he could physically push away the regret and guilt there. "Guinevere, I have lied to you. I have let you believe something that is not true. And I am so sorry."

Guinevere took a step back, suddenly afraid. What else did Arthur know?

"The Lady of the Lake cannot get to me, I promise. Merlin did not send you to Camelot because of a threat to me. He sent you to Camelot because he knew what was coming for him. He did not need you to keep me safe. He asked *me* to keep *you* safe."

She sat, stunned. Broken. All this time, they had let her think she had a purpose. A mission. That she was fighting on Merlin's behalf, working for Camelot. That she had become Guinevere as a necessity to protect Arthur. Not herself.

It made no sense.

No. It made perfect sense. Every magical attack they had faced had been focused on her. Not Arthur. She had not seen it because she had never thought to look.

Merlin's exact words came back. *You are afraid of the wrong thing,* he had said when she worried she could not protect Arthur. He let her go, knowing what she thought, deceiving her without lying to her. Knowing that she would have refused to leave if she had known the coming threat was to Merlin, not Arthur.

The truth left her hollow. She was neither queen nor sorceress, protector nor warrior.

She was a burden.

CHAPTER TWENTY

Guinevere walked through the next days as though in a dream. Arthur wanted to speak with her but she could not manage it. Not yet. He was called away to the border, which for once was a relief.

She let Brangien brush and braid her hair. She visited and was visited. She grew to depend on Dindrane to accompany her so the burden of conversing was lifted. Dindrane and Brangien formed an unspoken alliance, shielding her and prompting her when she had to act a certain way. They were, in a way, her own knights. Fighting her small battles, protecting her from gossip and censure.

Everyone assumed her altered manner was because of the trauma of the boar attack. They pitied her and spoke softly, walked carefully. But Lancelot had doubly rescued her. News of the patchwork knight's heroics rippled through the city, all the focus on that part of the story, Lancelot's name on every tongue. The tournament was fast approaching, and Camelot thrummed and hummed with anticipation.

One afternoon there was a light knock on Guinevere's door. Brangien opened it, then bowed and moved to the side. Arthur stood, framed by the doorway.

"Guinevere, would you join me on a walk?"

She nodded mutely, taking his offered elbow and letting him lead her out of the castle onto one of the walkways that circled the many levels. The wind nipped teasingly at them. It was nearly midsummer. She had meant to do some protective magic on the solstice, but it had never mattered anyway.

Arthur stopped. He sat on the edge of the walkway, his legs dangling over the side as he gazed down on his city. The lake bordered everything, impassable, guarding. Waiting. "I returned last night. I sent word. I hoped you would come to my room so we could speak."

"I do not wish to waste your time, my lord."

He flinched. "I am not your lord. Please do not call me that."

Guinevere sat next to him. But she kept her legs tucked safely under her, staying back from the edge. "I have nothing to offer you. It would be selfish of me to demand any of your attention."

"That is not selfish."

"It is." She shook her head. She had been thinking of it—thinking of little else. "Why did you marry me? If all Merlin asked was that I be safe in Camelot, why not declare me a distant cousin? Or, more fitting, a servant? If you did not need me to protect you, why make me queen?"

Arthur shifted so he was turned away from Camelot. Toward her. "You speak of selfishness. That was the root of my decision. Merlin wanted you by my side, and I leapt at the chance. I have been hounded since the day I took the crown, besieged not only by armies, but by politics. I did not lie when I said any marital alliance would only have made my life more difficult. If I married a Pict, my southern neighbors would feel threatened. If I married someone from Camelot, my knights would be insulted that I did not marry *their* sister or daughter or cousin. And after Elaine—" His voice broke; then he continued firmly. "After that, how could

I trust anyone to love me for anything but my power? The idea of adding another complication to my life—another person to be treatied with, a stranger in my home who would treat me like a king—was so *wearying* I could not face it. Ever since I claimed Excalibur, I ceased being Arthur and became king. I love my men, but they are my men. Even my family is complicated. Sir Ector and Sir Kay. Mordred. I did not want a wife like that. Merlin has been the only constant in my life. And you are part of him. I hoped that if I brought you here and filled the role of queen so no one else could demand it, I would have peace. More than that . . . I would have a friend." He dropped his head, staring down at his hands. "It was unfair to you. And I hated the deception. And I hated that you did not view yourself as my queen. Not really. Please . . . please do not go. Do not leave me."

He finally looked up, his face now as familiar to her as Camelot. And she realized that Camelot was beloved to her. So was Arthur. She did not want to leave. And she did not have it in her to hurt him. She reached out and took his hand.

He squeezed her fingers, trailing his thumb down hers. His hope was almost palpable. Guinevere smiled, wiping at her face. She had not meant to let the tears escape. "I like it here."

His face relaxed. His strong features held tension well, but when it was gone, the boy he had so recently been was revealed. His shoulders slouched, the sharp lines of his tunic suddenly a bit softer, too big for an unkingly posture. Something in her released, too. Arthur still wanted her. He still needed her. It was not the way she had been led to believe, but with nothing else in her future claiming her, she would cling to it.

It broke her heart, though. She had become someone new for him, but even those deceptions were lies. How could she explain to him how lost she was, still, without hurting him? How being his friend, even being his wife, was not enough to make her feel real?

She could not tell him. Maybe someday, when she had grown into whoever she would be next. Until then, she would stay. Because it was easy. Because it was safe. And because she wanted to be needed. Arthur needed a friend. She would be that friend.

How often had she wondered what life would be like if she could simply be his queen, or even just a girl? Now she had that, and she did not know what to do with it. But she would try.

"Do you want to know a secret?" she asked.

"Yes."

Guinevere grinned wickedly. "Sir Bors did not kill the dragon."

"*What?*"

Guinevere told Arthur the story. She left out how wrong it had felt to push out real memories in favor of false. How she had wanted to wash herself as she had filled Sir Bors's clothes with rocks and then thrown them in the stream. She did not tell him how she had understood the dragon, how the weight and melancholy of loss clung to her still.

Instead, she gave the dragon words. Made the narrative funny, herself the hero. It sounded like a children's story. Gone was the infinite sadness of the ending of great things. In its place, a knight, a dragon, and a clever maiden.

Arthur leaned back, laughing. His face was bathed in golden light by the lowering sun. She wanted to trace his profile, to rest her fingers on his throat and feel the way his laughter moved through it.

She understood why everyone loved Arthur. Why they looked to him. Why they always wanted more from him. How could they not?

How could she not?

They walked for hours. She told him the truth of the boar attack, how Lancelot had saved her, Rhoslyn's village removed the poison, and then she and Lancelot went on their ill-fated visit to Merlin. But she did not tell him Lancelot's secret. She had promised not to. Though she suspected Arthur would still let Lancelot compete in the tournament, she could not risk taking away that opportunity. Besides, it was not her secret to reveal.

"Why do you think the boar and the spider went after me? Do you think it was the Lady of the Lake? The wolves in the forest, too, attacked me over anyone else."

Arthur frowned. "It does not seem like her magic. But it could be. Or it could be just the lingering remnants we are stamping out. They could not come for me, so they chose you. To be safe, we should keep you out of wild areas."

Another loss. Guinevere changed the subject rather than dwell on it. "How are the border issues?"

"Maleagant is nibbling away to the northeast. I am afraid he is making deals with the Picts. Trading away rights he does not have."

"Why not stop him?"

"If I go against him and he has made treaties with the Picts, they are obligated to come to his aid. Right now he is a nuisance, not a threat. But that could change at any moment."

Arthur paused to run his fingers fondly along the image of a wolf carved into the stone. The exterior of the castle was covered with such details. Wolves, trees, dragons. Deer and fish and flowers. Whoever had dug the castle free from the mountain had not stopped there. They had spent an equal amount of time making it wondrous. Guinevere wanted to go up to the alcove, but that was Mordred's private spot, and she was loath to take Arthur there. She felt it would be betraying Mordred.

Arthur dropped his hand from the wall, staring down at it as it clenched into a fist. "I should have known better than to ever trust a man who fought at Uther Pendragon's side. No one but the most brutal, the most cruel, could have kept a place there. Maleagant saw us as lords of the land, not stewards. If the people were ours, every-thing they had—everything they were—was ours, as well. There was a settlement on the far borders of Camelot. Small. Unimpor-tant. He took—" Arthur stopped, rubbing his face. Guinevere rec-ognized a memory that did not want to be looked at. She expected him to turn away, as she always did from those types of memories. Instead, he opened his eyes and lifted his chin. "He took two of their daughters. Agnes and Alba. And when he was finished, he discarded them."

Arthur shook his head. "I would have executed him. But accord-ing to my own laws, I needed proof. And Maleagant was so feared, no one would offer any. It was two peasant girls' word against a knight of the king. Elaine begged for mercy on her brother's behalf. And I listened. I sent her away, and I let him go. He took those most loyal to him. I did not expect him to find hold in a kingdom so quickly. But fear and violence are powerful weapons; people are so accustomed to them that they respond instantly. Camelot is a work in progress. It will be years—decades—before I can shape it to what I hope it will be. Burning down villages, slaughtering their lord, and declaring yourself the new king? That takes very little time."

Guinevere shuddered, remembering the way Maleagant had watched her. She could not pull a clear picture of him up in her mind because of the dimness of her vision that night. She was grate-ful for it, now.

Arthur's problems were very big indeed. There was no knot to fix this. "What can I do?" she asked.

He took her arm and led her through a door back into the castle. "The problems of my borders are my own. You are doing enough simply by being here."

"I want to help, though. I *need* to."

"You are helping. If you could—" Arthur paused. They were outside her door. He looked at it, at the wall, at anything but her. "If you could be my queen, that would be enough. You did not have a real choice before. I am giving you that choice now. Will you? Still be my queen?"

Guinevere's heart raced. It felt like a far more intimate question than their wedding vows had been. Then, they had known she was not his queen. Not really. What was he asking now?

"I will," she said, feeling as tender and hopeful as a spring bud.

Arthur's face broke into a smile. "I—"

"Uncle king," Mordred said, standing politely several feet away. "The Pictish envoy is here. And the stewards have questions about the tournament."

Arthur turned toward Mordred. It felt colder when his eyes were directed elsewhere. "Good. Good. Actually, Guinevere should be involved in the planning. Will you take her with you to the stewards, Mordred? I trust her to take care of this on my behalf. It is an excellent queenly duty." He beamed at her, then strode away.

That had not been *quite* the duty she had wondered if he was asking her to participate in.

Determined to make an effort, she fetched Brangien. They met with the stewards to discuss seating, flag colors, how many would be at the feast and where to put them, whether food and wine should be provided for the common spectators, and a hundred other decisions too small for a king but right for a queen.

Mordred leaned by the door, yawning exaggeratedly whenever she caught his eye. After several hours, with only a fraction of the plans settled and a meeting scheduled for the next morning as well, Guinevere was released. Mordred walked her to the dining hall. She looked hopefully for Arthur, but he was not there. Unless it was a scheduled feast, attendance at meals was unpredictable. The knights with wives ate with their families. Those who were single were usually found at mealtimes, but not always.

Guinevere and Brangien sat next to Arthur's seat. Guinevere waited for him join them, but by the time she finished her meal, his seat remained vacant. She realized she had hoped that their tenuous new understanding would mean more time together. But while it changed things for her, Arthur still had to be king every waking moment. She sighed, picking at the stitching on her pale pink dress.

"Do two such fair ladies have plans for the evening?" Mordred spun his knife on the table. "Perhaps a lively discussion of what color our queen will wear so as best to stand out at the tournament?"

Guinevere made a face. She could not help it. The idea of spending any more time on the logistics of the tournament was sour in her belly. She wanted to help Arthur, but she had lost being a magical protector for *this*?

Mordred laughed. "Good. Come with me. We are going to a play."

"A play?" Brangien repeated, her expression dubious.

"You enjoy watching men pretend to be at war in the arena, but not actors pretending to be in love? Surely we have enough of war in reality. Why play at it in all our free time? Come. Let us celebrate the wonders of humanity."

Guinevere looked at Brangien. Brangien wrinkled her nose, then shrugged in agreement. "I do not actually want to talk about the tournament any more tonight."

Mordred clapped his hands together, rubbing them excitedly.

"Excellent. You have not seen the majesty of mankind until you have seen Godric the Fair compare his mistress's charms to the variety and quality of winds he releases from his—well. I do not want to spoil it."

Both horrified and intrigued, Guinevere could not say no.

They walked back as twilight lingered and the bells chided them to hurry home.

Guinevere wiped away a tear, her stomach sore from so much laughter. "That was the worst thing I have ever seen in my life," she said.

"It truly was." Mordred danced in front of them, moving backward to face them. "It truly was. I have lived nineteen years and could live one hundred more and see nothing worse. Are you not delighted?"

"I am."

Brangien huffed, but she had laughed harder than any of them when Godric the Fair had mistaken his horse for his betrothed and made amorous advances. The theater was in the lowest part of the city. It was not nearly as nice as the arena, but it was just as packed. If tournaments made the heart race and the blood boil, plays made the heart dance and the tears flow.

"Thank you," Guinevere said. "I think that was precisely what we needed."

Mordred bowed, sweeping his arm out. "I am the queen's most humble and devoted servant."

Brangien scoffed. "You are as humble as Godric's poetry was lovely."

Mordred staggered. "You wound me, fair Brangien. Now hurry along, or we will be picked up by the watch and forced to spend the evening in a cell so we cannot commit any mischief." He raised an eyebrow, indicating that he was not opposed to mischief of any kind, then turned his back to them and continued stepping merrily toward the castle.

"You seem to have softened toward Mordred," Guinevere said, watching his lithe form. He was lean, slender and almost delicate. A reed to Arthur's oak tree. But he was lovely, and he moved with surprising grace. She remembered how he had swung his sword as though dancing with it. And she remembered the spark when his hand had touched hers.

She had been very careful not to touch his hand since.

Brangien nodded. "When I ran from the trees, certain the boar was still behind us and we were about to be killed, he was the first to me. I screamed that you were still in the woods and he did not hesitate. He ran straight in. He did not even have his sword. What he thought he would have done had he found the boar, I do not know. But his willingness spoke volumes. I might have misjudged him." She paused. "Slightly. And I only said *might*."

Guinevere had, too. She had thought him her enemy. But really, he loved Arthur as well as or better than anyone. She suspected he watched her so closely because he was the only other person who knew Arthur's history with Elaine. He did not want Arthur hurt again. They were united in that.

And he had understood why she healed Sir Tristan. He knew they could not have magic within the walls, but he was not so rigid as to betray her actions in the wild.

When they entered the castle, Guinevere felt settled. Something that might grow to happiness had taken seed in her chest. This was a life. A real one. Not the one she had dreamed of, or thought she had, but one that she could fit into in time. Mordred bade them goodnight and she returned to her rooms with Brangien.

Together, they knotted the hairs for Brangien to visit Isolde in her dreams. Brangien thought it a sacrifice that Guinevere was giving up her own dreams night after night, but Guinevere did not want to dream. There was nothing for her to hope to see. And if Brangien and Isolde could only be together when sleeping, Guinevere would make it happen. At least her magic could accomplish this one thing.

Guinevere curled up into her own bed. She toyed with Merlin's hairs, still wrapped around her finger beneath a silver ring. She could visit him the way Brangien visited Isolde. But she was still so angry with how he had misled her, and that he had chosen to let himself be trapped. How could a wizard so wise be so foolish?

She closed her eyes, grateful that she would see nothing.

CHAPTER TWENTY-ONE

Though Camelot had been buzzing with anticipation for two solid weeks, the tournament seemed to get no closer. Lancelot stayed out of the city—to protect her identity, Guinevere suspected, though in armor and with her voice lowered, Lancelot was not obviously female. But it frustrated those who wanted to have Lancelot in their homes and manors for meals, or to watch the patchwork knight train.

Finally, the night before the tournament arrived. No one was happier than Guinevere that the day was at last upon them. Not only because she hoped her friend would succeed. Or because she anticipated the excitement of watching.

No, mostly because it meant she would never again have to adjust seating plans twenty-two separate times to accommodate all the ladies and their knights and cousins and friends while keeping in mind who was feuding with whom, who hated whom, who would be terribly hurt if they were not in the front, and who needed to be reminded that they did not have the right to demand a place closest to the king and queen. She would rather have done battle on the field than battle over the seating arrangements.

But everything was as settled as it was going to be.

Guinevere wanted nothing more than to sleep until it was time to leave. But with Brangien far away in her Isolde dreams, Guinevere found sleep eluded her. She paced. She could not help glancing at Brangien's face, jealous not of the slumber, but of the company Brangien kept there. Guinevere was itching on the inside. Like she had been trapped beneath a layer of ice all winter and could sense the coming of spring thaw.

She wanted out.

She wanted a release.

She *wanted*.

She used the secret passageway to knock on Arthur's door and then enter his room, but he was not there. She went back to her own rooms, disappointed. She did not know what she would have done if he had been there, but she hated being denied the surprise of finding out.

There was an unexpected knock at her door; she opened it eagerly. There was no one in the hall. Puzzled, she closed the door. Then she heard the knock again.

It was at her window.

Which was in the middle of a wall high up on the side of the castle, with no walkway outside it. She rushed to the glass with a candle and peered out to see a face staring back at her. She barely muffled her scream, dropping the candle.

"Sorry!" a voice shouted, muted by the glass.

"Lancelot?" Guinevere could not believe it. She grabbed a cloak and wrapped it around herself. Then she snuck out the nearest door and leaned over the walkway. Lancelot still clung to the side of the castle, hanging by only her fingertips and boots.

"What are you doing?" Guinevere hissed.

With more ease than Guinevere navigated a flat walkway,

Lancelot climbed over to her, jumping the last several feet and land-ing as light as a cat.

"I could not sleep," Lancelot said, sounding sheepish. "I am sorry. This was presumptuous of me."

Guinevere laughed. "No, it was madness, not presumption. How do you do that?"

Lancelot shrugged. She twisted her toes against the walkway, staring bashfully down. "I am nervous. For tomorrow."

"Me, too." Guinevere led them around a curve to a more shel-tered portion of the walkway, then sat, pulling her cloak around her. She felt suddenly shy. Both because she was in a nightdress, and because when she had last been with Lancelot, it had been a time filled with mortal peril and intense distress. Now, cocooned by the summer night, changed by what she knew of herself, she was not sure what to say. "How have you been?"

"I have not encountered a single possessed boar, demon spider, or vengeful water spirit. The forest is quite dull without you there."

Guinevere laughed, leaning back. Lancelot copied her posture.

When Lancelot spoke again, the playfulness had left her voice. "I am terrified."

"Of what?"

"Of tomorrow. If I fail, then it is over. My dream is dead. I have nothing to build a future around. And if I succeed . . . I step past everything I have known into everything I have wanted. I feel like I am clinging to the side of a cliff in the dark, about to drop, and I do not know whether I will survive the fall."

Guinevere understood. More than Lancelot could ever know. Except she had been walking confidently in one direction only to find herself stepping off an unseen cliff. In a way she felt as though she were still falling. Where would she land?

"Why do you want this so badly?" Guinevere asked.

Lancelot looked down over sleeping Camelot. "I grew up under Uther Pendragon's rule. My father died, forced to serve in his army. And my mother— I am not sure what happened to her. It is probably a kindness that I do not know. I was orphaned. Alone. No family, no future. So I swore that I would become the warrior I needed to be in order to kill Uther Pendragon. I trained without pause. I stole food, clothing, worked in fields as a boy, whatever I had to do to survive. And then King Arthur killed Pendragon before I could. At first I was angry. But I saw what King Arthur brought. And I realized my plan was as small and selfish as I had been. I wanted to kill Pendragon to make myself feel better. King Arthur killed him to make the whole world better. And so I decided that instead of becoming the warrior who would kill a tyrant, I would become the knight who would defend a king. I believe in King Arthur. I believe in his story. And I want nothing more than to be part of it."

Guinevere nodded. She understood this, too. Arthur was building something new. Something good. Something truly noble. And it drew those who could find that nowhere else. That was why most of his knights came. They could not find the justice and fairness they longed to defend in their own countries.

Arthur was like a flame in the night. A burning brand. Even those like Rhoslyn who did not fit here did not begrudge him his light.

Lancelot was ready to devote her entire life to Arthur, just like so many others. Guinevere envied Lancelot her certainty, her determination to become the thing that she knew she should be. Lancelot was *born* to be a knight.

Guinevere was not born to be a queen. Would she land safely, filling this role? Would the fall kill her? Or would she continue falling, forever?

"Thank you," Lancelot said. "For everything. I hope the next time we meet in the castle, I will belong here."

"You already do." Impulsively, Guinevere leaned over and kissed Lancelot's cheek. "For luck," she said, smiling.

Lancelot put a hand against where Guinevere's lips had been. Grinning, she stood, bowed, and then climbed straight down the side of the castle. Guinevere stayed outside long after, watching and waiting. She could not say for what.

In the morning, Guinevere sent Brangien ahead to the field to see to any last-minute needs. Being without Brangien also meant she could take the secret tunnel with Arthur.

When a light knock sounded on her door, she hurried to it, happy with anticipation. She had barely seen Arthur since their talk in which he asked if she would be his queen. His days started before the sun was up and ended long after it had set—when he slept in the castle at all. But at least today she would get to be at his side the whole time. And she wanted to be with him when he saw how hard she had worked, how well the tournament had come together. It was proof to them both that she could do something other than minor magic. That she could be something like a real queen.

She opened the door, beaming—

Mordred's face was already set in an apologetic grimace. She tried not to let her own face fall, but she could not help glancing past him, searching for Arthur.

"He is not here." Mordred looked at the floor, his thick, dark lashes covering his eyes. "There was a matter in one of the villages he had to see to before the tournament. He asked if I would escort you."

"I am sorry you have to."

"I am not sorry at all."

Guinevere did not know how to meet the challenge in his

expression. Her stomach fluttered and she pulled up her hood, her fingers betraying her with the slightest tremble.

She wanted one relationship—just one—that was simple. She envied Brangien her Isolde. Sometimes she wondered what they did in their dreams. Sometimes she wondered what she could do in a dream, if her actions did not matter. And she did not know whom she wanted in that dream with her as fire burned low and deep within her. Sometimes it was Arthur. And sometimes . . .

She shrugged deeper into her hood to avoid looking at Mordred.

She wore darkest blue today, but, in a nod to the patchwork knight, had asked Brangien to make her dress out of different squares of blue cloth. The result was playful, shimmering. Rather more like water than she had intended, but she did her best to ignore that. Her hood was deep green and only went around her shoulders, unattached to a cloak because the day was so fine. Her hair trailed beneath it, long and laced with delicate braids.

"The queen looks radiant," Mordred said. He offered his arm. She set her hand carefully and lightly on his elbow.

"The king's nephew looks quite dashing as well." She bit her rebellious tongue for letting that out.

Mordred tensed beneath her hand, then relaxed. She did not look over to see his expression. But his steps were light. Happy, even.

"It is not easy," he said as they walked through the tunnel. "I understand."

"What is not easy?"

"Loving King Arthur."

Guinevere did not like this topic. She wanted to move away from it, and picked up her pace accordingly. "I am his wife. It is easy."

"We are alone. We need not pretend. I have seen the way you watch him, waiting for him to notice you. I know that feeling. Arthur—" He paused. Guinevere wondered how long Mordred had known Arthur. How it must have been to serve an uncle younger than yourself, knowing he existed because of violence done to your grandmother. Knowing your own mother had tried to kill him. Mordred had *chosen* Arthur. Chosen to believe in him and his cause. Just as Guinevere had. "He is like the sun. When he is focused on you, everything is bright and warm. Everything is possible. But the problem with knowing the warmth of the sun is how keenly you feel its absence when it shines elsewhere. And a king must always shine elsewhere."

Guinevere did not answer. But Mordred was right. She wanted more of Arthur than she had. Than she could have.

"You deserve to live in the sun, Guinevere," Mordred whispered, holding the sheet of vines so that Guinevere had to brush past him as she exited the cave into the sunlight. In spite of the heat and the brilliance, she shivered. Part of her longed to go back into the cave. With Mordred. To trust him with all the wild and lonely things of her heart. Her honesty would hurt Arthur. She suspected—knew, even—that Mordred would not be hurt. He would understand.

She hurried toward the horses instead. There was so much chaos and activity at the stable that no one even noticed the queen arriving with only one knight. By the time she was on a horse, she was surrounded by all the knights who would compete that day, and many others besides. Sir Tristan. Sir Bors. Sir Percival. Sir Gawain and Sir George, with whom she had never spoken, and several minor knights who were not in Arthur's inner circle. Also, carefully avoided, Sir Ector and Sir Kay. Mordred subtly shifted his horse so that he blocked her from view.

"Thank you," she whispered.

He winked. She looked quickly away.

The knights were in high form, their energy contagious. Lancelot would fight five of them before facing Arthur. They boasted and bragged, their excitement growing as they rode closer to the tournament field. This was Lancelot's day, certainly, but it was also their day to perform in front of all of Camelot.

More than just Camelot. Visitors had been streaming in for days, camping around the arena. Word had spread and the entire field was teeming with activity. Rickety booths and stands had been set up in every available space, selling food, drink, colorful strips of cloth representing favorite knights—Guinevere saw many patchwork bands tied to arms—and anything else that an enterprising person thought they could make someone pay for.

The knights rode directly through the crowd to shouting and cheers so loud Guinevere would have covered her ears had it not been rude to do so. Rows of rough-hewn benches had been placed all around the combat field. Flags snapped from poles. Jugglers and minstrels strolled around the edges, entertaining the crowds while they waited for the fights to begin. Beyond them, there were tents in case any of the ladies wished to retire, or the knights needed to pray or change clothing or otherwise prepare themselves. In the prime position overlooking the field was a raised platform, enclosed like a box with rippling yellow and green fabric walls. It held a large, high-backed wooden chair, a smaller one next to it, and several rows of benches for the ladies and for knights who would not be fighting.

Arthur's chair was empty. Guinevere rode to the stand, then dismounted. Servants led the horses away. It was amazing how many things she had to worry about—her clothing, her wrists, her ankles, her hair, whom she spoke to and for how long, so on and so forth—and yet how few things like choosing what to wear, paying for it, taking care of her own things, preparing her own food. She had not even held a coin since coming to Camelot.

She stepped up and into the shade of the royal box. She paused in front of her chair, waving. The crowd shouted in appreciation. Then she sat, and waited.

For Arthur.

She was still not very good at it. The thought of how much time in her future she would have to practice waiting for him made the brilliant day dimmer.

Brangien arrived at her side with a goblet of spiced wine. Spices were so expensive, they rarely used them. But tournaments were even more special than weddings, apparently. Guinevere sipped, idly watching the performers as they made the rounds. Dindrane joined them. She shifted in agitation.

"Is something the matter?" Guinevere asked.

"Yes. No. I am not certain. Time will tell." Dindrane put her hands to her mouth, grimacing. Then she smoothed her lovely brown hair and set her hands primly in her lap. "I gave my handkerchief to Sir Bors. I am not certain he even knew what to do with it. But if he wears it today, I think—I hope—perhaps I will be courted soon."

Guinevere wanted to laugh at the idea of clever, waspish Dindrane with that bull of a man. But he was good, at heart. Arthur trusted him. And he was older. He had had a wife many years ago, but she died in childbirth. He had a son still, and did not need an heir. Dindrane *would* be a good match for him.

Guinevere smiled and reached across Brangien to pat Dindrane's knee. "I hope he wears it. And if he does not, he is a fool."

"Oh, I have no doubt he is a fool. But I dearly hope he will be *my* fool."

Finally, Guinevere had permission to laugh. She settled into her chair, still searching the crowds, looking for something. She caught herself. Looking for *someone*. Where was Arthur?

There was a ripple, a drop of commotion that spread outward

from the crowd across the field. People jostled, exclaiming, push-ing to get a better view. A child sitting on his father's shoulders was lifted free and put on a different set of shoulders. Arthur emerged from among the crowd. No horseback entry for him. No immedi-ate delivery to the separate, raised platform. Arthur galloped across the field, the child shrieking in delight as the king pretended to be a horse. Then, swinging the boy back to his waiting parents, Arthur raised his arms in greeting.

If Guinevere thought the shouting for the knights had been too loud, this was deafening. Arthur ran the full length of the field, pass-ing each section so everyone would have a chance to see him. To be near him. Hands reached out and he held his own to them, brushing them as he passed.

He leapt onto the platform. Guinevere beamed at him, but he did not even look at her before turning around to face his people.

"Camelot!" The roar swelled and then faded to a low hum. "My people! Friends from near and far! Today is a wonderful day. Is it not?" Another tremendous roar. Arthur held up his hands and it quieted. "Today represents the very heart of Camelot. Today rep-resents everything we work for. Today, we recognize valor. We test bravery. And we reward strength and goodness! Today, the brave war-rior who saved my queen—" The crowd roared in approval again, and Arthur let them carry on. Guinevere raised her hand, acknowledging the people, though her only role in this narrative had been to be in peril and be saved. When they stopped cheering, Arthur continued. "He saved my queen from a rampaging beast. But you already know him from the arena. You have long watched the patchwork knight. Today, you meet Lancelot!"

On cue, Lancelot rode into the center of the field. Guinevere was delighted to see she rode her own horse. The loyal, smart blind steed that had taken such good care of them. Lancelot turned toward their box and inclined her head. Guinevere felt a thrill of nerves for her.

The crowd was wild, collectively giddy to finally see the patch-work knight face real opponents. Until now, Lancelot had faced only other aspirants. Today, Lancelot faced knights. Arthur's knights. And there was no one better.

In truth, Lancelot faced more than just the knights. But all an aspirant had to do at tournament was defeat at least three knights in combat chosen by those knights. Nowhere was it noted that the aspirant had to be a man.

Arthur sat. He turned toward Guinevere, beaming, his excite-ment contagious. "I have something for you," he said. He reached into a pouch at his side and pulled free a chain of silver, green jewels delicately clasped and streaming from it.

Brangien bit her lip in delight. "You cannot wear jewels in your hair anymore," she whispered, "but you can wear them on your head."

"For a queen," Arthur said, his voice pitching soft. "For *my* queen." He tried to fasten the piece around her head, fumbling it. Brangien huffed and stood, taking over. Guinevere felt the cool touch of the silver against her forehead, the subtle weight of the green stones. It was not a crown or a circlet, but it was a reminder. Of who she was. Of who Arthur had chosen her to be.

"I had it made the same day as your iron threads," he added. When she, as a witch, had been commissioning pieces to protect him, he had been commissioning them to make her a queen. "Beau-tiful," he said, and she did not know if he meant the jewelry or her.

"Thank you." She lifted a finger to run along the lifeless stones. She had meant to bind magic to her jewels. But they bound her to Arthur now, which was a sort of magic. She hoped.

The crowd roared, drawing Arthur and Guinevere's attention

from each other. Sir Tristan, newest of Arthur's knights, was first and had walked onto the field. A year ago he had been there as aspirant. He had bested only four of the five knights, so he had never faced Arthur. None of the knights chosen through combat had.

"Who defeated Sir Tristan when it was his tournament?" Guinevere asked.

"Mordred," Brangien said, watching nervously as Sir Tristan looked over the wall of weapons. He was on foot, which meant he had chosen horseless combat.

"Mordred?" Guinevere asked.

"You wound me," a voice murmured over her shoulder. She turned to find him with a smile on his face, his eyelids half closed. He was not watching the fight preparations. His posture said he was at ease, uninterested. "I am always the last defense between anyone and the king. And no one has ever gotten to him through me."

"Which is why I asked Mordred not to compete today," Arthur said. He was only half-listening to them. "I *want* to fight Lancelot."

All conversation was ended with the roar of the crowd. Sir Tristan let Lancelot choose first from the offerings of blunted swords. The rules were simple: First combatant to strike what would be a killing blow was the winner.

But *simple* did not mean *safe*. Dindrane nervously listed every injury that had happened during a tournament. Broken ribs were most common. Concussions. Broken arms. During the first tournament, where multiple aspirants had been trying to gain knighthood, one unfortunate combatant never woke up after a vicious blow to his head.

Tournaments were not games. They determined the fate of a potential knight. And knights determined the fate of Camelot.

Sir Tristan and Lancelot circled each other. Sir Tristan wore his own leather armor, plated with sections of metal, and a metal helmet that left his face clear. Lancelot, much to the delight of the crowd, was fighting with mask in place.

"Do you think he is ugly?" Dindrane speculated as the fighters circled each other. Sir Tristan feinted, the blow easily knocked aside by Lancelot.

Guinevere's heart raced as she watched, hoping. She liked Sir Tristan, but she very much wanted him to lose. "Lancelot is not ugly at all."

"And how would you know?"

Guinevere froze. She was not supposed to have seen Lancelot's face. As though any person would be wandering the forest in full armor and mask, all by themselves, on the off chance they would have the opportunity to rescue the queen from a wild boar.

She was saved from answering by the first true clash of swords. It was as though a spell had been broken. Fighting began in earnest. Terrible blows were blocked with such force Guinevere shuddered, imagining how even that would hurt. Every strike Sir Tristan tried was blocked. Lancelot used the space better than Tristan, dancing around him. Sir Tristan was fast and strong. But Lancelot was faster. Lancelot leaned back, dodging a huge swing and dropping to her knees. She slammed her sword upward, stopping just shy of Sir Tristan's chin. Had their blades been sharp, she could have run a real sword through his head. Even a fake sword would have injured him at that angle.

Sir Tristan backed up and dropped his sword. He bowed. Lancelot stood, returning the bow. Then she went perfectly still, waiting the next challenge.

"That was risky," Mordred said. His face was between Guinevere's chair and Arthur's.

"How so?"

"If Sir Tristan had been faster, Lancelot would have been on his knees and unable to dodge quickly again. Lancelot risked everything, counting on an opening that was not guaranteed."

"But it worked."

Arthur was clapping fiercely. "Yes. Lancelot is smart, but more than that, he is brave. He holds nothing back. But he also showed tremendous restraint. Most knights would have delivered an actual blow as a matter of pride. I am very glad he did not injure Sir Tristan."

Brangien was slumped in her chair, exhausted from the strain of watching Sir Tristan fight. Guinevere patted her friend's leg. "He is fine. He fought very well."

Brangien nodded, wiping at her forehead with a handkerchief. "The patchwork knight is special. Sir Tristan could beat any of the other knights."

"*Almost* any of the other knights," Mordred corrected. Guinevere turned. He was examining his fingernails.

Brangien rolled her eyes, ignoring him.

"What weapon would you choose?" Guinevere asked. "Perhaps a vicious deer?"

Mordred's eyes lit up with delight. "Oh, Lancelot is not nearly so fearsome as the Green Knight. For him, rabbits would do."

"Sir George is next," Arthur said, ignoring them. His leg bounced impatiently. Guinevere suspected if he could, he would leap out of the stand and take Sir George's turn.

Sir George rode on a proud black stallion, signaling a fight on horseback. He lifted his spear and shield to the crowd. They cheered. Lancelot retrieved her horse. The crowd tittered nervously. There were groans scattered throughout. No one wanted to see the tournament ended so soon.

"Is his horse blind?" Arthur was horrified. "I would have given him one of mine!" He slumped back in his chair. "I cannot believe Sir George is going to win because of a better horse." Arthur took a long drink of his ale, scowling as he watched Sir George prance around the field. Lancelot was still and straight on her horse. She accepted the shield and spear handed to her.

"Next time we will make rules about horses as well as weapons. I should have checked." With a sigh, Arthur leaned forward again, resigned.

Sir George roared, galloping straight for Lancelot. He lifted his spear in the air—and with no discernable direction from her rider, Lancelot's horse danced to the side. Sir George galloped straight past. He pulled on the reins, forcing his horse to a quick stop. But it was too late. Lancelot's mount had turned as she moved, putting her rider in perfect position. Lancelot's spear sailed through the air, thunking painfully against the center of Sir George's back before falling to the ground.

Sir George's curse echoed across the field.

The crowd erupted again. Everyone stood. Most people used the benches not for sitting, but to stand on. Arthur himself had burst from his seat, clapping and whistling.

"Did you see that?" he asked, his eyes shining.

Guinevere laughed, nodding, but Arthur turned around. He had been asking Mordred. "On a blind horse!"

"He let go of his spear. If he had missed, he would have been unarmed."

"I know!" Arthur crowed his response as praise in response to Mordred's criticism. He grabbed Guinevere's hand and kissed it, then threw his own in the air, unable to contain himself. He did not sit again, but stood leaning out across the beam that fenced in the stand.

Sir Gawain also chose horses, but this time with swords. Guinevere marveled with the rest of them at the superb control Lancelot had of her horse. They were as one creature. Because the horse

could not see, she did not spook or react to things on her own. She
followed Lancelot's guidance with perfect accuracy. This fight lasted
longer, repeated blows being exchanged, but it ended the same way:
Lancelot triumphant.

Lancelot *triumphant*. She had done it. Guinevere felt tears in her
own eyes as she clapped so hard her hands—particularly her still-
healing burned one—stung.

"Three!" Arthur shouted. "Three!" He raised his fingers in the air
and the crowd roared. Lancelot had just guaranteed herself a place
among Arthur's knights. Rather than raising her arms and exulting,
Lancelot bowed her head. Then she turned her horse toward the
king's stand and put a fist against her chest, bowing even deeper.

But she was not done yet. No knight would quit without going as
far as possible. It was a matter of pride. Sir Percival hurried onto the
field. He, too, had chosen swords. Though he was fresh and Lancelot already three knights deep into a fight, the match was over almost
before it began.

Dindrane snorted. "Oh, Blanchefleur will be so embarrassed."
She said it just loud enough for her sister-in-law, seated behind her,
to hear.

That was four. One remained. Sir Bors strode onto the field,
wisely forgoing horseback combat as well. Dindrane squealed, grabbing Brangien's arm. "Look! Look! On his sleeve!"

A white handkerchief waved like a flag there. Guinevere's friends
had given her so many reasons to be happy this day. Lancelot would
be a knight, and Dindrane had a suitor who, while slightly ridiculous,
would provide her with a happy and comfortable life.

Dindrane, tears in her eyes, turned to Guinevere. "Thank you,"
she said, her voice so low it was hard to hear over the cheering.

"Why are you thanking me? It is Sir Bors who recognizes a prize
when he sees one."

Dindrane shook her head. "No one in the castle paid me any mind until you did. Your kindness has . . ." She stopped, dabbing at her eyes. "Well. You are right. Sir Bors simply had the good sense to snatch me up before someone else did."

Guinevere beamed and leaned across Brangien to embrace Dindrane. Even Brangien laughed and hugged Dindrane as well.

Dindrane screamed Sir Bors's name, her shouts lost in the chorus of *Lancelot* ringing through the air. Sir Bors paced the length of the weapons stand. He had not lived this long by luck. With only one working arm, he was at a disadvantage with any combat that required a shield. And he had seen how fast Lancelot was with a sword. Far older, Sir Bors could not match Lancelot's speed.

But he could best nearly anyone in sheer strength. He picked up a wickedly heavy mace and chain, swinging the weapon experimentally. The crowd hushed. They could see the same strategy at play. Only the strongest could wield that weapon with any dexterity or skill. And no one had ever seen Lancelot use it in the arena.

"Damn," Arthur muttered.

Guinevere's heart fell, too. She had wanted Lancelot to best all five knights. Then not a single one of them could argue against her appointment.

Lancelot picked up the other mace and chain. Where Sir Bors made it look like a child's toy, in Lancelot's grip it became clear how heavy it was. It was a weapon of blunt force, made for smashing through things. Shields. Armor.

Bodies.

It was also difficult to imagine a blow from even a mace *without* sharpened spikes would not do serious damage to the recipient. Guinevere rubbed at the still-healing wound beneath her sleeve. She wanted Lancelot to win every match. And, for the first time, she feared it was impossible.

Sir Bors swung his mace and chain through the air so fast it made a whistling noise. He circled Lancelot, twirling his weapon with ever-increasing speed. Lancelot did not move her feet, keeping the mace ball on the ground.

Sir Bors swung for Lancelot's ribs. Lancelot darted back, the mace squeaking across her armor. The speed and force of the blow carried Sir Bors past Lancelot. Without losing momentum, he spun, following the wickedly heavy ball back around for another blow. Lancelot was ready. She dove and, rather than swinging her mace, kept it anchored to the ground. Lightning fast, she wrapped the chain around Sir Bors's leg.

Sir Bors, his own momentum too much, fell forward to the ground. Lancelot scrambled onto his back, pressing her knee at the base of his spine so he could not rise. Then she dragged her mace up and set it gently at the base of his skull.

"That was cheating!" Dindrane screamed.

Sir Bors was shaking. The crowd quieted. Had he been injured? Lancelot stood, removing pressure. Sir Bors rolled onto his back, and the source of the shaking was revealed. He was laughing.

Tremendous bellows filled the air. He held out his good hand and Lancelot took it, helping him stand. He waggled a finger chidingly at the younger fighter, then took her hand and lifted it in the air.

The crowd went wild. Lancelot had done it. She had bested all five knights.

Arthur cheered loudest of all. He stood on the wooden plank, then jumped onto the field. It was his turn.

And Guinevere did not know who to cheer for anymore.

CHAPTER TWENTY-TWO

Guinevere did not want to watch, and she could not look away.

Arthur walked directly up to Lancelot, clasping her shoulder and leaning close. No one could hear what was said. Guinevere felt a spike of jealousy as blunt as the tournament swords. Not because she knew Lancelot was a woman. But because if Lancelot became a knight, she would know Arthur in a way Guinevere never could. She would probably even see him more than Guinevere did.

And perhaps a *bit* because Lancelot was a woman. What would Arthur think when he found out?

She realized she also liked that she knew Lancelot when no one else did. She would lose that. The closeness, the intimacy of their midnight talk on the walkway, would be gone. Everyone would know Lancelot as she did, and Arthur would know her better, even.

Arthur broke away from Lancelot, drawing Excalibur. The crowd erupted. Guinevere's stomach turned. She clutched at it, suddenly hot and cold at the same time.

"My lady?" Brangien asked.

Guinevere stood, then fell. Brangien knelt at her side. Guinevere's head was swimming. She shivered all over.

"What is it?" Mordred asked, joining Brangien.

"The wine, maybe? The spices?"

"Does she need air?" Dindrane asked.

Mordred put his soft fingers against her cheek. The spark of him reached her, and she grasped hold of it desperately, as though it were a line dropped to her. She felt impossibly far away, trapped somewhere deep inside.

"Guinevere," Mordred whispered. "Guinevere, where are you?"

And then, as fast as it had come on, it passed.

She shuddered, closing her eyes, then opening them with great effort. "I do not know what came over me."

"You swooned," Dindrane said confidently. "Too much excitement. That is why ladies do not fight."

Mordred took her elbow and helped her back into her seat. Brangien gave her a handkerchief. Guinevere pressed it to her face, wishing she were back in the castle, alone. But she was here, and she was the queen. The weight of the jewels against her forehead reminded her. She looked out, worried, but no one was looking at the royal box. Not with Arthur and Lancelot on the field.

Arthur had re-sheathed Excalibur, leaving it against the weapons stand. That damn sword. He was chatting happily with Lancelot, pointing to various weapons like they were choosing fruit from a dish.

Mordred still crouched at Guinevere's side. "Are you sure you are well?"

"Yes, thank you. Too much excitement."

"Hmm." Mordred looked out at the field. "I suppose so. At least they did not choose to battle on boats, right?" He smiled wickedly at her. She scowled, throwing the handkerchief at him. He snatched it out of the air, tucking it into his vest and then disappearing back to his seat.

Guinevere tried to shake off the lingering feelings of dread and emptiness. She felt as though she had not eaten in days. Brangien, ever observant, passed her a bowl of berries and nuts. Guinevere chewed on them nervously.

Arthur picked long swords. It was not a surprising choice. He was good with every weapon, but Excalibur was a long sword. He tossed one to Lancelot, then strode confidently to the center of the field. The crowd hushed in anticipation. In all the tournaments, no one had ever made it to Arthur. Lancelot was the first. And while many of the men of Camelot would be called upon in a war, a majority of the watchers had never seen Arthur fight.

He did not swing his sword as a showman would. Like Lancelot's, his movements were calm, measured. Contained.

Thus it was a shock when he burst forward, impossibly fast, his sword a streak. Lancelot parried the blow, their blades ringing. But Arthur continued pushing forward, forearms out, shoving Lancelot off balance. Lancelot spun, twisting free and swinging her sword. Arthur met the blow, then delivered one, two, three of his own. Lancelot swung her sword as though desperately swatting insects from the air, only just managing to redirect each blow so that it would not hit her. Arthur was giving her no opportunity, no quarter. Lancelot had barely done more than deflect and parry.

"Good!" Arthur shouted as Lancelot dodged another strike. He laughed, his chest heaving. Lancelot swung and Arthur raised his blade to meet hers. He held it there, forcing Lancelot to keep pushing the blow. But Arthur was bigger, his shoulders broader, his arms more powerful. He pushed harder and Lancelot stumbled back, losing her footing for the first time in all the fights. Lancelot fell.

The crowd gasped. But Lancelot kept going, rolling so that her legs flipped up over her head. She landed with her knees on the ground, then jumped to her feet. She had never let go of her sword.

Arthur laughed again, delighted. And then he charged. Now it became apparent Arthur had been holding back. His sword winked and shone, blinding in the sun. Lancelot ducked and weaved, blocked and parried. A particularly brutal blow knocked her once again to her back. Arthur swung his sword, stopping it just shy of her neck.

Her own sword was held straight up, pressed against his belly.

They did not move.

No one made a sound.

And then Arthur threw his sword, shouting in joy. He grabbed Lancelot's hand and hauled her to standing, raising her hand in his own. "Sir Lancelot!" he shouted. "Knight of Camelot!" He embraced Lancelot, clapping her on the back.

After the tournament came the celebration. And if Guinevere thought the tournament had been violent and loud, she had no idea how a celebration with thousands of inebriated and very ecstatic people was.

She clung to Brangien, even the space around the box now filled with revelers in the twilight. Her head rang from the nonstop noise. Everything smelled of ale and wine. Her stomach had not settled from her attack earlier, and neither had her nerves. She wanted to congratulate Arthur, to toast Lancelot, but she had not seen either of them in hours. Dindrane and Sir Bors were standing scandalously close to each other in a dark corner, whispering. Sir Tristan had come to check on Brangien and Guinevere, but had been pulled away by Sir Gawain to find more to drink.

Whoever was supplying the drinks would come away from the tournament a bigger winner than anyone.

"Can we go to the tent?" Guinevere shouted. Brangien nodded. They pushed through the crowds. It was too dark or the people were too drunk to realize they should part for her. The tent, at least, was separated from most of the masses. Guinevere sat gratefully on a cushion. With a buffer between herself and the noise, she felt better already.

"I will go find some food and something to drink. But not spiced wine!" Brangien left Guinevere there with a lamp.

Guinevere lay back on the cushion. She should be happy. Lancelot won. No one could deny her prowess. She would be a knight now. Guinevere could *feel* it. If anyone had discovered Lancelot was a woman, Guinevere was certain she would have heard of it. Better to get Lancelot back to the castle, away from the crowds, and sort it all out there. She was confident Arthur would take Lancelot's side. There was no reason to deny her.

She sighed. It was a good day's work. She had helped more than one friend. Planned a tournament that would be talked about for years. Why was she not happier? She was being queen, like Arthur had suggested. Like Merlin had wanted.

But it was not enough.

Before, she had been sure of her purpose, of her place. Now, she felt like everything she was depended on Arthur. She knew that Camelot would always come first. Must come first.

But what about when *she* needed someone? She tapped her fingers against the cool stones Arthur had given her.

She heard the whisper of the tent flap. "Thank you," she said.

"Do not thank me yet. You have not even looked."

Guinevere sat up, startled, to see Mordred kneeling next to her.

"I thought you were Brangien!"

"Not a lot of people get us confused. I am much handsomer than she. Are you still feeling unwell?" He lifted his hand to feel her forehead. She swatted it away.

"Brangien is coming back with something to eat."

"Is she? Or was she waylaid by Dindrane to get advice on how soon a lady can wed a knight?" Mordred sat back, leaning on his elbows.

"Does Arthur know you are here?"

"Does he know *you* are here?" Mordred had all the confirmation he needed in her expression. His own turned serious. He sat up, leaning toward her. "Guinevere," he said, the lamplight low and flickering in his dark-forest eyes. "My uncle is a good man. But he is not a good husband. And he never will be."

"It is not like that," Guinevere whispered.

Mordred lifted an eyebrow. "What is it like?"

"Like . . . a partnership. But it is not the partnership I thought it would be. And I am trying to discover what I want it to be."

Mordred reached up and ran his fingers along a strand of hair that had escaped her braid. He tucked it behind her ear, his fingers lingering there. She shivered.

"Are you cold?" He leaned closer. His eyes held her there. His eyes that were always watching, always seeing. Mordred always noticed her. Whenever she was in a room, she was the center of it for him. She knew that. Just as she knew she would never be the center of anything for Arthur.

Mordred closed the distance between them, brushing his lips against hers. The same spark she had felt at his hand was there, intensified. She gasped, and he drew her closer, pressing his mouth against hers. His hands were at the small of her back, her hands in his hair. She could taste how much he wanted her, how dark and smoldering his desire.

She had never known what it was to be desired. It was sweeter than damsons, more intoxicating than wine.

He grabbed her arm, sliding his hand along it to move her hand from his hair to somewhere else. But his fingers pressed her wound. The jolt of pain startled her out of the hungry haze she had lost herself to.

She pulled back, putting her free hand to her mouth. She shook her head. "Mordred," she whispered. "We cannot."

The light burning in his eyes slowly dimmed, like that of smothered coals. He hung his head. "Please forgive me. I would *never* hurt Arthur. I would never take something he loves. But, Guinevere . . ." Mordred looked back up, pain and pleading in his face. "He does not love you. I will. I do."

She did not answer. She could not, frozen by her own internal strife. Had she betrayed Arthur? She was not his wife. Not really. And Mordred was right. Arthur did not love her. He had never asked anything more from her than friendship. She was a companion to him, but never a priority.

To Camelot, she was queen. In her heart, she was a girl who had lost her way. She was Guinevere, and she was not even Guinevere. She was without a purpose. And she desperately wanted to be wanted.

All this time she had thought of what she was denying Arthur by being his wife. Tonight, like a blade to her heart, she felt what *she* was being denied.

Mordred interpreted her silence as a dismissal. He stood. "Forgive me," he whispered again. Then he left the tent.

Guinevere pulled her knees to her chin, wrapping her arms around them. How had things gotten this complicated? Fighting the Dark Queen herself seemed simpler than trying to be a queen who was not a queen, to a king who did not need her.

How much had Arthur sacrificed over his lifetime, how much of what he wanted to do and who he wanted to be had he given up to keep Camelot safe?

Would she do the same? Would she live forever next to him, beside him, waiting for him to need her?

No. It was not enough. She would go out, find Arthur, and kiss him. Surely it would feel like it had with Mordred. Everything felt new and different, everything had changed. She would use a kiss to change everything with Arthur now.

But what if she kissed him and nothing changed? What then? That unspoken space between them was safe. If she closed it, they could never go back.

Lancelot was brave enough to jump from her cliff, not knowing what bottom would greet her. Guinevere would be, too.

There was a footstep outside the tent. She looked up, hastily wiping the tears from her face. She did not know who she hoped to see. Brangien? Lancelot? Arthur?

Mordred?

The man who came through wore a black cloak, a black hood, and carried a large burlap sack. She had never seen him before.

"Good night, little queen," he said.

She did not have time to scream before everything went black.

Men are hungry fools.

If they cannot eat it, wear it, or use it, they kill it anyway. They spread like fungus through the heart of the world. Lift a rock, and there: man.

But that is not quite right. At least fungus grows and feeds other life. Men only devour. Everywhere they reshape in their image. To their needs. Forests are felled for their homes. Fields are forced to bear their fruits, their grains, their decisions. A fungus only kills. Men change. Men demand order from nature. Men melt rocks and form metal, biting iron to pierce and slay. What can she do against such poison?

She has been pushed back too far, for too long. But Merlin, the great defender of men, is sealed away. Chaos curls from Camelot. Where there is chaos, there are cracks. And where there are cracks, secret things can grow.

She has been waiting for all the seeds she planted to sprout and grow, tangle, choke out what the usurper king has tried to claim. She needs the queen-not-queen and her heart of chaos.

But someone else has taken her.

CHAPTER TWENTY-THREE

Guinevere awoke to the sound of rushing water. It was worse than the splitting ache of her head.

"Good morning, my lady," a man said.

Guinevere sat up, then regretted it as the world spun. "I am not your lady," she said.

"But you are Arthur's lady, which suits my needs much better."

Holding a hand to her head, she blinked until the room came into focus. It was a dank hovel. A few holes near the ceiling let in knives of sunlight that did little to cut through the gloom of the small building. The walls were rock, roughly fitted together. The floor was packed dirt, scattered with chunks that had fallen from the walls. She could see no water, but she could hear it, all around.

The man stood over her, hands clasped behind his back. He was shorter than Arthur, but broader. There was a thick power to him, the brutal strength of the boar. His hair, which had been braided back from his face, was traced through with streaks of gray like iron. His eyes were neither cruel nor kind. They betrayed no emotion, no expression. It was somehow more chilling that way. She wondered if they moved when he laughed. She suspected they did not.

Maleagant, revealed. She had liked him better blurred. She had liked him better with Arthur at her side.

Guinevere tucked her legs beneath her. Her clothes had not been disturbed, though somewhere her hood and the jewelry Arthur gave her had been lost. Movement caught her eye and she looked behind her to see two other men standing next to a heavy wooden door. The door was the only part of the structure that looked new.

Her voice as dull as the rocks. "Sir Maleagant."

"No screaming or pleading. Good. I like southern ladies. You are always so well-bred. Like dogs, instructed from birth to serve your purpose. To obey your master." He crouched so they were face to face. "I am your master now." He slapped her. The impact snapped her head to the side, setting it ringing again from the blow that had knocked her unconscious in the tent.

She was used to pain, thanks to the demands of magic. This hurt, but it was not unbearable.

He waited until she turned her face back toward him. "I have some questions for you. Answer truthfully."

"I will answer truthfully or not at all," Guinevere said.

"That is good." He slapped her again. This time she fell to the ground. For a breath, she let herself rest against the grit. Then she pushed herself up. She was fiercely glad she was here in the real Guinevere's place, taking this punishment. At least poor, dead Guinevere was not being hurt.

It was not rational. But it gave her something to hold on to. It made her feel stronger than she was.

"You did not ask me a question yet," she said.

"I find it is best to punish dogs before they are disobedient.

Preventative. Here is your question." He leaned closer, studying her face. Then he ran his fingers down one of her now-loose braids. "Does Arthur love you?"

Guinevere could not think of a question she wanted to answer less. It had been the very question she had been about to find the answer to. Before they took her. Now she would never know. "He cares for me."

He raised his hand and she braced herself. Then he nodded. "I believe you. Would Arthur sacrifice Camelot to have you returned safely?"

This was not a difficult question. Arthur would sacrifice anything to keep his people safe. Including her. She knew it was right, that he was king because of it. And she felt equal parts triumph and despair knowing she could not be used against Arthur. For a tiny moment, she let herself wish he loved her so much he would give up everything to save her. And then she let it go. She had once thought she would die for him. She had not intended to prove it to herself so quickly.

"I know he would not," she said.

Maleagant rubbed his jaw. "That is unfortunate. I had hoped a pretty, fragile thing like you would play into his blind need to protect everything. My dear Elaine broke him, I fear." He paused, tilting his head to the side and staring not at her face, but her torso. "Are you with child?"

Her fingers clenched into fists. A blessing to have been Arthur's wife in name only, then. "No."

He sighed. "Just as well. I am not a patient man. I do not have months to spare. Do you see how I have not struck you, even though your answers were not what I was hoping? You told the truth. That is good."

Maleagant sat across from her, leaning back on one arm and narrowing his eyes in thought. "I could sell you to the Picts. They are not as familiar with Arthur's *nobility* as I am. They might think they could trade you for some advantage." He tapped his fingers against his knee. "Or I could offer your death to the Picts in exchange for an alliance. They were not pleased when Arthur did not want any of their daughters. With you gone, he would be open to marriage again. Your father is too far south to cause me problems should I kill you."

She had come to Camelot to protect Arthur. Not only had she failed to do that, but now she would be used against him. The river rushing somewhere outside surrounded her, whispered that she was never meant to be this. That she never could have been this. That she should have let the water claim her long ago.

She did not want to die. If this was a game of constantly moving pieces, she had to convince him that her moves were the better idea. "That is true. And my father has another daughter as well as sons, so it is not a terrible loss. I do not think you risk Arthur starting a war over my death, either. The cost would be too high for him to do it for revenge. But trading me to the Picts is a better option. Trick the Picts into thinking they can bargain with me and get your coin or your land that way. Though you risk their ire in the long run. You will have made enemies of Arthur *and* the Picts."

If she was sent to the Picts, there would be journeys. Anything could happen then. She was not powerless, but she could not risk magic here. Not yet. If she revealed what she could do and got away, or was traded back to Camelot, word would spread. Arthur himself would suffer the backlash of being a Christian king married to a witch, which would serve Maleagant far better than her death.

She brushed the floor grit from her cheek and smoothed her skirts. "I *do* think I have more value alive than dead, but I assume most people feel the same about themselves."

"Are you certain Arthur does not love you? You are a very unusual queen. I was wrong about how they bred them in the south."

She stared at him and did not look away. She was supposed to be a queen. The chosen partner of Arthur, the greatest king alive. She could be strong. "Hold me at ransom for less than Camelot. Borderland. Horses. Silver. You may be able to wring those from Arthur."

"Your problem is in thinking I will be happy with anything less than Camelot."

Guinevere closed her eyes, then nodded. Magic, then. She tried to call the fire. She had only ever called it for cleansing, did not know if she could use it for anything else, did not even know if she wanted to. Could she use it as a weapon? Could she turn magic from something to protect those she loved, to something that devoured?

Merlin would do it.

She shuddered at the thought. It felt like a line that, once crossed, could not be undone. Far worse than the memory magic. But her dilemma was unnecessary. Surrounded by water, filled with fear, she did not have the strength to create so much as a spark. She had nothing to feed the fire. It failed her.

"One last question. Are you listening?"

Guinevere opened her eyes.

"My man has been at the Camelot docks for weeks now. And he had something interesting to report. On several occasions, the queen did not get into a boat, and yet arrived on the lakeshore. And many times the queen did not get off at the docks—the only docks in Camelot—and yet arrived at the castle! Are you magic?"

Guinevere laughed. She could not help it.

Fortunately, he took it as an answer in the negative. "Which means there is another way into the castle. Tell me what it is, and I will let you stay queen of Camelot." He paused, and his dead-eyed smile extended her an offer along with his hand. "Under the new king."

She imagined Maleagant creeping through the tunnel. Entering the castle before anyone knew he was there. Defeating Camelot from its heart. None of her silly door protections could keep his evil out. They protected Arthur from magic, but Maleagant was the most human of men. Magic darker and more powerful than any she could wield would need to be used against a man of such vicious, indomitable will.

She could be satisfied knowing he would never best Arthur. She would *have* to be satisfied with it, because she feared her life held very little more for her. This, then, was how she protected Arthur. Not with magic, not with power. With silence.

"I will never tell you," she said.

"So there is a way." He smiled, and finally it touched his eyes. The lines there told a history of violence, of cruelty. And promised a future of it, as well. He stood, grabbing her arm and yanking her up so roughly she yelped in pain. The men at the door opened it and Maleagant pushed her over the threshold. She teetered on the rocks there, staring down at a grasping, rushing river.

She scrambled to get back into the building, but Maleagant was behind her. He held both her arms, lifting her in front of himself. She dangled, helpless, over the river.

"Do you know what else my man at the docks told me? The pretty young queen of Camelot is *terrified* of water. Everyone remarked on it. You should do better to hide the ways to break you." He shook her and she screamed, staring down.

The water. Dark and eternal, over her head. The light, so far above, but she could not get to it, could not—

And it was cold—

And there was a voice, calling to her—
Calling—
Not Guinevere. Calling who?
Maleagant shook her again. She held his hands, trying to grasp his wrists.

Mordred was a spark.

Arthur was steady, warm power.

Maleagant was *cold.*

She went limp, closing her eyes. She had always known water would be her death. Had she known what was coming for Merlin? Had it been coming for her, too? She wondered if Merlin himself had put the terror of water into her, the same way he had pushed in the knot magic. To keep her away from the Lady's grasp. To keep her safe.

It had failed.

She tried to think of Arthur. Brangien, who would mourn her, but who would always have Isolde now. She would miss Lancelot's knighting. And Mordred. Had he come back to find her missing? She remembered the spark, the fire of his lips on hers. It was dark and wild, unsteady, hungry. She caught onto it, pulling it deep inside, where Maleagant could not touch it. Arthur's strength, too, she tried to recall. To hold against herself like a shield.

"A channel island," Maleagant shouted, his mouth against her ear. "Surrounded by a rushing river. No prison could hold you better." He let her hang for an eternity of seconds, and then at last pulled her back in. He threw her into the building. She landed hard on the floor, crawling toward the center. As far from the river as possible.

"Next time, I take you swimming. Think on that, and decide whether the king who does not love you enough to save you is worth it." Maleagant turned to his men. "No one touches her," he said. "Yet." Then he left.

She curled around herself, shivering. She could find a way. She would have to. No one was coming for her.

One of her fingers pulsed, swollen from how hard her heart was beating. Swollen around the three hairs from Merlin's beard. She unwound them, then pretended to fidget with her own hair, knotting her dreams to his. She was finally desperate enough to seek him out.

"Please," she whispered, closing her eyes and trying to find sleep—her only hope of help.

She walks backward through time.

She trails through her stay in Camelot. Sees each person there who grew to mean so much to her. Slowly releases them to be strangers of her future. Dindrane. Lancelot. The knights. Arthur, bright, shining pillar, fades last. Once more he is simply a name, a belief, a hope. She walks back through the forest that ate the village. Back to her first meeting with the knights, with Brangien. With Mordred. The nuns and the convent pass in the blink of an eye, hardly worth noting.

She steps past her time as Guinevere, and finds . . .

Arthur has not faded. Not truly. If she is in her own past, how does Arthur stay so bright, like a beacon? Why does she feel such hope—such sadness?

Where is she?

She has left Guinevere behind to find Merlin. And instead, besides the dream of Arthur, she finds . . .

Nothing.

She stands suspended in a field of black, beneath a starless sky.

Everything around her shimmers, moving gently and slowly. Her hair drifts around her. Blue amidst the black.

"What are you doing here?" Merlin asks.

She turns toward his voice. He struggles to get to her, moving his arms in a strange sweeping motion. His beard flows behind him, trailing like a silver river.

"You should not be here," he says.

She knows. Now that she is here, she does not like it. She came here for a reason. She expected the cottage. The lessons. She had planned to interrupt Merlin during a lesson, to talk to him in her memories. But she cannot find them. Once she stepped out of the convent, this was all that remained.

"I need your help," she says. Her voice is layered, infinite. Sweet and cold.

"You have to go back! She is not watching me because she thinks me trapped, asleep. But if she senses you here, you are in terrible danger."

"I think I may already be in terrible danger." She lifts her hand. Her arms are bare, pale and glowing. Something is missing. Her wound. The skin. Lancelot. The tournament. Arthur. She grasps hold of the threads of her future, clinging. "I have been kidnapped. Merlin, I have been kidnapped!" She laughs, delighted to finally remember. "I need help."

"I cannot help you in the affairs of man. You know that."

She shakes her head. "I know nothing. You told me lies. Arthur did not need me."

"He does need you. More than either of you knows. He is the bridge; you must guard his way safely over the blackest waters. Be the queen. Fight as a queen, not as a witch. And remember, whatever else happens, that you chose this."

She lowers her arms, and the future falls away again. "I am in a

bad place. I do not want to go back to it. I will stay here." She pushes
Guinevere away from herself. "It is too hard, Merlin. Merlin." She tilts
her head, trying to find more truth here in the darkness. "Why do I not
remember my mother? Why could I not find my way to my past?"

The world trembles. The blackness around them ripples, then swirls.
She has left all fear in her future. She is not afraid. She feels . . . infinite.

But Merlin is afraid. "Go now, foolish creature! Do not look for me
again, or she will find you!" He pushes against her forehead, sending
her spinning head over feet, circling and circling as the black field blurs
and then—

CHAPTER TWENTY-FOUR

Guinevere gasped. Waves of dizziness crashed over her, as though she were still spinning in that black place, pushed away by Merlin. Instead, she was on a dirt floor in a damp, dimly lit stone room.

She reached up to her hair, terrified. Merlin's beard hairs dissolved like starlight in the morning, fading as she watched. He had taken even that away from her. She was alone.

A guard spat noisily behind her. She was not alone.

Guinevere stood, brushing off her dress. She faced two guards. They sat on the floor, playing a game with several round, flat stones and a few small sticks. Interrupted, they turned and watched her with hooded eyes. They wore leather tunics as tightly as they wore meanness. They had wrapped themselves in it, armed with hatred and suspicion.

"If you help me, King Arthur will reward you."

"Way I see it," one of them said, wiping his nose along his arm, "King Arthur not likely to be king much longer, yeah? And even if he is, I trust Sir Maleagant's sword more than I trust your king's kindness."

"Give Sir Maleagant what he wants," the other guard said,

shrugging impassively. "It is not going to go easy for you, whatever you do. But he likes the young ones. If you do what he wants, he might be nice to you. For a while."

"For a while," Guinevere repeated, letting the words trail away. "How can you serve a man like this?"

"Liked you better when you were asleep." The first guard returned to the game, picking up the stones and sticks. "Never seen anyone sleep as long as you."

"Downright lazy," the second guard said. "Been sleeping nearly a day. Is that what fine ladies do?"

The first guard snorted. "You would not know a fine lady if she bit you in the ass."

"I have *paid* fine ladies to bite me in the ass."

They both laughed. The game was resumed, Guinevere summarily dismissed.

She had thought Sir Ector and Sir Kay unpleasant. She repented of that now, having seen what truly unpleasant men were like when given perfect freedom to be as wretched as their basest nature. After sliding down against the wall farthest from them, she sat still and quiet, considering it best not to draw their attention again.

How had she been asleep for a day? It had gained her nothing, and cost her precious time. She did not know when Maleagant would return. And she did not know what she would do when he did. Merlin's abandonment stabbed her anew. Not even in dreams would he speak with her, help her. Guinevere closed her eyes, trying to remember the black place.

Merlin had been afraid that she would be found. By whom? All that time in Camelot she had feared attack. The only threat was the one who had come for Merlin. The one he had sent her away from.

The Lady of the Lake.

Guinevere's fear of water, her refusal to so much as touch it—if her hands could sense the truth, perhaps they were saving her from what she would find there. An elemental force of unfathomable age and power, determined to end her in order to punish Merlin. She would have been used against Merlin the same way she was now being used against Arthur.

She would not stand for it. Merlin was gone. But she would not give Maleagant what he wanted. She would take the option away from him entirely. At the next opportunity, she would fling herself into the river. Let the Lady take her. Let herself be unmade. It was the least Merlin deserved. If he could see past and future, he had seen this and he had not helped her.

And this way she could never be made to hurt Arthur.

"What are you smiling about?" the first guard said. "You look creepy. Stop it."

"Can I go for a walk about the island?"

"Yes, of course. I have packed a picnic! And would her ladyship like a bit of music to accompany her stroll?" The second guard doffed his hat, bowing. They did not move away from the door.

"I need to relieve myself."

The guard kicked a chipped and cracked wooden bowl toward her. It skittered across the floor. "Have at it, queen."

That ploy had failed. And, worse, she really did need to relieve herself. "You cannot expect me to do it with you in here."

He pitched his voice high in imitation of her. "Then you cannot expect to do it at all."

She picked up the bowl, retreating to the farthest edge of the building. It was heavily shadowed. The men snickered. But the second guard turned his back on her. "Come on, Ranulf," he said. "Let the poor lost queen take her piss."

The first guard, Ranulf, shrugged. "Speaking of, I need to go water the river before Sir Maleagant comes back and I have to stand at attention while he tortures his new pet." He stepped out the door, closing it behind him.

Guinevere had never peed so fast in her life. She squatted over the bowl, keeping her skirts pooled around her. When she was finished, she stood and refastened her drawers with her back to the door.

There was a shout from outside, and a large splash.

"What is—" the second guard said, standing.

Guinevere picked up the bowl and rushed across the room, throwing its contents in his face. He shouted in disgust, spluttering. She opened the door, ready to leap into the river—

And jumped right into the arms of a knight.

Beyond the edge of the island, Ranulf was being carried swiftly away, facedown. She only caught a glimpse of him as Lancelot swung her around and set her safely against the wall of the house. The second guard roared out of the door, squinting and half blind. Lancelot grabbed him around the waist, using his own momentum to toss him off the rocks and into the river.

He struggled to keep his head above the water. Lancelot picked up a large rock and threw with expert aim. It smashed into the guard's head and his eyes rolled back. He dropped beneath the current and disappeared.

"When will Maleagant return?" Lancelot asked.

Guinevere shook her head, pressing her back as hard as she could against the stone building. She had been prepared to leap into the river to her death. But she did not want to anymore. Not for anything. "Soon, I think."

"Come on." Lancelot edged around the building, away from her.

"I cannot swim!" Guinevere cried.

"I will help you."

"No, you do not understand!" Guinevere hurried past the door to catch up to Lancelot. She followed the knight around to find that Maleagant had tricked her, at least in part. Because the other side of the channel was broader, but sparkling and calm in the late afternoon light. It looked easy to cross.

Still a river, though.

"It came only to my thighs," Lancelot said. "You will be fine. Hurry." She stepped into the water and Guinevere shouted.

"No! I have—I have to tell you the truth, Lancelot." Guinevere hung her head, staring at the rocks that separated her from the water.

"That Merlin is your father?"

Guinevere looked up, shocked. It felt wrong, coming from Lancelot's mouth, just as it had from Arthur's. "Did Arthur tell you?"

Lancelot shook her head. "It did not take much to put it together. After all, how would a princess from the southern lands know where Merlin lived in the woods? Why would she be so desperate to save him? Everyone knows what Merlin was to Arthur. Of course Arthur would choose his first protector's daughter as a wife." Lancelot smiled, but her smile was bitter. Her hazel eyes narrowed and hardened. "I even understand the deception. Sometimes we have to hide from what others see in order to be what we know we are."

There was a reason Lancelot's hand in hers that day in the forest had felt right. Had felt true. Lancelot understood her.

"I cannot touch the water," Guinevere said. "If I do, I fear the Lady of the Lake will find me, too, and take me like she did Merlin."

"Then why were you going to throw yourself in?"

"Maleagant would have used me against Arthur. I am not certain I could keep Arthur's secrets forever against a man like that." Guinevere shuddered.

Lancelot waded to her. She turned and leaned so her back was presented to Guinevere. "Come on."

"What?"

"On my back. Hold tight. Wrap your legs around my waist. We are crossing this river."

Guinevere climbed on as instructed. She crossed her arms around Lancelot's collarbones. Lancelot adjusted her legs, hiking her up a bit. Guinevere's skirts were around her waist, her ankles white and forbidden in the sunlight.

Lancelot held Guinevere's thighs in place on either side, and then stepped into the river.

Guinevere closed her eyes, but now that she knew what the fear was—that it was real, not simply foolishness—she found it easier. The shame of her terror of water had been almost as great as the fear, and without shame, the fear could be faced.

Lancelot's pace was careful, each foot firmly planted before the next was lifted. It seemed to take a lifetime. As the water got higher and higher along Lancelot's legs, Guinevere feared Lancelot had judged the depth wrong.

"A little looser, my lady," Lancelot said, her voice strained. Guinevere loosened her arms, which had drifted up around Lancelot's throat.

"Sorry!"

"Almost there. Close your eyes. That will make it easier."

Again Guinevere did as instructed.

Lancelot spoke lightly, her low, rich voice carefully even. "How did you get past the guard inside? Did you use magic?"

Guinevere snorted, lowering her face to Lancelot's shoulder and resting it there. "You do not want to know."

"Well, now I want to know more than I have ever wanted to know anything."

"I will spare you the details," Guinevere said, breathing deeply of the leather scent of Lancelot's patchwork armor. It cut through the river smell, helping Guinevere combat the fear. "But it involved a full chamber pot."

Lancelot laughed, her hands tightening around Guinevere's thighs. "You did not!"

"He deserved worse. I only wish it had been Maleagant's face on the receiving end."

"I am proud of you. A true warrior can make a weapon of anything. I will have to remember that trick."

"I doubt a bowl of piss will be one of the weapon offerings at the next tournament."

Lancelot made a low noise in her throat. The splashing stopped. Lancelot went several steps farther, then tilted her head so it bumped against Guinevere's. "My lady, your noble steed has seen you safely to land." She crouched low and Guinevere dropped to the blessedly dry ground. "And now we run."

Guinevere and her knight raced across a broad, rocky plain. Scrubby bushes dotted the landscape but offered little cover. "My horse is there, at the tree line. I could not risk riding her closer. It took me ages to cross this plain, darting from rock to rock. I need not have bothered. They never once came out to keep watch. Maleagant did not fear discovery."

"How did Arthur know where to look?" Guinevere gasped around a stitch in her side. She had not eaten since the tournament. And she did not know how much time had passed, having spent so much of it unconscious. But she kept pace with Lancelot. She could be tired when they were safe.

"Brangien, your maid, found you. I am unclear on the specifics. Something with sewing and your hair left behind in her combs."

Dear Brangien! Guinevere's heart swelled with gratitude. Brangien had risked banishment in order to find Guinevere. Maleagant had not counted on the strength and cunning of women. "And Arthur sent his best knight."

Lancelot pointed. "We can talk when we are on my horse riding away from here."

They made it to the trees without any sign of pursuit. Lancelot whistled a high, sharp note. Her horse meandered up amiably. Lancelot boosted Guinevere, then mounted in front of her.

"How far are we from Camelot?" Guinevere asked, her arms loosely circling Lancelot's waist.

"About a day. But we are not going back to Camelot."

"Where are we going?"

"North, toward the Pictish lands. Maleagant will expect us to race back to Camelot. He will try to cut us off. I hope that by going north and then angling down, we can avoid him. I love this horse with all my soul, but carrying two riders that long, she could not outpace a hunting party."

"Will Arthur meet us there?"

Lancelot drew a deep breath, then released it slowly. "Arthur did not send me. Brangien said he was not going to send anyone. Not until he knew more. Most moves against Maleagant end in war, and the king will not enter into a war unless he absolutely must. I never thought I would miss his father, but . . . sometimes war cannot be avoided."

Guinevere wilted. It was what she had expected, of course. But knowing it for fact hurt. Some part of her had still hoped that Arthur would risk everything for her, and that hope had seemingly been answered when Lancelot appeared. "Arthur was right to choose as he did," she said softly. "He must weigh the good of all his people. I cannot tip that balance. I should not. But how did you come? You cannot disobey Arthur. You are a knight now."

Lancelot's voice grew unexpectedly gruff, as though she were trying to speak around something lodged in her throat. "I am not."

"*What?*"

"I would advise against shouting."

Guinevere hissed instead of shouting. "What do you mean, you
are not a knight? Did they delay the ceremony because of my dis-
appearance?"

"My gender was discovered just as your kidnapping was. I was
dismissed without conversation."

"But Arthur must—"

"King Arthur had more on his mind than one woman's problems."

"Than two women's problems," Guinevere said, her voice soft
and sad. "When we get back, I will demand you receive your place
among his knights. You earned it. You are better than any of them."

"That does not matter now. Your safety is all that matters." Lancelot paused. "King Arthur was wrong not to choose you." Her voice
was as fierce as her sword. The horse reacted to her tone, moving
faster. Lancelot stroked the mare's neck, patting it and slowing back
down. "My queen, you saw me as who I am from the first. I will fight
for you for the rest of my life. It is the only honor I could ask."

Guinevere's arms tightened around her knight's waist. She lowered her heavy head, resting her cheek against Lancelot's strong
upper back. "Thank you," she whispered.

"Thank me when we are safe." Lancelot rode warily, her head
turning constantly from side to side, searching for threats.

Guinevere did not want to distract her, but she had more questions. "How did you find Brangien?"

"She went to Mordred, and he found me."

"Mordred! Brangien went to Mordred?" Mordred ran the courts.
It was one thing for him to excuse Guinevere's magic in the forest

when he thought she did not do any more. Another entirely to excuse magic done in the heart of Camelot. "If word of this gets out, she will be banished."

"Mordred is certainly not going to tell. This was all his idea. He argued with the king, demanding they ride to find you. When the king said they would wait, Mordred stormed out. Brangien had already searched for you and she took the information to him. It was Mordred who recognized the place Brangien described. He is waiting for us at a camp. We thought it best if only one of us scouted. Easier to hide. And if it had come to it, I could have dressed in women's clothes and tried to get to you that way. Though I am glad it did not. I feel false in women's clothing. It is like wearing a lie."

The forest grew thicker and Lancelot had to focus on guiding her horse. Guinevere kept watch, every rustling bird or skittering animal making her certain they were being followed.

As twilight faded into evening, Lancelot directed the horse into a series of low hills, covered with trees.

Galloping hooves pounded toward them. Lancelot drew her sword.

"Lancelot!" Mordred called. He pulled his horse to a stop with skidding hooves. A second horse was being led by a rope behind the first. "You are being followed. I counted six men. I suspect Maleagant is with them. Quick, Guinevere." He paused, closing his eyes as relief washed over his face. "Guinevere," he said again, his voice as soft as a prayer. Then he was back to the urgent business of keeping them all alive. He tugged on the reins of the second horse to bring it closer. Guinevere slid down and then climbed onto the fresh steed.

"Are you hurt?" Mordred moved closer and searched her face in the fading light.

"Nothing that will not heal. Lancelot was just in time. You both were. Thank you."

"Can your horse ride in the dark?" Mordred asked the knight.

Lancelot laughed. "My horse always rides in the dark."

"Then we need to move. I will not let that monster have her again."

"We cannot outpace him," Lancelot shouted as they pushed their horses to a gallop. It was not as fast as the horses could go, but still faster than was safe in the low light of the moon.

"I know!" Mordred gripped his reins in anger.

"We could pick a place to fight before he can gather more men. If we surprise them, we may stand a chance." Lancelot sounded calm. Resigned. Guinevere did not like their odds. And she would be useless. Unable to help as she watched two people she cared about fight—and probably die—for her.

Mordred shook his head. "Maleagant has powerful allies, and his soldiers are loyal. If Arthur's nephew kills him, it would mean war just as surely as if Arthur had."

"But he will never stop." Guinevere had seen it. Had felt it. War with Maleagant was as unavoidable as the night closing in on them. "He wants Camelot. He will not give up, even if we make it back. He is a threat to the kingdom. To Arthur."

Mordred slowed his horse. Hers followed suit. "I . . . might have an idea. But it is a very bad idea."

Lancelot circled them as she watched for threats. "I am open to any idea that does not end with us dead, Guinevere recaptured, or Camelot overthrown."

Mordred continued. "We need Maleagant dead. That much we can agree on."

Guinevere nodded grimly.

"What if *we* did not kill him? What if his death could never be traced back to Arthur?"

Guinevere considered it. Perhaps they could ride into Pictish territory. And somehow convince the Picts to kill Maleagant? Unlikely. And even if they managed to kill Maleagant's entire party, there was no reason the story would not spread. "If people know Maleagant took me, any assassin's blade or arrow will be attributed to Arthur."

"We will not use blade or arrow," Mordred said. "We will use a weapon that King Arthur, defeater of the Dark Queen, banisher of magic, would never use."

Guinevere went cold. "What weapon?"

"We wake the trees."

Guinevere shook her head. "We cannot! Merlin put them to sleep for a reason."

"Obviously we will not wake *all* the trees. There is a copse a few miles from here. Ancient. Powerful. I knew the channel island Brangien described because I fought here at Arthur's side. If anyone knows what threats sleep in the roots and the soil, it is I."

"Even if we thought it wise, it cannot be done."

"It can," Mordred said. "I know what you are, Guinevere."

She tried to protest, but he lifted a hand. "You do not have to explain yourself to me. Not all of us agreed with the need to banish Merlin." He leaned toward her, so near their legs brushed as their horses avoided bumping into each other. Intensity rolled off him. "We lure Maleagant into the trees. You wake them. They kill him. And then we put them back to sleep. Maleagant is dead, Camelot is safe, *Arthur* is safe. Please. I do not know how I can save everyone otherwise. And I cannot lose him. Or you."

Merlin had told her Arthur needed her. He had advised her to fight as a queen. But that meant not being able to fight at all in this terrible world of men. Mordred was right. This was a task only she could do. She was terrified, not only of the tyrant chasing them, but of the forest awaiting them. There were so many ways for this to go wrong. Iron was finite, contained. It held magic without expanding. Her knots bound whatever they did, and every knot eventually frayed, the magic fading. But the trees . . . they were living. And trying to control living things never went as planned.

She had to try. And Mordred, who had always seen her, believed in her.

"To the trees," she said.

CHAPTER TWENTY-FIVE

Guinevere knelt at the base of a towering oak. It was gnarled and twisting, with deep score marks running up and down the trunk like scars. She put her hands on them and then pulled back from the pain. They *were* scars. This tree had done battle.

Lancelot waited on her horse in the center of the perfectly circular meadow that Mordred had brought them to. Guinevere had heard of fairy circles, formed by mushrooms or stones. But this one was fenced in by the trees. As though something had stood in the center and pushed back all around itself. Or rather, himself.

Merlin.

Guinevere longed to speak with him. To ask him what he had done, how he had done it, how she should do it. But he had refused to tell her any truths.

Mordred's hand came down lightly on her shoulder. "Can you do it?"

"I have no idea what I am doing. Or supposed to do. I have never done this type of magic. I know tricks, Mordred. Cleansing. Knotting. This is so much more."

"*You* are so much more." He knelt at her side. He put his hand over hers, the spark and flame inside leaping back to life. Then he put her hand on the tree. With Mordred's heat guiding her, she moved past the bark, past the skin and surface of the tree. Down to its heart, its roots, pulsing back up to the leaves. A hundred years of sun and rain, storm and snow, growth and hibernation, rushed through her. She could feel it as though sunshine powered her own pulse. And somewhere, deep within, she could feel the spirit of the tree itself.

"I feel it," she whispered. "But I do not know how to wake it."

"Perhaps a shock. Fire?"

It had been fire that had driven them to sleep. And she could not wield fire like a weapon as Merlin had. She was more likely to set the whole forest on fire than to wake anything up, and then she and her friends would die from flames and smoke if Maleagant did not get to them first.

"I can see riders!" Lancelot shouted. "They are minutes away. If you are going to do something, do it soon. Mordred, I suggest you mount and be ready to fight."

"Iron!" Guinevere said. "Iron is a cold shock to every magical thing."

Mordred shook his head. "I could not get my sword to the heart of this tree in time."

What else was magic hungry for? Something that fed magic and had iron, as well. Something that would go to the roots, feeding the entire tree. Waking it.

"Give me a knife." She held out her hand.

"What for?"

"Just give it to me!"

Mordred pulled one from a sheath at his belt. Guinevere held it in her palm. She closed her eyes. If this did not work, nothing would. She would have to watch Mordred and Lancelot die. Arthur would fall.

She drew the knife across her palm. Mordred hissed in surprise, but she did not open her eyes or look at him. She held her hand over the roots, letting the blood drop there. Letting it seep into the ground. Then she placed her palm over the trunk, tracing one of the simplest knots she knew. *Wake.* And then one of the most terrible knots she knew, that she had used on the bird to find Merlin.

Obey.

A breeze rustled through the tree, the leaves shivering. But the meadow was perfectly still. There *was* no breeze. The tree shuddered again. Guinevere still had her palm against it, letting the blood run freely down it.

The leaves quivered and then stopped.

It had not worked. She opened her eyes, devastated.

And then, beneath her hand, she felt the tree wake. She had felt trees before, felt their agitated sleep. Felt the leaf of the forest that had claimed the village, felt the sense of teeth. It was nothing compared to what she felt in this tree.

Triumph. And a joy more terrible than any fear she had ever known.

She stumbled back, falling, then scrambled to her feet. "This was a mistake. We have to go. Lancelot!"

Still her hand was bleeding. Watering the meadow. A root snaked around her feet, pulling her to the ground. She screamed as it dragged her across the dirt. A branch reached down, and the leaves, each as thin as a razor, lashed at her arms. Her sleeves were sliced apart, a hundred cuts.

"Guinevere!" Lancelot shouted. The tree pulled Guinevere higher, holding her out over the meadow as her blood dripped, dripped, dripped into the ground. To the roots of all the other trees.

And in the center of the meadow, something else was moving. Writhing beneath the dirt. Waking up.

"Command them!" Mordred shouted. "Make them obey! Maleagant is almost here."

Guinevere could not. She had done the wrong thing. In the dream, Merlin had told her to fight as a queen—it was the only thing he had told her—and she had tried to fight as a wizard. A tree swung, a low branch swiping viciously at Lancelot. Lancelot ducked under it, falling off her horse. She whistled sharply, and her horse ran from the meadow.

Mordred ran to his horse, but the trees got there first. Roots engulfed his horse and slowly pulled it down. There was a crunching noise, a breaking and tearing sound. The horse screamed once—Guinevere felt the scream throughout her body—and then it went silent.

A root snaked around Mordred's leg. "Command them!" he shouted.

"Stop!" Guinevere screamed. She was still bleeding, still held suspended. But the trees stopped. Waiting. Listening. She held Maleagant in her mind. Added five more men to him. She put iron in their hands, fire in their eyes. Then she put her hand against the tree branch that held her. She fed the trees the image of Maleagant, of his men. She fed them fire and iron and death.

The trees shivered. The thing beneath her still writhed, like a beast circling unseen beneath the water, sending out ripples. But it had not surfaced yet.

The root around Mordred's ankle slipped back beneath the dirt. He ran to a spot beneath Guinevere. Lancelot joined him.

Release me, she told the trees. They pushed back. They were hungry. They were thirsty. And she was something *new*. She could not explain the excitement the trees felt. Recognition, but also delight. They were trees. They had experienced men, they had known blood in the battles with Arthur. Why were they feeling this?

Stop, she demanded. She let sparks dance up and down her arms. The tree recoiled, dropping her. Mordred caught her—staggering, but breaking her fall.

They froze as Maleagant's cold voice cut through the night. "What did you do to her?" he asked. He clicked his tongue disapprovingly. "I do not like my things being damaged." He loomed in the deeper dark at the edge of the trees, using them as cover. His men circled. Guinevere could hear them, but no one had stepped into the meadow yet.

Mordred set Guinevere down and stood in front of her. Lancelot shifted to protect both of them. "Run," she said, her sword raised.

Maleagant laughed. "These are your champions? A woman and Arthur's eel? You were right. The king does not love you, does he? I would send better after one of my dogs." He paused. "Actually, my *dogs* are better than your protectors." He lifted a hand and five riders burst into the meadow.

Their horses reared back, eyes rolling, nostrils flared with panic. Three of the men fell to the ground. The fourth held on. The horse fell instead, rolling over and crushing its rider before struggling to its feet and galloping into the forest after the other horses.

Lancelot spun among them, killing two of the men before they could get to their feet. Mordred did not leave Guinevere's side. She did not want to look away from Lancelot, did not want to look away from Maleagant. So much was happening.

But she was staring down.

Beneath her feet, hundreds of jet-black beetles burst through the ground like fountains, spreading and scurrying away. Dusty black moths flew up, circling her, disappearing into the night air.

"To me!" Maleagant said. The two men remaining—two had been killed by Lancelot, one by the horse—backed up to Maleagant. As soon as the horses had gone mad, Maleagant had dismounted from his own. He had not set foot on the moonlit meadow. His men stood in front of him, swords raised. Maleagant stared at the quivering trees around them. "You are in trouble, little queen. You do not know what you have awoken here. I can get you out safely."

Guinevere looked up from the horrors rising from the ground.

Maleagant held out his hand. "Walk to me very slowly and be grateful I am feeling merciful."

The same darkness pouring out of the earth seemed to rise within her, filling her. The trees had tasted her—but she had tasted them, too. The ancient rage, sleeping for so long, was awake now. Beetles crawled up her, down her arms, over her face. The thing beneath her was almost free. She should be frightened.

She was only angry.

"*I am not* feeling merciful." She closed her eyes and released the trees.

The man to Maleagant's right stumbled, falling against a trunk. Branches grew in an instant, pulling him tighter and tighter. In a handful of seconds, the tree enveloped him, growing around him as it would a rock. But men are so much softer than rocks. So much more breakable. His screaming did not last long.

The man to Maleagant's left met the same fate as Mordred's horse. He was pulled down to the earth, embraced by roots. Squeezed and wrung out and broken down. The trees were not wasteful. They would use all of him.

Maleagant slashed at a branch that reached for him, cutting into it with his iron sword. The trees shuddered, drawing closer, leaning over the meadow. Maleagant ran toward Guinevere. He did not run fast enough.

Vines wound up his legs. He hacked at them, but each vine cut was replaced with three more. They thickened, keeping the shape of him, curling over him. They wrapped up to his arm, tightening, until he dropped his sword. He was rooted to the ground now, held fast. He fixed his eyes on Guinevere. The moon had broken free from the clouds, bathing them all in pale white light.

"You are worse than I," he said, his jaw clenched, neck straining as he resisted the vines twining lovingly around it. "I sought to rule men. What you have awoken will destroy them."

Guinevere felt nothing. Had she been afraid of something so fragile? So temporary? She imagined the vines entering his mouth, stopping his tongue. They did. They covered everything but his face. It tipped up toward the moon, his cold, dead eyes finally settling on an emotion:

Agony.

Maleagant was dead.

"Guinevere," Lancelot said. The fear in her voice pierced Guinevere. She shuddered, suddenly aware of the beetles that crawled all over her. Aware of what she had done, and how little she had felt about it.

She brushed the beetles away frantically. The trees shuddered, creaking and groaning as they stretched. "Enough," Guinevere said. "We are finished."

But the trees were not. And neither was the darkness. A hand burst free from the ground, grabbing Guinevere's ankle. Lancelot cut the hand off. It scurried along the ground like a spider, away into the forest.

"What have we done?" Guinevere covered her mouth as she watched another hand form where the first had been cut off. Something was down there. And it was breaking free.

Mordred knelt next to the hand. "Guinevere, I am so pleased to introduce you to the Dark Queen. My grandmother."

CHAPTER TWENTY-SIX

The hand extended, growing to an arm. A hint of a shoulder. The first curve of what would be a head.

"No," Guinevere said, backing away in horror.

Mordred released the hand. He stood. "Arthur destroyed her body, but not before she sent her soul down into the ground. She needed help in order to take a new form. I could not manage it; neither could my mother. This is miraculous. Thank you."

"You tricked me!"

He recoiled as though offended. "I *tricked* you? I am the only person who has not lied to you. I am the only person who came for you."

Lancelot gripped her sword hilt, stepping in front of Guinevere. "No," she said. "You are not."

"How?" Guinevere could not believe it, could not understand. "You are not fairy. You touch iron."

Mordred twirled his sword elegantly through the air, the metal singing. "My mother is Morgan le Fay, Arthur's sister. But my father was the Green Knight. I am from both worlds. Iron bites, but it does not kill. And I am accustomed to pain." He lifted an eyebrow in wry judgment. "That was a nasty trick you did on the doors at the castle. Like ants swarming over my body every time I went in or out."

Guinevere forced her eyes away from the monstrosity in the ground to meet Mordred's gaze. "You cannot let her rise. You know what it would mean."

"A return to nature. A return to the wild magic at the heart of this country. Do you know who carved Camelot out of the mountain? It was not men. Men came in and claimed it, because that is what men do." He held his sword and stared at how it caught the moonlight. "I do not want men to die. But they need to be reminded of their place in the world. Someone has to stop them claiming everything worth having. Stop them claiming *everyone* worth having." He held out a hand toward Guinevere. "You do not belong in Camelot. You belong here, with the dark and wondrous magic that runs beneath and through everything. You know it is true. Tell me you have not tasted it. Tell me you have not felt it when we touch."

Guinevere could not tell him that. Not honestly. And the loss of magic *did* hurt her. She felt it everywhere: in the weight of Camelot's stone, the expectations of its people, the relentless erosion of time. She had let it form her into someone she did not know. She had let men claim her.

"What is your true name?" Mordred asked. "You are not a princess from the south."

She opened her mouth, and—

She did not have it. It had been lost to her. All she was now was Guinevere. She could feel the future coming, creeping ever closer, where even the little magic she knotted into the world around herself would cease working. Wonder would sleep so deeply that it could not be called. Just like Merlin, sealed away in a cave. He had let it happen. He had left Camelot. Given it to Arthur. Given the world to men.

Guinevere understood Mordred's anger. She felt it herself. Everything wondrous was being unmade, and it was terrible beyond comprehension. But wonder, too, was terrible. The meadow around her was proof enough of that. Was not Maleagant's death terrible and wonderful in equal measure? The tree's sentience beautiful and abominable? Trees, magic, wildness were the uncaring opposite of justice. Men demanded justice, revenge. They banished magic to make way for rules and laws. In nature, only power mattered. And she had power.

It had crawled all over her as she watched a man die.

She could not give herself to this darkness. Not after everything she had felt and seen and done as Guinevere. Because of Camelot, she knew what it was to have a family among friends. To love Arthur. To believe in him. She had from the moment they met. There was loss in what Arthur was doing, yes. She finally understood what the dragon had shown her. The kinship it had seen in her. The choice ahead of her.

Merlin had already made the choice to remove himself from the clash of old and new. To let his own magic be sealed away.

To die, even.

Guinevere was not ready to die. And she was not ready to let darkness return without a fight, either.

"We have to stop her from rising," she said, turning to Lancelot. "I might be able to. But only if you keep Mordred busy."

Lancelot's grin was a grim sight in the moonlight. "I can do that."

Mordred sighed. "Do you know why I never lose?" He rushed forward, kicking Lancelot viciously in the stomach. He swept his sword through the air. Lancelot barely managed to block it with her own. Mordred pushed, shoving her away. "Every moment touching iron, every breath taken in well-ordered, stifling Camelot, every *minute* near Arthur and Excalibur is pain. My life is pain. What have I to fear from you?" He ducked a swing from Lancelot and kicked out at her knee.

Guinevere hurried to where the Dark Queen was emerging. She had two hands now, shoulders, a spine. Her head was bowed, still not lifted. She moved and shifted, made not of skin but thousands of crawling things, of dirt, of plants. They were rebuilding her. Reaching out a trembling hand, Guinevere placed it on the Dark Queen's back.

Everything moved faster, the Dark Queen shivering and rising. Guinevere yanked her hands—still covered in blood—back.

She had felt—

Life. Predator and prey. Birth and death. Pleasure and pain. The Dark Queen was all of them. More than human, and less, as well. She was fairy. She was *chaos*. She would tear down everything Arthur had built. Throw men back centuries. Take away their cities and fields, give them only foraging, hunting, being hunted. Because then she would have dominion over them. She was coming to reclaim the Earth.

And Guinevere could not stop it. No knot she knew could bind the chaos of the Dark Queen. Even touching her fed her more power. Merlin had warned Guinevere to fight as a queen. She had not. And she had awoken something she could not put back to sleep.

She turned to find Mordred standing over Lancelot. Lancelot was on the ground, unmoving, her sword gone. Mordred had his sword raised.

"Stop!" Guinevere shouted.

Mordred lowered his sword. "I have no quarrel with Lancelot. I like her. She defies the boundaries of men. I could not let her strike the Dark Queen, though. She is still vulnerable until she is formed. But it will not be long now." Mordred moved to the side as Guinevere rushed to Lancelot. Her knight was still breathing, though a gash on her head was bleeding freely.

"Lancelot," Guinevere said, shaking her shoulder. Lancelot groaned, but did not open her eyes or move.

"We have a lot to talk about." Mordred sheathed his sword. "I would say the Dark Queen will explain, but she is not big on explanations. Come, we should move Lancelot out of the meadow. I do not think it will go well for her once my grandmother rises. Lancelot will be safer in the trees. If we can find her horse, maybe it will carry her far enough away. This is not a place for humans. The Dark Queen will show no mercy."

"Then I will die, too!"

"Guinevere." Mordred grabbed Lancelot by both arms to drag her across the meadow. "Now you are being obtuse."

Guinevere ran to the first tree, the oldest. She pushed her palm against it, reaching for the knot that commanded it to obey. She sensed the tree feeling it. And she sensed the tree disregarding it.

"No!" she shouted. She pushed again, harder. If she could get the trees under control, they could bind the Dark Queen. She sank through the bark, remembering how she had changed Sir Bors's memories. She felt for the tree's heart, for its memory. Maybe she could—

The tree pushed back. When she finally managed to open her eyes, she was on her back, staring up at Mordred.

"You are not their queen." His voice was soft. "The forest is hers. It always has been."

Guinevere crawled back to the tree. She smashed her hand against it. The tree shivered, more with annoyance than anything. She was the bird drilling in, not deadly, merely a pest.

Then a shudder ripped through the tree, through the grove. Fear Guinevere knew, fear she had held her whole life, gripped her. The dread of death. Worse than death. She looked up from the blackest depths, the light shimmering on the surface of the water above her. *Remember*, the tree pushed. *Remember what it is to be unmade.*

Guinevere felt a sick twist of nausea. She looked up to see Excalibur pierce the tree.

The cold gripped her; it was terrible and empty. She crawled away, hoping that the trees would go back to sleep. But something else was happening. The tree cracked, going gray. It died before her eyes—dried up and dried out. The leaves fell, crumbling into dust before they hit the forest floor.

Just as her blood had spread, so, too, did the poison of Excalibur. All around the meadow, the trees that had awoken were consumed.

The thing in them that gave them life, spirit, anger and joy and hunger, was gone. Arthur withdrew the sword. It did not glow in the moonlight. Even the moon was devoured, no reflection along the smooth metal of the blade. Arthur turned.

"Quick, before she is formed!" Guinevere said. "She is still vulnera—" Guinevere felt metal under her chin, against her throat. Mordred lifted her to her feet, holding her against his chest. His arm around her waist. His blade at her neck. They stood between Arthur and the Dark Queen.

"Mordred," Arthur said. "Release her."

"I am not yours to command."

"You cannot want this. You know what the Dark Queen will bring. You know how destructive the magic, how terrible the cost."

"Who are you to tell magic it cannot exist? You, who exist because of magic! Magic of violence, magic of greed. Men have done worse things with magic than fairies ever dreamed of! You were born because of magic, and you rule because of a foolish wizard, because the Lady of the Lake gave you that hideous thing!"

"He is the bridge," Guinevere whispered, remembering. "He is the bridge between the violence that was and the peace that might be."

"Move, Mordred." Arthur tried to go around, but Mordred followed, keeping himself and Guinevere between Arthur and the Dark

Queen. Guinevere could hear her behind them, could hear the skittering and creeping. The growing.

Arthur stepped closer. Guinevere shuddered, her whole body convulsing with the same existential dread she had felt from the tree. She pushed back against Mordred, needed to get away, to be away, to be far away from that thing. From Excalibur.

"If you come closer to her, she will be unmade. Look, she can barely stand." Mordred stepped toward Arthur, pushing Guinevere nearer to the sword. The world spun. Darkness swirled, eating away at her vision. *She was underwater. She was trapped. She was—*

Arthur backed away. Guinevere drew a shuddering breath.

"I will let you choose," Mordred said. "Your mother never had a choice. I am more merciful than Merlin. If you want to end the Dark Queen, you can. But you will have to go through Guinevere to get to her. Excalibur will kill her, too. That is your choice. Kill them both, or kill neither."

Guinevere knew it was true. She would not survive if Excalibur could reach her. It was not hunger radiating from the blade. It was the absence of hunger. It would devour magic and never be sated, never be full. It did not eat to survive. It ate to end.

But the Dark Queen would truly be dead. The chaos she nurtured forever over. The people of Camelot would be allowed to grow and learn and live and die on their own terms, subject only to each other, not to magic they could not understand or control. She looked into Arthur's warm eyes. The boy king. He carried the weight of a kingdom.

She nodded. "Do it."

Arthur held her gaze. And then the king disappeared, leaving only her friend. Her Arthur.

He sheathed the sword.

She is free.

For so long, she has had a thousand eyes, a thousand legs and bodies. And now she is formed, she is real. But she is not safe. She can feel that horrible tool, the unmaking of her, the unmaking of magic.

Her beautiful boy is nearby. And so is the queen-not-queen. Her savior. There is a mystery in her blood, her sweet blood. The dark queen, the true queen, swirls with happiness. She has form, she has a mystery, she has a goal. Before, she tried to defeat men in battle. Now, she will destroy them from within. She will rot them, decay them, grow new life from their corpses feeding the forest.

But for now, she has an enemy still too dangerous to face. Too much has been taken from the land. She tries to draw from the trees, but they are dead. Worse than dead. They have been erased. It is horrible. She cannot make a stand here.

Follow me, she whispers with the buzzing drone of a thousand black flies bringing plague in the wet heat of summer. *Bring her.*

CHAPTER TWENTY-SEVEN

Guinevere heard the Dark Queen slithering away, into the trees. Faster than shadow. Faster than flight. She was risen, and she was gone, and both were Guinevere's fault.

Mordred laughed, backing away from Arthur. He dragged Guinevere along. She was too weak from the loss of blood and the sickness of Excalibur to fight him.

"Leave her," Arthur commanded.

"Come after us and you will have to fight me. That ends with one of us dying. I am ready to kill or die. Are you?"

Arthur dropped his head, shoulders slumped. Defeated. Whatever Mordred had done, he was still Arthur's family. Guinevere knew, as Mordred did, that Arthur was not willing to kill him.

Mordred picked up speed. Guinevere dragged her heels, pulled against him, but he did not slow. One of Maleagant's horses wandered by. Mordred whistled and the horse trotted to them. Mordred threw Guinevere up onto it, then mounted behind her. He kicked at the horse's flanks, sending them deeper into the forest.

"Whatever they have told you," Mordred said, his arm tight against her waist, his mouth at her ear, "they have lied."

"Merlin—"

"Merlin is the worst liar of them all. You think he cares about you? The man who walks through time? He would have seen this. He would have known it was coming. And is he here?" Mordred gestured to the darkness around them. "No. He is not."

"He is my—my father."

"You cannot even say it without tripping over the word. Your heart and your tongue know a lie when they feel it, even if your brain tells you it is true. Merlin is no more your father than Arthur is your husband. They trapped you in the prison of Camelot, bound you in dresses, stripped away everything that was real and created their *queen*. They molded you into a form that suited them. Because you are terrifying. You are more powerful than any of them. Do you know what Excalibur is? What it does?"

Guinevere shook her head, closing her eyes.

"People think it is magic. It is the opposite of magic. It is the end of magic. Magic is life. Excalibur is an executioner. That is why you cannot stand to be around the sword. Your core is magic, your veins flow with it, your heart beats with it. Your soul knows that Excalibur is not your defender. It is your enemy." Mordred's grip was now not holding her captive so much as holding her up. He rested his cheek against her head. "Merlin has always forced his will on the world. Through magic, through violence, through deception. And now that he has decided magic must end, he has made you complicit. He made you a prisoner of his plans. Did he tell you anything true?"

She wanted to answer. She could not. Had she known everything, what might she have done differently? What might she have chosen? Merlin insisted she chose this, but she had a head full of things he put there and so very little else.

"You deserve to be free," Mordred said. "You deserve to be wild. You are not a queen. Camelot will never feed your soul. It will drain you as surely as Excalibur. Give in to the magic at the heart of you. Leave them behind." He put his hand over hers, the spark and the fire stronger than ever.

Something inside her recognized something inside him, rose to meet it, yearned for it. Mordred had not killed Lancelot. He had not killed Arthur. He had fought only to reawaken the magic, to reclaim the things that had been driven into the earth. The things that were part of himself.

The things that she could no longer deny were part of her.

"What will she do, now that she is free?" she asked.

"I do not know. I only know that she is as natural a creature as the birds, the deer, the rabbits."

"The snakes. The wolves. The spiders."

He laughed gently. "Yes, she has more of those in her, it is true. But have they not a right to live as any other creature does?"

"She will hurt people."

"Maleagant hurt people, and Arthur did not stop him."

"He was trying. It was complicated."

"My grandmother is not complicated. Look at the dance of men, the treaties and borders and rules. Look at how little good it does anyone. They all still fight and bleed and suffer and die. And their souls die long before their bodies ever do. Tell me you would rather be in Camelot than out here."

"But to ally with darkness!"

"We do not have to join the Dark Queen. She will not care, and neither do I. We do not have to do anything unless *we* wish it. There are no laws, no borders, no rules here. Let me untie the knots that Merlin has bound you with. That Arthur has tightened."

Merlin had lied to her. He had kept her from the truth in ways she feared she would never know. And Arthur had let her believe it. But when she thought of cutting all the lines of memory and experience and love that tied her to Arthur—things Merlin never pushed into her head, things deeper and older than magic—she felt only sadness.

She had not started on this path with the truth. Now she had it all. Now she could choose, fully and completely. Sacrifice herself to Camelot, or walk away.

It was going to hurt. She smiled sadly. At least she knew pain. Pain would not kill her. Pain would not unmake her. It might reshape her, but she could accept now that whatever knots she tied around herself would always fray. In coming undone, they gave her the space to become something new.

"Be with me," Mordred whispered, "and be free. Be with me and be loved."

She turned her face to his. His lips brushed hers and the fire flared, stronger and brighter and hungrier than any she could ever conjure on her own. Fire was against her nature, but it was the core of Mordred's, and he passed it from his lips to hers.

She gathered it, relishing it, knowing she could have a lifetime burning this bright, this hot, this true.

Then she channeled the fire into her hands, igniting them. She grabbed Mordred's hands. He shouted in shock and pain, jerking away from her touch. She shoved, and his momentum carried him off the horse, sent him tumbling to the ground.

She took the reins, urging the horse back toward the meadow.

"You will never be happy with him!" Mordred shouted, his voice raw with anguish. "He is the end of our kind!"

Tears streamed down her face. She knew Mordred was right. That, in choosing Arthur, she was choosing to sacrifice magic, to end wonder, to tame and cultivate the wild heart of the land. To kill that own part of herself.

She was choosing Arthur, again. She did not know how, or when, but she had made this exact choice before. She knew it as suddenly and surely as she knew that Mordred had told the truth when he said Merlin and Arthur had lied about everything.

Arthur was on his knees in the center of the meadow, defeated. Excalibur was sheathed, lying abandoned on the forest floor beside him.

Guinevere slipped from the horse and ran to him, then knelt.

"I am sorry," she said.

He looked up, eyes shining. He grasped her, pulling her to him. "I thought I lost you."

"You should have. I woke her. You should have sacrificed me to end her."

"I can fight her. I have done it before. But I could not lose you. Not again."

He held her close. She rested her head against his chest, the closeness of Excalibur at her side a throbbing ache even sheathed. Arthur was an ending. But he was also a beginning. And she believed in him. Merlin had put his faith in men. She did not understand him, but she understood that, at least. They were capable of so much evil—and so much good. With Arthur, she knew the balance would tip toward the latter.

"How did you know to find us?" she asked. Brangien had told only Mordred.

"Merlin came to me in a dream. I am sorry that I did not get here sooner. And I am sorry that I did not come for you when Maleagant took you. I wanted to. I wanted to so desperately. To leave it all behind and save you. But . . ."

"But you have a nation to take care of." Which was why he should have killed the Dark Queen, even if it meant killing Guinevere. The same mixture of devastation and happiness she had felt telling Maleagant that Arthur would never sacrifice his people for her she now experienced in reverse. She did not know which version was better.

The pain from Excalibur pulsed with her guilt. She had broken the darkness open, and they had no idea what the result would be. Mordred was right—Merlin had to have seen all of this. And still he sent her. She wished she could trust that the wizard knew what he was doing. She would try to trust herself instead.

Lancelot limped toward them and sat heavily on the ground. She whistled. She whistled again. And at last the gentle *clop* of hooves sounded. Her horse nudged her, and Lancelot wrapped her arms around her horse's neck, nuzzling her face there.

"We lost," Guinevere said. "The Dark Queen is still out there. Mordred is, too."

Arthur looked grimly at the agonized corpse of Maleagant. Guinevere shuddered, turning away from it. *She* had done that. That was what Mordred wanted her to become. Powerful and terrible. When they were riding here, it had felt so important to kill Maleagant. So urgent. But now she wondered.

"There will always be another threat. Someone will fill the void Maleagant leaves behind. The Dark Queen will plot. Mordred—" Arthur paused, the name sticking in his throat. The betrayal was sharp and new. "Mordred will make his own decisions. Camelot is worth having, and that makes it worth taking."

"We are still alive," Lancelot said. "I count that as a win."

Arthur reached out and squeezed Lancelot's shoulder. "Thank you for being there for Guinevere when I could not."

"It was my honor to serve my queen."

Guinevere pulled away from Arthur. She shook her head. "But I am not anyone's queen. We cannot pretend I am. Look at what I have done, what chaos I have set free. Arthur, I— Everything I am is a lie. Mordred knew it as soon as he met me. He knew I could be used against you. Maleagant did, too. I put you in danger."

Arthur stood. He held out his hand to Guinevere. In it, he held the chain of silver and jewels he had given to his queen. "I have been in danger my whole life. I do not want to face it alone anymore. Please," he said. "Please come home."

Guinevere hesitated. She would not join Mordred and the Dark Queen. But she could slip away into the dark. Live in the wild. Become a hermit, a rumor.

She had been wrong about everything. But so had Merlin. She did not need protecting anymore. Arthur still did. Sealing herself and her magic away would do no one any good. Whatever Guinevere was, she would use it to defend him. She took the silver chain and refastened it against her forehead. And then she took Arthur's hand.

It was not the spark and flame of Mordred's touch, or even the instant connection of Lancelot's. It was older, and stronger, like the mountain of Camelot. It was worth building on. She could accept that it might not be what she wanted it to be, that they would have to grow into each other to discover what they might be together. But she would not let go of it. "I have two conditions for remaining queen," she said.

"Name them."

"The Dark Queen is back. We know the threat now. I will be the first line of defense. I will not shrink from this fight, and you will not hold me back from it."

Arthur nodded solemnly. "The second?"

"I get to choose my own knight. The queen's protector. That way,

you never have to worry about protecting me. It will not be your responsibility."

Arthur flinched. "It will always be my responsibility."

"No." Guinevere's voice was hard. "Never again, Arthur. If you
face that choice again, you choose Camelot. You are not my knight."
She turned and held out her free hand to Lancelot. "She is."

Lancelot froze. She did not step toward Guinevere. She looked
at her king.

And her king smiled, nodding. "Sir Lancelot, do you accept your
position as the queen's protector?"

Lancelot dropped to her knee, bowing her head. "With everything I am."

Arthur's hand moved to Excalibur. Guinevere flinched and he
stopped. "Sorry. Habit. We will knight you when we get back to
Camelot," he told Lancelot. "With a different sword."

Lancelot stood. Then she laughed, wrapping her arms around
Guinevere and lifting her, twirling her in a circle. "Thank you," she
whispered. She set down Guinevere and straightened, clearing her
throat. "My lady," she said, "allow me to help you onto your horse."

Arthur led them to his own horse, and they rode through the
darkness until dawn illuminated Camelot in the distance, calling
them home.

Guinevere rode in the boat across the lake. She remembered Maleagant's spy. She would not risk more people noticing her comings and
goings and discovering any weaknesses that could be exploited.

The water held dread for her still, but she could live with the
dread. There were worse things than drowning. She had faced the
Dark Queen. The Lady of the Lake would just have to wait her turn.

Word preceded them. Arthur lifted her from the boat, then climbed to the dock and stood next to her. Crowds were gathering in the streets, lining the pathway up the endless hill to the castle. They gasped. They cried. Arthur took Guinevere's hand and raised it. "Our queen is home!"

The crowd cheered. Lancelot stood behind them, quiet. Arthur turned to her, holding out his arm. "Rescued by her champion. The queen's protector and my newest knight, Sir Lancelot!"

This time the cheer was a bit more muddled and confused. But they would get used to it. And it was not their decision anyway. Lancelot, hand on the pommel of her sword, strode confidently beside Guinevere. She scanned the street as though expecting assassins in the heart of Camelot.

"Guinevere!" Brangien shot free from the crowd, throwing herself at Guinevere. They embraced, holding each other close.

"You found me," Guinevere whispered. "Thank you."

"You are my sister. I will always find you." Brangien stepped away, fussing over Guinevere's bloody and torn sleeves. She took off her own cape and draped it around Guinevere's shoulders, pulling up the hood. "Where is Mordred?"

"Later," Guinevere said. She knew Brangien would feel guilty for giving Mordred the information that helped him. But the guilt was only Guinevere's.

Together, they began the long walk to the castle. Arthur waved to his cheering people, including an openly weeping Dindrane on the arm of Sir Bors, but Guinevere could see the strain in Arthur's smile. How much it cost him to be their strength. She put her hand on his elbow and squeezed, bearing the burden with him. She had chosen Camelot.

A light mist of rain began to fall. Guinevere shrank from it. But then she tipped her head back, letting it fall on her face. Letting it wash away the blood and terror and regret. It was the first time she could remember water touching her skin. Each drop nourished her, replenishing some of what she had lost. She felt stronger. Powerful. Ready.

She was Guinevere, Queen of Camelot.

She was home.

Rain to face. Washing clean. Carrying away the sweat and the blood and the taste of her.

Droplets to droplets. Gathering, dripping, streaming. All the things that water knows rushing down the streets of Camelot, through the ditches, down the stones, down down down.

Down through the forsaken lake. River to stream to an older lake, a colder lake. The tiniest trace remains, but it is enough.

The water stirs. Forms. A face looks up from the depths, twisted with the longing and fury of an infinite being who had never before known loss.

Her lips curl around a single word.

Mine.

ACKNOWLEDGMENTS

Special gratitude to Sir Thomas Malory, T. H. White, Geoffrey of Monmouth, and an endless series of movies and television specials for planting the Arthurian legends deep in my brain.

Special gratitude to my editor, Wendy Loggia, and her assistant, Audrey Ingerson, for helping me prune and shape what grew.

Special gratitude to my agent, Michelle Wolfson, for being able to sell the wild things that spring up out of my imagination.

Special gratitude to my husband, Noah, and my three beautiful children for keeping the landscape of my life joyful and green.

Special gratitude to Regina Flath for coaxing magic out of reality for the cover.

Special gratitude to Janet Fletcher and Colleen Fellingham for making certain no weeds got through on their watch.

Special gratitude to Missio and "Bottom of the Deep Blue Sea" for keeping my brain watered and focused.

Special gratitude to everyone at Delacorte Press and Random House Children's Books, particularly Beverly Horowitz, Barbara Marcus, and my publicist Allison Judd, as well as the marketing and publicity departments for helping my books find new readers.

Special gratitude to Stephanie Perkins and Natalie Whipple, who always work at my side.

And finally, special gratitude to the girls and women overlooked in stories and in life, who still find ways to create magic and grow in power and truth.

ABOUT THE AUTHOR

KIERSTEN WHITE is the *New York Times* bestselling author of the And I Darken and Paranormalcy series, *Slayer*, *The Dark Descent of Elizabeth Frankenstein*, and many more novels. She lives with her family near the ocean in San Diego, which, in spite of its perfection, spurs her to dream of faraway places and even further-away times.

KIERSTENWHITE.COM
@KIERSTENWHITE

BOBA TK